The Alphas
A Nico Scarlatti Novel

By
Christopher Merlino

*There is nothing more fun to me than building a world
and populating it with friends...and enemies.*

Acknowledgements

This series has quickly become my favorite of all my projects. Not only has it stretched me as a storyteller, but it has stretched me in my research as well. I hope my passion for the merging of religion, myth, and lore has shown in these first two Nico Scarlatti books. I hope it has piqued the readers' interest in future installments, because I intend to expand Nico's world and add newer and deeper twists.

One of the hardest things about completing another novel is creating an acknowledgements page that doesn't read like the last five. As always, I want to thank my beautiful wife, Charm, for her longsuffering as I sit and write for hours on end. Thank you for your constant support and encouragement, but most of all, your love. More than anything else, that is what spurs me on.

As usual, my best friend, Duane, is my biggest fan. Thank you for continuing to support me and push me for the next manuscript, the next story. There is nothing more important to a writer than the love and encouragement of his friends and family. I am grateful to call you my friend.

As always, I offer my final thanks to all those who spend their money on my books, and take the time to read my stories. It means the world to me. I would ask that, if you enjoyed reading this story, you would take a moment to leave me a review on Amazon. Reviews are always appreciated and help future readers to decide if a book is worth their time and money. Thank you all and please, check out my other stories, all available on Amazon.

Prologue
(1290 A.D.)

"They're coming!"

The young boy skittered past a group of men seated around a campfire. Without a word, they extinguished the blaze and followed the boy through the snow-covered pass to a group of tents, clustered together among the trees. The boy continued to shout, rousting the entire camp.

"They're coming! They're coming!"

Men scurried out of the tents with swords drawn, bows and quivers of arrows were slung over shoulders. They gathered in front of the largest tent, where a rustling could be heard. A man emerged, his long, brown hair hanging in jagged locks to his shoulders. He wore a dark green tunic over a coarse, tan-colored shirt. His trousers matched the color and material of his tunic, and his leather sandals laced all the way up his calves and over his trouser pant legs. Though the hour was late, he appeared to have been ready for action at a moment's notice.

"What do you say, boy?"

The kid, no older than twelve, gasped for air as he stood before his father. His dark brown eyes glinted in the moonlight. The thrill of danger shone on his face as he recounted all that he had seen.

"They're coming," he said. "From the south."

"How many?"

"I counted four, father."

One of the men spoke up. "That means at least twice that number, Lucien."

"Yes," Lucien nodded. He returned his steely gaze to his son. "How far?"

"They just cleared the ridge…Two hours at most."

Lucien called out, "Make ready! Remember, these are the most dangerous creatures alive. Keep alert and follow the plan. Look out for one another."

The men scattered, fanning out and taking their positions throughout the area. They were all experienced mountain men. The freezing elements didn't bother them. Snow and ice were their norm. Having been raised among warrior clans, they all understood cover and concealment in rugged terrain.

Hours later, the moon slipped behind some clouds and everything went dark. Not a star could be seen. Without light, the temperature seemed to drop even further. The shadows, previously cast by the light of the moon, now blended together into one, plunging everything into inky blackness.

Samuel spoke first. "Can't see a damn thing." It was just a voice in the darkness, less than five feet away.

"Shhh," replied William. "These things can hear a whisper from two furlongs."

From their cover, behind an outcropping of dense evergreen bushes, they surveyed their surroundings, worthless as the effort was, in pitch darkness. Their prey was close by; the tension in the air told William that. It was vital to maintain the element of surprise. At some point, the moon would emerge from behind the clouds and they needed to be ready to act in an instant.

There was a gentle movement of air, a *whoosh*, from behind. They whirled around, but saw nothing. Armed with crossbows, they crouched, back-to-back, scanning for any movement, anything to indicate the enemy had arrived. There was a shout from one of the other teams, and the distinctive sound of a crossbow releasing a bolt.

It had begun.

Both men tensed, prepared for an attack from all sides. William heard another *whoosh* of displaced air as something moved close by. It moved so quickly, his mind could scarcely record the sound, let alone follow it. There was one thing he and Samuel both knew: No human could move that fast. They heard the sound again, this time terrifyingly close by.

The moon picked that moment to emerge from behind the clouds. It was almost blinding, after such pitch-darkness, and the wide-open mountain plateau glowed as the snow reflected the light, intensifying its effect. William could see the positions his comrades clearly, even from fifty or a hundred yards away. They were all engaged in combat. That meant...

William shifted his eyes back to his own position. It was standing right in front of him, a wicked grin on its face. Before William could squeeze the cross-bow release, the thing flicked its wrist and the cross-bow skittered across the rocks. William's hand went automatically to the oak stake he'd secured under his tunic. In a smooth, practiced motion, he pulled it out and stabbed straight for the heart. The stake struck nothing but air as the creature moved like lightening, shoving Samuel to the ground and positioning his arms around William's neck.

William knew he was dead. In another second his neck would be snapped. He saw it all in his mind's eye. His mind flashed to the countless times he'd come across a body with a snapped neck. He knew exactly what it would look like. He steeled himself and prepared for the sharp pain that would be the last thing he ever felt.

It never came. Just as he felt the creature's arms tense to snap his neck, William felt them loosen, and he heard a grunt of pain. He spun around to see the creature stiffen in pain, its hands reaching for something behind him. That was when William saw Samuel, on his back, his crossbow still aimed at the vampire.

The creature roared in pain, and William watched as the pointed canine fangs extended to three times their normal length.

He could see the bloodshot eyes, and the veins clouding the skin all around the forehead and eyes. The vervain-soaked crossbow bolt had struck the vampire high in the center of its back. It was in a place hard for the vampire to reach, but it missed the heart.

William knew a wooden crossbow bolt was painful for a vampire. A bolt soaked in liquid vervain was excruciating. As the vervain seared through the vampire's system, it weakened the creature, reducing its reaction time, but it wouldn't kill it. For that, they needed a heart strike. As it frantically grabbed at the little crossbow bolt, William plunged his stake into its chest. The vampire jerked to the left at the last moment and the stake missed the heart by inches. The vervain-soaked stake only wounded it further, and the vampire scampered away, finally getting the crossbow bolt out and quickly jerking the stake out.

It glared at William and Samuel as they scrambled to reload their crossbows. It would take several seconds for the vampire's rapid healing process to overcome the vervain-filled wounds. Vervain slowed down everything for vampires. As it stood, William realized he and Samuel would never be able to load their crossbows in time. They scrambled apart. At least, when it attacked one, the other could strike.

The vampire wasted no time. Lunging first for William, it shifted back to Samuel. Before William could take aim, the creature had his fangs deep into Samuel's neck. Within seconds, Samuel would be dead. William's crossbow was useless so he charged, holding another stake at the ready. When he was close enough to strike, he raised the stake and moved in.

Suddenly, the vampire's head jerked up toward the sky and it screamed in agony. Samuel fell to the ground as the vampire's hands grasped its head at the temples. It dropped to its knees. William didn't hesitate. He plunged the stake into its back, directly through its heart. The vampire stiffened, crying out as it dropped to its knees. William watched as its face darkened to a wrinkled, ashy, charcoal-grey. Then it went limp; its eyes still open as it toppled over onto the frozen ground, lifeless.

William rushed to Samuel, fearing the worst. He turned his friend over and found his neck covered in blood. He frantically wiped it with a rag, using snow to clean the area so he could assess the wounds.

"Please, God," he said. "Be alive."

He saw Samuel's breath freeze in the night air and he sat back in relief. He quickly recovered, and wrapped a fresh rag around Samuel's neck to staunch the bleeding.

"Rest here, friend," he murmured.

When he rose and scanned the area, he saw similar scenes as the hunters, having dispatched the vampires were now tending to the wounds of their comrades. He saw a few vampires still alive, writhing on the ground in pain. He checked under his tunic for stakes, and took two out. With a stake in each hand, he strode to the nearest vampire. He staked that one, then the next, until he was out of stakes. Then he went back and helped Samuel up. Together, they staggered to the group assembled at the mouth of a tiny cave. They passed several corpses, humans who had not survived.

The ritual was already underway. A vampire stood, shackled in vervain-soaked twine. A vervain-soaked stake protruded from his midsection. In obvious pain, he stood, his defiant eyes staring straight ahead. William could see Wynnifrea, perhaps the most powerful witch to ever live, performing the incantation.

"Elementum holis tule an solarium! Cantis mayleo grudarious! Mecsara ne ingostio! Havadum nexa descartra! Inicio serventum allemas!"

She turned to Lucien. "The key." When he held up the long, intricately carved cylinder, she nodded.

William had seen the key close up. It was otherworldly. The metal gleamed, even in the dark. It was hard, harder than steel, only far lighter. The carvings, so detailed and intricate, were unlike anything he had ever seen. He couldn't imagine the tool it would take to carve such an object.

Lucien carried the key to the mouth of the cave. It was a tiny space, perhaps six feet deep and four feet wide. At the back of the cave, a flat stone jutted out from the cave wall. Lucien stood the cylinder on end in the middle of the outcropping. He lowered his head and performed the sign of the cross before exiting the cave.

He nodded at Wynnifrea, who then closed her eyes.

"Invictum moratori! Terra omniperi! Al anfernum divini eferenti!"

The entire cave glowed deep crimson. The ground shook, but William, along with the others, stood firm. They'd been through it before. After a few seconds, the glow intensified, shifting to golden-orange. Wynnifrea stood with her arms spread wide, her head tilted to the night sky.

Lucien shoved the bound vampire toward the cave. "I have waited a long time for this, betrayer. Enjoy your eternity."

Without further fanfare, he shoved the vampire into the cave. With a scream the vampire disappeared into the light. Wynnifrea lowered her arms and the light diminished, fading into a soft glow before vanishing altogether.

No one said a word. They stood in rapt silence for many moments as the realization of what had just taken place sank in. They were finished.

William watched as two men approached Lucien and Wynnifrea. They'd been a part of the group from the beginning, yet never mingled with the rest of the men. They came and went at strange times, seeming to appear out of nowhere. Now, they took Lucien and Wynnifrea aside. William drew closer as they presented the long, metallic cylinder to Lucien.

"You must guard this at all costs," one said. "We cannot interfere in this affair again."

Lucien accepted the cylinder and nodded. "I understand."

He and Wynnifrea walked together away from the group. William followed, keeping his distance.

"Do you have the box?" Lucien asked.

She led him a large rock. From behind it, she pulled a sack, and from that, she pulled a clay box, covered in carvings. She pulled the top off and held it out. Lucien gently placed the cylinder into the box and Wynnifrea added several stones, and then closed it. Placing it on the rock, she closed her eyes and held her hands over it. She began a new incantation.

"Insperius insperio addonai. Malefacia om nuevius parteum. Everio lodi hhu cathung nario ebis altui. Garolio fe oud wilim. Desai nar updio bencoudi qar lidio. Secreto al fwenio carpus dei inconfio."

She opened her eyes and lowered her hands. "It is done."

Lucien picked the box up and tried to open it. He couldn't even see which side was the top. He grasped it tightly and hurled it with all his might at the mountain wall. It crashed against the wall and clattered to the ground. He pulled a mallet out of his sack and tried to smash it to pieces. He couldn't even dent it.

He looked at Wynnifrea, who smiled. "Hide it well, my friend."

Chapter 1

The old man beckoned them to follow. He didn't wait for them before he scampered over the fence and around the abandoned metal shacks. He had already led them through the Visitors' Center, into the breathtaking Wadi Rum, through the tourist area, and into an area the government had restricted, years prior. He had told them the army had deserted their guard duties decades ago, when war broke out in neighboring countries. They never returned to their round-the-clock posts, choosing the merits of mobile patrols over committing manpower to the useless task of guarding the restricted mountains. They did erect fences to keep the general public out, and the signage made clear the consequences of trespassing.

The three foreigners exchanged glances before following the old man over the fence and behind the metal shacks. The red dust covered their shoes and clung to their clothing, as well as their sweaty, exposed skin. None of them were used to such extreme heat, but the old man seemed unaffected by any of it. He was waiting for them at the mouth of a small cave. Had he not pointed it out, they would never have thought to explore it on their own. The opening was so tiny the old man had to slide in feet first. As soon as his head disappeared, the foreigners exchanged skeptical glances.

"This guy better not be wasting our time," one said, pulling his curly, shoulder length brown hair back and securing it with an elastic band. He was dressed in well-worn blue-jeans and a black concert T-shirt which revealed a number of tattoos on both arms. His amber-tinted eyes glared at the opening as he considered the punishment he would inflict on the old guy if he was indeed putting them on.

"Relax, Gamut," another replied. He was the most refined of the group, dressed in pressed slacks and a button-down, light blue shirt. His black hair was pulled straight back, held in place by expensive product. He exuded the kind of confidence that comes from decades of breeding and wealth. "We're here to follow every lead, no matter where it takes us."

"Is that right, Yared? Well it better take us somewhere worthwhile soon. I'm sick of spending day after day with a blood-sucking parasite."

Yared turned his ice-blue gaze on Gamut, his nostrils flaring as he tried to restrain his temper. "Be careful, Gamut. Your canine slobber would…"

"Oh, bloody hell! Will you lot stuff it? It's too bloody hot in this God-forsaken place for me to stand here while you two embarrass yourselves." Garland MacElroy shook his head and ran a hand over the back of his neck. Feeling the warmth, he cringed, knowing the sunburn would be intense on his fair skin. Scotts weren't meant to be in the desert. He shook his head. "Bloody vampires and werewolves. Two centuries old abominations fighting a centuries old war like a couple of galoots! C'mon! Heid doon arse up!" He brushed between the other two and strode toward the opening.

Gamut frowned. "What'd he say?"

"It's Scottish slang," Yared replied. "It means 'get on with it.'"

They lowered themselves down through the opening and gathered at the beginning of a tunnel, large enough for a man to walk through without bending over. The old man sat on a rock outcropping. He gestured down the passage and babbled something incomprehensible. Yared gestured for the man to lead the way but the guy didn't move. He shook his head emphatically and repeated his previous statement.

Yared frowned and exchanged a glance with Garland. They both turned to Gamut, who sighed and gritted his teeth. "He won't go any farther. He says the passage is evil."

Yared stared at the old man for a moment. The fear in his eyes was real. He focused his gaze on the man's eyes for a second and applied a slight mental twist before gesturing down the passage. The old man got up and led the way into the passage.

Garland grunted. "Hmph! You don't even need to speak to compel him?"

"I don't speak Arabic," Yared replied, stifling a satisfied grin.

They followed the old man in silence as he led them through the jagged passage. The darkness enveloped them within a few strides. It was no problem for the werewolf, Gamut, and the vampire, Yared, but Garland was a warlock, human, and therefore, without the kind of night vision the others possessed. He made due with a small flashlight. Caves dotted either side of the passage, some small, the size of child's room, others much larger. They inspected each cavern in turn, splitting up to cover more ground. They came to the end of the passage, and found themselves at the center of a massive cavern, big enough to contain a modern, two-story house.

"How could this be?" Gamut frowned.

Yared shrugged, scanning the giant cavern and breathing in the dank air.. "We've been walking gradually downward for close to two miles as far as I can tell." He gestured. "Spread out. If it's here, we'll find it."

They split up and scoured every nook and cranny of the jagged cavern. Garland felt a shimmer. He stood tall and narrowed his eyes trying to determine what was different. It was a similar feeling as the one he got when summoning chakra for his spellcasting. Only now, it coursed through him without any effort on his part.

"It's here," he declared, his brow furrowed in concentration. "I can feel it."

Gamut laughed. "Good for you." Turning to Yared. he smirked, "Here that, Yared? The mage can feel it."

"I am *NOT* a mage!" Garland glared at him. "You would do well to remember that."

Gamut frowned. He tugged at his collar and swallowed hard as his comfort was affected. He looked at Garland in confusion.

"Feeling warm, werewolf?" Garland's eyes were shades darker as his glare intensified. "You see, my canine friend, mages draw their power from the light. Their effects are powerful but superficial. Warlocks..." he glared even more intensely. "Well...let's just say a warlock's power is a bit...darker."

Gamut scratched at his chest. His bones suddenly felt heavy. As the seconds passed, he could feel his blood boiling in his veins and his heart felt as though it would explode at any moment. The itching intensified, causing his mind to overload, especially because he could barely move his joints. A tremendous sense of dread washed over him. His eyes bulged in their sockets as fear overcame him. He collapsed on the ground, writhing. It all took less than thirty seconds.

Yared sighed. "Knock it off! Garland, we don't have time for this."

Garland, chuckled and waved a hand. Gamut immediately lay still, his breathing gradually returning to normal. When he collected his thoughts, he sprang up from the floor, darted behind the smirking warlock, and prepared to bite down on his neck.

"Careful," Garland warned with another chuckle. He didn't fight the werewolf at all, tilting his head to one side and offering a clear shot at his neck. "You should know I consume copious amounts of wolfsbane, just as I do vervaine."

Gamut snarled in his ear. "Maybe, but I can still snap your neck like a twig."

"All right, everybody *calm down!*" Yared shook his head. "Gamut, let him go."

Gamut waited a second or two before shoving Garland aside. "I don't know why we ever thought this could work. We need to stick with our own kind."

"That kind of short-sighted thinking," Yared replied evenly, "is why we find ourselves on the precipice of extinction. Perhaps we should complete our task. We can worry about killing one another later."

He turned to Garland. "You said you could feel something?"

Garland didn't respond. His eyes still locked on Gamut's.

Yared rolled his eyes. "It's like dealing with children," he mumbled. "Garland!"

The warlock blinked and turned slowly, to face Yared, who raised his eyebrows. "What do you *feel*, Garland?"

The warlock snapped out of it. "Right. Something magical is here…in this room." He looked around the room. "Something powerful."

Yared nodded. "Let's find it."

Garland pointed at the other two. "Just stay here. Your chakra pull might interfere. Let me stand in the center of the room and see if I can pinpoint it."

He made his way carefully through the dark cavern. Standing in the middle, he closed his eyes and began turning in a slow, clockwise rotation, focusing all his senses on the magic emitting from somewhere in the underground room. Gamut shifted his feet and gritted his teeth. Within seconds, the warlock pointed and crept deeper into the cavern and to the right. He stood at the wall and felt around, mumbling something Gamut couldn't make out. Garland finally grinned and looked back at his companions. He grasped a little ledge and pulled hard. A large rock slid out from the wall and fell at his feet.

Yared and Gamut stood, spellbound, as Garland grinned and peered into the hole with his flashlight. He glanced back with an excited smile.

"Something's in there."

Yared and Gamut raced to join him. Garland reached into the hole and pulled out what looked to be a clay box. It was about the size of a shoebox and not very heavy, indicating it was also hollow. It was covered in symbols and glyphs, most of which were indiscernible to the three men.

"This is it," Yared said, taking it from Garland and inspecting it. "The key is in here." He marveled at the intricate artwork and frowned. "I know some of these but the rest are foreign to me."

"Who cares about the glyphs?" Gamut said. "Let's open it and get the key."

Yared shook the box but heard nothing. He spun the object in his hands but could see no means of opening it. He frowned.

Garland pursed his lips. "Could *this* be the key?"

Yared shook his head. He pointed to the clay container. "That is just the box. It's precisely as it was described to me."

"Well, there's no lid," Garland shined his flash on it, scouring every inch. "I don't see any cracks. There's nothing to move or push. I see no levers or buttons. What the bloody hell?"

Yared shook his head. "It's not supposed to be easy. Remember what the key is for."

Gamut grabbed the box. "I say we crack it open and get outta here."

He poised to smash it against the wall but hesitated and glanced uncertainly at the other two. He raised his eyebrows. Yared and Garland shrugged before nodding. Gamut threw the box into the wall.

It hit and clattered to the ground, unscathed. They exchanged amazed glances and Gamut picked it up. He threw it to the ground as hard as he could. Pieces of rock exploded from the ground as the impact shook the room. The box remained undamaged.

"This is maddening."

Yared shrugged. "It's protected by powerful magic." He turned to Garland. "Is this something you can work on?"

"I can try, but I'm guessing a witch cast this spell."

"We've done our job." Yared picked up the box and strode toward the passage. "Let's get this back to the compound."

They made their way out of the underground passage. Having no further use for the old man, they left his corpse in one of the smaller caves off the main passage. His neck was snapped in one fast, efficient motion and he was left without a second thought.

When they emerged into dwindling daylight, Yared pulled out his smart-phone and sat on a small rock. He tapped and swiped before holding the phone to his ear.

"Yes?"

Yared smiled. "We found it."

"I swear, Yared, if you jest…"

"Fear not, brother." Yared smiled and patted the artifact at his side. "The key has been uncovered. Or I should say…the box has been uncovered."

"Was the key inside?"

"It would appear, dear brother, that our work has just begun." Yared sighed. "It appears to be spelled shut. We cannot open it."

His brother swore under his breath. "Of course. Bring it home, brother. You have done well."

"How will we open it?"

"The same way it was closed. We require a witch." Yared heard his brother sigh deeply, letting out a long slow breath. "We require a very powerful witch."

Ƀ ᴀ ᴈ̌ Ψ Ç

"That's gotta be them."

Alvi Cornega peered through the high-powered binoculars handed to him by his new number two, Isidro Vargas. He found the approaching vessel and scanned for any sign it might be naval or police. The salt air stung his eyes, but he maintained his focus on the distant ship. The blue and white vessel bobbed in the mild surf. Alvi noted the sleek lines as well as the twin engines at the stern. The Mexican vessel was built for speed. Then again, so were police and navy cruisers. Alvi saw nothing suspicious but that didn't mean much. The authorities weren't totally stupid.

They knew how to disguise their vessels. He only bothered to look out of sheer habit.

Alvi hated these kinds of deals. He hadn't been in the field making exchanges in years, long before he took over the Manizales Cartel. It was dangerous work. Drug trafficking was a violent business and those at the top needed layers and layers of protection, not just from the authorities, but from their rivals, and even from their friends...sometimes even more so from friends. One could never be too sure who was in bed with whom, and what deals were being struck. A friend today could slit his throat tomorrow.

Since a huge part of his operation was recently burned down, and his cash flow was crippled, Alvi had to make ends meet. The five cartels were decimated, but not completely destroyed. There was a huge power vacuum in the Colombian drug trade, and the tattered remains of each cartel scrambled to protect its own interests. It wouldn't be long before they were at each other's' throats. They were fortunate enough that Nico Scarlatti hadn't torched their underground labs and warehouses. Product continued to be harvested, processed, and packaged. There just wasn't cash for kind of security Alvi was accustomed to, and even fewer trustworthy individuals left to make things work without his direct supervision.

On top of all that, the Mexican Montenegro Cartel demanded a face-to-face at this exchange. They were concerned about the situation in Colombia, and nervous about dealing with unfamiliar and potentially inexperienced faces. They also told him they wanted to make sure Alvi was in a position to rebuild. In reality, they just wanted to make sure Alvi was on-site in the event things went south in the wake of the Scarlatti disaster.

Without taking the binoculars off the approaching ship, he said, "Get everyone to their stations. If they don't stop at a half-mile out, we're unloading on them."

Isidro turned and spoke into the black microphone clipped to his lapel. Moments later, Alvi heard boots scrambling across the deck and clambering up the stairs to the upper level. He heard hardware being opened and assembled. He watched three of his guys on the lower deck spread themselves out across the port side of the 220 foot Heesen yacht. They each carried military-grade RPGs, supplied by his contacts in the Colombian army.

As agreed, the inbound craft slowed and maintained a distance of one half mile. Alvi waited until he saw the signal repeated several times. Alvi squinted his eyes as he confirmed the signal. He raised his hand, signaling his own guy to respond.

"Okay, Sid," Alvi called. "Bring us in."

Isidro raised his voice for everyone to hear. "Okay, men! We're moving in. Be alert!"

The two yachts pulled up alongside one another and men on either side lashed them together. Tensions were high, but this was a common method of transacting their business, so everyone knew the drill. Eyes darted back and forth but no one really expected trouble.

Alvi greeted the Montenegro chief, and they discussed the transaction for a moment before shaking hands. Alvi waved to Sid, who ordered some of his guys to bring the product up. In all, they carried up twelve crates of pure Colombian cocaine; each crate contained sixty kilos. This represented Alvi's entire available supply. He needed the money from this transaction to rebuild.

The Mexicans began bringing box after box of their own over to Alvi's vessel. Alvi was taking a huge risk, putting everything into one transaction, but it meant about a hundred million American dollars in his pocket for an afternoon of work. He was nervous about popping up out of hiding, but things had been calm for the past few weeks and he desperately needed funds. He could feel the vultures circling. His only comfort was the knowledge that they were just as crippled as he was.

The exchange was done quickly and efficiently, with each box checked and then stowed below decks on both vessels. When both leaders were satisfied, the transaction was complete. They signaled their men to unlash the boats. As the vessels drifted apart, Alvi waved to his Mexican counterpart and then waited as the motors revved and they backed away under power.

As they sped away from the meeting place, Alvi and Sid exchanged pleased glances and Alvi left him to command the ship. He descended the stairs and relaxed into a soft chair below decks. His heavy eyes pleaded for relief and Alvi closed them, letting the anxiety of the day flow out of him. He took deep breaths as his heart rate made the gradual return to normal, and he slipped into a gentle sleep. It lasted until a chill washed over him and he dreamed a presence of pure evil loomed over him.

Alvi's eyes snapped open and he sprang up from his seat, bringing his pistol up in one fluid, practiced motion. His eyes found the shadowy figure and he took immediate aim. He felt a sharp jerk, and the gun flew from his hand, landing on the carpeted floor. He felt a blow in the middle of his chest. It was as if the wind had formed a fist and lashed out at him, slamming him backward into the seat again. When he caught his breath, he looked up and saw two glowing white eyes staring back at him.

They flashed silver and then back to pure-white as Alvi focused on the figure standing before him. He was dressed in strange garb, flowing black robes, trimmed in gold. The look on his face was serene, as though he hadn't a care in the world, as though he wasn't on a yacht full of men with automatic rifles ready to kill at Alvi's command.

When Alvi opened his mouth to scream for help, the man held up a finger and Alvi saw the crackle of purple electricity surrounding it. His mouth snapped shut in stunned disbelief. The man smiled and the electricity disappeared from his finger.

"No need to involve your crew," he said. "There is no point in getting them all killed when all I want to do is talk."

"Whaaa…who…who are y-y-you?"

The man gave him an amused look. "Oh…I'm terribly sorry. How rude of me. Though you must admit, *you* were the one who pulled the gun." He bowed slightly. "You may call me Azazel."

"Azazel?" Alvi repeated. "What…I mean…who…?"

"What…would have been the better question," Azazel said, examining his fingernails. "Though it would have also been the ruder choice." He waved a hand. "Shall we dispense with the small talk?" Without waiting for a reply, he continued. "Amazing as this sounds, you have something I require."

"Just take whatever you want and go," Alvi said.

Azazel chuckled. "Did I say some*thing*? I meant some*one*. I require the services of a very powerful witch." He leaned forward with a menacing smile. "I understand you are acquainted with such an individual."

Alvi frowned. "Nayra? Why her? There are lots of witches."

"True," Azazel agreed. He held up a finger. "But none as powerful as...Nayra, was it?" He shook his head. "No, there aren't many left with the knowledge or the power to subdue and control two high-level demons. The amount of draw on chakra from that effort was impressive by any standards, let alone today's."

Alvi's eyes widened. "You want to control demons?"

Azazel chuckled. "Control demons? No. I have but a simple task. I merely require..." He shook his head and looked at Alvi.

"Nayra?"

Azazel grinned. "Right...Nayra. I just need her to help open a door."

"Open a door?" Alvi frowned. He sat up a little straighter, interested despite himself. "What door?"

Azazel smiled. "A very special door." He looked at Alvi for a moment. "Let's leave it at that for now. My question for you is, what would you like in return for her services?"

Alvi knew a dodge when he saw one. Even with a frightening presence in the room, he knew when he held an advantage. Since the...whatever he was...was on *his* yacht asking for *his* help, it meant Nayra's cloaking spell was working and their new home was undetectable by the supernatural. Azazel must have staked out his yacht and waited for him to show up.

Actually," Alvi said. "I'd like to know more about this door you want opened."

If Azazel was surprised or annoyed, he didn't let on. He smiled at Alvi and nodded.

"Of course, you would." Azazel thought for a minute. "It's the impudence of youth. I once knew one with such impudence.

He thought to question a power higher than himself. When those who were in a position to see things more clearly warned him against taking such foolish action, do you know what he did?" His pearl white eyes flashed silver for just a second before returning to their deep white hue.

Alvi suddenly felt as though his advantage was more of a liability after all. He couldn't remember why he had thought he was in a position to exert any pressure on Azazel. He did his best to remain calm but felt like his emotions lay bare before Azazel.

Azazel continued his story. "Though he knew his path was self-destructive, he continued with such dogged determination, he actually convinced many that he knew something the rest of them didn't." Azazel shook his head sadly. "In the end, he led them all to their destruction."

Alvi frowned and nodded as though he understood the point. "Okay."

Azazel shook his head. "The point, my impudent young friend, is that you might think you are making wise choices; you might think you are doing what is best." He wagged a finger at Alvi. "But you are playing in a realm for which you are woefully ill-equipped."

Alvi continued to frown. "What exactly does all this mean?"

"It means you should avoid questions, the answers of which are a burden to you once you get them."

The words sounded so sinister, perhaps because of their strange eloquence, as they tumbled off Azazel's tongue. He spoke with the confidence of one who was as ruthless as he was powerful. He could back up his words and he knew it. Alvi knew when to take a hint and when to press. Azazel was not a man to be trifled with.

"What is Nayra's help worth to you?"

Azazel smiled and spread his hands with a slight bow of his head. "Ahhhh. *Now* you are starting to ask the right questions."

Chapter 2

The world drifted back into focus, but her head felt like a giant tuft of cotton. She couldn't concentrate on anything for more than a few seconds without painful throbbing behind her eyes. She saw shapes but could make nothing out. She heard voices but could not comprehend the words. As her mind struggled to cope with the events swirling all around her, she began to remember her reality, and her body wracked with fear.

"Ahhh," a nearby voice said. "The princess awakes."

She recognized the voice, the accent. The boys she worked with on the boardwalk were Russian. His accent sounded like theirs. She felt hands on her, groping her, and she struggled against his touch. His breath came in ragged gasps and she could smell his cologne. The combination was nauseating. She fought harder.

"Are you struggling, little one?" the voice asked, his hands continuing to roam. "I can see in your eyes you are. Unfortunately, my young virgin, you are still suffering the effects of the cocktail. Nothing moves! Haha! Never fear. It will wear off soon, and you're your mind will clear. We need you alert. Today is your big day."

Her eyesight began to clear. A smiling face, staring down at her, came into focus. His smile was kind...sort of, but the glint in his eyes was anything but. She'd seen that look before. As her mind cleared, she recalled her situation. She remembered the sting of a needle in her neck as she was leaving work. She remembered waking up with a room full of other young girls, all similarly drugged and taken.

She remembered being told her old life was over and her new life was about to begin. The men all laughed as her future was described in horrific detail. Most girls were sold into brothels throughout the Middle East and Europe. The "special ones" were sold at exclusive, invite-only, auctions, where the participants would bid. She was told, life with these buyers was often far worse than the alternative. She didn't know what that meant but she was petrified to find out.

"How I wish I could be the one to take you, to...*teach* you," the man continued, his voice almost wistful. "Such perfection is hard to come by, even at your young age." He smirked. "Girls don't save themselves anymore, but you have. And today, you will be rewarded for your virtue."

He laughed and stood. "Today, my love, you will be sold." His cold, dark eyes met her frightened blue ones. "Unless you don't fetch the minimum that is. In which case, you go to the brothels." He leaned closer. "Usually, we make big money in the brothels for the virgin's first time, but I promise you, if you fail to fetch the minimum, your first time will be with me...*tonight*." He made sure she saw his sadistic grin before he left the room.

Hours later, she was fed, and taken to a shower to bathe and groom herself. She was given specific instructions and told she would be inspected following her shower. At first, she refused, but when she was informed that there were a dozen men prepared to bid for the privilege of forcibly bathing and grooming her, she relented. She was powerless to defend herself and powerless to change her situation. The effects of the drugs were mostly gone, but she still felt sluggish and weak. Even at full strength, she would have no chance of escape.

Following her shower, she was led back to her room where she found a stunning sheer white dress laid out on her bed, and expensive white heels in her size. She was instructed to put the outfit on, and had to do so in front of several men. A woman entered with a hairdresser's kit. After laying out her tools and setting up a mirror, she began trimming and shaping. After nearly an hour of work, the stylist declared the job complete.

Staring at herself in the mirror, she could barely recognize the girl who should be hanging out with her friends on the boardwalk, giggling at the shirtless boys walking by and flexing their muscles, preparing to begin her junior year of high school. She should be thinking about homecoming, cheerleading, parties, and prom. Instead, she was about to be auctioned off to some foreign pedophile, who would use her for as long as she amused him, and then she would be discarded.

Her thoughts were interrupted by the opening of her door. Her Russian tormentor entered with a sly smile. "It is time. Are you excited, little princess? How much money do you think you're worth?"

She put her head down and walked ahead of him. He chuckled and placed a hand at the small of her back, guiding her to a room where several other girls waited. The looks on their faces told her they were all praying, in their minds, for a salvation they knew would never come. One side of the room was almost entirely glass. They could see into the adjoining space.

At that point, men were preparing a stage in the center of the room. They tested lights, each one shining in turn on the stage. There was nothing else in the room. She could see darkened glass on every wall surrounding the stage. The bidders must be in rooms behind the glass.

She thought she saw sudden movement. It was like a blur of color shooting across the room. Just like that, it was gone. She slumped in despair. Her fate was sealed. There would be no salvation.

A short time later, the auction began. The first girl was led from the room. From their place behind the glass, the girls watched as the Russians led her to the stage and auctioned her off like a piece of artwork. The girls were warned against any movements or gestures they were not asked to make. They could cry all they wanted. The Russians made it clear, the more frightened they appeared, the higher the bidding would go, until only the most sadistic of the bidders remained.

The first girl was sold in less than three minutes. After the bidding ended, two guards led her off the stage. The auctioneer, a tall, thin man, wearing a headset microphone, wrapped a computer-generated band around her wrist and nodded to the guards. They led her from the auction room, back to the holding room, where the next girl was led to the stage.

There was another flash of color. From her vantage point inside the room, she was even more certain than before that she saw something. She thought she must be hallucinating, perhaps an after-effect of the drugs they had pumped through her. Her head *was* still somewhat foggy, but she felt like her eyes were working okay. She shook her head, wondering if she was going crazy.

The second girl was sold, then the third, then the fourth. Eleven girls were sold in about an hour. She was the last to be led out into the auction room. Her knees trembled and her mouth was dry. She fought back tears and did her best to look like she wasn't scared. She walked into the room, stepped onto the stage, turned from one side to the other, and stood with her back to the other girls watching in the room.

The auctioneer smiled and began with a description of her, speaking about her as though she was a portrait in an art gallery. Halfway through his speech, she thought she saw the movement again. Her eyes darted to her right. She was staring off to the side as the auctioneer looked back at her. His eyes narrowed and he glanced at one of the guards with a quick nod of his head. The guard moved to catch the girl's eye. He gestured for her to face forward. She didn't respond. He stepped forward with a menacing glare.

"You better stand up straight and face forward, you little b…"

He was interrupted by another flash of movement. In the next second, he was hurled into the nearest window. The double-paned, bulletproof glass didn't shatter. The guard's body took the full force of the impact. He suffered injuries equivalent to falling four stories onto concrete.

Before anyone could react, the blur flashed through the room like lightning. The auctioneer's head jerked back, then twisted violently to one side. He dropped to the floor, his lifeless body crumpling in a heap. Standing behind him was a man with a smug grin on his face. He acknowledged her with a wink before dashing to one side, tearing through the nearest guard, who never had a chance.

Screams erupted from behind the darkened glass. She heard a sound like electricity crackling, and was blinded by a massive surge of light as the windows blew out. Glass scattered across the floor and everything went dark. The smell of ozone filled the room, followed by the stench of burnt flesh. Her stomach churned and her heart raced so much, all her limbs shook.

"Do not be afraid."

The voice came from directly behind her. She froze in place, but felt a strange calm in her gut. A warm hand touched her arm. It was gentle and kind, not like the groping fingers of her Russian captor. Before she could blink, she was back in the holding room with the rest of the girls. Standing among them was a handsome man with short, dark hair, and piercing brown eyes. He gazed at them with compassion and kindness, things she'd given up hope she'd ever experience again.

"Everyone hold hands," he commanded. "I am here to take you to safety."

Without so much as a beat, they were in a different room. It was well-lit, spacious, and comfortable, with plush couches and chairs scattered throughout. The tables were made of expensive-looking dark wood and the carpets were pristine. The smell of lavender air freshener lingered. Her mouth dropped open and she exchanged stunned glances with the others.

The man gestured toward a table loaded with food. The girls all stood, hesitating. She knew they were all thinking the same thing; they were unsure what trouble they would get in if they were caught here by the Russians.

"Please," the man insisted. "Eat. This is all for you. You have nothing further to fear. By the end of this day, you will all be back with your families."

"B-b-but, they said if we tried to leave, they would…"

He waved a hand. "My friends are…dealing with them, even as we speak. You will never see them again." He smiled, his eyes soft and calm. "Now, eat. Enjoy. You must be starving."

The girl stared at him. "Who are you?"

The man smiled. "You may call me…Zha'riel."

"Nico!" Xabier scanned the room from his place at the center of complete and utter carnage. He had lost count long ago of the number of guards he had ripped to shreds. At this point, the pile of bodies and body parts would take days for the medical examiner to sort through.

"Here, Xabs!"

Xabier made his way to the voice. He found Nico standing over an equally impressive pile of bodies. Looking around he squinted at Nico.

"No blood?" he asked. "I mean…at *all*?"

Nico wrinkled his forehead. "There's blood." He lifted one of the bodies with his toe. "See?"

Xabier leaned over and peered at the red spot on the floor. "It looks like paint." He looked at Nico. "You know; you're not proving anything by killing them all without shedding blood."

Nico stared at the bodies, all humor fading from his face. Xabier caught the look in his eyes and pressed his lips together. He frowned and looked around the room.

"Where's the halo?"

"Taking care of the girls."

Xabier shook his head and rolled his eyes. "Still won't get his heavenly hands dirty, eh?"

Nico continued to stare at the bodies with a thoughtful look on his face. "He's protecting the innocent; that's his job."

Xabier nodded and shrugged. He caught the look in Nico's eyes. "What are you thinking?"

Nico's bright, green eyes darkened and he let out a long slow breath. "I'm thinking it's time to send a message."

$$\mathcal{B} \, A \, \underset{2}{\mathcal{Z}} \, \psi \, \mathcal{G}$$

"What do you make of it, Agnes?"

"This is extraordinary work."

Benyamin sniffed without cracking a smile. Dealing with his own species was complicated enough, but interspecies cooperation meant Benyamin would also have to allow for the personalities of a number of supernatural creatures. At least Agnes was pleasant, for the most part. She was an elemental, a creature who could take the form of the various elements of the world: earth, wind, fire, and water. Her personality seemed to drift between forms, making her unpredictable, particularly when startled or pressured.

Benyamin did his best to keep things quiet and stress-free where she was concerned. He needed her expertise in supernatural artifacts and relics. She held three PhDs, in archeology, anthropology, and linguistics, all three of which would be useful in uncovering and interpreting the items required for their endeavors. His main goal was to keep her focused on the task at hand.

"Thank you for that penetrating evaluation. I was hoping you might probe a little deeper into the nature of the...*extraordinary* piece."

Agnes looked up with a sheepish grin. "Sorry. It's just...I've never seen anything like this. It is clearly hollow." She shook the box and lifted a shoulder. "And yet..."

"And yet," Benyamin finished, "there is no visible lid, opening, or mechanism?" He raised his eyebrows. "Yes, we know this, my love. Thank you for stating the obvious. Now...regarding the symbols?"

"Oh yes," Agnes nodded, her bright blue eyes dancing over the box. She pushed a lock of reddish-brown hair behind her ear. "I recognize about half of them. They're not all from the same species though."

"Species?"

"Yes." Agnes pointed to a symbol on the box. "*Your* language…Aramaic." She pointed to another familiar symbol. "That's a werewolf symbol…the Blood Moon Clan. And this Celtic-looking one with the three dots? It's Garland's warlock clan." Agnes identified several more symbols. "I just need time to research the rest, but I'd bet the rest of the coalition can identify the ones related to their species."

Benyamin frowned, his brow furrowed in thought. "We know there are twelve species. There are two symbols for each, assuming we're on the right track."

"That would leave six," Agnes squinted at him. "What are you thinking, Benyamin?"

"I'm thinking that leaves three species unaccounted for. We need to figure out what those species are and bring them into our fold."

Agnes shook her head. "The portal stone was clear…twelve supernatural species went into the portal. The key is hidden inside a locked box. Their languages are all needed to unlock the box's protective spell."

"But not *only* their languages, apparently."

Agnes raised her eyebrows. "So, there are three species that were *not* cast in? Why would *their* languages…" She closed her eyes. "Ahhh."

Benyamin reached for a bottle of old, expensive Scotch. Pouring himself a drink, he said. "I think we've figured it out. In addition to those cast *in*, we need…"

"We need the languages of those who *locked* the gate," Agnes finished, peering at the box with renewed interest. "I wonder who…"

"We must assume humans," Benyamin said. "They are the stewards of creation. They would have been involved."

Agnes moved the box slowly in her hands. "Here," she said, pointing at an ornate cross. "Christianity."

"That's one," Benyamin agreed, looking over her shoulder. He pointed. "And there."

Agnes frowned. "The dove?" She nodded her head back and forth in acceptance. "It makes sense. The whole Holy Spirit thing." She shook her hands when she said it, like she was talking about something spooky. She sat back. "Okay, that leaves four symbols. Who else would have been involved?"

Benyamin continued to sip his drink. He closed his eyes in thought. Who else could be involved? The humans are not supernatural. They would need more than their courage and stubborn persistence to open a portal.

When he spoke, the words were scarcely audible. "A servant of nature."

Agnes frowned. "What?"

"The humans. They needed magic." Benyamin turned to her and spread his hands. "They couldn't open a portal on their own. The supernatural creatures that *could* open one were the ones being thrown into the portal. None of them would have knowingly helped."

"*Knowingly*," Agnes said. "What about *un*knowingly?"

"Too risky. It had to be someone with ties to the humans *and* ties to creation. It had to be a servant of nature."

Agnes groaned and rolled her eyes. "I hate witches." She looked at the box again. "Witch symbolism is tricky. We'll have to get the rest of the coalition to identify their languages. Then we will have four remaining. Two of them will be the witch language."

"But the last two," Benyamin said. "I can't imagine who else would have been needed."

"We'll figure it out," Agnes said with confidence. "The answer is out there. They wouldn't have made it impossible."

Chapter 3

"I don't understand why we are putting ourselves in danger. How do you know this isn't a trap?"

"It is *not* a trap," Alvi insisted as they entered the Vista Bela hotel in Jurado, Colombia. "I don't know what it actually *is*, but I do know our old friend, Mr. Scarlatti, is involved."

Nayra's eyebrows raised and she ran her tongue along her teeth. "Interesting."

They walked through the cool, marble lobby. The scent of salt-water wafted through the spacious room, mixing with the citrus air freshener. Palm trees surrounded four massive pillars which framed a sitting area in the middle of the lobby, creating the feel of a tropical oasis. Several guests lounged in plush seats, sipping drinks, completely unaware of the company they kept.

Alvi and Nayra took the elevator to the top floor and entered the penthouse suite. The wide-open space provided an extraordinary panoramic view of the South Pacific Ocean via a wall of glass stretching from one end of the long room to the other. Off in the distance, cruise ships could be seen entering and leaving the Gulf of Panama. Tourist vessels cruised at low speeds in search of whales and dolphins. Closer to shore, water-skiers and jet-skiers glided through the waves in a multicolored dance that almost appeared choreographed for the consistent distance each maintained from the others.

"I don't like it here," Nayra said. She hunched her shoulders and scanned the room. "There is evil in this place."

A chill swept through the room. Alvi spun around, his eyes darting from one corner to the next. Nayra's gaze fell upon a white-robed figure whose mouth twitched at the corners. His glow-white eyes were aimed in her direction.

"Now *that* is not very complimentary."

He was seated in a chair in the middle of the room, one leg crossed over the other. He looked like he'd been there the whole time Alvi and Nayra were perusing the suite.

"Azazel," Alvi said, with a gesture. "This is…"

"Nayra, I presume?" Azazel inclined his head toward her as he rose. In three easy, powerful strides, he approached the wetbar on one side of the room. He poured three glasses from an ornate, crystal decanter. Holding one up for inspection, he made a face and said, "I suppose it will have to do." He handed one to Alvi and another to Nayra. He raised the third glass in a toast. "To unexpected alliances."

Alvi and Azazel both sipped the liquor, while Nayra made no move to drink. She stared at Azazel, her eyes narrowing even more at his toast. She was frightened at Azazel's imposing presence; he didn't have to try. With no effort, he exuded a power far greater than anything she had ever confronted. One of the first lessons in the dark arts, her ancestors had passed down to her, was to never become entangled with those more powerful than she.

Azazel lowered his glass and pressed his lips together in what she took for mild amusement. "Is there a problem?"

Nayra gathered her courage. "I haven't agreed to any…alliance."

Azazel furrowed his brow. His eyes flashed silver.

"Now she doesn't mean that, Azazel," Alvi jumped in. His forehead beaded with sweat, and he rubbed his palms together. Nayra often allowed herself to appear frail and fearful, but beneath the surface she was a fierce soul. And stubborn; she could be quite stubborn.

"What I mean," Nayra said, her dark eyes leveled at Azazel. "Is that I don't know you, and I don't know what you want from me."

Before Alvi could interject, Azazel said, "Perhaps you would permit me to show you something."

He held out his hand, palm up. A three-dimensional image appeared, hovering just inches above. When he removed his hand, the image, a clay box, about the size of a shoebox, remained, suspended in mid-air. Alvi's mouth dropped open. Before he could say anything, Azazel turned his eyes on Nayra.

"What do you make of this?"

She stared at him for a tense moment before turning her attention to the image. A glimmer of recognition struck her. She peered at all sides. Her forehead scrunched and she mumbled to herself. "It cannot be...this...this...it's...impossible..."

Alvi looked closely as well, but his forehead scrunched and he let out a helpless breath.

Azazel said, "Do you know what this is, my dear?"

Nayra ignored him. She continued to roam her gaze from one inscription to the next. Azazel straightened his posture and cleared his throat.

Nayra looked up. "This is..." She shook her head, glancing back at the image in disbelief. "Has it been *found?*"

"Less than one month ago," Azazel confirmed, his eyes never leaving hers.

"*Madre de Dios,*" Nayra mumbled.

Azazel furrowed his brow in amusement. "A fine young woman, I'm told." His eyes took on a far-off look before refocusing on the present. "I will say this...had *I* been available to deal with her when her husband first brought her to Bethlehem, we could have avoided a myriad of problems over the past couple millennia." He shook his head in disgust. "Instead, we let that paranoid slob, Herod, bungle things year after year. Before long..." He waved a hand and shook his head. "But that is a story for another time. Anyway..."

"Herod?" Alvi asked in bewilderment. "Who...?"

"Haven't you read your Bible, Alvi?"

Alvi shrugged. "Not really."

"Good for you." Azazel laughed, his eyes glimmering. "It's a boring read anyway, lacking any semblance of artistic integrity, and quite one-sided in its approach, in my opinion. I've always wondered why so many people wasted their time on such a poor collaborative effort."

Azazel spoke as though he were discussing the merits of any random work of art. Nayra could see, Alvi was struggling to follow him.

"Herod was the king of Judea back when Mary and that poor fool came to Bethlehem." Azazel shook his head, as though he still couldn't quite believe what had transpired. "It was such a simple task. All he had to do was dispose of *one* infant. Of course, Herod turned it into a prolonged massacre of every single child under the age of two." Azazel chuckled at the memory. "You do have to admire his enthusiasm. The man knew how to throw himself into a project."

Alvi was raised a Catholic, but Nayra would be stunned if he recalled any of those names from scripture. For Alvi, scripture was little more than a collection of stories. The people within weren't real. While Alvi stood with a blank look on his face, Nayra stared at Azazel in bewilderment. Azazel had personal knowledge of Biblical characters. It was mindboggling.

Nayra returned her attention to the image. Her eyes flicked from one end to the other, her expression alternating between disbelief and suspicion. She looked at Azazel, trying to discern whether he was playing some kind of mind game. With a carrot like this box dangling in front of her, he could get her to do most anything, but if he knew the significance of the box, he also knew there was nothing in the world more important.

Azazel circled Nayra and the hovering image. "Allow me to tell you a story." He waited until Alvi and Nayra both turned their attention to him. "Once upon a time, this planet teemed with the supernatural." He spread his hands. "It wasn't always that way, but a supernatural...*God*, for lack of a better word...cannot create a *natural* world and expect to keep the supernatural out." He shrugged. "It was just a matter of time."

"A matter of time before what?" Alvi asked.

Azazel looked at him as if the answer was obvious. "Before the *creation*...mutated."

ᛒ ᚨ ꝫ ᚦ ᚲ

"It is murder, no matter how you justify it."

"I don't need to justify *anything*."

Nico shrugged Zha'riel's hand off his arm and walked into the kitchen. He glanced over his shoulder and caught Xabier's eye. He loved being able to see from one room to the other. The wide-open floor plan was one of the biggest selling points for Nico. He grew up in a tiny house built in the 1950s and his childhood, memories were always of cramped spaces, cut off from adjoining rooms.

Nico pulled a beer from the refrigerator. He took a quick sip and as he let the liquid slide down his throat he also felt a surge of power come over him. It froze him for just a second before it passed. It was as thrilling as it was horrifying. It had to be Lucifer's blood. Hell's king had saved his life, and in so doing, tipped the balance of power within him. Now, instead of being a mix of dark angel and mage, Nico's blood now contained the blood of the most powerful force for evil in existence. Lucifer's power surged through him.

Zha'riel folded his arms across his chest and shook his head. "It is happening exactly as I suspected it would."

"Oh, here we go." Nico rolled his eyes.

"You are arrogant, Nico...and naïve. You believe you are in control, but you are not. You are most *certainly* not."

Nico drained his beer and reached for another. "You know what your problem is, Zha'riel? You still think like an angel."

"I *am* an angel!"

"But they turned on you, didn't they?" Nico pointed his finger at him. "The angels. They exiled you."

"Yes," Zha'riel agreed. "Because of *you*."

Nico laughed as he opened his beer and took another long sip. The contents almost came out his nose. "I see. It's all *my* fault, right? Isn't that against your own philosophy, Zha'riel? How am *I* responsible for *your* actions?"

Zha'riel opened his mouth to speak but shut it just as quickly. He gritted his teeth and bowed his head. "You are right. I am responsible for my predicament." He raised a finger. "Just as *you* are responsible for yours."

"I'm okay with that."

"And when Heaven comes for you?"

It was a familiar conversation. Zha'riel had been reluctant from the start. The idea of saving the innocent appealed to him, but he constantly admonished Nico and Xabier, always insisting three supernatural beings ought to be able to avoid unnecessary bloodshed. When Nico and Xabier began killing the criminals, even after saving the innocent, Zha'riel objected. Murder would not be tolerated, even the murder of violent predators.

Nico and Xabier always ignored his pleas for justice over murder. Irrespective of how hard Zha'riel argued, Nico felt compelled to exact vengeance. The justice system never did its part when it came to dealing with evil. It always softened the blow of justice at the precise moment when it should have dropped the hammer.

"Tell the halo," Xabier said without taking his eyes off the television screen, "that Heaven...will soon be a non-issue." Even from across the room, with the surround sound blaring, he could hear every word.

"The vampire does not reassure," Zha'riel said. "And you are insane if you think he is able to protect you from Heaven. Anyone who stands between you and Rafael's soldiers will be cut down without a second thought."

"Speaking of violence..." Nico retorted.

"Tell the halo, I don't intend to face off against Heaven." Xabier's phone chirped. "Instead, I plan to find someone who..." His voice trailed off as he read the text message on the screen. His brow furrowed.

"You okay?' Nico asked.

Xabier looked up, confusion in his eyes. "Ye-uh...yes, I'm fine." He stood up and looked again at his phone. "I'll be back. I have to check on something."

"Need help?"

Xabier forced a smile. "I'll be fine."

When he left, Nico turned to Zha'riel, who had a concerned look on his face. "What now?"

"You are changing, Nico," he replied. "You can feel it. I can *see* that you feel it."

Nico let out a long, resigned sigh. "Yes, Zha'riel. I can feel it, and it sometimes scares the hell out of me, but I also feel like I'm getting stronger every second. *You* act like it's a bad thing."

"It *is* a bad thing!" Zha'riel's entire body shook with the statement. "I know you cannot see it, Nico, but you are descending into darkness. Please listen to me."

"I'm always listening, Zha'riel, and I'm handling the urges. It's not like I'm out there killing random people. I am only hurting the ones I set out to hurt."

"Do you hear yourself?" Zha'riel replied. "You say nothing about the innocent."

"The innocent are *your* department," Nico shot back. "*My* department is making sure the bad guys don't hurt anyone else...ever again."

"Judge, jury *and* executioner." Zha'riel shook his head and sat in a chair at the kitchen table. He put his head in one of his hands. "The only reason you have not hurt an innocent is because you are drowning the urge in criminal blood. It will not be long before you move this..." He flailed his free hand. "...line in the sand you think you have drawn."

ᛒ A ᶾ ᴪ Ꮸ

"Are you certain? You are sure it was Seir?"

Abdiel hung up the phone and turned to his master. "My Lord, I believe, as the humans like to say, 'They took the bait.'"

Lucifer stood in the center of the rotunda at the National Archives. He loved the feeling of space, and him at the center of it. American architecture always seemed to be about their status at the center of the universe. Perhaps one day, they would learn a lesson. For now, he would have to be content with their more gradual descent into depravity.

"The witch has been taken?"

Abdiel nodded. "By Seir."

Lucifer allowed himself a slight smile. "So, it begins."

"How can we be certain they will join the coalition?"

"The motivation behind *that*," Lucifer explained, "is simple, as old as time itself. You see, my old friend is vindictive." He looked at Abdiel. "You would be surprised at how petty archangels can be."

He didn't mind the time he spent explaining to Abdiel the nuances of his business. A general of renown in Lucifer's army, Abdiel was an expert at commanding troops in battle, but he was less skilled in the art of the bigger picture. He was sharp, though, and all he needed was guidance.

Abdiel frowned. "He would take the witch just to keep *you* from getting her?"

"Absolutely," Lucifer replied.

"It seems soooo…" Abdiel shook his head in bewilderment. "I don't know, so…"

"Silly?" Lucifer offered. He shrugged. "It's no different than any other relationship, Abdiel."

"How do you know he will use her to open the portal?"

Lucifer frowned. "That's fifty-fifty. If he thinks I really want it open, he might kill her and drop the body somewhere obvious."

Abdiel nodded. "That's why you wanted those rumors started."

"If Azazel thinks we're trying to keep the portal closed, he will do whatever it takes to open it."

"So why not just partner with the slag coalition?"

Lucifer cast a sideways glance at him. "*Slag?* Come now, Abdiel, there is no need for such disdain. These creatures are useful to our ends."

"What *are* our ends?" Abdiel asked.

Lucifer pressed his lips together. His brow furrowed and he tilted his head. "What of young Nico? I understand he is progressing.

"Yes. This latest incident was a real bloodbath. I'm surprised Zha'riel allowed it to happen."

Lucifer stood before the massive Faulkner painting, depicting the signing of the Declaration of Independence. Of all the moments he'd orchestrated throughout history, isolating the Western Hemisphere from Europe was his favorite. Sure, he would have to stand back and keep a low profile while the Holy Narcissist stepped in and took over. Truth be told, Lucifer didn't even care. He knew it wouldn't be long before the Son would grow bored or, more likely, that these ridiculous humans He'd created for Himself, would rebel and anger Him. Either way, He would one day turn His almighty back on His own creation.

"So close," he murmured, his eyes roaming over the massive canvas.

Abdiel scrunched his forehead. "My Lord?"

Lucifer's eyes snapped back into focus. He turned to Abdiel, his hands clasped loosely behind him. He smiled, only his eyes betraying the darkness within. He was dressed in a black Burberry suit. Abdiel, clothed in Armani, looked right at home, standing next to him. Though he was accustomed to Lucifer's gaze, Abdiel was certain he would never be comfortable under it.

"We are so close to bringing young Nico into our fold." Lucifer returned his gaze to the painting. "He will be an invaluable resource in the coming war."

"War?" Abdiel frowned. "Are we going to war, my Lord?"

"Surely you can see it, Abdiel. This nation is ready to rip itself apart. Centuries of work are about to bear fruit."

He moved from the painting to the exhibit containing the Declaration of Independence. His smile grew even wider as he read the words...words he'd long before memorized. He glanced over at Abdiel who was doing his best to play the part of second-in-command. Lucifer appreciated the effort, and the company, but Abdiel was not Azazel. Perhaps in time, but he simply lacked the countless millennia Lucifer shared with his best friend.

"So," he said. "Nico will continue to grow in strength as the darkness grows within him. He will fight the darkness while giving in to his urges."

"Just as you foresaw," Abdiel said.

Lucifer nodded. "He needs to be careful. The urge will only…"

He cut himself short as two ladies walked toward them. They appeared to be professionals, perhaps historians or museum associates. The brunette caught his eye and flashed him a seductive smile. She tried to be subtle about it, but to Lucifer, it was the equivalent of peeling off her clothes and lying on her back. He smiled at her and nodded as she passed. Abdiel stifled a laugh.

"I think she fancies you, my Lord."

Lucifer chuckled and shook his head. "This creation of His." He jerked his head slightly upward. "It makes you wonder what He was thinking, doesn't it?"

Abdiel hung his head, the smile threatening to turn into a full-blown guffaw right in the middle of the echo chamber that was the National Archive. His body shook with the effort to stifle that laughter. Lucifer grinned and patted him on the shoulder.

"Worried my brother will come flying in on one of his heavenly chariots?" He chuckled. "Not to worry, my friend. Michael has more important things to do than worry about our irreverence."

Abdiel recovered. "You were saying about Nico's urges?"

"Ah, yes." Lucifer waved a finger and turned back to America's founding document. As he scanned the words he smiled. "Right now, young Nico is indulging a mere thirst…a thirst for violence., for blood. He's indulging that thirst by taking the lives of scumbag humans."

"Not the best thing for our side," Abdiel noted.

Lucifer brushed it off with a dismissive shrug. "A worthwhile sacrifice. Humans, by nature, are corrupt and despicable. We will never run short of these pathetic minions. Nico, however, could very well go over the edge all on his own."

"And then?"

"Aside from drawing attention to the supernatural," Lucifer said. "He could mobilize Heaven."

Abdiel closed his eyes. Lucifer smiled in silence. Abdiel really should have thought of that. Of course, Heaven would notice the body count in Southern New Jersey. If he wanted to remain at Lucifer's right hand, Abdiel would have to think a whole lot faster.

When Abdiel looked up again, Lucifer saw the concern in his eyes. "Do not fret, my friend. It takes centuries. You have had mere months." He laid a hand on Abdiel's shoulder and looked into his eyes. "You have proven yourself a loyal soldier." He squeezed. "And a trusted friend."

"Thank you, my Lord."

Lucifer released him and turned toward the exhibit containing the United States Constitution. Abdiel followed and they stood side-by-side, taking in the document. Abdiel could scarcely understand his master's fascination with America's treasured documents, but he stood, waiting to learn.

"So," Lucifer mused. "How best to nurture young Nico's descent into darkness?"

Abdiel frowned. "As long as keeps company with the angels, it will be difficult influence him."

Lucifer smiled and held up a finger. "Yes and no. The vampire is the key. My guess is he's pulling young Nico two steps for every one Zha'riel moves him." He thought for a minute. "Actually, Zha'riel is probably doing part of our job for us."

"What do you mean?"

Lucifer shrugged. "Zha'riel is what the Americans call a 'boy scout.' He is probably nagging young Nico at every turn. Nico might limit his body count just to appease him...for now." He smirked. "But Nico will ultimately break free of Heaven's restraint. Then, Heaven will have to act." He peered down at the two-hundred-year-old words as he thought. He looked up at Abdiel. "We must avoid that eventuality."

"Perhaps a distraction, my Lord."

Lucifer tore his attention from the founding document, stood up straight, and stared at Abdiel in silence for a moment. "Continue."

Abdiel took a breath. "Perhaps, instead of concerning ourselves with nurturing Nico's descent, we should nurture his...*other* weakness."

Lucifer frowned. "Go on."

"Azazel took something from him." Abdiel was clearly pleased with himself for thinking of it first. "He took something Nico loved very much."

Lucifer's eyes stared off into the distance. "The girl," he said softly, closing his eyes. "Of course."

"Perhaps," Abdiel said, "we could nurture his broken heart."

Lucifer nodded. "I assume my most trusted advisor already has someone in mind?"

Abdiel smiled and nodded formally. "Of course, my Lord."

Chapter 4

"Are you sure this isn't some kind of turf war, Yuri? You know, your competition comes in and makes a move on your territory?"

Yuri Malakov shook his head and spoke with a thick Russian accent.. "If one of my enemies did this, there would be no question about it." He surveyed the carnage. "These incidents are getting more and more elaborate."

"You think they're all the same group?"

Yuri rolled his eyes in frustration. The Atlantic City Police Department wasn't going to be any help at all if Chief Thomas North, was any indication. Four attacks had occurred over the past six months. The first three were relatively small, costing the organization forty-two men in total. The body count for this one would be over sixty, a total loss.

He let his eyes roam over the scene. The rooms were a mess. Every window pane was shattered, and the glass shards covered the floors. Blood spattered walls in the main room, and pooled around a pile of bodies, or more accurately, body parts. Those were the remains of Yuri's team. He turned his head to another, neater pile of corpses. Those were the buyers, wealthy, and powerful men from around the world. This was bad...very bad for business.

"Over one hundred men killed in one city over six months." He looked at the police chief. "That's more than we've lost worldwide in the past three years combined. And we operate in war zones, Chief North. Doesn't it strike you as mildly ironic that some piss-ant city in America is more dangerous for us than Eastern Europe or the Middle East?"

The chief sighed. "Look, we'll find them."

"I pay you, not only for security, but for information...you know?" Yuri pumped a fist. "Informatzi, Chief North! I want to know who is doing this."

Chief North nodded. "Like I said, we'll find them."

"Make sure this remains quiet," Yuri said.

The scene was not yet public knowledge. When Yuri had tried to contact his auction team and received no response, his first call was to Chief Thomas North. When the police chief had checked the location, and found the massacre, Yuri instructed him to keep it sealed and immediately boarded a plane. Now, his team was sifting through the carnage, trying to ascertain what had happened.

"Sir!" One of the men came up to Yuri, shaking his head. "All twelve buyers are here, along with everyone involved. It doesn't look like there were any survivors."

Yuri thought for a moment. "That is disappointing."

Chief North frowned. "It's disappointing that your whole Atlantic City crew was killed? Or that no one survived?"

Yuri shrugged. "A survivor would at least give us someone to look for. Usually, when things go bad like this over and over again, someone on the inside is involved." He pressed his lips together in thought. "Somehow this...whoever they are...is getting information without turning our own people. Or, they are killing the traitors as they go. That means it isn't one of your government agencies."

"Well, you're right about *that!*"

They turned to see a man in black jeans and an untucked, black, button-down shirt strolling up the tunnel toward them. He wore black sunglasses and walked as though he hadn't a care in the world. The chief made a move to stop him, but Yuri held a hand up.

"Wait. We're about to get answers."

The man approached, and Yuri made him to be young, in his twenties. He chuckled at the impudence of Americans. They had no respect for their elders or for authority. It would one day be the downfall of their civilization.

"Your people," the man said, "were loyal right to the end."

Yuri could tell the man was unarmed, which made him crazy. Either that, or he was in possession of some very valuable information. He suppressed the urge to shoot the guy in the face, though his fingers did tap the butt of the gun, in his shoulder holster, under his blazer.

"And how would you know that?" he asked.

"Because I was the one who killed them." He frowned. "Well...*most* of them. My buddy took out a bunch too."

Yuri's eyes darkened. "If that is true, why should I let you walk out of here?"

The man smiled. "My close friends call me Nico. And you won't be *letting* me walk out of here."

The police chief chuckled and lit a cigarette. "So, you just willingly walked to your death?"

Nico chuckled and shook his head. "I didn't say that...Yuri, was it?" He surveyed the scene, turning his back on Yuri and the chief. "So unnecessary," he said, shaking his head. Turning back to Yuri, he continued, "You know, I don't understand you people. This is the fourth time I've had to make a mess in my own town..."

"*Your* town?" Chief North exploded. Smoke from his latest puff chased his words out of his mouth. "Look here, you young fool..."

"Eeeaasssy, Chief," Yuri patted his back.

Nico never turned around. He just stood there, shaking his head in wonder. "What happened? The first three messages weren't clear?" He turned around with an apologetic look on his face. "I'm really sorry about that, Yuri" He shrugged. "I'm kinda new at this, so I might be a little clumsy at sending messages."

Yuri took in a sharp breath. "For someone who is unarmed and alone, you are very arrogant."

Nico chuckled. "My brother used to say the same kind of things to me." He stared at Yuri. "Scumbag criminals killed him six months ago."

"And you think we…"

"No, no, no," Nico shook his head and waved a dismissive hand. "No, I destroyed that entire organization months ago." He left out the part about Alvi Cornega and the witch, Nayra, escaping with their lives.

Yuri frowned. "I don't understand."

"This has nothing to do with my brother's death," Nico said. "This has to do with you kidnapping innocent girls and selling them to pedophiles and rapists. This has to do with you and your crooked police chief over there, pretending you're above the law."

Yuri nodded. "I see." Turning to the chief, he said, "I think we're done here."

Chief North nodded and drew his firearm. "All right. Come with me, son."

Nico pressed his lips together and turned back to the bloody scene. "You people and your guns." He shrugged. "You just don't understand, do you?" Turning back to the men, he said, "Do you think I did all this with a gun?"

With that he stretched out his hand and sent the chief's gun spinning across the room. It clattered to the ground fifty feet away and skittered into a concrete wall. Yuri pulled his gun and took dead aim at Nico before the gun flew out of *his* hand too! Another gesture from Nico and both men shot backwards, slamming into the concrete wall behind them. Before they could regain their senses, they were engulfed in a quick burst of green electricity, causing them to scream out in agony.

"Now then," Nico said, ceasing the torture. He pulled out a phone. "I just need to make a quick call." He held the phone to his ear. After several moments of listening, he hissed. "Where the hell are you? We had a plan."

After ending the call, he turned back to the stunned pair of criminals lying on the ground. "I guess we're on our own, fellas." He bent down and dug in Yuri's inner coat pocket until he found a smartphone. He looked through the contact list. "So, Yuri, who is the top dog in your organization?"

Yuri, his breathing ragged, spat, "I tell you *nothing!*"

Nico held the phone out with one hand and placed a finger against Yuri's temple. The crackle of green energy lasted only a split second, but Yuri's bloodcurdling scream went on for three. Nico blinked at the sound and mock-cringed.

"Ouch. That hurts, huh?" He looked at his finger. "I've never tried that before." Looking back to Yuri, he said, "So, about the top guy…" He held out the phone and shook it with a playful grin.

Yuri swiped down on the screen and tapped a name. "Him."

"Nikoli Petrov?" Nico nodded. "Gotcha." He pulled Yuri to his feet and leaned him against the wall. "Now, I was supposed to have a cameraman for this, but he seems to have flaked out on me, so we'll have to work together here."

He swiped the screen until he came to the app designed for video communication. He opened the app and found Nikoli Petrov's name in the contact list and hit SEND. He waited until he heard a voice, then a face appeared on the screen.

"Yuri?" He added a string of Russian gibberish.

"No, this isn't Yuri," Nico interrupted. "Do you speak English?"

"Yes. Where is Yuri?"

"He's here," Nico said, aiming the camera at Yuri. "See?"

"Yuri? Are you all right? What is going on?"

Nico pointed the camera back at himself. "All right, shut up. I have a message. Am I talking to the right person?"

The camera on the other end moved to reveal a second man. He had silver hair, a scar on his right cheek and a pair of fiendish dark eyes. He was not a man used to being trifled with. Even over the phone, Nico could feel his ice-cold gaze.

"You are now."

Nico grinned. "Great. Now, just to get you up to speed, I sent your man Yuri here, three messages to knock off his kidnapping, human trafficking, pedophile supply operation, but he decided to ignore me."

"*You* are the one responsible for the deaths of forty-three of my men?"

Nico grimaced. "About that. We're up to a hundred and five or so now."

He turned the camera on the bloody scene. He panned slowly from one end to the other, showing the unidentified man the destruction he had wrought. He heard the man mutter in Russian, probably making threats and vows of vengeance.

"Yeah, yeah, yeah," Nico waved his hand at the phone. "This was message number four, but your man, Yuri over here, didn't see it that way." He faced the phone at Yuri's chest. "So, I'm sending the message directly to *you*."

Yuri stood, barely able to hold himself up. Nico aimed the phone at Yuri's chest. Without warning, he plunged his hand into Yuri's gut, and blood gushed over his arm. He forced his hand upward until his fingers found the pulsing organ and wrapped around it. He stared the gasping Yuri directly in the eyes and smiled.

"Nice meeting you, Yuri."

And he ripped his hand downward, letting Yuri's lifeless body slide down the wall. Nico held Yuri's heart in front of the camera for several seconds before turning the camera to his face.

"You know," Nico said. "I actually thought it would beat a few times...you know, like in the movies? I guess Hollywood doesn't know their stuff, do they?"

For the first time since the man came on the screen, Nico saw the cold steel façade crumble. He stared at Nico in disbelief. A second passed before his eyes focused and he regained his composure. He gazed back into the screen, doing his best to stare Nico down. When he finally opened his mouth, his words were in perfect English, with a menacing Russian accent.

"You are a dead man."

Nico had no patience for threats. "Let me make this perfectly clear. Atlantic City, New Jersey is closed. Don't make me bring this to your doorstep."

Without waiting for a reply, he ended the call, dropped the phone in Yuri's lifeless lap, and turned to leave. He heard a groan. The police chief was waking up. Nico was about to end him in much the same way he ended Yuri, when he had a thought.

Dropping into a crouch next to the chief, he shook the man's shoulder. "Chief North? You with me?"

"Whaa?" The man's eyes were wide with fear as he saw Yuri's bloody corpse.

"Don't try to talk," Nico said gently. "I had to rip your friend's heart out of his chest to make a point to the Russians. I'm thinking I should do the same to you."

"P-p-p-please…"

Nico pressed his lips together. "Perhaps we could come to an…arrangement?"

ᛒ ᴀ ᣟ ψ ɢ

Xabier's phone buzzed. He knew it was Nico. He knew he was supposed to help send the "message" to the Russians. Xabier hated keeping his friend in the dark, but his old life was catching up to him. He didn't want to drag Nico into that mess. His friend had grown in strength and control over the past few months, and there was no end in sight to that growth, but Xabier wasn't sure how Nico would measure up to an army of the most dangerous creatures on the planet.

He hadn't fared well against Azazel. Since that day, Nico Scarlatti had faced only human adversaries. They were no match for him, but that meant nothing in the supernatural world. Not all creatures could be killed. Some just had to be avoided. For nearly fifteen centuries Xabier had carved out a life staying hidden from certain groups. Today, an old friend had discovered him. He had to know if he was in danger.

He hated New York City. It had nothing to do with the city itself. Xabier just hated large crowds. In most cases, a vampire would thrive in a place like the Big Apple. With millions of people living in such proximity, countless millions of tourists coming and going from all over the world, and a high crime rate, New York was the kind of place where a vampire could survive in obscurity. The night life alone provided nocturnal predators ample opportunity to feast on the unsuspecting.

The problem with big cities was they were also the first places supernatural hunters would look. Xabier'd had close calls in London, Paris, Rome, Los Angeles, and New York, over several centuries, before he realized true safety lie in distance from such places. Ever since, he'd maintained a safe perimeter around any major city.

Now, he was breaking his cardinal rule, and stood in the middle of Central Park...vampire heaven. The two-and-a-half mile-long by half-mile-wide reserve was the perfect place for predators to stalk their prey, and why wouldn't it be? By 1850 New York City was home to the largest concentration of supernatural beings in the world. Their influence reached the top of the state legislature. It wasn't long before their influence created a pool of "socially conscious reformers" who argued, "the creation of a great public park would improve public health and contribute greatly to the formation of a civil society." The group created the perfect hunting ground for all manner of predator.

By the time the human population realized what had happened, they were stuck with the monstrosity and unable to admit their mistake. To make matters worse, the project set off the "urban park" movement, and large parks began to sprout up in major cities throughout America. Parks are dangerous places to be after dusk. While the stories of the supernatural beasts preying on humans in these places were soon relegated to myth and lore, there remains countless unexplained deaths and disappearances in major parks all over the country each year.

Xabier stepped deeper and deeper into the wooded area. His senses were on high alert. His ears fixated on every sound, identifying it, and categorizing it in his mind as he crept along, prepared for an attack from any direction, particularly from above. His eyes penetrated the night. He was grateful for the enhanced night vision his species possessed. He could see clearly, even with minimal light from the moon or stars.

He caught a sudden movement to his right and darted to the other side of the path, peering through the trees for any sign of life. He heard a slight rustling and squinted in that direction. A face appeared, pale and anxious, peeking out from behind the trees.

"Xabier?"

The voice sounded familiar, but, Xabier took no chances. He scooted from one spot to another, checking for any indication there were others waiting to pounce on him. When he came up empty, he returned to the path.

"Come out, Leonard," he said softly. "I'm here."

He heard the snapping of twigs and watched as a man stepped out of the trees and onto the path. Xabier hadn't seen Leonard in ages and could not be certain it wasn't a trap, so he watched in tense caution as his old friend approached. Leonard, sensing Xabier's apprehension, raised his hands and spun around slowly, showing Xabier he was unarmed.

"It's not a trap, Xabier. You have my word."

Xabier smiled. "How are you, old friend?"

He embraced Leonard and held him at arm's length for a better look.

"You look well. You haven't aged a day."

It was an old joke among vampires, but it served to break the tension between the two estranged friends. They laughed for a moment but quickly returned to their previous apprehensive states. Leonard cast uneasy glances from one side to the other.

"You weren't followed?"

Xabier frowned. "Of course not, Leonard. What is this about? Are you in trouble?"

"I think we're *all* in trouble," Leonard said, shaking his head. "There are rumblings."

Xabier let out a breath. That wasn't unusual. There were always rumors that something big was about to happen. There was always someone "on the verge" of uncovering a powerful artifact or relic. News like that barely raised an eyebrow these days, but Leonard had gone to a lot of trouble to find Xabier, and he'd broken years of necessary silence to do so.

"What exactly?" Xabier prompted.

"They're here."

Xabier frowned. "They" could mean anyone, but when vampires used the term, it usually meant a very specific "they," and it was not a group Xabier was interested in seeing right now, or ever.

"When you say 'they,'" Xabier said in a slow, even tone.

"I mean *the* "they," Leonardo insisted.

Xabier let out a sharp breath. "Here in New York?"

"No!" Leonardo scowled. "Do you think I'd still be here if they were?" He looked from right to left just in case. "Last I heard, they were down south somewhere."

Xabier swore under his breath. "Even *that's* too close. Any idea what they're after?"

Leonardo shrugged. "That's the weird thing. When they want something, the community buzzes. Everyone wants on their good side. This time, they were super quiet about it, and they haven't reached out to the community at all."

Xabier furrowed his brow. "What are they up to?"

Leonardo shrugged. "I'd hoped you might have some idea. I heard a strange rumor about some sort of…coalition."

"What kind of coalition?"

"Like…all of the supernatural species or something like that. Something about a global search."

Xabier's face froze. "That's not good."

"I know," Leonardo nodded. "I remember what you told me about the last time…"

"You need to keep this absolutely quiet," Xabier interrupted. "If they find out you know about them…"

"Don't worry about me," Leonardo assured him. "I know how to keep my head down." He looked at Xabier. "Do you think Lazlo is coming for you?"

Xabier blew out another breath. "I think if Lazlo ever finds out where I am..." He blew out a breath and leaned against a tree. "How old is this information?"

"Two months. Maybe a little more."

"Two *months?*" Xabier exploded. "And you're just telling me *now?*"

"Hey!" Leonardo pointed out. "You're the one who lives off the grid. It's a miracle I found you at all."

"You're right," Xabier conceded. "This coalition is bad news. Leo. Do you have any idea what it's all about?"

He shrugged. "No idea. I could poke around a little., but..."

Xabier nodded. "Do that, but keep it quiet. Don't take any chances, and let me know as soon as you hear anything."

Chapter 5

"Amazing."

"Absolutely stunning."

The mood in the room was that of a group who had taken a huge step forward, then realized just how far they had yet to go. The thousand-year-old artifact sat on a pedestal, in the center of a massive banquet room, at a plantation house in Wallace, Louisiana. The coalition of supernatural creatures seldom gathered together in one place, but the discovery of the box containing the Purgatory Key caused a surge in excitement, and even a degree of camaraderie.

Gamut approached and stood next to Benyamin. "This is your doing," he said, his eyes surveying the array of creatures mingling around the artifact. "Twelve mortal enemies all gathering in a common cause. Quite impressive, my friend."

"Everyone understands the situation," Benyamin countered. "Self-preservation trumps hatred. Perhaps we can usher in a new period of peace whilst saving our individual lines from extinction."

Gamut chuckled. "Who would have ever thought? Vampires consorting with werewolves? Wraiths with Daevas? Elementals with Shapeshifters? It's like the world is turned on its axis."

Even with the vow each member of the coalition had agreed to, there was always trepidation about putting the most powerful creatures in the world in such proximity. One never knew if today would be the day ancient feuds reignited. Benyamin was the only one the other members trusted to keep his word. He was the one who'd put the coalition together in the first place. His reasoning was less about needing help and more about a desire for peace between the supernatural factions.

"Perhaps," Benyamin said, "by working together successfully, we will build a level of trust that will transcend our historical differences."

Gamut nodded, his eyes still roaming over a scene he would never have believed possible. "I wonder if your dream of peace is something one can reasonably expect. The humans seek peace. They seldom achieve it."

"Peace is not something humans are predisposed to desire."

Benyamin and Gamut turned to face the newcomer to their discussion. Ktulis, a wraith, was one of few members of the coalition Benyamin truly liked. He was intelligent, pragmatic, and decisive. The only real issue with the wraiths was their tendency toward violence. Like many supernatural creatures, they survived by eliminating their enemies. Wraiths took that even further. Existing in total secrecy, fading into the shadows, they took privacy to the extreme, eliminating anyone who discovered their true nature. For this reason, human hunters pursued them relentlessly, driving them to near extinction. Ktulis was truly battling for the survival of his species.

"Humans speak of peace, but they never take the steps necessary to achieve it."

"And what steps would those be, Ktulis?"

The fourth voice to join the conversation was Rasputin. Yes, *that* Rasputin. Long since thought to be dead, he had spent nearly a century in the shadows of humanity. He'd learned his lesson. His rise to power and influence had been far too public. It was better to be unknown to the masses. He took the lesson to heart, and remained hidden from the world, using his powers sparingly.

An instigator by nature, Rasputin was not a fan of the wraiths, and had argued against their inclusion in the coalition from the outset, but Benyamin knew everyone's involvement was necessary. And what good would it do to have one or more of the species working against the effort once they found out they had been excluded?

Ktulis shrugged. Benyamin knew how Rasputin felt about wraiths and hoped Ktulis would take the high road.

Ktulis met the sorcerer's eyes. "Sometimes, the only way to achieve peace is to eliminate one's enemies."

"Ha!" Rasputin laughed. "A strategy that has worked well for the wraiths, no?"

Benyamin interjected. "There is no need to trade insults. We are all on the same side."

Ktulis stared daggers at Rasputin for several seconds before breaking eye contact. "For now," he muttered.

Suddenly, the room chilled. Everyone present felt the change in the atmosphere, and began to look around apprehensively. As if by instinct, each stood apart from the others, ensuring space between them and any possible attackers.

"Well, well, well," the voice seemed to hiss from all around the room. Then, a figure appeared in one corner. He was dressed in loose black garments, his black hair pulled back in a long, tight pony tail. He surveyed the room with an amused smirk on his face. "What a friendly gathering of weaklings."

Benyamin stepped forward. "I don't know who you are, sir, but you've wandered into the wrong party. I suggest you remove yourself from my home before I get angry."

The man's eyes flickered in amusement. "Oh, please *do* get angry."

Benyamin was about to take him up on his challenge until the man's eyes glowed a deep crimson. The vampire stopped in his tracks. Benyamin Maccabee was one of the most powerful creatures the planet had ever produced. Very little in existence scared him. A red-eyed demon topped that short list.

"Don't let my associate's brusque tone put you off."

Everyone spun away from the red-eyed demon and faced the newcomer, who had appeared in the corner opposite the demon. Clothed in sheer robes that appeared metallic but draped loosely over his form, he was seated in a chair, looking casually at his fingernails, as if inspecting a fresh manicure. Without warning, he stood up and everyone jumped, causing the demon on the other side of the room to chuckle.

"Now, Seir," said the newcomer, obviously in charge and therefore, the most powerful being in the room. "There is no need for rudeness." To the rest of the room he said, "Ignore the ill-tempered demon."

He smiled as he strode to the center of the room. He stood before the pedestal, on which rested the box everyone had been discussing. He peered down at the delicate carvings and shook his head. The look on his face indicated he was not impressed.

"Funny," he mused. "Such a fuss."

"I'm sorry, sir, but who exactly are you?" Benyamin asked. "And what do you want with us?"

The man straightened and stared at Benyamin as though the answer should be obvious. "You may call me...Azazel."

ℬ 𝐴 ⚡ 𝜓 𝐺

"All right...I've texted, emailed, and now I'm leaving a voicemail. You need to get back to me."

Nico hit the END button and stared at the screen of his phone. Xabier had been out of contact for several days. He'd never told Nico where he was headed or what he was doing, so Nico had nowhere to even begin a search for his friend. He tried calling Zha'riel, first out loud, and then by phone. He received no response.

"Why can't people keep in touch?" he muttered. "How hard is it to shoot someone a text letting them know you're alive?"

He leaned against his car, outside his new favorite bar, McGillian's. He and Xabier found it less than one hour after moving into their new home. Nico ran through all the possible reasons why Xabier might not call, and few of them were good. The problem was, Nico was still relatively new to the supernatural world. He didn't have an extensive network of supernatural contacts like Xabier had. Now, he was regretting his loner lifestyle.

Shaking his head, Nico went inside. He needed a drink and a quiet place to think everything through. Fortunately, the bar was almost empty. The evening crowd was just beginning to trickle in. Nico found a seat at the end of the bar and before he signaled Frank, the bartender, he had an ice-cold beer sitting in front of him. He grunted his thanks, and tossed a couple twenties on the bar.

He sipped the cold beer and closed his eyes, pinching the bridge of his nose. He glanced at his phone, but had no messages, no responses to any of his efforts to contact his friends. He shook his head, his mind floating where it always went in lonesome times.

He thought of her soft, blonde hair, the way it smelled when she'd cuddled up to him, her head on his chest. He thought about her eyes, the gentle blue that sparkled when she'd looked at him. He loved those memories, but it was her smile he truly missed. She'd smiled at him in a way no one ever had before.

In a single moment of vindictive pettiness, she was taken from him.

From that moment, Nico had only Xabier and Zha'riel. One was a vampire who liked the violent world of the supernatural a little bit too much. The other was an angel, exiled from his home for helping Nico. On one hand, Nico should have taken comfort in that demonstration of friendship. On the other, how long would it be before Zha'riel got homesick and regretted his decision?

"Oooh. I know that look."

Nico looked up into a pair of piercing green eyes. She was close enough for him to see little flecks of gold and red throughout, reminding him, strangely enough, of Christmas. She had lush, wild, red hair, cascading to the small of her back in spiral curls. Her perfect curves were covered in a sexy yet tasteful black dress which fit her form perfectly. She leaned on the bar with a tentative smile.

"Bad day?" she asked. "You look like you could use something a lot stronger than that beer."

Nico looked back at his glass and drained it. He shrugged. "Maybe you're right." He signaled the bartender. "Frank! The Balvanie!" He turned to the woman and raised his eyebrows.

"Tatiana," she said. To the bartender, she smiled, "I'll have what he's having."

Nico shook his head and rolled his eyes. "Do you even know what you just ordered?"

"Thirty-year-old Scotch?" She raised her eyebrows. "Yes, I know what Balvanie is. You're a man after my own heart…uhmmm…"

Nico grimaced and turned away. Out of the corner of his eye, he saw Tatiana purse her lips, and her shoulders slumped. He felt like a jerk, but thoughts of Stephanie dominated his mind.

"Oooookaaayy," Tatiana said, turning away and sitting on a stool.

Frank brought their drinks. Nico sipped his and closed his eyes as he let the alcohol slide down his throat, the burn warming him all the way down. He felt Tatiana's eyes on him as he withdrew once again.

She put a hand on his shoulder. "You okay?"

Nico blinked and shook his head. As pretty as the woman was, he had little interest. Thoughts of Stephanie clouded his mind every time a similar situation came up. Women were attracted to him, which was something he wasn't used to or comfortable with. At first, he liked it. That was how he got Stephanie.

"Look," he said, not turning to face her or even opening his eyes. "I'm sorry. I don't mean to be rude. I'm just not interested."

She nodded, a disappointed look crossing her face, but she didn't push. "Fair enough."

She pulled out her phone and studied the screen. Nico let his mind wander. Thoughts of angels and demons clouded his every thought. Stephanie's scorched, bloody, broken body was never far back in his mind. How could he sit and flirt with a pretty girl when he knew it was entirely possible his history would someday repeat itself?

He stole a furtive glance at Tatiana while her eyes roamed over her screen. She *was* breathtaking. He sucked in a gasp and refocused his gaze on his drink. Temptation flooded his body. Zha'riel had warned Nico of the risks his loved ones faced. Every woman Nico loved would be at risk. Anyone who was close to him would be a target for Azazel's minions to attack whenever they chose. Add to that the uncertainty of Lucifer's presence in his life. It was clear he hadn't saved Nico's life out of the kindness of his blackened heart.

And, of course, there were Heaven's angels.

Since his ill-fated confrontation with Azazel, Nico had been twice visited by members of Rafael's legion. He was twice warned to stop killing the violent criminals he and Xabier had been hunting. It was a mind-numbing twist of logic, but the angels never stayed around to debate their orders. They were clear about the danger Nico faced if he persisted on his current path. Nico wondered if they would ever follow through on their threats.

"Can I just say one thing?"

He looked over at Tatiana. Her eyes shimmered in an otherworldly manner. His heart skipped a few beats and then raced. That was new. No matter how pretty the other girl was, Nico seldom felt himself react. Stephanie's memory always overtook him before that could happen.

Tatiana was waiting for him to respond. He shrugged and waved a hand, indicating for her to continue.

"I'm not trying to be pushy," she said. "I'm really not. I could go find another guy to talk to." She blushed and cringed. "Okay that was really catty. I'm not like that. It's just...you look like you could use a friend." She turned even redder, nearly matching her hair. "Oh, my god! I feel like such an idiot. I'm gonna shut up now and leave you alone."

Nico laughed. "No, you don't have to do that." He gestured to Frank for another drink. "We'll drink this round together."

He held up his glass and Tatiana clinked hers against it. She stared at him over the rim of the glass as she took a sip. For the first time since he lost Stephanie, Nico didn't tear his eyes away.

He let himself stare back. Something about Tatiana made him feel like it was okay, like it wasn't a betrayal, but he knew he wasn't ready to start anything.

"Just to be clear," he said. "I don't want to talk about family, exes, or why I'm withdrawn. Oh, and I also don't want to talk about vampires, angels, or best friends."

Tatiana nodded, wrinkling her forehead. "That's a very...*specific*...list."

Ᏸ A Ꮫ Ψ Ꮳ

Azazel's eyes glowed pearl-white, flashing silver, before settling back to his usual ice-grey gaze. He waited as the realization dawned on every member of the coalition. Most had come across demons in their lifetimes. Some had even encountered angels. None had ever run across an archangel, and the fallen archangels were the most feared beings in creation. They were the boogie-men the supernatural told their children about to scare them. They were not beings one ever expected to meet.

Azazel nodded when he had everyone's attention. "A story perhaps," he said. "To break the ice?"

He strode around the room, making eye contact with everyone present. He spoke with the authority of one who not only knew details, but who was witness to them first-hand.

"Your kind once threatened humanity," he accused. "Your arrogance, your insolence, and, quite frankly, your stupidity, aroused the ire of those in a position to crush you. Humanity banded together with Heaven, and threw the strength of your species into Purgatory. They locked the door and..." He gestured to the thousand-year-old clay artifact. "...threw away the key, so to speak."

"We know all of this," Gamut spoke up.

Azazel raised his eyebrows. "Oh? And yet you have not opened the box?"

Benyamin furrowed his brow. "We have been unable to uncover an opening mechanism."

"It is because none exists." Azazel shrugged. "The key is heavenly and the box is the creation of humanity. To open it, one must access the very thing which binds the supernatural to the natural."

"Chakra," Garland MacElroy said softly. "It is sealed magically."

Rasputin frowned. "So, one of *us* can open it?"

Azazel shook his head. "Not exactly. Yes, the box is both sealed and protected with a magical spell, and no, none of you can open it. To open it you must employ one who practices the specific type of magic used to seal the box." He raised a finger. "Oh, and they would also have to be powerful enough to open the portal itself once the key is in place."

"Which type of magic was used?" Garland asked.

Rasputin sniffed and shook his head. "It would have to be extremely powerful. Teleportation is serious stuff. I would imagine a portal to Purgatory would be a thousand times more so."

"Ancestral Magic."

Agnes Littelson was an Elemental, one who took the form of the various elements of the natural world: earth, wind, fire, water. In her human form, she was virtually powerless. In her elemental forms, she was almost impossible to fight. She recalled her previous conversation with Benyamin.

Everyone turned to stare at her.

"It has to be ancestral magic," she repeated. "It is the most powerful form of witchcraft."

"Who said it had to be witchcraft?" Garland asked.

"It doesn't," Agnes conceded. "But there is a warlock and a sorcerer in Purgatory. I doubt one of your own put them there. It has to be a mage or a witch. Magi are solitary. Who knows how much power any random mage will possess? If they needed to open the box or the portal, they would have to be sure any generation could do it. An ancestral witch is human. They draw from the forces of their witch ancestors."

Benyamin nodded in agreement. "So, potentially any generation of witch could do it, given time to learn and grow in power. The portal could always be opened again."

Azazel spread his hands. "Are we all caught up?"

Jargis, a vetala, or skeleton creature, frowned. "But you're an angel, right? Why can't you open it?"

Azazel's eyes flashed once again. Benyamin got the impression he didn't like to be challenged, especially by a creature without basic coverings. As skeleton creatures, vetalas were almost never seen in the daylight, for obvious reasons, and doomed to remain in the shadows even at night to avoid attention. To go out in public, they had to come up with some fairly elaborate disguises, usually effective only in the coldest of climates, where bulky clothing, hats, and masks were the norm.

"Contrary to popular belief," Azazel said evenly. "Angels are *not* all-powerful, not even archangels. This *natural* world was not created for us. There are those who draw their power from the natural world, not just chakra."

"The servants of nature," Benyamin said.

Azazel gestured toward him. "An educated man." He nodded his approval. "The son of the betrayer proves himself a bit more...*intellectual*, than his father."

Benyamin frowned. He knew the stories surrounding his father. He was the joke of all humanity. The fact that he survived his own stupidity was an even bigger joke in the world of the supernatural. That he and his family were among the most powerful entities on the planet was the only reason the joke was never uttered to their faces.

Benyamin shrugged off the barb and pointed to the box. "So, a witch's spell can only be broken by another witch."

"Basically, yes."

"We don't have a witch."

Agnes spoke up. "Most of them were wiped out in the past few centuries. Christianity drove them into the shadows.

Rasputin chuckled icily. "Those that survived weren't very powerful. We'd be lucky to find one who can handle such a monumental load."

"Fortunately," Azazel announced. "I happen to have made the acquaintance of one who possesses the very combination of power and knowledge we require." He nodded. "Seir?"

Without a word, Seir disappeared. He reappeared seconds later, next to Azazel. This time, he was accompanied by an older woman with jet black hair and piercing gray eyes. She didn't acknowledge any of those present. Instead, her eyes focused like lasers on the box in the middle of the room. Azazel laid an affectionate hand on her shoulder.

"Nayra," he said, gesturing to the box.

She nodded and approached the pedestal. Her eyes roamed over the thousand-year-old relic. After several seconds, she pointed. "These two."

Benyamin craned his neck and looked at the symbols. "That leaves this one." He indicated a symbol on one end. "And this one." He pointed to another. "The rest are all accounted for by the members of our coalition."

Nayra peered at the symbols in question. She shook her head. "I don't recognize…" She turned to Azazel. "I don't know those symbols."

Azazel's eyes narrowed. "How can this be?"

"She identified the witch symbols," Benyamin said. "We have the languages of the twelve alphas. We have the humans." He shook his head. "We can't figure out the last group that would have been involved."

Azazel stared at him for a moment. "You said humans and witches?"

"That's right." Benyamin watched the eyes of the fallen angel. He saw a flicker of understanding. "You know the last language?"

Azazel shrugged. He walked over to the box, shaking his head the whole time, as though he knew the answer, and the answer was so silly and obvious, he didn't want it to be that simple. He looked at the two symbols Benyamin indicated and let out a rare chuckle.

"Of course, *they* would be involved."

Agnes, fascinated despite herself, blurted, "You know that language? What is it?"

Azazel smiled. "That happens to be my native tongue, my dear. It is Enochian, the language of the angels."

Chapter 6

"You are a patient man to put up with such riff-raff."

Benyamin sat, and sipped his wine. His eyes followed Azazel over the rim of the glass. "Something tells me you include my kind with that "riff-raff," as a general rule."

Azazel chuckled, but shrugged without denying the assertion.

After the meeting adjourned, Seir had escorted Nayra back to Colombia. The coalition members went their separate ways. Nayra's job was to organize the translated symbols, and the members would reassemble for the opening of the box. The excitement of coming so close to the end of the first leg of their journey was palpable. There was a great deal of camaraderie between previously warring factions.

Azazel had remained behind until everyone had gone. He paced in front of the picture-window, overlooking the front lawn of the plantation estate. Dusk had fallen, and the brilliant moon shone in the cloudless sky. He considered his plan, mulling the details over in his mind. He knew Lucifer had been keeping Nayra hidden for a reason. There was no way she'd come by that cloaking spell on her own. What Lucifer's reason could possibly be, Azazel had no idea.

Lucifer's end game was always to destroy the created world. The trick was to do it in such a way that Heaven was caught off guard. It was no easy task. Once Michael and his archangels saw a supernatural threat, they descended like locusts and destroyed everything, ensuring the Father's creation was protected, so, Lucifer's efforts had to be subtle, well-planned, and executed over time. It was a cosmic chess match, played against multiple opponents on the same board.

It didn't make sense that Lucifer wanted to keep the alphas locked away in Purgatory. They were one beat removed from humanity, which meant, on the totem pole of the supernatural, these species represented the lowest of the low. Yet, they served a purpose. Their proximity to the humanity within their essences rendered them unable to completely remove themselves from the human race. They remained close, becoming the monsters, the bogeymen, that haunted humanity.

Lucifer had always taken advantage of their instinct to be close to humanity. He set them up as evil, creating a dynamic of fear playing out for centuries, even millennia. As long as humans and angels were busy hunting monsters, the real evil work could be done in the shadows. When the alphas were taken out of the equation, it was just a matter of time until their species were weakened to the point of extinction. Lucifer had mourned that coming day. Why would he set himself against the idea of returning the alphas to the world, strengthening the supernatural order? What possible reason could Lucifer have for wanting the alphas to remain locked away? Whatever it was, Azazel was committed to thwarting his plans. Working with the coalition was a way to do that without drawing attention to himself.

"I have a special place in my heart for your species," Azazel finally replied. "Your humanity was twisted as a result of a direct action against our greatest enemy." He leaned with his back to the wall and sipped old Cabernet from the glass he had been absently swirling. He shook his head in recollection. "We were so close. We honestly thought we had Him." His eyes flashed silver as he returned his gaze to Benyamin. "But it was all a trick. Hades couldn't hold him, and he lost his own life in the effort, along with thousands of my brothers."

Benyamin narrowed his eyes. "You are talking about..."

"Yes, *Him,*" Azazel sneered, waving a hand to cut Benyamin off before he could utter the name. "Your father was a brave man." He shook his head. "Foolish, but very brave. In fact, I owe a debt to your father. His actions resulted in my freedom."

Benyamin said nothing. He was clearly used to his father's reputation. Usually the butt of the cosmic joke, he was seldom praised for courage. More times than not, he was condemned for his treachery or his gullibility.

Azazel changed the subject. "Is your brother in line?"

Benyamin nodded as he poured himself another glass of wine. "He is."

"I will believe that when I see it." Azazel stared at Benyamin, trying to determine if Benyamin really did have his impulsive younger sibling under control. "So, where are we on the location of the gate?"

Benyamin shook his head. "We know it is somewhere in Europe, probably in the Alps. We're hoping once the box is opened we will find the key as well as the location."

"And if there is nothing but the key?"

Benyamin shrugged. "Then I don't know. We would be at a dead end."

"Perhaps not." Azazel sat in a winged-back chair across from Benyamin. "If we had someone who was present back when the gate was first opened."

Benyamin shook his head. "Obviously, all the humans would be long since dead. The angels wouldn't help us. If *you* don't know the location, I doubt anyone in the underworld knows either."

Azazel agreed with a grim smile. "Yes, the angels cast a large perimeter around the region whenever the gate was opened and they covered their tracks, so we couldn't get anywhere near the site. Which leaves your coalition."

"*Us?*"

"The supernatural," Azazel said. *Is this guy really this slow or is he just playing dumb?* "Have you ever wondered how the angels and the humans managed to get *all twelve* alphas to the same place, one after the other?"

Benyamin shrugged. Azazel knew how things worked in the supernatural underworld. There wasn't really a network of communication between the species. They were at war most of the time. Even among allies, there was mutual distrust. Within the modern-day coalition, that distrust remained. Pulling information from a particular species without some kind of recompense was difficult. No one wanted to be a sucker. Therefore, no matter how much of an alliance they thought they had, each group would always act in its own best interest, and that meant it could be easily isolated.

"Humans are skilled at hunting the supernatural," Azazel said, "but they are the weaker species. They should not be able to take on the entire supernatural world. They had help, and not just from the angels." He let his words sink in. "Did you know your brother had an enemy?"

Benyamin laughed. "My brother has many enemies, most of whom he has disposed of."

"One in particular," Azazel said. He settled himself in his chair. "He once had a human friend, named Xabier, who persuaded Lazlo to turn him so their friendship would survive the ages. For centuries, they ravaged Europe and the Middle East, until Xabier fell in love with a woman. This was fine until he informed Lazlo of his intention to turn her. Lazlo, fearful that he would lose his friend, forbade him from turning her, even though she was willing. Xabier decided to turn her anyway, but Lazlo discovered his rebellion. In a blind rage, he killed the girl before Xabier could feed her his blood. She died in Xabier's arms, a mortal human."

Something in Benyamin's posture made Azazel lean forward. He pursed his lips and squinted his eyes. "You know this story."

"Xabier," Benyamin said softly. "Yes, I knew him. He vowed revenge, and Lazlo laughed at him, knowing he couldn't be killed. Xabier disappeared, and Lazlo never saw him again. None of us did."

"Ah ha!" Azazel held up a finger. "You are incorrect. Xabier spent three centuries following in your brother's wake, killing everyone and everything your brother ever loved or even liked.

Xabier, preferring the psychological game, never let Lazlo know why such bad luck had befallen him, he let Lazlo sink deeper and deeper into depression and misery. Lazlo became isolated from his family and embittered at his life."

Azazel looked at his fingernails. "An elegant effort, I must admit. Some people are born to inflict pain on others. It really *is* an artform."

"A fascinating story," Benyamin said in a bland voice, "but what does it have to do with our current effort?"

"Xabier," Azazel nodded. "With some strategically placed evidence, over a period of decades, managed to turn Lazlo's father against him. The two became bitter enemies and the family split over the feud."

"Wait a minute," Benyamin said, his nostrils flaring. "All of that was *fake*? *Xabier* set my father and brother against one another?"

"He did," Azazel confirmed.

"Hundreds of years," Benyamin breathed. "My family has been at war with itself over nothing."

He was not a man given to fits of rage. His personality was more reserved, but Azazel could sense the emotions boiling just under the surface. No one understood family war better than Azazel, and no one understood the need for vengeance better than Azazel. As angry as Benyamin may be, he had to maintain his focus on the bigger picture. Lazlo, should he uncover the truth, would have only blood on his mind.

Benyamin shook his head and frowned. "I still do not see how this relates to the Purgatory Gate."

Azazel tilted his head. "Did we not just agree that a supernatural creature had to have been involved in the effort to put the alphas away? Who better than someone who had already willingly set himself against one of his own?"

Benyamin's eyes stared off into the distance. Azazel's logic was sound. He would wait for the snobbish vampire to see the truth. Within the supernatural community, each species had its own customs and traditions. Some species tended to be more solitary while others stayed in groups. The one thing they all had in common was they never turned on their own kind. Individual disputes were usually settled quickly and decisively. That Xabier relentlessly stalked and waged psychological warfare on Lazlo was highly unusual.

"I can't believe it," Benyamin said with little conviction in his voice.

"When Xabier lured your father to the portal, he also tipped Lazlo off to his father's location and vulnerability. Of course, Lazlo, seeing an opportunity to end his feud decisively, showed up. Xabier, after ridding the world of the Alpha vampire, he faced off against Lazlo, assuming the angels would back him up and take one of the original family as a bonus. He was wrong. He barely escaped with his life after taunting Lazlo with the truth about all of his previous misfortunes."

Azazel paused and swirled his glass of wine, staring at the liquid as it ran back down the sides of the glass.

Benyamin blinked. "How do you know all this?"

Azazel shook his head. "I don't *know* it. I am merely putting the pieces of the puzzle together. It is entirely possible I am wrong, but…"

"But you're not," Benyamin said. His eyes told Azazel the vampire was convinced. "Lazlo has been hunting Xabier for six centuries. He refuses to discuss his old friend. This explains it."

"You must see to it that Lazlo is kept at bay. He cannot find out about the plan to open the portal and he most certainly cannot be anywhere near Xabier until the location of the portal is revealed. He might be the only being in existence, outside the angels, who knows the location."

"Lazlo must know," Benyamin said.

Azazel raised his eyebrows. "Do you think it possible he would reveal it?

"Absolutely not. He would never be party to releasing our father. He will not accept…"

Azazel held up a hand and cocked his head to one side. "What was that?"

Benyamin listened intently. He closed his eyes. Suddenly, he rocketed out of his seat and through the double doors. In the hall outside the room, he stopped and listened again. Azazel strolled along behind him.

"Lazlo?"

Benyamin stood as still as a statue. "I don't know."

ℏ Λ ⌇ ψ ς

"He grows ever stronger."

"That he does."

Zha'riel hated visits from Rafael. The archangel tended towards smugness; especially since Zha'riel had been punished for disobeying his orders. That the exile came from above Rafael's offices made it all the more pleasurable for the powerful angel. He got to deliver the news personally, all the while pretending to be saddened by the whole unpleasant situation.

"I am almost out of patience, brother." The warning tone in Rafael's voice was apparent. He was making no effort to hide his feelings.

"I must admit, I am as well."

Rafael stared at Zha'riel with eyes wide open. Since his exile from Heaven, Zha'riel had expressed nothing but defiant loyalty to Nico, refusing to renounce even his most obviously evil acts. For this reason, Zha'riel's reinstatement to full angelic privileges wouldn't be considered. A lack of contrition in angels was not the best quality to demonstrate, but if Zha'riel changed his attitude, and showed a commitment to his duty as a representative of Heaven, he could be restored to his former position of glory.

"So," Rafael said. "You are coming around to see things as they truly are."

Zha'riel shook his head. Having tried the same technique himself, unsuccessfully, on Nico, he was beginning to see the deceitful nature of it. Rafael presented Zha'riel with the choice of either agreeing with Rafael's assessment or admitting he was ignoring reality. It was effective, but sharper thinkers, like Nico, were frustratingly willing to lose the word war.

"Not exactly," Zha'riel said. "I do not agree with the murderous rampages, and I definitely believe his bloodlust is growing. He is on the wrong path. And *yet*..." He trailed off as he tried to formulate his thoughts into words.

"And yet?" Rafael prodded.

Zha'riel shrugged. "What alternative have we presented?"

"You joke!" Rafael's face was a mixture of surprise and disgust. "We need present no alternative to murder! With every life he takes, he mocks Heaven's law. He even mocks the laws of his own people!"

"Yes," Zha'riel agreed. "Though, if he did not act, how many innocent girls would be violated and sold to the vilest of people?"

"It is not relevant."

"To Nico it is." Zha'riel folded his hands. "Look, brother, we can go around in circles, and I will agree with you."

Rafael was incredulous. "Yet, you defend him."

Zha'riel sighed. It was always the same black and white interpretation of events. There was never any middle ground with the angels. Nico repeatedly pointed it out. With angels, it was always their way or no way. They were stiff, wooden personalities with no concept of compromise or debate. Nico couldn't stand them and refused to participate in their bullying.

"I do *not* defend him," Zha'riel shot back. "I merely state his case as he would. You reject his argument, which leaves him in an impossible position. In his mind, if he does not act, he sentences many innocent girls to horrific fates. In his mind, Heaven does not care about these innocent girls."

Rafael's eyes blazed in anger. "And you allow that accusation to stand?"

Zha'riel shrugged. "What am I to say? If he allows these vile creatures to live, they return to their lives, which means more kidnapping of innocent girls, more rape, and more human trafficking. The only way to protect countless future victims is to end the lives of the offenders."

"That," Rafael insisted, "is of no consequence. They exist in a fallen world. He will not be permitted to murder at his own discretion." He spread his hands. "*Yet*...as a part of Heaven's earthly army, he would have a bit more freedom to act. You must convince him, Zha'riel. It would be a shame to have to destroy so impressive a weapon."

The silence hung in the air between the two angels. There wasn't much Zha'riel could say. Rafael was in the position of power and Zha'riel was a disgraced angel in danger of losing his status permanently. Still, something kept him from abandoning Nico. As much as he disagreed with Nico's merciless methods, he understood criminals had the advantage of playing by no rules. Nico equalized their advantage.

He had already saved dozens of young girls from a fate that was truly worse than death. No one could argue that innocents were dying at his hand, but Heaven wanted him to stop. When Zha'riel tried to present Heaven's position, Nico always got confused. How could Heaven side with evil?

"Take heed, Zha'riel," Rafael warned. "Your involvement in his endeavors do not go unnoticed. The only reason you have not been dealt with is because you yourself have not murdered. Be sure you do not cross that line. If do, I will be unable save you."

Zha'riel nodded.

"Do you wish to reenter Heaven, Zha'riel?"

"Of course."

"Dissuade young Nico of his current course," Rafael said, "or end him. Do either, and you will return to glory and all will be forgiven."

Kill his friend.

Zha'riel could imagine nothing more repulsive, though the thought had occurred to him more than once. He was so conflicted over Nico's actions, he was never sure on which side he landed. In the presence of his former commander, Zha'riel tended to side with the angels. His arguments usually collapsed under Nico's and Xabier's withering logic. It wasn't that they shattered Heaven's arguments; it was really a matter of priorities. Nico and Xabier wanted to save the innocent. Heaven wanted the Father's dictates followed to the letter. They were both admirable pursuits. Unfortunately, one often came at the expense of the other.

Zha'riel shrugged in disgust and turned to walk away. Rafael cleared his throat.

"There is another matter we must discuss."

Zha'riel turned back to his superior with a wordless frown.

"There is a situation," Rafael said. "One of grave consequence for the future of mankind on Earth." When Zha'riel did not respond, he continued, "We have heard rumblings in the underworld."

There was nothing unusual about that. The underworld always had rumors floating around. Violence was always on the precipice of breaking out and spilling over into the natural world. There was always a relic or ancient weapon about to be rediscovered that would upset the balance between good and evil. The trick was to decipher which rumors contained truth.

Zha'riel shrugged. "I assume there is something *to* these particular rumblings?"

Rafael pressed his lips together in a tight line before replying. "Unfortunately, this one is all too real and all too serious. There is a band of supernatural families trying to awake a sleeping dog from a thousand years ago."

Zha'riel wracked his brain to figure out which sleeping dog. Rafael waited for a few seconds, but Zha'riel shook his head.

"The key has been uncovered."

Zha'riel's eyes widened and he puckered his forehead. "Do they have the location?"

"No," Rafael shook his head. "I do not even think they have managed to open the box at this point."

Zha'riel let out a relieved breath. "Then there is still time. We must guard the points."

Rafael shook his head. "Heaven cannot be directly involved. This is an opportunity for you to bring Nico into our purpose. Perhaps he will begin to grasp the larger picture."

Zha'riel blew out a breath. This was bad. There was only one reason to uncover the key. Whoever had it, had the means to unleash terror on the world. Once they opened the box and assembled a spell, it was a question of locations. The portal itself was just one of the necessary locations. There were five others necessary for the portal to be opened. The process was complex and required timing and knowledge. He wondered how far along this supernatural group had gotten with all of it. He himself only knew the stories. It had been the archangels who guided the humans a thousand years ago.

"There is one other thing," Rafael said.

"Yes?"

"The abomination you have befriended is involved."

"Xabier?" Zha'riel scowled. "How?"

Rafael shook his head and made a face. "He was a part of the team that imprisoned the alphas."

Zha'riel's eyes widened in understanding. "Xabier knows the locations."

"Correct," Rafael nodded. "As much as I would like to see that abomination suffer, you will need him to identify the locations." He held up a hand. "And we have reason to believe he is already being pursued, possibly by more than one group with competing interests."

Chapter 7

"We need to meet."

He could hear the anxiety over the phone. The call from the police chief came at such an unusual hour, nearly one in the morning, he was immediately suspicious. He hadn't expected Chief North to do anything more than pretend to cooperate with him. Now, even with a sleep-deprived brain, he was pretty sure the chief was setting him up.

"Why?"

"The Russians are here."

Honesty? Nico sat up in bed and let the bed sheet slide from his chest. Maybe the chief was actually going to work with him. Either way, if the Russians were in town, there was only one way to deal with them. He hadn't expected them to run and hide from him, but they must have jumped on the first plane they could find.

"Chief," he asked. "If I come to meet you tonight, am I going to have to kill a bunch of Russians?"

The chief was silent. It was all the answer Nico needed. He chuckled, knowing the Russians were listening in on the conversation.

"Please," Chief North said. "They have my family." He paused. "I have two daughters."

The irony did not escape Nico. Suddenly, when it was *his* daughters at risk, the chief cared about stopping human trafficking. Though he felt no compassion at all for the chief, Nico was not about to let his innocent children suffer for his criminal behavior.

Another voice came on the line. "Do you know who I am?"

The voice sounded familiar. It was the man Nico had spoken to when he killed Yuri. He had come to America personally. Nico smiled to himself as he slid his feet from under the covers and strode through the hall and into the kitchen, wearing only a pair of boxers.

"Hello again, Nikoli," he said in a cheerful tone, as he flipped on a light and opened the fridge for a bottle of water. "How was your flight?"

"You are funny man," the mobster hissed. "Maybe I kill your police chief's daughter, Meester Funny Man…see if you think that's funny."

Nico sipped his water. "I think you have bigger problems than a corrupt police chief's family, Nikoli."

"Oh, really? What problem do I have?"

"I told you to stay out of my city and you ignored me." Nico maintained a matter-of-fact tone. "Now I have to rip your throat out."

Nico could hear a burst of laughter. It was a deep and sinister chuckle, and sounded like it hurt the man's throat. He wondered if he was the type of guy who looked like he was in pain whenever he smiled. Probably.

"You meet us in same building you butchered my men…top floor…one hour…or I take the chief's family to Russia and see how much I get paid for them."

The line went dead before Nico could reply.

"Zhari!" he shouted and received no reply. Where was Zha'riel?

Nico had one hour. It was plenty of time, but he had no idea where to start looking. After several calls, he could not get the police chief's home address. He considered simply alerting the police of the kidnapping, but it was entirely possible the Russians had more insiders on the force. The other possibility was the police could go charging in, and get the wife and kids killed in the crossfire. Nico had precious little faith in the ability of the police to keep people safe, especially in Atlantic City.

He thought for several seconds. If he could figure out where the chief lived, he could go in and free the chief's family before dealing with the Russians. If not, he would have to be creative with the Russians.

"Zha'riel!" he shouted. He waited for a few seconds and shouted it again. "Where the hell are you?" He slammed a hand down on the kitchen table. "Absent vampires and absent angels," he mumbled, and then shouted, "*SOME FRIENDS I HAVE!*"

"You need not yell," Zha'riel said from behind him.

"Shut up," Nico said, tossing the empty water bottle into the recycling bin. "We've got a problem. Are you able to find out the home address for the chief of the Atlantic City Police Department?"

"I can orb into their Records Department," Zha'riel said, "and look at his file." He frowned. "Then again, so can you. What is going on?"

Nico shook his head. His ears began to redden as he realized his answer had been right in front of him. He resisted the urge to put his fist through the refrigerator door. He hated looking foolish, and he was finding himself less and less patient with his own failures. He needed to get his temper under control. The first thing to go when he was upset was his reason and logic.

Zha'riel frowned. "We need to talk, Nico."

"Not right now," Nico replied. "I have business with some Russians."

Zha'riel cocked his head to one side and grabbed Nico by the wrist.

"You must not kill today, Nico. Please."

Nico shrugged him off. "Killing is the only language these people speak, Zhari."

He told Zha'riel about the kidnapping and the ultimatum. He checked the clock on his phone.

"I have forty minutes to get to the casino," he said. "I'd like to get there early and scope out the situation. I don't want anyone getting away." Looking at Zha'riel, he said, "Can you go and take care of the goons guarding the chief's family?"

Zha'riel shook his head. "Of course, but Nico, you must do this without killing anyone."

"Why?" Nico narrowed his eyes, seeing the pained expression on Zha'riel's face. He was always moody and ill-humored, but today his faced betrayed something he never showed: fear. "What?"

"If you kill today," Zha'riel said, leaning in closer. His eyes focused on Nico's. "Rafael will order your execution."

Nico leaned back and blew out a breath. "He said that?"

"He has been trying to contact you, but you keep avoiding him." Zha'riel spread his hands in frustration. "So, he came to me."

Nico shook his head. "Great. What am I supposed to do? I'm not letting these Russian scumbags get away."

"Rafael only mentioned killing." Zha'riel smiled. "He did not say you are forbidden to punish."

♭ A ♬ ψ G

"Are you sure about this?"

"Am I sure about walking into a bar full of vetala?" Xabier droned as he stood on the sidewalk across from the roadhouse dive bar, just outside Flagstaff, Arizona. "*Hell* no, but if Max is in there, we'll be okay."

"Yeah," Leonardo said, casting furtive glances in all directions. "And if not, they'll tear us apart and eat us."

His fears were not without foundation. Vetala were not known for their tolerance of outsiders, particularly their vampire cousins. Vampires managed to blend in far easier with humans, enabling them to exist alongside people without arousing suspicion. Vetala couldn't manage that kind of proximity for very long. Their bloodlust made them ferocious feeders, and they did not possess the vampires' capacity for compulsion, a trait that made it possible for a vampire to influence the thoughts of a person.

Vetala tended to ravage an area if they stayed for too long or in large groups. That attracted too much attention. They usually nested together in groups of six or eight and hunted in pairs, each pair going in separate directions and hunting as far as possible from the nest. Vetala were among the most hunted species in the supernatural world. Since they fed on human blood and flesh, they were often mistaken for vampires.

Xabier looked at his phone. It buzzed with another text from Nico. He would read it later. He nudged Leonardo. "Let's go."

Inside the dingy bar, Xabier sniffed. The place smelled like stale beer and smoke. The No Smoking laws apparently hadn't reached the out of the way location yet. He scanned the room and wrinkled his forehead. It was about a third full, mostly a trucker and biker crowd, guys who spent a lot of time on the road and not a lot of time in one place. Typical for vetala. Xabier led the way through the room and took a seat at the bar.

"A couple beers," he said, nodding to the bartender. He held the man's gaze as Leonardo took the seat beside him.

Leo knew how to act the part. As fearful as he seemed outside the bar, he could put his game face on in the blink of an eye. Now, he looked just as rough and ready to brawl as anyone else present. He nodded at the bartender, who nodded back without saying a word and poured two drafts in heavy steins.

Xabier sipped his beer and leaned on the bar. "Hey, is Max around?"

The bartender's eyes widened slightly and he glanced to his right. Before they knew what was happening, Xabier and Leo were surrounded, dragged from their chairs, through the bar, and out the back door. They were thrown against the wall under a flickering light. Neither fought back, though they were prepared to defend themselves if it came to that. The whole scene took less than ten seconds.

"What do you want, *vampire*?"

The rough voice belonged to a tall, thin man with bloodshot brown eyes. Vetala tended to be thin, often, skeletal, prompting many cultures to refer to them as "skeleton creatures." Their sickly appearance was deceiving. Vetala were strong and fast. They were also extremely volatile.

Xabier winced. "So, I guess my cover's blown, eh?"

He was shoved into the wall once again and a forearm jammed into his throat. The vetala in front of him was ready to explode. His eyes, also bloodshot, were fierce, even darker than his friend's. He bared his teeth, his top center incisors replaced with needle-sharp fangs. Xabier knew those fangs not only pierced skin and vein, allowing the vetala to feed, but they were also hollow, acting as syringes to deliver paralytic venom to their prey, enabling the vetala to carry the victim off for later feeding.

Xabier grunted as the forearm pressed him hard into the wall. "I just want to see Max."

"About what?"

"Look, chief," Xabier said. "I don't know you. I'm not talking to you idiots. Now, go get Max."

With a lightning fast shove, the vetala in front of him went flying across the blacktop. Leo followed Xabier's lead and tossed his guy in a similar manner. They were outnumbered three to one, but vetala only understood violence. Any sign of weakness only served to encourage their violent tendencies, especially toward vampires. Vetala had a massive inferiority complex when it came to vampires.

Xabier and Leonardo squared off, ready to fight for their lives.

"Look," Xabier said. "You can come at us and kill us, but I promise, we'll take a lot of you with us." He shrugged. "Or you can go get Max and no one has to get hurt."

The vetala looked at one another. Xabier and Leonardo tensed as they saw the unspoken agreement between the mutant vampires. As usual, the vetala were prepared to do things the hard way. They all grinned wickedly, and set to pounce.

"What is this?"

Xabier looked to his right and grinned. "Max, old buddy! Back these goons off!"

Max pushed his way through and stood in before Xabier. His eyes bored into him. Xabier felt a slight twinge of doubt about his relationship with Max. It had been many years since they last saw one another, and who knew where his mind was these days?

What was I thinking?

"Xabier. It's been a long time." Max was tall. At 6'5", he towered over Xabier's 5'10" frame. Even still, Xabier thought he probably still outweighed the slender vetala by at least twenty pounds. He figured he could probably snap Max in half if it came to that, but then he would have to deal with Max's crew. Things could get very bloody, very quickly with vetala. It was best to keep calm and try not to aggravate the situation.

"That it has," Xabier replied with a slight grin, trying to convey a nonchalance he wasn't completely feeling. "How have you been, Max?"

Max shrugged and tilted his head to one side, his eyes never leaving Xabier's He shrugged after a few silent seconds. "The same." He glanced at Leonardo. "Who's this?"

"A friend."

"What are you doing here?"

That was the end of any pretense at pleasantries. Xabier looked around at all the faces staring at him. He could see their anger had turned to curiosity. It wasn't every day a vampire showed up in their midst and survived.

"I have to talk to you," Xabier replied. "Alone."

Max's tongue flicked across his upper lip. He finally nodded. "Walk with me."

Xabier stepped away from the wall and followed Max.

"Hey. What about me?" Leonardo asked. He didn't look thrilled about being left alone with a bunch of hungry vetala. He glanced from right to left.

Max turned and frowned. "Why don't you go back inside and have a drink?" He nodded pointedly at his guys. "He's a friend."

Leonardo looked less than convinced, but Xabier nodded reassuringly at him and he let the group of vetala usher him back inside the bar.

When they were alone, Xabier asked. "I need you to be real honest with me, Max. What have you heard about a coalition?"

ᚻ ᴀ ⩣ ᴪ Ꮹ

"Nitey-nite."

Nico left the four men guarding the parking garage entrance unconscious, resisting his urge to end them, and hustled from one level to the next, prepared for anything. He found no further guards before the top floor of the vacant, unfinished casino. It wasn't a big surprise. Nikoli probably figured the four he left at the entrance would have been enough to escort Nico up. He wasn't expecting resistance. He was expecting Nico to beg for his life and the lives of the police chief's wife and children.

He looked at his phone. He had eleven minutes before the deadline. Not that it mattered. Zha'riel should have handled the men guarding the chief's family by then. Nikoli could be kept waiting indefinitely. In fact, Nico thought he might amuse himself, watching the Russian grow ever angrier as the minutes passed by, but before he acted, he needed to be certain Zha'riel did his part.

"Come on, Zhari," he mumbled as he orbed from room to room on the top floor, scanning for signs of life.

"Impatience is not a virtuous character trait," Zha'riel said, appearing out of thin air.

"Yeah, well neither is tardiness," Nico grumbled. "Is the family safe?"

Zha'riel nodded. "They are. Sixteen men." He shook his head. "They were prepared for a police response."

Nico pursed his lips. "But not an angelic one, eh?" He chuckled and cast narrowed eyes at Zha'riel. "You didn't kill a single one of them, did you?"

"Of course not," Zha'riel insisted. "To do so would..." He stopped in midsentence, seeing Nico' grin. "Ahh...you joke."

"You need to be a little quicker than that, Zhari."

"Anyway," the angel said. "They have about forty men in the northeast corner, overlooking the ocean."

Nico nodded. They orbed together to a room unoccupied by the Russian mobsters. The penthouse floor was unfinished. Some rooms had only studs for walls, and in some places one could see clear across the entire floor to the other side. The penthouse suite was about half complete with drywall so Nico and Zha'riel were able to sneak in, close enough to listen to the Russians without being seen.

"His time is up."

Nikoli Petrov's gravelly voice responded. "Call him."

Nico's eyes widened and he reached for his phone. He slid and tapped as fast as he could to shut it off, sending the call directly to voice mail. He grinned at Zha'riel and waved the phone in front of him. Zha'riel shook his head, unamused.

"Straight to voice mail."

Nikoli growled. "He thinks I won't send your little girls to the brothels."

"P-p-please." The fear in the chief's voice was palpable.

Nico felt a surge of cold energy in his core. This was something he had been looking forward to all night. He made a move toward the room, but Zha'riel grabbed his arm.

"You must *not* kill, Nico. Please, do not test Rafael's resolve."

Nico shot him a sly grin. "Trust me."

"If I trusted you," Zha'riel replied. "I would not..." Again, he noticed Nico' playful expression. "Even in the direst of circumstances..."

"Zhari, you really have to lighten up. This situation is not in any way dire."

Zha'riel shook his head. "You should not take your enemies so..."

"Look," Nico said. "It's not like we're talking about Azazel and Seir. If we were talking about Azazel and Seir I'd listen to you, but we're not talking about Azazel and Seir. We're talking about humans...humans with guns and knives. These idiots can't hurt us." He slapped Zha'riel on the back. "So, let's go get em." He held up a finger. "Without killing them of course."

$$Ƀ\;A\;\check{Ȝ}\;Ψ\;Ç$$

Nikoli glared at one of his men. "Will this American make me chase him all the way to…"

"Stop whining. I'm right here."

Nico strolled into the room as nonchalantly as he could. He really wanted to rip all their spines out through their stomachs, and probably would have if Zha'riel hadn't been lurking in the background. Instead, he put on his best adolescent grin and sauntered through the Russian hit squad, nodding at each one as they stood there, mouths agape.

Nikoli turned to face him. The unconcerned look on Nico's face threw him for a beat. "How did you get past my men?"

"What?" Nico chuckled. "The four goons in the parking garage? Nikoli, if you want to challenge me, you're gonna hafta leave more than four guys. I don't think they even saw me."

"So, you killed them."

Nico shook his head with a grim smile. "Nah. The angels are starting to get pissed about all the violence, so I have to dial it back a skoshe."

"Angels?" Nikoli scowled and looked at one of his guys, who shrugged helplessly.

Nico waved a hand. "Yeah. A bunch of stick-up-their-ass hypocrites if you ask me, but what can ya do? Anyway, if I go around killing violent predators like you, Rafael is gonna send his garrison after me."

Nikoli stared at him like he was a complete lunatic. "And Rafael is…angel?" He grinned.

"*Arch*angel actually," Nico said, sitting on a two-by-six held up by a couple of saw horses. "He's in charge of a whole garrison of angels. They don't like me very much."

"Ooooh," Rafael nodded sagely, his guys stifling laughter.

"Yeah," Nico said. "So that's why I didn't kill your guys down there." He shrugged. "*And* it's why I can't kill all of *you*." He hopped off the board and clapped his hands together. "So, shall we get to it?"

Nikoli shook his head. "You are psycho American." He stood face to face with Nico, his arms folded across his chest. "It is shame what I have to do to you." He gestured over to the chief, sitting between two mean-looking Russians who didn't look as though they had the capacity to smile. "And what I have to do to your police chief's daughters."

Nico bit his bottom lip as if deciding whether to say what he wanted to say. "Nikoli, have you actually spoken to your guys over at the chief's house lately?"

Nikoli's hard gaze wavered. He took a calming breath. He stared at Nico as he raised the phone to his ear. With every ring that went unanswered his face tightened. He finally lowered the phone and, with barely contained rage, ended the call and handed it to one of his guys. He stared at Nico.

"My men?"

"They'll live," Nico said, with an off-hand wave of his palm. "The angel that went over there wouldn't kill anyone. My guess is they're in police custody." He smiled. "Don't worry. You'll all together soon."

Nikoli pursed his lips. "I think no more talk."

Nico nodded. "I was thinking the same thing."

Without warning, he raised both hands in front of him. Flames erupted in his palms and he immediately hurled the fiery masses at the men on either side of him. He stretched his arms his head and bolts of violet-hued electricity swirled all around the room, knocking everyone off their feet. The whole scene was over in a matter of seconds. Nikoli and his men were all incapacitated, lying on the ground. Some of them were still convulsing from the lightning coursing through their bodies.

"You did not have to do that, Nico," Zha'riel strode through the three-dozen helpless bodies lying on the cement floor. "I could have taken them without any violence."

Nico laughed. "You know what? You're a real buzzkill, Zhari. I didn't kill anyone. You should be happy."

"I am pleased," Zha'riel nodded. "But unless violence is necessary, it should be avoided. You are still governed by darkness."

"Whatever." Nico shook his head. He pulled Nikoli up and laid him on the same boards he had been sitting on just moments before. "All right, read this guy's mind and tell me everything he knows about the sex trafficking and sex slave operation in Europe."

Zha'riel shook his head with a furrowed brow. "I will do no such thing."

Nico shrugged. "Okay." He turned to Nikoli. "You're my witness. I tried it his way…the *non-violent* way. He didn't want to help. So, we're gonna do this *my* way. It's nowhere near as effective, but it hurts a hell of a lot more, so, in a way, it's worth it."

He poised his hand over Nikoli's head. "Tell me the locations of every brothel in Europe under your control."

Nikoli, still paralyzed from being nearly electrocuted, hissed Russian obscenities. Nico shrugged. "Have it your way." He flexed his fingers and the purple crackle returned.

"Nico, wait!" Zha'riel held up a hand. "I will get the information."

Chapter 8

"You're sure?"

"They went in the front door. By the time we walked in, Xabier was gone."

Lazlo Maccabee stared at Edward, his number two, for several seconds, causing the other to tremble slightly. One didn't become Lazlo's number two by merit alone. More often than not, the job was won by attrition. Lazlo tended to tear apart those who failed him. His second-in-command was a job no one really sought.

The second of five children of the Maccabee family, Lazlo possessed a similar refinement as his elder brother, Benyamin. As a member of the original vampire family, they had over two thousand years of culture and experience. In all that time, Lazlo clung to one simple truth about vampires: He could always make more.

"Are you telling me we came all this way, after picking up a trail that has been cold for a thousand years, only to lose him once again?"

Edward gulped. "N-no. Please. We think he is with a vetala named Max. They must be close by. His friend is still here, so we think he'll return."

"You *think*?" Lazlo sneered jamming his hand into Edward's gut and thrusting upward until he held his beating heart in his hand, as Edward grunted in pain and anticipation of death. A single pull and a being that would otherwise live forever would die in an instant. "Let me explain something to you, you sniveling wretch. The vampire we're pursuing is one of the smartest, sneakiest, most lethal creatures you will ever encounter. He has managed to elude *me* for a thousand years."

He squeezed the vampire's heart a little more, causing Edward to grimace in pain. It wouldn't take much more for Lazlo to crush the powerful muscle in his hand. Lazlo looked into Edward's eyes and watched as the emotions flashed one by one. He loved the up-close and personal nature of killing. He didn't just love to kill; he loved to watch others die, loved to see the life drain from their eyes. He never got enough.

"So, brother, I see you are still killing your own as quickly as you replace them."

At the sound of her soft, silky voice, Lazlo's eyes softened, and he felt the corners of his mouth twitch upward. With his hand still grasping Edward's beating heart, he cocked his head slightly, acknowledging the presence of his little sister, Riva.

Lazlo smiled. "Sister. You received my message."

"Mmm," she replied, striding over to observe Edward's face. "Cryptic though it was."

She scrunched her forehead as if puzzled by something and then pursed her lips, as if the sight of her brother with his hand in someone's chest was nothing out of the ordinary. Riva's auburn locks fell in thick waves, well below her shoulders. Her eyes were a lighter shade of green than her brother's but possessed the same intensity and ferocity as Lazlo's. She stood two inches shorter than her brother's five-foot-ten-inch frame, her lean, slender body a picture of feminine perfection. She looked out the window of the dingy motel and shook her head. Like her brothers, Riva Maccabee spoke with a refined, gentle accent, always mistaken for European, though never properly placed.

"What a ghastly place. I'm breathing dust, Lazlo. Why are we here?" She glanced at Edward, still doing his best not to move as Lazlo grasped his heart. "And will you let the poor fool go, for

God's sake?" She cocked her head and shrugged. "Or kill him. Honestly, Laz, standing there with your hand in a man's chest is positively appalling!"

Lazlo chuckled and ripped his hand out of Edward's chest. Edward fell to the floor, gasping. Lazlo held up his empty hand and wiggled his fingers.

"You're lucky my sister has such a..." Lazlo frowned thoughtfully. "...a *calming* effect on my mental state."

He stared at Edward, whose wounds were already healing, and raised his eyebrows. "Get up."

Edward pulled himself to his feet. He stood before Lazlo, still struggling to control his breathing. Lazlo glowered at him, his jade eyes boring into Edward's, who just hung his head.

"Now," Lazlo said softly, his tone conveying the consequences of failure. "Get back to your team and locate my turncoat friend. Do not attempt to contact him. Do not attempt to subdue him. Just find him and call me. Do you understand?"

"Y-yes, sir." Edward's head bobbed up and down.

"Disappear."

After Edward made his hasty retreat, Lazlo turned to Riva with a smirk on his face.

"Don't give me that look, you ass," Riva said, her own lips curling up despite her feigned annoyance. "Are you going to tell what this is all about or did I just come out to the middle of the desert for your amusement?"

"Be calm, little sister," Lazlo said. He patted her cheek. "All will be explained."

He went to one of the end tables where he had a bottle of wine. He found two plastic cups and poured for himself and Riva. He handed one to his sister and they both drank in silence for a moment. Lazlo refilled their cups and peered out the dusty window. He shook his head.

"It really *is* a horrid place, nay?"

Riva giggled. "I feel like I'm covered in sand. What are we *doing* here?"

Lazlo didn't answer right away. Instead, he sipped his wine and leaned against the dresser. He ran a hand through his hair and Riva narrowed her eyes.

"I like it that way," she said, nodding toward him. "Your hair. It's shorter. It looks quite handsome."

"Yes," Lazlo nodded. "I opted for a more modern look. It tends toward unruliness when I grow it long."

Riva pursed her lips. "Tell me."

Lazlo closed his eyes. "Do you remember Xabier Legartza?"

"You mean your friend from Aragon?"

"Your memory serves you, sister." Lazlo gave her an affectionate smile.

"Yes, well, he is hard to forget. His death sent you into a spiral from which you have not yet recove...what?"

Lazlo was shaking his head and grimacing. "Xabier is not dead, Riva."

"What?" Her eyes widened. "But you said...you told us..."

"I lied."

That, in itself, was nothing new. Lazlo had always held his cards close to the chest, even with his family. The death of a close friend, though...why make that up? "But...why?"

"Because if you all knew the truth, you would have hunted him down and killed him."

Riva's face contorted. "After what he did to you, I should think..."

"*Precisely*," Lazlo hissed. "What he did to *me*. After his myriad of betrayals, I was unwilling to allow anyone else the pleasure of tearing his heart from his chest."

Riva's eyes widened. "What have you not told us?"

"It concerns your father."

ᛒ ᚨ ᛉ ᚹ ᚷ

"So, are we allowed to talk about vampires and angels tonight?"

Nico smelled her subtle perfume before she ever spoke. His brain was making the connection when her voice hit his ears. He turned in his chair, and the first thing he saw was a mass of brilliant, wavy, red hair. Two beautiful green eyes stared back at him, their corners crinkled due to her radiant smile.

"Tatiana."

"You remembered." Her smile grew wider.

Nico chuckled. "You're a little hard to forget."

She studied his face with a skeptical squint. "I'm going to choose to take that as a compliment."

"Good." Nico returned her skepticism with an affirming nod.

He held up his glass so the bartender, Frank, could see, and then pointed at Tatiana. Frank nodded and grabbed a rocks glass and the familiar bottle of Balvanie. Tatiana laughed and tilted her head in approval.

"Your nonverbal communication skills are excellent."

They lapsed into a comfortable silence, sipping their thirty-year-old scotch. Tatiana seemed to realize he wasn't in the mood for banter. She sat with him, enjoying excellent scotch and stealing silent glances at him every now and then.

Nico sat, thinking about his situation. He and Zha'riel took down fifty Russian sex traffickers and saved the chief of the Atlantic City Police Department. Success like that ought to come with a sense of accomplishment, but Nico felt only the emptiness of failure. He hated the slightest thought of any one of those men taking another breath. Men like that weren't men; they were animals. Why couldn't Zha'riel see that? Why was he siding with the same angelic hypocrites that threw him out of Heaven for helping a friend?

Ever since his supernatural transition, Nico's world made no sense. Everything he thought he believed turned on its' head. Right and wrong were so blurred in this new world, confusion seemed to be the predominant state of affairs. One thing he did know was the angels were decidedly *not* on his side. He needed to figure out how to avoid them.

He glanced furtively to his left. The smell of her perfume wafted into his nostrils, sending his heart into overdrive. The sight of her tripled the effect. A brief vision of Stephanie clouded his mind, but dissipated as Tatiana's alluring smile filled the space. He finally took a deep breath and gulped down the rest of his drink, signaling Frank for another. He turned to Tatiana and smiled back at her.

"I'm lousy company," he said. "Tell me something about yourself."

"Mmmm," Tatiana wrinkled her forehead. "I tell you something; then you tell *me* something. Fair?"

"Deal."

Over the next hour or so, they exchanged meaningless personal trivia. They laughed and drank plenty of fine scotch. As the night wore on, Tatiana's subtle flirting grew less subtle. She found plenty of reasons for her hand to brush Nico's hand, his leg, and his arm. At first, Nico let her flirtations go without responding. He was still caught between memories of Stephanie and his need to move on.

"So," she said with a laugh. "The whole thing about not wanting to talk about angels…what is that all about?"

"Biggest bunch of hypocrites I've ever met," Nico blurted it out before he could think about it.

Tatiana's forehead puckered and she shot him a playful smirk. "Angels are *hypocrites?*"

Nico shook his head. Something inside screamed for him to shut up, but alcohol affected even the supernatural; it just took a whole lot more. Nico knew he was well past that point, but enjoyed the company of the beautiful woman sitting next to him too much to stop. With every sip, his inhibitions faded away. His ability to temper his words had long since disappeared.

"They spy on people," he said with disdain in his voice. "And they don't understand justice."

Tatiana stifled a laugh and stared at him through shimmering eyes.

He shrugged. "What?"

"I can't tell if you're teasing me," she said.

He reached out and covered her hand with his. It was the first time he'd initiated any contact. He immediately felt the smooth warmth of her skin and his heart began to skip beats.

"I would never tease you."

Tatiana almost burst out laughing. When he cracked a grin, she bit down on her lips to try to stifle the next giggle. Nico let the moment wash over him. This felt good. At least he was out of his funk, even if it did take an entire bottle of Scotch.

"Anyway," he continued, leaving his hand on hers. "There's really only one angel I trust, and he's been kind of a pain in the ass lately." He shook his head and mumbled, "What I really need to do is figure out how to blind them."

Tatiana frowned. She turned her hand over so she could hold his. Their fingers intertwined. Nico ran his thumb over her knuckles. Their eyes met and the atmosphere changed. The angel discussion was forgotten the electricity between them intensified.

"Sh-ummm…Should we get out of here?" Tatiana asked.

Nico saw her tense, bracing herself for serious Nico to return and send her away. He surprised them both when he pulled her hand into both of his and stood up.

"Definitely."

Ҍ ᴀ ᴈ̌ ѱ ɢ

"You can*not* be serious!"

"I am absolutely serious."

Benyamin seldom lost his temper. He had a reputation for cold, calculating, and methodical behavior. He solved problems by outthinking his enemies, not by brute strength and intimidation. He left that kind of ruthlessness to Lazlo, who reveled in the power of blood-lust. Both methods were effective in their own ways but Benyamin always remained steadfast that one could accomplish far more, far quicker, if those in his charge were encouraged rather than intimidated, but Nayra was pushing the limits of his patience.

"You have the box," he pointed out. "You have the translations. What more could you possibly require?"

Nayra shrugged helplessly. "Diosito Santo! El orden del encantancion! If I do not say it perfectly en orden, it will no work!"

When she became excited or stressed, Nayra tended to speak half-English, half-Spanish, switching back and forth in mid-sentence. Alvi laid a hand on her shoulder. Benyamin stared daggers at her as he tried to fathom how they could be so close to their prize only to be stymied by another puzzle.

"This is ridiculous."

"It is intelligente," Nayra said. "This..." She waved her hands. "...is no supposed to be facil...easy. Whoever cast this spell was very powerful and very wise."

Alvi shrugged. "It makes sense to me. You want to free the most dangerous creatures that ever walked the face of the Earth. Of course, the people who locked them up would make it hard to let them out."

Benyamin seethed. "You would be wise to keep your mouth *shut*, human. You are superfluous to these proceedings." He turned back to Nayra. "Now, witch, you figure out how to open the box. I am losing my patience."

"I no can open it without the orden del encantacion," she said, folding her arms across her chest. "You find, then I open."

Benyamin smirked, his eyes darkening as he did so. He was not amused. "Perhaps a little encouragement is what you need, witch."

In an instant, he was behind Alvi, his fangs exposed as he set to plunge them into Alvi's neck. Before he could bite down, Benyamin felt intense pressure in his head. It ran all the way down his spine, feeling as though his bones were about to explode. He went rigid and collapsed onto the floor.

Nayra, still seated and having never moved so much as a muscle, continued to gaze at him with her steely, ice-gray eyes. All Benyamin could do was stare back at her and try to put on a brave face. Nayra, with a mere thought, could add or relieve the pressure. She applied a little more and Benyamin cried out in pain.

"ENOUGH!"

Azazel appeared with Seir by his side. He glared at Benyamin before looking at Nayra.

"Stop...*now*."

Nayra allowed herself one more jolt of pressure directed at Benyamin before releasing him. He took a moment to catch his breath before getting to his feet. He glared daggers at Nayra.

Azazel focused his pearl-white eyes on him, flashing silver as his own anger bubbled up. He hated dealing with these lower supernatural forms. Demons were bad enough, impossible to control, and not at all trustworthy, but they were light-years more reliable than what the Earth produced. Talk about a corrupted creation. This dismal little planet had no hope at all if these ridiculous creatures were the best it had to offer.

"I assume you are the one responsible for this?"

Benyamin gritted his teeth. "Your witch is useless. She cannot open the box."

"Can't?" Azazel turned to Nayra. "Or won't?"

Nayra shook her head. "The vampiro is a fool. He thinks I just make up spell and box opens." She held up the paper with the translated symbols. "All spells must be done correctly. All words in proper orden. If no, maybe box closes for good."

Azazel nodded, his forehead wrinkled in thought. "You think if the incantation is not performed perfectly in order, the spell might lock the box forever." He turned to Benyamin. "What is the problem? In more than two thousand years of life you've never of a spell like this?"

Benyamin gritted his teeth. "Of course, I have heard of..."

"Then why are we at odds?"

Benyamin lowered his eyes at Azazel's withering stare, which was answer enough for Azazel. The fallen archangel's eyes bored into Benyamin's for several moments before he turned back to Nayra.

"What do you require?"

Nayra thought for a minute. "The box is only one part of the puzzle. There must be another piece somewhere containing the order for the encantacion." She spread her hands. "But I do not even know who the witch was that cast the spell!"

Azazel smiled. "*I* do, and you no doubt have heard of her. The witch in question was named Wynnifrea."

Nayra gasped. "W-Wynnifrea?" Her hands began to shake and she shrunk back into her seat. "It is hopeless. She was the most powerful witch to ever live."

"*Nothing* is hopeless," Azazel said, his finger extended. "Wynnifrea *was* a powerful witch. You *are* a powerful witch. Alive is more powerful than dead. So, forget who cast the spell, and focus on what we need to do to find the missing piece."

Nayra wrinkled her forehead, considering his words. What Azazel said wasn't entirely true. The power of the ancient witch did matter. Her spell would not be easy to take down if Nayra was forced to use a brute force approach, but he was right in that a live witch was in a far better position than a dead one. She could do this. She was powerful and she knew her craft.

Nayra practiced ancestral magic, the practice of drawing power from one's deceased ancestors to strengthen her own magic. Nayra descended from a long line of powerful witches. She could summon a great deal of power when she chose. Wynnifrea, on the other hand, practiced an entirely different form of magic. It was the most ancient form of witchcraft and by far the most powerful.

"I need to learn Khara," she mumbled, almost to herself.

"Khara?" Benyamin frowned, finally getting back into the conversation. "Kharashuoa? Impossible. I was under the impression the witches…"

"They did," Nayra snapped.

The problem with Kharashuoa was in its corruption. The power one could wield was so extraordinary, it tended to corrupt the practitioner, causing her to descend into darkness, gathering more and more power unto herself. This was corrosive to the human psyche. Witches were supernatural beings but, unlike most supernatural creatures, they were still very much human, subject to human ailments and death. Witchcraft grew out of the earth, connecting humanity to the supernatural. When darkness overtook one's psyche, all bets were off, and the damage the Kharashuoaist could inflict upon humanity was frightening.

Throughout history, the witches causing the most trouble in society were all Kharashuoa practitioners. The perceived oppression of witches throughout human history could all be traced back to a Kharashuoa practitioner. Humans generally didn't distinguish between the various forms of witchcraft, leading society to assuming all witches were the same.

Benyamin frowned and glanced at Azazel. "How can we help?"

Azazel nodded with a slight smile as Nayra looked up in surprise. Benyamin lowered his head as an act of contrition. "I apologize for my impatience. I am anxious to see my father once again. Please...what can I do to help you learn what you need to open the portal."

"I need resources," Nayra said. "There must be archives. All witches maintain grimoires, or spellbooks. They contain the...recipes...for every spell they ever cast. These grimoires are usually passed down from generation to generation and each witch uses them and writes their own as well."

"So, you need Kharashuoa grimoires." Benyamin nodded. "I will begin researching immediately."

"That will help me learn Khara," Nayra said. "What we really need are Wynnifrea's grimoires, and we need to find where she recorded the order for the encantacion."

Azazel nodded and gestured for Benyamin to follow. When they were outside the room, he led Benyamin down the elegant hallway to the main staircase which overlooked the massive foyer. The two-hundred-year-old oak woodwork was stunning throughout the large space. The staircase railings, the crown molding, and the wood paneling on the walls had the patina of age. To anyone else, that age would mean something, but to a pair of supernatural creatures, two hundred years was nothing.

"It is imperative we maintain a cohesive unit," Azazel said. "Picking fights with old witches is unproductive."

"It will not happen again."

"See that it doesn't." Azazel drew in a breath. "Your brother...has he contacted you?"

Benyamin shook his head. "Unfortunately, no. If he heard our conversation before, he is certain to put his every resource into finding Xabier Legartza."

"And is it safe to assume he will kill the vampire?"

"No question about it," Benyamin said. "Even without your story, Lazlo will not allow the portal to be opened. He does not want to face our father. More importantly, he hates Xabier, portal or not."

"Will your sister help?"

Benyamin shrugged. "Riva is a wildcard. She loves Lazlo and usually takes his side. She's fiercely loyal to him, however, the opportunity to reunite with our father could be the one thing that might tip her loyalties in our direction." He frowned at Azazel. "Shall I tell her the truth?"

Azazel pressed his lips together. "If she takes the information to Lazlo, it will put us even further behind in the search for Xabier." He shook his head in frustration. "Yet, without her, Lazlo may find him first anyway. He will kill Xabier before we get the information we require." He nodded at Benyamin. "I think the risks are worth the potential gain. Find out where they are and we will position ourselves to monitor your brother."

Benyamin nodded and returned to the massive conference room where Nayra was busily researching historical witchcraft. Azazel leaned on the railing overlooking the foyer. He was in a race and he was behind. He hated playing from behind.

"Your thoughts?"

He said it before Seir announced his presence. Seir was used to that. Azazel's sense of his surroundings was second to none. He needed it if he expected to survive outside Lucifer's inner circle. They could never forget *that* little issue, yet to be resolved.

Seir sucked in a breath through his teeth. His glowing red eyes narrowed as he took his place at the right of his master. "I think leadership suits you."

Azazel chuckled. "It is an unusual position for me to be in, is it not? When I am the rational voice in the room, how bad must things have gotten?"

"You controlled the situation, and they are now prepared to work together toward a common goal. Lucifer would have fared no better."

Azazel bristled at the mention of his former friend. He thought for a moment. "Our situation has changed. You must be prepared to follow wherever Riva Maccabee leads you. After Benyamin explains the situation to her, she will decide. If she sides with us, you will go and assist her. If not, you will track her, and you will have to remain invisible." He held a finger in Seir's face. "In *all* cases, the priority is the safety of Xabier Legartza. Our fanged friend leads a charmed life starting *right now*."

Chapter 9

"*My* father?" Riva exclaimed. "Lazlo, he is just as much your father as he is mine. Just because…"

"That man…" Lazlo pointed a finger at her. "…is no longer my father. He is a betrayer. He betrayed his friends and he betrayed his own flesh and blood. *Then* he brought the curse of *his* damnation upon our family."

Riva fell silent. Lazlo left no room for argument. It always came back to their father's ultimate betrayal, rather, his series of betrayals. He knew Riva's lifelong desire was to reconcile Lazlo and their father, but his untimely imprisonment had ruined any hope for such a moment.

She shrugged helplessly. "So, what does Xabier have to do with father?"

"Xabier…" Lazlo raised his eyebrows and waited a beat. "…is responsible for his demise."

Riva's soft, jade eyes darkened and veins surfaced around her eyes. This happened whenever a vampire prepared to exercise its supernatural power. It was also an indication a vampire was losing control of its emotions. Vampire emotions, like their senses, were always more heightened than those of humans.

"Calm, sister," Lazlo said in his soothing tone.

Riva let out a long breath. "Tell me everything."

Lazlo started from the beginning. He and Xabier met in the mountainous region of Aragon in the early years of the fourteenth century. Formerly comprising the Western coast of modern-day Spain, Aragon is now a landlocked region, roughly forty percent its former size. Its northern border is the Pyrenees mountains between France and Spain. Xabier's people, the Basque, once roamed those mountains in great numbers, but today, they are reduced to near extinction in a tiny region to the west of Aragon.

When they met, Xabier and Lazlo became fast friends. Xabier's devilish good humor was tempered by his extraordinary skill with a sword. In those days, the sword was a daily necessity. It did not take long for Xabier to realize his new friend was different. Lazlo hated keeping his vampire identity from him. When Xabier followed him one night and saw him feeding on a villager, Lazlo thought he would run screaming. Instead, Xabier was fascinated. He plied Lazlo with questions about vampirism. His loyalty was something Lazlo had never experienced, even among his own family. His miserable wretch of a father had ingrained a sense of dread in his children none of them had overcome.

Xabier begged Lazlo for months to turn him into a vampire, but Lazlo refused, not wanting to condemn his friend to an eternity of misery. When Xabier was mortally wounded, defending against a raid in his village, Lazlo found him and saved him by feeding him his blood. Vampire blood contains extraordinary regenerative properties. This gives it the power to heal nearly any human wound or condition within seconds. It is also the primary ingredient in turning a human into a vampire. If a human dies with vampire blood in his system, he is turned. The moment Xabier was alone, he slashed his own throat and expired within seconds. He awoke several hours later in Lazlo's home, alive and starving for blood.

"I can't believe I never knew that," Riva said. "Though the two of you were not exactly regular visitors at the family home."

Lazlo bristled. "Well I'm sorry if I didn't often make it back to the happy family home in Parthia."

"Of course not. You and your new pet spent two hundred years ravaging the North!" Riva stared at him. Her eyes set in like lasers, boring into him "You never thought twice about the family you left behind! You never thought twice about the sist…" Her voice cracked and her eyes watered.

Lazlo rushed to her side and took her hands. "Sister, I stayed away because our father made life at home unbearable. Even as an adult, I could do nothing to please him. He hated me." His voice softened. "Please never mistake my absence for insouciance. Missing my sweet sister was excruciating."

Riva's eyes watered even more and tears spilled onto her cheeks. The bond she'd shared with Lazlo as children was strong. Their eldest brother, Benyamin, had always been the favorite. Their father had doted on him and held him up as the standard to which all his other children should meet. Lazlo, as the second eldest, bore the brunt of their father's disappointment. Lazlo was also the one who drew their father's rage even when he directed it toward *them*. As their elder sibling, he felt an intense responsibility to protect them, even if it meant drawing their father's venom entirely onto his own shoulders. Riva drew the ire of their father whenever she stuck up for Lazlo. He accused her of horrible things, calling her a "harlot" and "her brother's lover."

"Okay, whatever." She shook her head. "Go on."

"One day, Xabier met a young woman." Lazlo's eyes glassed over as though he were seeing straight into the past. "No big deal. She was supposed to be food, but Xabier refused to touch her. He said she was different."

"Xabier fell in love?" Riva asked, her eyes widening with expectation.

"He fell in love," Lazlo repeated. "He was so entranced by her, I could not make him see reason. He wanted to turn her so they could be together forever."

Riva nodded knowingly. "But you wouldn't allow it."

"It was a bloody mistake!" Lazlo insisted. "She would have domesticated him, like a dog."

"Oh, brother," Riva closed her eyes. "What did you do?"

Lazlo closed his eyes. "Xabier defied me and decided to turn her anyway. Before he could feed her his blood, I snapped her neck. She died in his arms." He looked at Riva, who had closed her eyes and was shaking her head. "It was for his own good." Lazlo heard the pleading in his own voice. "I thought Xabier would get over it rather quickly, and we could return to business as usual, but it didn't work out that way."

"I should think not," Riva said with a bland snort.

Lazlo explained how Xabier, cursing their friendship and vowing vengeance, disappeared into the night. Lazlo laughed the threats off, assuming Xabier would eventually cool off and return. As a vampire from the original family, Xabier knew Lazlo could not be killed. As it turned out, he didn't want Lazlo to die. He wanted him to suffer. Lazlo related to Riva everything Xabier had done to him.

"He did all that without you knowing?" Riva asked in disbelief.

Lazlo shook his head, reliving the betrayal, seeing every death in his mind's eye as if it was happening to him all over again. "I never even suspected. Xabier was a great warrior. I assumed any vengeance he took would be direct." He gritted his teeth. "Xabier took it to another level entirely."

Riva's eyes widened and her mouth dropped open. "It was all just a ruse to get father to hurt you."

"To get father to *kill* me," Lazlo corrected. "Make no mistake. Xabier's endgame was to have me murdered by my own father."

"So Xabier Legartza caused all the misery our family has suffered for centuries?"

"There's more," Lazlo intoned. "When the alphas were being rounded up, it was Xabier who lured many of them to their capture, including father."

Riva's eyes darkened. "He betrayed a vampire to the humans?"

"Ironic, nae?" Lazlo said with a humorless smirk. "The greatest betrayer in human history betrayed by one of *his* own."

"It's not funny, Lazlo."

Lazlo's grin widened. "Ahh, come now, sister. Allow me to enjoy the *one* part of the story that brings me some amusement. But you haven't heard the final bit. Whilst he was luring father to his demise, Xabier also leaked word to me, informing me of when and where our dear father would show up. He meant to have me thrown into the portal along with father, but I was cautious. I arrived *during* the battle and remained out of sight. All of father's minions were killed and he was thrown into the portal whilst I watched."

"Dreadful."

Lazlo chuckled. "It was the greatest moment of my life. Then, after everyone had gone back to their camp on the other side of the mountain, I found Xabier lying in wait. He stood and faced me. That was when he told me the truth about all my misfortunes over the years. I suspect he thought he would have help from the angels because he seemed surprised to be all alone against me. When he realized no help was forthcoming, he ran, and search though I might, I haven't heard his name for a thousand years."

Riva pursed her lips. "Until now."

ᛒ ᴀ ⦰ ᴪ ᏽ

Tatiana awoke in a king-sized bed, tangled in soft, silky sheets. It wasn't her own bed, she knew that immediately. It was unfamiliar, but soft and comfortable. It took her a few moments to recall where she was. Then she reached over to the other side of the bed. It was empty.

She propped herself up on one elbow and glanced around the room, but saw no one. She pulled a pillow to her body and lay back, staring at the vaulted ceiling as she considered the previous night. She couldn't recall ever being with a man so intense and passionate. Nico made her feel things she'd never dreamed possible.

"What are you smiling at?"

His voice cut through her thoughts. Tatiana didn't wipe the smile off her face. Instead, she rolled onto her side, her head still on her pillow. Her eyes focused on him as he stood in the doorway.

"As if you didn't know," she purred. "What time is it?"

"Almost ten."

"Mmm. Late.

He sat on the edge of the bed and Tatiana scooted closer, resting her head on his thigh, tracing his muscled chest with her hand. He covered her hand with his and stroked it with his thumb.

"I have to go," he said. "Work."

Tatiana pouted Then she smiled, pulling herself up to a seated position. She tugged Nico to her, drawing his lips to hers. She ran her fingers through his hair, pushing his shaggy bangs back off his forehead.

"Do I have time to take a shower?" she asked.

"Hmm?" Nico frowned. "Oh, no. I didn't mean..." He grinned and wrapped his arms around her. He buried his face in her luscious red hair, alternately kissing the top of her head and inhaling her scent. "Please stay."

She pulled back and met his gaze. "Really?"

Nico smirked. "I supposed we could pretend this was just a one night thing, but..." He got serious and looked into her eyes. "Look, Tatiana, I don't bring girls home...ever. Not since—"

His eyes filled with the pain of loss. For a moment, Tatiana thought tears would fall, but he took a deep breath and touched her cheek.

"I had someone," he said softly. "She's...gone."

"Bad break-up?"

"No," Nico shook his head. "She's just gone."

Tatiana's mouth opened, but words failed her. She just nodded in understanding. "Nico, I'm so sorry." She lay her head on his chest.

"It's okay," he said. "My point is, I don't do this. I don't date. You're the first since...well, for months. I like the way I feel when I'm with you. So, if you think there's something good between us, I want you here."

Tatiana nodded. "Okay, Nico." She kissed him sweetly on his neck, his cheek, and finally his lips. "Go to work. I'll be here when you get back."

She watched Nico exit. She heard his car door slam and then the engine roared to life. Tatiana looked out the window in time to see the charcoal grey Maserati disappear behind the heavily wooded front of the property. She stared wistfully for several moments before smiling to herself and plopping back down on the bed. She pulled the pillow to her chest and hugged it again, resuming her recollection of the previous night's events.

After a short daydream, her eyes opened and she glanced around the room again. Nico's silk robe lay across the foot of the bed. She slipped into it and left the room. She swept through the entire house, making sure no one was present. Finally, she returned to the room and grabbed her phone. Returning to the living room, she found the correct contact and sent off a quick text.

In.

She immediately deleted the conversation and tossed her phone onto the coffee table. There would be no response. Since she had the day to herself, she thought about what she was going to do. Before long, her thoughts returned to Nico…

Nico drove his Maserati to a secluded parking spot around the corner and checked the map on his phone. He had the entire day planned. The information Zha'riel pulled from Nikoli's mind had gone into a sorting metric Nico had created on his computer. The program plotted the locations he would visit in Eastern Europe. He had to admit, that Nikoli character got around. According to the map, he had Russia's entire western border covered. From Estonia to Latvia to Lithuania to Belarus, and throughout the Ukraine, Nikoli had dozens of brothels, safehouses, and auction sites to go along with his extensive network of kidnappers throughout the continent of Europe.

Today would be a crippling day in the world sex trafficking market. Nikoli was a high-ranking member of the Russian mob.

His arrest would soon be known to his superiors, and soon after that he would tell his lawyer Nico was coming, giving them a chance to fortify their locations. Not that Nico cared. The more the merrier as far as he was concerned, but on the off chance they chose to move the girls, Nico thought it best to act quickly. His primary concern was for the innocent victims.

"Zha'riel!" he shouted.

"Zha'riel is busy today."

The voice, coming from the back seat of his car, startled Nico. He nearly hit his head on the roof as he jolted and spun in his seat. The man in the back seat was dressed in what had to be a five-thousand-dollar Italian suit. Navy blue with light pinstripes, the three-piece suit conveyed power and control, exactly what an archangel had to be.

Nico breathed a sigh of relief. "Rafael," he muttered. "What a pleasant surprise."

"You've been avoiding me," he accused, his dark eyes flashing. "You don't respond to messages. You don't show up to meetings."

"That doesn't sound like me," Nico said blandly. "Anyway, I'm busy. What do you want?"

"The warding sigils on your house and the bar you frequent were a nice touch."

Nico chuckled. "I should have thought to put them on my car." He made a mental note to remember to do that later.

"Why are you making it so difficult for us to help you, Nico?"

Nico turned in his seat. "Let me explain something to you, Rafael. We're not on the same side. We're not partners, and we're *not* friends. You left Stephanie to die. You refused to help, so *I* had to go face a fallen archangel whackjob on my own. *Then*, you punish Zha'riel for intervening and saving Xabier. All you ever do is threaten me." Nico shrugged. "So, tell me, why in *hell* should I trust you?"

Rafael raised manicured eyebrows. "Be careful," he warned. "You are floating on the edge of your own demise."

Nico sighed. "Something tells me I've been floating on that edge ever since I transitioned. If you want to kill me, get on with it. Otherwise, piss off. I'm busy."

"*Killing* you is not what *anyone* wants." Rafael said. "So far, everyone on *my* side of the war has tried to keep you from succumbing to darkness, but you ignore everyone but your vampire friend and Lucifer's minions." He raised his eyebrows. "How has that worked out so far, by the way? Your brother is dead because of *your* greed. An innocent girl is dead because of *your* failure."

Nico opened his mouth, but Rafael shook his head. "*Silence*...would be your wisest approach, human." He stared at Nico in the rearview mirror, putting his two forefingers to his pursed lips. "This is what you need to know, Nico. The next human corpse to fall at your hands will result in Heaven descending upon you and ending you. So, whatever little plan you have to go after Russian gangsters better account for every single life you come into contact with." He opened the door. "We are watching, Nico. Do not make me come for you."

He stepped out of the car and walked away. Nico gritted his teeth and let out a long, slow breath. He felt an icy chill flowing through his veins. It wasn't new, but what *was* new was the rage he suddenly felt. Before he could get it under control, he flung open his door and jumped out of the car.

"Hey!" he shouted, whirling in all directions. "Where are you, you self-righteous sonofabitch?" he shouted at the top of his lungs. "Why wait? Let's just settle this here and now!" With a simple thought, Nico was holding Mattaeus' angel sword. He held it up and waited for Rafael to return. "Come on," he muttered. "Let's see if these things really work on angels."

"Oh, they work."

Nico spun around, surprised at the new voice. He held the sword at the ready, though the new arrival merely stood there, empty-handed, and smiling as if he hadn't a care in the world. His platinum blonde hair and electric-blue eyes were unfamiliar to Nico, who still stood in a fighting stance, keeping the sword extended before him.

He posed no threat, made no move, yet Nico sensed the power emanating from the man's depths. He felt the hate, the anger, and the ice-cold core. It was familiar, like an instinctive connection. It was like nothing he had ever felt before and yet it was as natural to him as breathing. Within seconds his mind put it all together.

"Lucifer."

Chapter 10

"You know; I can do without putting myself in the middle of a bunch of cretins."

"Couldn't be helped."

In their room at Sonesta Suites, just outside downtown Flagstaff, Xabier reclined in a heavy chair, his head tilted back so he was staring at the ceiling. His eyes were unfocused as he pondered everything Max had told him. A rocks glass half-filled with fine Scotch sat on his right thigh, supported by his right hand. He hadn't touched it since his initial sip fifteen minutes before.

Leonardo stretched out on the couch, his own glass held loosely in his hand as it dangled over the back of the couch. He was on his third drink. He shook his head, clearly still shaken by their recent run-in with the vetala. Leo was a willing fighter, but had spent the past few decades avoiding trouble as much as possible.

"Did we at least learn anything of value?"

Xabier breathed in deeply without moving his eyes. He bit his bottom lip, still trying to piece things together.

"Something's definitely going on. Max told me there are whispers about some kind of supernatural coalition."

"Dammit!" Leonardo exclaimed. "I *knew* it."

"But he has no idea what they're up to." Xabier finally took another sip. "He does know the vampires are running things."

"Vampires." Leonardo narrowed his eyes. "You think Benyamin is calling the shots?"

"It makes the most sense. If vampires are heading up a supernatural coalition, Benyamin is the one in charge. He's the most diplomatic."

Leonardo scoffed. "Yeah, as long as everyone stays in line. I can't imagine him working with vetala and wendigos."

They both knew how ruthless Benyamin could be. He was always referred to as the one with the level head, the one who could be reasoned with. The reality was, Benyamin's temper was as violent as his notorious brother's. The only difference was Lazlo never pretended to be anything other than vicious and unforgiving.

"Which brings us to the real question," Xabier mused. "What could compel mortal enemies to work together?"

"A common goal," Leonardo said, his voice softening in thought. "I can't think of anything."

"I can," Xabier said. "They all have exactly one thing in common." He straightened in his chair and took a long sip of Scotch before looking right at Leonardo, who stared back in rapt expectation. "They all have alphas imprisoned in a special section of Purgatory."

Leonardo's mouth dropped open. "*Special* section?"

"It was sectioned off specifically for the twelve alphas," Xabier said. "Over three years, the alphas were rounded up and tossed in."

"When was this?"

"Sixteenth century. The witch, Wynnifrea, controlled the portal. Afterward, she locked the key in a box and spelled it shut. I thought it had been hidden away for good." Xabier shook his head and gritted his teeth. "If they find that box and manage to open it—"

"How do you know all this?" Leonardo asked. His eyes were wide, greedily taking in every expression, just as his ears were taking in every word.

Xabier stared back with tired eyes. "I was there."

Before Leonardo could process that piece of information, Xabier's eyes narrowed and he darted to the window. He peered through the blinds, his heartbeat picking up pace as he considered what he thought he'd seen. Leonardo leapt to his feet and hurried to the door, taking a position with his back to the wall. He furrowed his brow as he listened.

"What is it? See something?"

"I don't know." Xabier continued to look through the blinds. "I thought I saw red."

"*Red?*" Leonardo's brow furrowed. "What does that mea—?"

"Not just red," Xabier corrected. "*Glowing* red."

Leonardo's eyes grew wide. "Aw, no! No, no no! Come *on*! Seriously?"

Xabier stared through the blinds, and scanned every foot of space he could see. Nothing seemed out of the ordinary, but he was convinced he saw what he saw. If Seir was nearby, he was in serious trouble. He and Nico had known it was just a matter of time before Azazel returned to finish the job Lucifer had interrupted, but Xabier had never expected Seir to show up randomly, on the other side of the country. What could it mean?

"He's after me," Xabier said. He gave Leonardo the short version of his experience with the homicidal archangel and his red-eyed demon minion. "I just can't figure out how he tracked me all the way to Arizona. It doesn't make sense."

Leonardo closed his eyes and shook his head. "And the timing sucks." He cast a nervous glance at the door, then back to the window. "Look, I say we just bail. We don't need to be messing with demons."

Xabier nodded. "I don't disagree, my friend. I just want to spot him, so we can avoid him. It wouldn't do to sneak out of this room and run right into his arms."

"What about your friend, Nico, was it?"

Xabier shook his head. "I would love to have Nico's help on this, and ten minutes ago I was ready to call him and explain everything. At the very least, his ability to orb would help us move around a whole lot faster. But if Seir *is* out there, I can't risk bringing Nico into it. Azazel still wants revenge. I have to protect Nico." He turned back to the window and looked out again. "He's my friend."

A knock at the door silenced both vampires. Xabier's head snapped to attention. Leonardo, his eyes wide, looked from the door to Xabier. He pressed himself even closer to the wall, listening for any sound from outside the room. They both knew better than to speak. Most supernatural creatures possessed extraordinary senses. Anything they said in the room, at this point, would be heard.

"Xabier, I know you're in there. Open the door!"

Xabier's brow furrowed at the familiar feminine voice. "It can't be," he murmured.

"Well, it is! Open the door!"

Xabier gestured with a head bob. Leonardo nodded and reached for the handle. When the door opened, in walked a stunning woman with long, wavy brown hair and jade-green eyes. Her dark hair and olive skin provided a stark contrast for the lighter eye color. The result was an effortless exotic and sensual appearance.

Xabier shook his head in disbelief. "Riva Maccabee."

"You remember." She said it as a statement though her head was tilted and she wore a quizzical expression on her face. "How long has it been? Over a thousand years, I suspect."

"That long?" Xabier frowned. He thought for a moment and shrugged. "Well, in any case, you're not the kind of woman one easily forgets."

She allowed a slight smile. "Always the charmer." Her face turned serious. "My brother knows you're here and is going to kill you."

Xabier's pulse quickened. For more than five hundred years, he'd managed to avoid the vengeful Lazlo Maccabee. Lazlo wasn't hard to avoid. He caused fear everywhere he went. He never bothered to learn the art of subtlety. Xabier always figured it was because Lazlo never had to worry about consequences for his actions. The original vampire family was all but immortal. No earthly weapon could kill them, which meant the best way to survive was to stay away. Whenever Lazlo got close, Xabier would disappear, moving from place to place as necessary.

If Lazlo was nearby, the only question was why hadn't he made a move? Xabier had always known there would come a day when he would have to face his former friend, but the timing here was bad. There was no way Xabier could fend off Lazlo and still pursue the coalition's efforts to open the portal. Riva's presence was even more confusing. Her relationship with Lazlo was always in flux. At any given moment, she was his closest confidante or she hated him. Since she was a member of the first vampire family, and therefore equally immortal, Xabier had no other choice but to let the scene play out and keep his eyes open for an escape route.

"And you're telling me this...why?"

Riva chuckled. "Relax, Xabier I am not here to help him. Though after what you did to my father, I should tear your heart from your chest and watch you die in front of me."

Leonardo tensed. Xabier watched as he moved, maintaining strategic position. As Riva continued further into the room, Leonardo maintained a safe distance but always stayed directly behind her.

"I swear to God," Riva said without taking her eyes off Xabier. "If you don't get out from behind my back I will rip out your spine."

Leonardo held his hands out in front of him. "No offense."

Riva's eyes sparkled and the right corner of her mouth curled upward just a fraction. To Xabier she said, "Your friend isn't much of a fighter, is he?"

"He can hold his own," Xabier replied. "What are you doing here?"

Xabier took as much edge off his voice as he could, but Riva's presence meant Lazlo was close. It could mean he was already lying in wait. Xabier continued to peek out the window. Was it really possible he was going to have to deal with a red-eyed demon *and* a couple of original vampires at the same time?

"What?" Riva asked. "You're not happy to see me?"

Xabier rolled his eyes. "I'm pretty sure you and I aren't friends, Riva. You're the one sibling that would do anything for Lazlo. He hates me and wants me dead. So, I ask again…what are you doing here?"

Riva sat in a chair and crossed her perfect legs. Her black, soft-leather pants clung to her shape before disappearing into a pair of suede, black, high-heeled boots. She looked down at the dust-covered designer boots and frowned in distaste. She tried to brush the dust off but gave up when she succeeded only in creating a cloud of dust and breathing it in.

She shook her head in disgust. "What I am doing here is saving your life." Her eyes lifted to meet Xabier's. "He's going to kill you, you know."

"Yeah, you said that already."

Riva raised her eyebrows. "So, shall we get on with it? We need to get you out of here before Lazlo finds us."

"We?" Xabier's eyes narrowed. "Who exactly is 'we?'"

"We," Riva said, "are people who care to see you survive."

Xabier stared at her. As soon as he met her stunning jade eyes, he knew. He pointed out the window in disbelief. "That's Seir out there, isn't it? He's with *you*? You're working with *Azazel*? Are you out of your mind?"

"Quite the contrary," Riva replied evenly. "For all these centuries, the one thing I have wanted was to see my father again—to reunite my family. Azazel seems to have found a way to do that."

"And you think it's in your best interests to join forces with him?" Xabier frowned. "Lazlo will kill you."

"I'm an original vampire," Riva countered. "I can't be killed."

"No, but you *can* be made to suffer for your sins!"

All eyes turned to see Lazlo behind Leonardo. The scowl on his face was barely intense enough to match the fiery rage in his eyes. Normally, a shade or two darker than Riva's, it was impossible to see any color at all as his eyes darted from his sister to Xabier, as if trying to determine which of the two was the bigger betrayer. His eyes settled on Riva who shrank under his gaze.

"You disappoint me, sister."

"Lazlo, I…"

"Silence!" He glared at Riva for a few seconds longer. "I'll deal with *you* in due course." He leveled his gaze at Xabier. "First I want to be perfectly clear with my duplicitous and cowardly old friend over there. I want him to understand what will happen in the event he decides to disappear on us."

At that moment Xabier noticed the Leonardo's unusual posture. He stood at a strange angle, with a grimace on his face and sweat pouring from his forehead. His face was a mask of fear and pain. Behind him, Lazlo's right arm disappeared behind Leonardo's back like a puppeteer. Xabier saw blood dripping off Lazlo's elbow.

Lazlo saw the look of understanding in Xabier's eyes. "That's right, my old friend. If you even *think* about running, the last thing your friend will see is his heart after I rip it from his body."

ƀ ᴀ ᶎ ψ ç

"New Orleans."

Benyamin stood behind Nayra as she poured over the old books. A quick trip with Azazel back to her South American home had produced a library's worth of aged and ancient manuscripts, in various languages, ranging from Latin to Greek to several long-dead Middle Eastern languages, including Benyamin's native tongue of Aramaic. Following their spat, Benyamin and Nayra settled into a working relationship which could almost pass for respect. Between the two of them, they managed to plow through dozens of texts, extracting anything pertinent that might provide a clue as to where and how they could pursue the ancient form of witchcraft called Kharashuoa.

He wrinkled his brow. "What about New Orleans?"

Benyamin shook his head in amusement as Nayra ignored his response. He was used to it. She worked in a constant state of muttering and musing. He could never tell when she was mumbling to herself or when her comments were directed at him. Whenever he replied to her, she would return his effort with a steely, gray-eyed stare, much like a child would receive from a parent after speaking out of turn. Or he would ignore her comment and Nayra would glare at him in silence, impatiently tapping her fingers until he replied.

After several moments of continuous murmuring and scanning between a map and an old document, she looked up at Benyamin. "We must go to New Orleans...now."

"Why? What is in New Orleans."

She stared at him as though the answer was plain as day. "A witch, of course."

Benyamin narrowed his eyes. "There are lots of witches in New Orleans."

"One witch in particular," Nayra said. "Marie Laveau."

Benyamin closed his eyes and pinched the bridge of his nose. New Orleans supernatural history was his specialty. "Marie Laveau?" He shook his head. "Nayra, Marie Laveau died in 1881. That news spread around the supernatural world in a matter of weeks."

"And?"

Benyamin's hands clenched into fists as his blood pressure rose and his heart rate increased. As much as his attitude toward the old witch had softened, he sometimes felt as though he was skating right on the edge of ripping her throat out. He wondered, fleetingly, how quickly she could react if he took another shot at her. He took a calming breath.

"So how are we going to—?"

"Shhh!" Nayra put up a hand and tilted her head. "Did you hear that?"

"Hear what?"

Vampires possessed exceptional hearing. They could pick out individual voices at over one hundred yards, a scream at close to a mile. They could pinpoint the location of a nearby sound to within a few feet even in pitch dark. Benyamin was certain there was no sound, even if a powerful witch insisted there was.

Nayra's head was still tilted to one side, and her eyes closed as she focused on whatever sound she thought she was hearing. A glint lit up her eyes and she held up a hand as she took long, deep breaths. Benyamin couldn't stand witches. He was always uncomfortable with their ability to reach out with their minds and 'touch' the intangible.

Without warning, Nayra's eyes snapped open and terror filled her expression. "They're here."

Benyamin frowned and tensed his muscles, straining to hear whatever it was the witch was hearing. "Who? Who is here, Nayra?"

"We need to get out of here," she insisted. "They're coming for me!"

"What are you talking about? Who is coming for you?"

Nayra's gray eyes were wide with fear. Her lips quivered as she tried to form the word. Finally, she gasped, "Demonio!"

Benyamin felt his heart sink. Demons were no fun to deal with. Even with his supernatural strength, he was no match for even a single demon. One-on-one combat with a demon was a suicide mission. He looked to Nayra.

"You know demons. What do we do?"

Nayra's eyes suddenly calmed and Benyamin watched as she steadied her breathing. She thought for a moment and pointed at Benyamin.

"Salt! We need salt...as much as you have." She waved a hand at him. "Go! Quickly!"

Benyamin rushed to the pantry and returned in an instant with two cylinders of table salt. "Will this work?"

"It will do," Nayra said, grabbing one of the cylinders from him. "Now pour a thick circle in the center of the room and do *not* step outside the circle. Demons cannot cross a salt line."

"Right," Benyamin said. "I knew that."

Moving as fast as she could, Nayra poured a salt border around the entire room, leaving only the doorway open.

Benyamin frowned. "Why would you leave that opening? Isn't the whole idea to keep them out?"

Nayra lifted a corner of the giant rug and took a black Sharpie marker from the table. She began drawing on the floor. Benyamin wanted to ask her what she was drawing, but chose not to interrupt in a life-and-death situation. He clamped his mouth shut and hoped the old witch knew what she was doing. Azazel told him all about how she had once captured and controlled two high-level demons, so she was not one to be trifled with.

When she was finished, Nayra replaced the corner of the rug and stepped across the salt line into the middle of the room with Benyamin. She took a seat in an ornate winged-back chair and watched the doorway. Benyamin sat on the couch and continuously scanned the room.

"Are you sure about the salt?"

"Positive," Nayra said.

"What did you draw on the floor?"

"Shhh!" Nayra said. "They're coming."

At that moment, the door slammed open and three men stood in the doorway, staring at Nayra, their eyes black as night, the grins on their faces sadistic and evil. A chill filled the room and Nayra shivered, her heart pounding in her chest loud enough for Benyamin to count the beats. Even Benyamin felt the icy cold, even though vampires were immune to most temperature extremes.

The lead demon, seeing the circle of salt surround his target, laughed. "You think salt can protect you, witch? We will shake this house apart!"

He raised his arms and the other two followed suit. The house began to shake. Benyamin stared in terror as the salt began to move. Within seconds, the salt line was diminished, the granules spreading out on the floor until, finally, there was a break in the line. Their defense was rendered useless.

The demons all smiled and without any further warning rushed straight at Nayra...

And slammed into an invisible wall. They stood in shock, staring at Nayra as they pounded on something they could not see but was strong enough to keep them at bay. When they tried to retreat to the doorway, they could not. The invisible wall surrounded them.

Nayra stood and walked over to the edge of the carpet. Lifting it up, she revealed the drawing. The demons' eyes grew wide in shock and anger. Nayra turned to Benyamin and smiled grimly.

"It is called a Devil's Trap. It will hold them until someone outside the trap breaks the seal."

He nodded in approval. "I've heard of this. Very clever."

"What is going on here?"

Azazel appeared in the middle of the room. He faced the trapped demons who'd gone from pissed to petrified. He squinted his eyes. "Who sent you?" He held up a finger and let them see a crackle of purple electricity. "And I think you know what will happen if you dare lie to me."

The leader spoke up. "A-A-Abdiel sent us. He said to kill the witch."

Azazel's eyes flashed silver and back to their menacing white glow as he considered the demon's words. He paced the room while everyone present remained silent. He closed his eyes and worked through all the possibilities. Lucifer had a purpose for everything he did. The presence of these demons and their intention to kill Nayra meant Lucifer was actively working against releasing the alphas. But why? What did Lucifer care if evil supernatural creatures reentered the world? If anything, the resultant chaos would work *for* the Dark Lord's purposes, not against. Azazel could only think of one reason for Lucifer's interest.

"He's trying to thwart me," Azazel said, looking at Nayra and Benyamin. His eyes flashed silver again and he shot them a humorless smile. "My old friend intends to intervene merely to deny me allies."

Nayra's eyes narrowed as she considered his words. "If Lucifer stands against us, we *are* thwarted, no?"

Azazel shook his head. "No. Lucifer cannot be everywhere. As powerful as he is, he cannot hide himself from me, and he knows he is the only one who can defeat me." He clenched his teeth. "We press on. What have you discovered?"

"We must go to New Orleans to search out a Kharashuoa witch."

Azazel nodded. "Then let's go to New Orleans." He glanced back at the captured demons. "After I deal with these three."

Chapter 11

"*Now* you show up?"

Lucifer pressed his lips together. "Nico, I…"

"You know what?" Nico held up a finger while his other hand held his sword at the ready. "Don't. You sent Abdiel to befriend me and then you *both* abandoned me when I needed you."

"I really *am* sorry about your Stephanie."

Lucifer grimaced, as if he were actually pained at the inference…Lucifer. Was Nico supposed to feel some kinship with the most evil being in existence after he was cut off and ignored throughout the worst days of his life? It was absurd. It was crazy, even for someone who was aware of the supernatural world and all that went with it.

Just hearing her name slide off Lucifer's lips soured Nico's stomach. The memory of how she died, tortured, alone, and scared, enraged him. What hurt even more was how Lucifer and Abdiel had disappeared after her death. He lost his brother and his girlfriend in a matter of hours. The one chance he had to restore them was his access to some of the most powerful beings in existence. A select few of the most powerful archangels held within them the power to resurrect a dead human. Apparently, they were forbidden from actually exercising that power; not that rules had ever held Lucifer back. He'd made a choice, and Nico was left to suffer for it. It was only Nico's tenuous grasp on life that held him back from attacking Lucifer.

"You know what?" Nico said. "You angels are the most confusing bunch of lunatics I've ever come across."

Lucifer nodded in sympathy. "I understand your feelings. You think I betrayed you, that I abandoned you when you needed my powers the most."

"How perceptive." Nico stared right into the dark prince's eyes and the sight froze his blood. It was like staring into pure gold. For a split second, Nico was transfixed at the sheer beauty. In the blink of an eye, the color flashed back to electric-blue, but Nico could still see the supernatural beauty behind the human. He felt a tug, just the slightest urge, to give Lucifer the benefit of the doubt, but the hatred inside was far more powerful. "Is this some new empathy training you fallen angels are trying out? It's a bit after-the-fact though. I don't need sympathy and I don't need empathy. What I *need* is to have the people I love back."

"Nico," Lucifer said. "First of all, angels are *all* hardwired to compassion. Even us evil, fallen angels understand emotion. We feel pain and loss on a scale you humans could never imagine."

"You expect me to believe this?"

"What you choose to believe is not important," Lucifer replied. "I say that, not to be harsh or cruel, only to illustrate the truth of the world."

"And what is that?"

"That you don't understand what it is you are asking." Lucifer leaned on the hood of Nico's Maserati. He pinched the bridge of his nose between his thumb and forefinger. "Nico, you must understand that raising the dead is not natural. It is not...allowed. There are consequences for exercising that kind of power in this world."

"As if you care about rules," Nico spat, still holding the sword in his hand, pointed it at Lucifer like it was an extension of his finger. "This coming from the guy who spat in the face of his master."

He knew, in an instant, it was the wrong thing to say. Lucifer's eyes flashed the same brilliant, golden hue as before, but now there was an ominous tension behind his gaze. Nico pulled his arm back and relaxed his posture. It was probably best not to press that button again.

"I'm sorry," he mumbled. "I shouldn't have gone there."

Lucifer raised his eyebrows and tilted his head. "Do you intend to use my brother's sword to slay me today?"

Nico bit his lip considered the question. Who was he kidding? When he thought to take on Rafael, he had known it was a suicide mission. He'd just wanted to get it over with. Lucifer was another story altogether. He had actually *helped* Nico in the past. Abdiel was the reason Nico was able to avenge his brother, and probably a good part of the reason he was able to hold out as long as he did against Azazel.

He lowered the sword and chuckled. "You recognize it?"

"Of course, I recognize it." Lucifer's mouth twisted in an ironic grin. "Our Father crafted three swords with His own hands. Michael's was the first, and therefore, the most powerful. He lost it the only time he and I ever clashed." He eyed Nico. "Of course, that was after I...how did you put it...*spat* in the face of my *Father*?"

Nico slumped his shoulders. "I said I was sorry."

Lucifer regarded him for several seconds in silence before pressing his lips together and nodding his acceptance. "Very well."

"But you *did* screw me over."

Lucifer shrugged and tilted his head. "On the other hand, I saved *your* life. Azazel destroyed nearly every atom in your body. Even Zha'riel's touch couldn't have overcome that."

"Yeah, thanks for that, by the way." Nico didn't bother to disguise his contempt. "I needed you. I was willing to do whatever it took to bring them back." He spread his arms. "I thought you wanted me to join you."

In the days following Nico's near-death experience at the hands of the maniacal Azazel, he had cried out to Abdiel, begging him to bring Nico before Lucifer. At the time, he had been willing to do anything to have his loved ones restored. Abdiel, at first, had been sympathetic and tried to explain

Lucifer's decision, but Nico was not interested in anything but seeing Stephanie and Dominick again. Eventually, Abdiel stopped responding.

"Of course, I wanted you," Lucifer assured him. "I still do. But you were in no shape to make a decision like that." He shook his head sadly. "My closest friend turned on me, out of anger, over a decision I'd made. He took business personally, and now I fear we will never reconcile. If I had taken advantage of you in your weakness, you would grow to resent me, and one day, you would betray me, as Azazel did."

Lucifer came to him and grasped Nico's shoulders, gazing into his eyes. "To bring your people back, the natural world would have to find a balance. Do you understand what that means?"

Nico shook his head.

"To bring the dead to life, another life must be sacrificed."

"So?" Nico shrugged his hands off. "We could have found some criminal to...what?"

Lucifer was shaking his head. "I am not a witch, Nico. There are those who practice necromancy. Some servants of nature can convene with the dead, and some can also perform life exchanges, but there are always unintended consequences. I cannot do what you wish. If I resurrect a life, another dies. We do not get to choose the one who dies."

Nico drew in a breath. Now he understood. To bring those he loved back to life, Lucifer would have to condemn two unnamed souls to death. It didn't seem like something the Prince of Darkness would care about, but Nico was coming to the realization that every living being was complex. Those who were eons old had layers humans could never begin to comprehend.

Nico sighed. "You still could have told me all this at the time."

"Would you have listened to reason?"

"Why do you care about reason?" Nico asked. "And why not give me the opportunity to make the decision? I would have come to you willingly.

"That would not have been willing at all," Lucifer replied. He leaned in closer, once again making eye contact. "You *will* come, Nico. You already know it. Can you feel that? It's a little cold, but it is so enticing. It is pulling you."

Nico stared back. He did feel it, the cold pull. The words didn't even make sense as they floated across his mind, but that was what it felt like. As much as he wanted to resist any pull in any direction, he had to admit he was losing the battle when it came to this cold tug.

Lucifer smiled in understanding. "Ahh. You wish to fight it, but you don't even know what it is you are fighting. How can you fight an unseen enemy, Nico?"

"You're playing a psychological game with me?"

Lucifer chuckled. "Not at all. In fact, this began the moment you took in the essence of darkness. Sansata was powerful. He was Azazel's son, a next generation, direct descendent of a fallen angel." He looked at Nico curiously. "No one told you who Sansata's mother was, did they?"

Nico's eyes widened. "Is? She's still alive?"

"*Alive?*" Lucifer said as though the question was ridiculous. "Of course she's alive…she's a god."

ℶ ℵ ℥ ψ ℭ

"Well, here we are. Bourbon Street."

Azazel watched Nayra with expectation in his eyes. She ignored his gaze and narrowed her eyes, looking in every direction. It was her first time in the city of New Orleans. She knew what she was looking for, but had no idea where it was. Benyamin came to her aid.

"I know this city well, Nayra. Where do you wish to go?"

Nayra held up a piece of paper with some words scrawled in her handwriting: *Marie Laveau's House of Voodoo.*

Benyamin smiled ruefully. "Of course. How did I miss such an obvious reference?"

"Sometimes the answer is not as complicated as one may assume."

Benyamin led the way several blocks south on the famed street. Even in daylight, the sounds of Bourbon Street filled the air. On the corner of St. Philip Street, an elderly black man sat on the sidewalk, his back against the old brick of Lafitte's Blacksmith Shop. He played a slow, heart wrenching dirge on a small saxophone. Nayra stopped for a moment and watched him. His eyes looked far away, almost hypnotic, as the notes floated from the gleaming brass instrument.

Azazel drew in an impatient breath and clenched his fists. Benyamin's eyes flicked back and forth between the fallen angel and the witch. He took her arm.

"We must hurry," he said in a gentle, but firm tone.

She nodded and allowed him to guide her the remaining distance. The whole way, her eyes roamed, studying the city. She even took in long, slow breaths as though the city's air could somehow connect her with the supernatural power coursing through the city. She finally snapped out of her trance-like state.

"Do you not feel that?" she asked with a quizzical expression.

Azazel frowned. "Feel what?"

She breathed in again and closed her eyes. "The chakra in this city is electric. I can *feel* my people."

"*Your* people?" Azazel held up a hand. "I thought you'd never been to…"

"Servants of nature," Benyamin said, raising his eyebrows. "She senses other witches."

Nayra hurried forward, leading the way as if she were a New Orleans tour guide. Azazel and Benyamin trailed as she made a beeline for the corner of Bourbon and St. Anne. She stopped in front of Oz, a gay bar, situated cattycorner from their destination. Marie Laveau's was a small, unassuming place, built with cream and grey-colored brick. The roof looked like it could use some attention.

Two tall men wearing slinky satin dresses strutted past and entered Oz. Azazel's gaze followed them and he rolled his eyes in disgust as Benyamin stifled a chuckle. Apparently, even the fallen angels had their limits. For a brief moment, Nayra thought Azazel might lash out and smite the transgendered couple right then and there. She only knew the dark angel by his homicidal and maniacal reputation, plus the short time they had worked together. Even Benyamin had admitted to her, Azazel had not lived up to his psychotic reputation, yet it was also clear the psychosis was not far from the surface.

Nayra made a move to cross the intersection but stopped and turned to Azazel. "You stay here."

"I beg your pardon?" Azazel's eyebrows shot up and the look on his face was a combination of amused and annoyed. "Let us get one thing clear…"

"Your energy," Narya said, looking him in the eyes without blinking. "It is black…pure evil. They will never talk to me if you are present."

Benyamin glanced from Nayra to Azazel. It was a contest of wills between one of the most powerful beings in existence and an old witch who was still searching for her place in history. What she said was true. Witches tended to read the chakra each person emitted. It was a practiced skill, but one that served the witches well. They could often distinguish between their allies and those who would do them harm simply by interpreting invisible energy. Azazel must know that to be true. The question was whether he would be willing to hang back.

Azazel's mouth tightened as he considered Nayra's words. "You are correct. They probably would withdraw." He smiled and gestured to Benyamin. "Accompany her. See to it no harm comes to her."

Moments later, Benyamin and Nayra entered Marie Laveau's House of Voodoo. The dim lighting provided just the right ambiance for a voodoo shop. The walls were full of trinkets and jewelry, dolls and charms, stones of various shapes and sizes, and even chicken feet dyed various colors. Nayra knew, at a glance, very little had anything whatsoever to do with voodoo. She'd run across voodoo practitioners in the past, and knew most of these items were for tourist consumption and fed more into the myth of voodoo than its actual practice.

"May I help you?"

The soft, monotone voice belonged to a middle-aged woman with long black hair and grey eyes. Her build was slender and she was of average height. She wore an elegant, royal-blue dress trimmed in gold. Her hair was pulled back and held by an ornate, art-deco-style silver clasp. Matching earrings dangled from her earlobes. She had a choker-style necklace with a simple silver pendant.

"My name is Aria. Are you interested in a reading? Perhaps you wish to see what the cards have to say? Or your palm?"

"We are not here for a reading," Benyamin said. He stood a short distance away, fingering a crude little wooden doll. "We are here for the real thing."

Aria glanced at Benyamin with pursed lips, and a furrowed brow, then back to Nayra. She replaced her anxious expression with one of amusement. "The real thing?" she replied with a laugh. "You wish to speak to your dead relative, or perhaps we might put a curse on an enemy?"

It was no surprise tourists often came into places like Marie Laveau's House of Voodoo with the hopes of commiserating with the dead or putting hexes or love spells on others. They made a fortune selling love potions, voodoo dolls with pins, and casting hexes on evil ex-boyfriends. Most of this was the college crowd coming in after, or during, a night of heavy drinking, their skimpy outfits covered in beaded necklaces given to them by men for flashing body parts upon request.

"No," Nayra said, her eyes staring without humor at the slender woman. "Nothing like that." She leaned in close with a furtive glance to see if anyone was listening. "We seek a descendant of Marie Laveau."

Aria giggled. "Well then," she said, leaning in with a conspiratorial look on her face. "You're in the right place. We're *all* descendants of Marie Laveau."

Benyamin, his calm, soothing voice masking any impatience he was feeling, leaned in as well. "We are not tourists. We are not interested in the junk you sell here. What we seek is a Kharashuoa witch."

Nayra cringed. In the short time she had known him, Benyamin had proven to be a patient man, but his quest to open the portal to Purgatory was consuming him and bringing forth a behavior bordering on sloppy. They could ill-afford to make mistakes, especially with Kharashuoa witches. By coming out and saying it in such a straightforward manner, Benyamin might have made a critical mistake.

Aria's eyes widened at first. She drew in a sharp breath and glanced from one side to the other. She straightened and smoothed her dress, an obvious stall as she collected herself and regained control. It all took a matter of seconds, and the woman was back to normal. She pulled her shoulders back and replaced her anxious expression with a resolute stare.

"I know nothing about such matters."

Benyamin huffed and moved to approach but Nayra held a hand slightly out from her side. He gritted his teeth but allowed the witch to take the lead. Nayra pursed her lips and regarded the woman silently for a moment before speaking. When she did, her voice was soft and gentle and she offered a warm smile.

"Please, Miss Aria, we do not wish to cause a problema. We only wish to meet with a true descendant of Marie Laveau. It is of the utmost importante."

She pulled out a small card and showed it to Aria. On it were the words for the incantation. At the bottom, Nayra had scrawled: *Wynnifrea's spell.* She thought could see the recognition in Aria's eyes, for a moment, before the woman returned her gaze with a steely look of her own.

Aria's eyes closed and she shook her head as she pressed her lips together. "I am sorry, but there are no descendants of Marie Laveau left. She had no sons, and her great granddaughter, the last remaining Laveau, never married. I am afraid you have wasted your time."

She was polite, but it was clear the conversation was over. Her light demeanor was replaced with an abrupt tone and an almost defensive posture. Nayra's eyes flashed. To her, a lie was the greatest insult. Benyamin, now fully in control of his own emotions, was the one who urged restraint, placing a hand on her arm and gently turning her to face him.

"Come, my dear. Let us away."

Nayra continued to stare daggers, her eyes still blazing, her jaw still clenched. It took a beat, but she nodded and relaxed her expression. "Ever the poeta." To Aria, she said, "I'm sorry for troubling you. Thank you for your time."

Aria smiled and nodded. She ushered them to the door and bid them farewell as they exited. As soon as they were outside, the door closed behind them and Nayra shook her head at Benyamin.

"She was lying. Could you not see that? Mentirosa."

Benyamin nodded. "*Of course*, she was lying. Her people have been hunted to extinction over hundreds of years. I haven't even *heard* of a practicing Kharashuoa witch in over a hundred years. If they exist at all, my guess is they are very careful about who they talk to."

As the words cleared his lips, a woman with long, dark hair approached from around the corner. She was dressed in black jeans and a tunic-style halter top in a black, teal, and pink design. Her boots, designer, black, with medium-heels clopped as she moved quickly along the sidewalk. She never looked at them, never acknowledged they were even standing there until she passed them.

"Follow. Not too close."

Chapter 12

"Now then...I offer you a trade."

Lazlo held Leonardo upright as the pain and fear completely consumed him. Lazlo's grip on his heart never let up, and every movement on his body, every breath, was agonizing. His increased heart rate only made things worse as Lazlo restricted the pumping of blood. And didn't seem to notice the pain he was causing. He spoke in the same menacingly cheerful tone, his ancient Middle Eastern accent now mixed with a heavy dose of European.

Xabier had never heard the English language come out of Lazlo's mouth, and the words and accent didn't match his recollections. Nevertheless, the cold intensity of Lazlo's gaze was exactly as he remembered. Two thousand years of meting out death and pain the world over served to make Lazlo as comfortable with his hand in someone's torso as he was lounging in a poolside cabana in the Caribbean.

"The trade," Lazlo continued, "is quite simple." He stared straight at Xabier. "Your life for that of your friend. Surely you don't want the burden of *two* betrayals weighing on that already guilty conscious of yours."

Xabier gritted his teeth and struggled against the urge to launch himself at the vampire who killed the love of his life. The only thing that would accomplish was Leonardo's death, followed shortly thereafter by Xabier's own torture and death. He glanced at Riva, rooted in place, her face pale with fear. Of all people, Riva knew the consequences of crossing her brother and she would do anything to avoid his wrath. Xabier could expect no help from her.

"Fine," he said. "Just let him go. He's not a part of this."

Lazlo smirked in triumph. "Ahh. A selfless gesture from the great Xabier Legartza!" To Leonardo, he said, "What did you ever do to earn that kind of loyalty?" When Leonardo tried to speak, Lazlo squeezed his heart even tighter, causing him to grunt in delirious agony. "That was a rhetorical question."

"Come on, Laz," Xabier pleaded, stepping closer, his hands spread out from his sides. "You don't care about him. It's me you want."

"Perhaps I should end your friend's life before I take you. It would be fitting for you to watch your friend suffer and die before I end your miserable and worthless existence."

"Fine," Xabier said. "Go ahead and waste time settling old scores while your brother and his *new* family continues on with their plan."

Leonardo flew across the room. He slammed into the wall with a thunderous crash, causing bits of plaster to fall from the ceiling. He landed on a rickety wall table which gave way under his weight. Both legs on one side splintered and collapsed. dumping Leonardo's limp body onto the floor in a crumpled heap.

Xabier's eyes flickered from his friend's body to Lazlo's hands to the floor at Lazlo's feet. Nowhere did he see a lifeless heart. He turned back to Leonardo and saw the faintest rise and fall of his chest. He was alive. He would heal in short order. Xabier let out a breath.

His relief was short-lived as Lazlo approached with fire in his eyes. His clenched jaw barely allowed the words to escape. "What…did you say to me?"

Lazlo's fingers clenched and unclenched, the tell-tale sign he was about to go for the heart. Xabier briefly wondered how many other people knew Lazlo well enough to catch such a signal. The next thought to float across his mind was to wonder if perhaps the "Benyamin's new family" crack went a little too far. The one thing the Maccabee family all had in common was a psychotic loyalty to one another. Their constant internal skirmishes meant little. If an outsider threatened one, they all banded together. To suggest Benyamin had a new family was beyond insulting.

"Benyamin is conspiring with witches and other enemies of vampires," Xabier said, standing his ground. "They want to open a porta…"

"Yes, yes," Lazlo cut him off. "I am well aware of my wayward brother's efforts. I shall deal with him in due course."

Xabier shook his head. "You think this is about your father?"

"I don't care what it's about, old friend, because they need *you* to tell them the location of the portal." He smiled, his eyes glinting with merciless venom. "I intend to deny my duplicitous brother the information he requires."

Xabier's mind raced. Lazlo was not one to waste time, never had been. He was a vicious killer with a flair for dramatic speech, but not enough patience for the kind of witty speeches seen in movies. Bloodlust tended to consume him when the kill was at hand. Xabier put his hand up before Lazlo moved to strike.

"Wait!"

Xabier was stunned when Lazlo hesitated. The ice-cold glare remained and Lazlo's body was still tensed like a venomous snake ready to strike. His lips twitched and Xabier thought he saw the corners of his eyes crinkle in amusement. It wasn't hesitation. He *wanted* to draw this out, to make it even more torturous. Lazlo wanted to enjoy the anticipation of the kill he had waited over a thousand years to finally get. Whatever the reason, Xabier had exactly one chance to save himself.

"Your brother is going to get the information anyway."

Lazlo's eyes narrowed. "You have mere moments to explain."

Xabier let out a breath. "I understand they already have the key box."

"Which means all they need is a location," Lazlo finished. "Which does not help your situation. Without you, they have no way of finding the portal."

"Not true," Xabier said. "Don't you think they'd be here by now if they had no other concerns?"

Lazlo's eyes softened a bit as possibilities raced through his mind. He was a murderous vampire but he was far from stupid. Lazlo knew how to cover angles. For all the bloodlust, he was an exceptional strategist and tactician. If there were possibilities, he wanted to know about them.

"Explain."

"That box they have cannot be opened without the incantation, which is inscribed all over the outside. *But...*it was inscribed in fifteen different languages and jumbled up like a word puzzle. If they say it wrong, it won't work, and could trigger a supernatural failsafe, locking the key away for good." He held up a finger. "That's one. Second, they need *six* locations, not just one. The portal is at the center of a massive pentagram. They have to light the five points before the portal can be activated." Xabier smiled and folded his arms across his chest. "But, none of that matters if they don't have a witch that can handle Kharashuoa magic."

Lazlo's eyes widened. His lips moved wordlessly, but Xabier knew what he was thinking. The Kharashuoa were once the most powerful and feared witches in the world. Their witchcraft preceded all others and drew its power from a source only they understood. It was the Kharashuoa who were originally responsible for the balance of nature, a task made more difficult and dangerous as more supernatural creatures came into existence, to say nothing of the demons the fallen angels brought into the world. Lazlo knew all this. He also knew there was one witch who would have been at the center of it all back in 1290 AD.

"Wynnifrea," he whispered. When Xabier raised his eyebrows, Lazlo rolled his eyes. "Of course, that wretched wench would be involved."

"In any case," Xabier said. "Benyamin and his witch have no doubt figured out they are farther away than simply opening that box. They need specific information from the witch who cast the spells."

Lazlo smirked, coming out of his awestruck surprise. "Allow me to guess." He pointed at Xabier. "*You* happen to know precisely *where* this information is hidden."

"I do."

"All the more reason for me to end you and have done with it."

"Then you'll have no chance of stopping your brother." Xabier shrugged. "Look, if he has a witch, they're probably tackling this from the witch angle, but all roads lead to Wynnifrea's crypt."

Lazlo frowned. "Everything required to open the portal is in this crypt with the dead witch?"

Xabier nodded. "Everything and more." He shook his head. "Listen, you might not care, but if the wrong witch gets her hands on Wynnifrea's grimoires, the reign of terror would be absolute. It took two hundred years after Wynnifrea died for the witch community to get a handle on the Khara witches, and the cost was catastrophic."

"An army of powerful witches without a real leader." Lazlo thought for a moment. When he looked up, he asked, "Why would my brother want them to return?"

Xabier shrugged. "That may be the price for opening the portal."

"Then we must hurry."

$$Ђ\ A\ ζ\ ψ\ ς$$

"A *god?*" Nico recoiled at Lucifer's declaration. "What the hell does *that* mean?

He blinked as Lucifer let out an unexpected guffaw. "I'm sorry, Nico. Did Zha'riel teaach you nothing?"

"I'm guessing he left a few things out."

Lucifer shook his head in wonder. Heaven was making it easy. Why did they never learn? One would think the scene in the Garden would have taught them a lesson about withholding information. It makes them appear untrusting and, as a result, untrust*worthy*. Lucifer's trick was never to suggest God was wrong. It was to question whether He trusted his own creation, or whether humans understood Him correctly. Rather than an unlikely giant seed of fallibility, it was far easier to plant many tiny seeds of doubt and try to activate that part of the human mind that naturally wants to question authority. *Why would He ask us to do this? Why ask us not to do that? Why put temptation before us? What is He hiding?* And so on. Human beings were naturally curious. For some inexplicable reason, it was part of their design. Lucifer never had to do much to get them to question their maker.

With Nico, Zha'riel had the opportunity to take a young, new creature under his wing and teach him. Instead, probably at the behest of his superiors, he chose to suppress Nico's growth. It was like trying to keep an infant from growing up. Sure, one can stunt the kid's growth to a point, but eventually he will grow, and he will come to see his suppressor as the enemy. Why Heaven always failed to understand that simple truth of human nature never ceased to amaze Lucifer.

"There are no such things as gods," Lucifer explained. "There is only one God...The Father. What you call gods are really angels who were exiled from Heaven."

"Those who followed you?" Nico asked.

Lucifer shrugged. "We each made our own choice. No one was coerced, but yes, those who saw what Heaven was about to become decided to act." He gritted his teeth at the memory. Eons later, and the worst day of his existence still felt like yesterday. "In any event, we soon turned on one another. Factions were created, alliances formed, enemies declared." He looked at Nico. "This was long before the world was created. It all took place in…"

"In the ether," Nico blurted.

Lucifer tilted his head in amusement. "In the ether, yes." He wagged a finger. "So, Zha'riel explained *some* things to you, no doubt leaving you with more questions than when you first began talking to him."

Nico couldn't argue that point. Zha'riel, for all his bluster about choosing the right side and fighting for good, hadn't really given him anything to believe *in*. The angels had rules; they had *their* way of doing things, and they didn't care to explain why any of it was the way it was. Ultimately, Nico felt like a pawn. To be fair, he also felt like a pawn when it came to Lucifer and Abdiel. He wasn't an idiot. The real difference was they seemed to sincerely believe he would ultimately choose them over the angels.

"At one point," Lucifer continued, snapping Nico back to reality. "All the other factions aligned and stood against me. They called themselves Titans." He nodded when Nico caught the familiar term. "Yes, them, though not quite what your mythology teaches, but then again…"

"Wait," Nico said. "You're saying the gods, like…the *Greek* gods…they're *real?*"

"Again," Lucifer said through gritted teeth, "they're not gods, Nico. Sure, to a human they seem god-like, but they're angels, very powerful, but definitely *not* gods." He chuckled as Nico tried to take it all in. "Don't forget, it wasn't just the Greeks. The Romans had their so-called gods too. So too, the Buddhists. There are dozens of Eastern gods and countless minor gods all over the world."

"And Sansata's mother?" Nico lifted his face to the sky. "Do I want to know about her?"

"Her name," Lucifer said, "is Parvati. You've probably never heard of her."

Nico shook his head.

"Parvati is the wife of Shiva. Now, Shiva is an interesting fella." Lucifer chuckled. His eyes flashed a brilliant golden hue. This time, the melancholy was replaced by humor and…joy?

Nico got the distinct impression Lucifer was drawing from happy memories, not just thoughts of ridicule, which was how he'd begun characterizing the gods. It made sense. From what Nico knew, the fallen angels were all once followers of Lucifer. They stood together against God Himself. That meant the fallen angels, or gods, were once Lucifer's strongest allies, perhaps even his closest friends. Certainly, they would have countless eons of shared history.

"Do you know what the Hindus call Shiva?" Lucifer grinned. "The Destroyer God."

Nico groaned and hung his head. He took a deep breath and shook his head before replying. "So, I've made enemies of the most psychotic archangel of all time, and now the..." Nico gulped despite himself. "...the *Destroyer* God?"

He almost burst out laughing. It sounded so perfectly insane. A year ago, Nico would have laughed in the face of anyone who mentioned the "Destroyer God."

"The Destroyer God's *wife*," Lucifer corrected. "Shiva could care less about Sansata. In fact, I'd bet he gloated when he heard the news of Sansata's demise. He'd probably look at it as karma." He chuckled. "They came up with the whole concept of karma, so it's fitting. Parvati though...she's another story. Parvati is...complicated. That is how Azazel would describe her."

"*Complicated!*" Nico flailed his arms. "What the hell is that supposed to mean?"

Lucifer glanced up at Nico' horrified face. "Just...stay out of India and the surrounding region for the time being. They don't usually stray too far outside their regions, and they almost never come to the west."

"Why is that?"

"Remember when I said the factions all stood against me?" Lucifer, with his hands clasped behind him, paced the ground in front of Nico. "They all blamed me for their misery. We battled for countless eons. Instead of standing together against Heaven, we killed one another while Heaven stood back and watched."

It was impossible for Nico to imagine the joy of life in Heaven. He doubted he could ever come close to imagining the loss the exiled angels felt. He knew Zha'riel's temporary exile caused the angel such grief, Nico wondered if he regretted having ever met his human charges. How much more would a permanent exile affect his angel psyche? Clearly, not all of them appreciated the end results of Lucifer's rebellion.

"Until," Lucifer went on. "One day, the natural world was created and I found a distraction from war. To make a long story short, once that simpleton defied his Creator, it opened the floodgates for all of us to enter."

Every time Nico heard another one of these ancient stories, his brain struggled to wrap itself around what he was being told. As a child, his family wasn't particularly religious, but he knew some of the major Biblical characters. He remembered some of the stories, and he thought it all just that: stories and characters. He never considered the possibility that any of it was real. He figured it was mostly a book of morality tales, maybe based on real life events, or maybe just created out of thin air to teach lessons. Now, he was learning those stories actually *happened!*

A random question floated to the forefront of his mind. "Was it an apple?"

Lucifer blinked and narrowed his eyes. He tilted his head, the gold flashing slowly across both eyes. Somehow, that flash, though it was the same brilliant golden flash, managed to convey every emotion the dark prince was feeling. Nico wished he hadn't asked the stupid question, but it was too late.

"Th…the fruit," he stammered. "…that Adam ate. Was it an apple?"

"An *apple?*" Lucifer asked, the incredulity erupting all at once. He started to say something else, but clamped his mouth shut. He pursed his lips and took a deep breath. "I just told you a story about warring angels that began before your world was even created. I gave you a glimpse into my own personal history, one that merged with this world long before any supernatural being entered, and after all that, the question that popped into your head was, 'Was it an *apple?*'"

Nico shook his head. "I know. I'm sorry. It's just one of those things people always wonder about."

"Well, people are ridiculous," Lucifer said, not bothering to mask his disgust. "They focus on stupid stuff."

"What *should* people focus on?"

Lucifer stared back at him, his golden eyes practically hypnotizing Nico once again. His expression went from one of disgust and disdain to sympathy and understanding. He looked at Nico almost the way a stern disciplinarian father would. His eyes regarded him as though he were gauging Nico's progress, placing a value on him. Then, he softened, and one of the corners of his mouth lifted.

Well, *you*...ought to focus on avoiding psychotic and vengeful archangels."

Chapter 13

"What happened here?"

Seir ground his teeth like a rabid dog. "It looks like her brother snapped her neck and took the human."

Azazel surveyed the scene. The room was empty save for Riva's lifeless body, lying on the couch. A broken wall-table lay in a scattered mess on the floor, and there was no sign of Xabier or Lazlo. There was a lot of blood on the carpet at Azazel's feet. He bent down and touched the cool wet spot and brought his bloody finger to his nose. He closed his eyes as he inhaled the scent.

"Vampire blood."

Seir frowned. "There was that friend Xabier had with him. It could be his." He grimaced and shrugged. "Or Xabier could be dead."

"Doubtful." Azazel shrugged. "This is not enough blood to kill a vampire."

Seir nodded. "Why take him away? He waited centuries for this moment. Why not kill him here when he had the chance?"

"Perhaps he wanted to take his time and enjoy it." Azazel smiled grimly. "It is what *I* would have done."

Seir closed his eyes and bowed his head. "I have failed you once again, Sire."

Since confronting Lucifer, they had been running for their lives. Seir's previous mission to kill Scarlatti had ended in failure, almost costing the red-eyed demon his life. Now, when their time-sensitive mission was on the line, he'd allowed their target to escape. Centuries of faithful service were one thing, but in Azazel's world, even a single failure could result in agonizing death…if one was lucky. Azazel was known to dispense far worse punishments than that.

Azazel shook his head. "Not this time. It was my orders you followed. I *told* you to remain out of sight." He sighed. "If the Lazlo kills our friend, we will simply find another way."

"My brother is *not* going to kill Xabier."

They turned to face Riva, who was sitting up on the couch, in perfect health. Her wavy brown hair fell perfectly around her shoulders and her jade eyes were clear and alert. There was no indication that, just moments before, she was lying dead, her neck snapped in half.

"Ah!" Azazel gestured to her. "Welcome back."

"It's about time," Seir mumbled.

Riva waved him off. "Well, I'm sorry. I can't control how long I stay dead for, can I?"

Azazel shook his head and pressed his lips together. "Ignore him. Seir's been in a bad mood for several thousand years. You don't think your brother is going to harm our asset?"

Riva shook her head and recounted the events leading up to her temporary demise. Once Lazlo had heard killing Xabier would not necessarily keep the portal hidden, his number one priority became getting to the crypt before Benyamin and his coalition. Xabier refused to tell him where the crypt was located, even under threat of instant death, so Lazlo's vengeance was delayed. He and Xabier had agreed to set aside their differences, for the time being, creating a coalition of their own, with the mutual goal of thwarting any effort to reopen the portal to Purgatory.

Riva rubbed the back of her neck. "My brother snapped my neck to give himself a bit of a head start."

Seir shook his head in disgust and turned back to Azazel. "He's going to call the mage now. I don't know why he hasn't already, but he will *definitely* call him in now. Then, Hell will get involved."

Azazel pursed his lips and stared out the window. Nico Scarlatti was the center of his focus. For months, all his efforts were poured into watching and plotting the demise of Lucifer's latest obsession. Ever since Nico had ingested the blood of the Morning Star, his chakras had been off the charts. The power emanating from him was unlike anything Azazel had ever seen, short of Heaven's inhabitants. What Nico probably didn't realize, was the powerful were easily recognizable by their chakra output. He wouldn't yet know how to hide himself.

Azazel used this knowledge to maintain a distant surveillance on Nico. Like the angels of Heaven, he had a general idea of Nico's activities. Thus far, Azazel had been biding his time, waiting for an opportune moment to strike and exact his vengeance, not only on the man who murdered his son, but on Lucifer, for his betrayal. Azazel would take away the thing Lucifer had placed above their friendship.

For now, Azazel had more pressing concerns. Would Xabier call Nico in? He came all this way without involving Scarlatti. The question was why? Just in terms of time and travel, having a mage to orb him from one place to another would make life so much easier. They were in a race after all, and there was no way Xabier could know how far along Benyamin and the coalition had gotten. It seemed a waste not to use Nico.

Unless…

Azazel's eyes closed and he nodded to himself. "He knows I'm involved."

When he turned from the window, Azazel found the other two staring at him in expectation. Riva's face was a mixture of fear and confusion. It was clear she knew the players involved, but was not a part of anyone's plans. She looked like she had a million questions but was too afraid to ask them.

Seir, on the other hand, frowned. "If he knows we're involved, would he not get as far away from it as possible?"

Azazel shrugged. "Not necessarily. Our vampire friend has a...personal...connection to this." He turned back to the window and sighed. "He's loyal. We know that much about him, don't we? Remember how he fought alongside his friend even when death was the only possible outcome?"

Seir rolled his eyes and Azazel smiled. Of course, Seir remembered Xabier's willingness to die in defense of Nico. He also remembered he had Xabier at the point of death before the angel intervened. Twenty more seconds, and Xabier Legartza would be a moot point. Seir was not one to fail his missions. That Xabier was still alive was an insult to Seir. Every breath the vampire took mocked him. Azazel appreciated Seir's dedication.

He let a wry smile come over his face. "Loyalty is what keeps him from hiding from me."

"Yes, but...loyalty to who?"

"To Wynnifrea," Azazel said. He wrinkled his forehead in thought. Pursing his lips once again, the dark angel pondered the possibilities while tapping his forefinger on his lips. "There is some connection there."

He watched as Seir thought about the facts. A strategist, who spent two thousand years at the right hand of a master tactician, Seir knew how to arrange a game board. He was a master in his own right. He understood how to approach targets of opportunity as well as how to draw unwilling targets into the line of fire.

Before he could spit out an idea, Riva broke her frightened silence. "Why not distract Xabier from his interference?"

Seir shook his head. "Silence, Fang! The adults are speaking."

Azazel held up a hand. "No. Speak." He never turned from the window. He stood, staring at the dusty landscape outside, his hands clasped in front of him, a portrait of serenity. "How might we distract a man who is loyal unto death?"

Riva shrugged. "You said he was loyal to this Scarlatti guy. Perhaps we could endanger him in some way, and get word to Xabier that he has become a target."

"That won't work." Seir shook his head. "Xabier knows Heaven is protecting him. Zha'riel is capable of handling anything we can throw at him." He nodded to Azazel. "Unless you go after him yourself, Sire."

Azazel contemplated their words in silent thought. He surprised himself with the thoughts spiraling around in his mind. He had never been at the helm of such complex planning. He was always the assassin or the punisher. As masterful as he was in that arena, he was far less experienced in the art of manipulation. He understood fear and pain, and how these things influenced behavior, but those things usually put him at odds with the target. It was fine when Lucifer was running the overall game. Azazel's role was important, but it was merely a part of a greater whole.

Azazel could recall times when he would question the more elegant approaches Lucifer employed. He often thought those intricately woven threads of deceit and discontent were a waste of time. Now, he was on the other side of the table, discussing with his own "team" the pros and cons of each potential action. Like Lucifer, Azazel was now a leader. If he was to be successful, he would have to master the art of war, not simply the art of killing.

His thoughts were interrupted by the buzzing of his smart phone, an intrusion for which he regularly cursed human technology. He much preferred face-to-face dealings, though he had to admit, the idea of instant and accurate information at one's fingertips was an advantage. Since everyone else was using technology, he would be a stubborn fool to ignore it.

Staring at the screen, his eyes flashed silver and the menacing white glow returned. He continued to stare at the report from his team as his mind raced. *Lucifer met with Scarlatti.* So, after months of biding his time, Lucifer was finally making a play for Nico. He would be successful, no doubt. There was no one in existence more charming and reasonable than Lucifer. The most beautiful of all the angels, he was also the one with the silver tongue. It wouldn't be until long after Nico had sold his soul that Lucifer's silver tongue would be revealed as forked.

The lies and deceit would be subtle. Everything would appear as if it were Nico's own idea, and Lucifer would come out of it looking like he was the one trying to talk Nico *out* of making the biggest mistake of his life. Ultimately, Nico would succumb to the wishes and whims of the source of all evil, and he will have only himself to blame. At least, that's how he will feel about it.

Azazel pondered the idea of killing Nico outright, of going ahead and doing it himself. He would kill anything and everything that stood in his way in one fell swoop, and be done with the whole thing. He would avenge his son's murder and avenge his friend's betrayal all in one moment.

What would that accomplish? And in that moment, a fresh perspective crept into Azazel's mind, one that was far more forward-thinking and involved far more finesse and thought than merely killing everything that stood in his way. Perhaps it was time to set aside his anger and build something for himself, something that would rival the Dark Army of Hell.

"Perhaps a new approach is called for," he murmured.

"Sire?"

Seir's voice penetrated his thoughts and Azazel snapped his head up, looking at both Seir and Riva as though just realizing they were there. "Go to the Driftless Area in Southern Wisconsin. Ensure that Benyamin and the witches do not kill Xabier or Lazlo. Xabier is precious to Nico, and we want to keep the option open of demonstrating good faith. Lazlo may also be of value in the future. Let us not spill unnecessary blood."

Without another word, he waved them off. Seir knew it was pointless to ask further questions. All would be revealed when necessary. He took Riva's arm and they were gone in an instant.

Azazel stood staring out the window, a soft chuckle causing his body to shake slightly. "Let us not spill unnecessary blood," he repeated. "I cannot *believe* I just said that."

ᛒ A ǯ ψ �

By the time the words reached their ears, the woman was halfway across Bourbon Street, strutting down St. Ann Street. Nayra and Benyamin exchanged suspicious glances before shrugging and watching the woman hurry past Napoleon's Itch, another popular New Orleans gay bar. Without a word, they set out after her, waiting for a horse-drawn carriage to pass by before crossing Bourbon Street.

When they reached the other sidewalk, the woman turned right, down a narrow, side alley. Nayra hurried ahead while Benyamin considered what might be lurking around the corner. New Orleans was known for supernatural activity, which meant, in addition to its indigenous witch, werewolf, and vampire population, other supernatural creatures flocked to the city. As a major tourist destination, New Orleans provided ample hunting grounds for the supernatural, and *that* meant another type of predator could be present.

Hunters were the bane of the supernatural. Their primary purpose was to work alongside witches to protect humans from the other species. Hunters had a special sensitivity to chakra, and an intense desire to hunt and kill supernatural predators. It was an instinctual urge, no different from the vampires' need for human blood, but it meant, even for an original vampire, caution was necessary before following anyone down a New Orleans alleyway, even if it was broad daylight.

Nayra waited impatiently at the entrance to the alley as Benyamin strained his ears. The woman was no longer in sight, having disappeared around a corner about two hundred feet into the alley. He could hear nothing to indicate a trap. He shrugged his shoulders and gestured for Nayra to proceed.

Midway down the alley, the right side opened into a large courtyard. The mysterious woman was waiting on the far corner, seated halfway up an iron staircase that led to a second-floor entrance of the building. Crates and pallets were stacked all around the courtyard and several dumpsters were lined up for easy access. Benyamin could only see the one woman but sensed the presence of several more.

"You can come out," he called.

One by one, the group appeared. In total, there were eight women, including the one Benyamin and Nayra had followed. A ninth appeared. She was slender and dressed in a royal blue dress, trimmed in gold. Her hands were clasped in front of her. It was

Aria, from Marie Laveau's House of Voodoo. She regarded them with disdain, her eyes flicking between the two of them.

"You say you seek out the Laveau's," she said, spreading her hands slightly. "You've found us. Beware, what you say right now will determine whether you leave this courtyard alive or not."

Benyamin smiled. Adjusting his tie and straightening his cuffs, he made eye contact with every member of what he assumed must be a Kharashuoa coven, perhaps the only one in existence. They all stared back at he and Nayra with suspicion, yet none of them appeared anxious or troubled. He could detect no racing heartbeats and no elevated breathing. Everyone was calm and waiting. He wasn't sure if that was a good sign or a bad one. Witches could usually tell what he was within a few seconds, at least those with experience could. It always caused some level of anxiety.

"To be clear," he began. "We mean to cause you no trouble or harm..."

Aria held up a hand. "We do not deal with vampires, even well-mannered...originals. Let the witch tell us." She turned her grey eyes on Nayra. "You *are* a witch, no?"

Nayra nodded. "Si. I am."

"And you practice..."

"I practice ancestral magic."

Aria pursed her lips. "Yet you are here. You are from a distant land. Your magic is far less powerful if you stray too far from the remains of your ancestors." She regarded Nayra through narrowed eyes. "You deceive us, do you not? Your magic is strong, even here."

Nayra clenched her jaw. Benyamin knew she had lost the advantage of surprise. Without knowing what the intentions of this group were, she was depending on their relaxed attitude when they discovered her powers were diminished so far away from her source. Benyamin also knew it was unusual for a witch to practice multiple forms of magic concurrently, but Nayra was unique. He'd witnessed her powers firsthand.

But, standing before Aria and her coven, Nayra appeared out of her element. When was the last time she'd faced off against another witch? As powerful as she was, there were nine surrounding her. If Aria could read her chakra that easily, it was a safe bet Nayra was overmatched. All she could do was be as truthful as possible.

"I also practice a form of magic called…"

"Expression," Aria finished. "Yes. I know. The question is, why would you come all this way to find a Laveau witch? We have no quarrel with you?"

"No, of course not." Nayra pulled the card from her pocket once again. "We merely seek assistance with the order of an incantation."

"Yes, I saw," Aria said with a curt bob of her head. "And as I said, we cannot help you with that."

"Yet you brought us here," Benyamin said.

He knew what was planned. Without warning, he moved, his vampire speed rocketing him into position behind the younger woman on the steps before anyone could react. It wasn't fast enough. Before his hands touched the woman's neck, he was thrown backward, slamming into the wall and tumbling down the stairs to the ground.

As he pulled himself to his feet, he was stricken with an agonizing pain in his head as a high-pitched squeal cut like a knife through every nerve ending in his brain. He groaned and fell to his knees, doubling over as he desperately clawed at his temples, finding no relief. The pain intensified each time he tried to move, and the pressure grew until he thought his head was going to explode.

Nayra wasted no time. The moment Benyamin moved to attack, she sensed things were about to go bad. When he went down, her first thought was to gain an advantage. She raised her hand and made a fist as if grasping something out of the air. The young woman they had followed grabbed at her throat and gasped for breath. Nayra shot her other hand up and made a sweeping motion. Three of the witches, standing on a balcony, two stories above, were hurled towards the edge. They had to grab whatever they could reach to keep from falling over the side.

Without warning, Nayra was lifted and tossed through the air, sprawling on the ground and tumbling to a halt near the dumpsters. She felt a force grasping her. Throughout it all, her singular focus was to maintain her grip on the young woman's throat. She felt it loosen briefly, but reestablished her grip and squeezed tighter. That was when she felt her own throat closing from an outside pressure.

"Release her," Aria commanded. "Now!"

The pressure was so tight, Nayra could barely speak. "I will...kill...her."

"Then you will die with her."

Nayra could feel the pressure exerted on her from all sides. She could see Benyamin incapacitated on the ground. He was not unconscious but writhing in pain. He was sweating profusely and every vein and artery in his head and neck protruded and seemed to swell to the point of bursting. His eyes bulged and his fangs were ultra-extended and bleeding. For the first time, Nayra saw the monster behind the refined, human façade, and was not repulsed. Instead, she felt as though one of her own was under attack. She felt the sudden instinct to protect, as a mother would her young.

Summoning chakra from deep within, Nayra gathered herself. The pain receded slightly, and she heard Aria's voice, but the words faded. She could see the look on Aria's face, the wide-eyed look of a woman who was stunned and anxious. In that moment, Nayra realized Aria was calling for the rest of the coven to increase the intensity of their spells. She had no time to waste.

Nayra released her grip on the younger witch and pulled with all her might from the earth. With a cry of anguish and pain, she lashed out in all directions with everything she had. The force of her power exploded from her core like a bomb, throwing everyone backwards. The downward force shook the ground in a fifty-foot diameter around her. The force then repelled upward, adding to the shockwave emanating from Nayra's center. The witches on the higher levels, protected somewhat by the balconies, were all knocked off their feet, slamming into the buildings behind them.

Those on the ground were less fortunate. They took the full force of the blast, and flew backward. One hurled headlong into a six-foot-high stack of wood pallets. Her body crashed into them, splintering some of the wood before collapsing to the ground. The stack of pallets then tumbled onto her unconscious body. Another, less fortunate witch, crashed headfirst through a lower-level window. A large piece of the window lodged in her throat. She slid to the ground with a stunned expression. The only sound she could make was a gurgling groan as blood filled her lungs.

Aria fared a bit better. With nothing directly behind her, she was simply lifted off her feet and thrown backwards, skidding on her right shoulder as she hit the blacktop. She suffered only scrapes and bruises, but her holds on Nayra and Benyamin were broken, along with any spells cast by the rest of the coven. She lifted her head and shook it from side to side. Several members of her coven scrambling to their feet on the balconies above. When she lowered her gaze, she saw the motionless body lying under half the pile of pallets. Finally, she saw the member who went through the glass and she gasped. It was her best friend.

"Dali!"

Tears sprang forth as she struggled to her knees. Surveying the scene, she saw Benyamin recovering from her spell and Nayra lying on her back, her breath coming in short bursts. Her first instinct was to finish the two of them off, but concern for her friend drove her to push thoughts of revenge aside for the moment. She scrambled to Dali's side.

She was still alive but not for long. Dali's eyes were wide with fear. Sweat poured from her head and her breathing was a mess as the blood poured out. The situation was hopeless. She held her friend's hand and kissed her cheek.

"They will die before you do," she whispered in Dali's ear.

She rose to her feet and gestured to her coven members. She raised her hands, tears still flooding her eyes as she began to draw chakra. Before anyone could unleash on Benyamin and Nayra, a piercing sound filled the air and an overpowering bright light engulfed them all. The witches all dropped to the ground and covered their eyes and ears. The vampire did his best to block Nayra from the light, but it was useless, and the sound drove him to his knees in pain.

The sound and light lasted for just a few seconds and then dissipated. When everyone came to their senses, an imposing figure stood in the center of the courtyard, clothed in black robes with silver trim. His eyes flashed silver before settling to a stunning pearl-white glow. His hands were clasped lazily in front of his navel, but he still seemed terrifying, an angel of death seeking someone to devour. He allowed everyone to take in his presence for a prolonged moment before his eyes returned to normal.

"Now then," he said in an ominous monotone. "It would appear this negotiation has reached an impasse." He smiled without humor, his eyes returning to their terrifying white glow. "Perhaps *I* can be of some assistance."

Chapter 14

"This changes nothing, you know."

Xabier closed his eyes and steered the charcoal-gray BMW X5 through the flattest state in the nation. As they approached Wichita, Kansas, twelve hours into their twenty-three-hour trip, he contemplated the glorious silence he and Lazlo had thus far driven in. The one thing he wanted to avoid, at all costs, was a conversation, because inevitably, the talk would devolve into a rehash of the past, and a rehash of the past could only end in blood because Lazlo would never admit it was his actions that got the ball rolling on their fifteen-century-old feud.

Xabier chose the path of least resistance. "I know."

Lazlo stared daggers while Xabier refrained from eye contact, and focused on keeping the vehicle between the lines as they sped through the state of Kansas. Out of his periphery, he could see Lazlo's jaw clenched and his left hand balled in a fist against his mouth. This was bad. Lazlo was struggling to maintain his composure. Even after fifteen centuries apart, Xabier knew the look. The conversation wasn't over.

He didn't have to wait long. Lazlo turned in his seat to face him. He regarded Xabier wordlessly as his eyes searched Xabier's expression. His jaw continuously clenched and unclenched. His teeth ground against one another. Xabier knew what Lazlo was looking for, some sign of remorse for what had transpired between them. That was the one thing Xabier refused to give him.

"We were mates, you and I."

Lazlo said it so matter-of-factly, it sounded almost as though he were reminiscing about their past relationship. His British accent continued to amuse Xabier. Having met at a time when Lazlo was just beginning to explore the world outside his Middle Eastern origins, his Aramaic accent had always been thick and dominant. Now, he sounded like a completely different person, more refined. It served to disguise the violent side of Lazlo's personality, making him seem less of a psychotic. Xabier wasn't fooled.

"We were," Xabier replied. After a beat, he followed up with a single word. "Once."

Lazlo's tongue flicked across his upper lip. Out of the corner of his eye, Xabier saw him narrow his eyes. He felt Lazlo's stare as the other vampire studied him. Though he knew Lazlo as well as anyone could, Xabier had never been able to predict him. It was that very failure that led to the events that would destroy their friendship. Of course, Lazlo would argue Xabier's disloyalty was the real reason.

"After everything I did for you," Lazlo pressed, "you repaid me by…"

"You *killed* her!" Xabier exploded.

Lazlo's eyes widened, and Xabier instantly regretted his outburst. Lazlo hadn't expected such emotion from Xabier, and Xabier hadn't planned on allowing Lazlo to get under his skin, but the wounds had never healed. Xabier had hoped to avoid this scene, alone with Lazlo, and emotions taking over them both.

"You chose a woman over your best friend," Lazlo said.

Xabier shook his head. "No. You were just afraid…afraid and paranoid."

Lazlo rolled his eyes and shook his head in scorn. "Me? Afraid? You must be delusional, my insolent little friend. What on earth would I have to fear?"

"Being alone. Everything you do, every friend you cross, and every bridge you burn, is always because of the same fear. You ruin every good relationship in your life before the other person can leave you."

Lazlo laughed but Xabier knew it was true. Lazlo's family was close in many ways but they were also the most dysfunctional group he had ever run across. With a father known primarily for his greatest failure, a failure that had gone down in history and would never be forgotten, the children and their mother had to endure the ridicule and scorn of an entire nation. At first, it had led to an incredible closeness, but ultimately, they turned on one another, leading to years of betrayals, deceit, and mistrust. All Lazlo's subsequent relationships were doomed.

"You forget your own role in the demise of our friendship."

Xabier shook his head. "My role was to fall in love. You couldn't handle it, so, you killed her."

"I *saved* you!" Lazlo exclaimed. "You wanted to *turn* her, you dullard. You can't turn every dollop you fall in love with."

Xabier slammed his foot down on the brakes and the BMW SUV skidded to a halt on the side of the road. He opened the door and jumped out. Slamming the door closed, he walked away from the car, his breath coming in short gasps as he struggled for control. Memories long since buried flooded his mind, reopening centuries-old wounds. Xabier remembered every detail of the love that was taken from him, though he had long ago suppressed those memories.

"She would have ruined you, mate." Lazlo was close on his heels. "She would have sucked the life right out of you."

"*Sarah!*" Xabier yelled, turning on the more powerful vampire.

Lazlo looked more confused than worried about a potential strike from Xabier. He cocked his head to one side.

Xabier stood facing his nemesis, his fangs bared, his face clouded with veins and the dusky pallor of a vampire ready to strike. "Her name," he hissed, "was Sarah."

"Right," Lazlo nodded. "Sarah."

The two stood face-to-face for the first time in fifteen centuries. Lazlo's hatred for Xabier was matched only by Xabier's contempt. For Xabier, it might as well have been 524

AD. His eyes filled with the pain of loss. The last time he felt this way, he was prepared to die, yet consumed with the fire of vengeance.

"You wish to strike me," Lazlo said. He spread his arms. "Well go ahead."

Xabier struck, his fist crashing into Lazlo's jaw and sending the more powerful vampire crashing to the ground. Lazlo, clearly surprised Xabier would dare to take the shot he offered, shook his head and ran his tongue along the inside of his bottom lip. He picked himself up from the ground as Xabier stood his ground, waiting for the retaliation. Xabier knew his life was in the balance, and Lazlo could only be pushed so far. He also knew he would die as soon as Lazlo had no further use for him. He would just as soon get it over with.

Lazlo chuckled as he straightened back up and dusted himself off. Without warning, he lashed out and struck a blow to the center of Xabier's chest, sending him flying backward and skidding to a halt on the dusty turf. He lay there, stunned, all the air knocked from his body. The bones in his chest were broken, but already healing as his vampire blood coursed through his system.

Lazlo stood over him. "Don't think, even for one moment, my insolent friend, that you can do me harm. I have been waiting for centuries to end your miserable life."

"Then get on with it."

"You have nothing to say? You drove a wedge between my family and me that tore us apart and you have nothing to say after fifteen hundred years?"

Xabier pushed himself up to his knees and stood unsteadily. The last thing he would do was speak to Lazlo while the other vampire stood over him like a conqueror. He had some pride left, though he was beginning to wish, for the first time, that he had brought Nico along. In any case, he was damned if he was going to sit there and take it. If Lazlo wanted him to say something, Xabier would say exactly what he should have said centuries ago.

"What I did, I did because you murdered the woman I loved. You took from me, so I took from you. If you want your revenge, go ahead and take it."

Lazlo stood poised to strike at Xabier's chest for the last time, but he didn't strike that final blow. Instead, he shook his head in disgust and turned back toward the SUV.

"We have no time for these trifles. We have business to attend to."

They rode in silence for hours, each lost in his own thoughts. Xabier's emotions calmed as the miles flew by. He stopped paying attention to Lazlo, though he was aware of the glances the other vampire was shooting in his direction. At first, the glances were menacing, clenched-jaw glares, as though Lazlo was still struggling to keep from tearing Xabier apart. As the miles passed, the dark tone of Lazlo's looks changed to one of curiosity. Xabier took it for as long as he could, but finally broke the silence.

"What?"

Lazlo chuckled. "It strikes me…you are the only one who knows the location of this witch's crypt."

Xabier shrugged and Lazlo nodded, his lips pressing together in amusement. His eyes narrowed as he regarded Xabier with keen interest. He held up a finger and shook it.

"It always vexed me, your ability to elude me. I always thought you hid yourself in some distant jungle or perhaps the Siberian wilderness. It never occurred to me, you might have had the help of a powerful witch."

Though he knew Lazlo would take it as an affirmation, Xabier remained silent. Lazlo smiled triumphantly while Xabier did his best to maintain an impassive expression. What difference did it make?

"So," Lazlo continued. "The great Wynnifrea stooped to protect the likes of you. Why? It was no secret she despised our kind."

Xabier glanced over at Lazlo. "She hated *you* more than she hated vampires." He shrugged. "Plus, I agreed to…never mind."

Lazlo tilted his head. "You agreed to what?" Then he closed his eyes as the answer came to him. "Of course. You agreed to help lure and trap the alphas."

Xabier raised his eyebrows and rolled his shoulders. His lips pressed together. He wasn't about to affirm Lazlo's suspicions, but Lazlo didn't need his affirmation. When he believed he deduced the truth, there was little chance of changing his mind.

"So Wynnifrea shielded you from me for a thousand years," Lazlo mused, "but she died in England. How did her remains make it all the way to America?"

Xabier closed his eyes. One of Lazlo's more annoying qualities was his incessant need to run down every lead, to uncover every detail, no matter how mundane, no matter how insignificant. His curiosity over Xabier's relationship with a witch as powerful as Wynnifrea would be insatiable, and they still had hours to go.

"If I tell you, will you stop interrogating me?"

Lazlo laughed long and loud, which caused Xabier to laugh as well. For a moment, they were the same two inseparable friends who laughed their way through the old Middle East and Europe. Xabier couldn't help but recall, with fond memory, the times they'd had. In all the centuries he'd spent avoiding Lazlo, he'd never made another friend like him. Xabier's relationship with Nico was different. While Nico could be trusted completely, he had yet to embrace the reality of what he was. Lazlo had no trouble letting his beast within run wild. He understood Xabier in a way Nico probably never would.

"Wynnifrea and I were…" Xabier made a face. "Let's just say it was complicated."

"Ahh yes," Lazlo grinned knowingly. "It usually is with women."

Xabier shook his head. "It wasn't like that. Well…not always. We weren't *just* lovers."

"And when she died?"

Xabier's eyes misted over. It had been a long time since he had to think about losing Wynnifrea, the one who had done so much for him. She was the person he had bared his soul to.

"You know what the worst part of being a vampire is?" he asked. Catching Lazlo's thoughtful frown, he continued. "Living through the loss of everyone you love…over and over again."

Lazlo shrugged. "Perhaps that is because you choose to love those who are destined to die."

Rather than argue the point, Xabier let it slide. "Anyway, Wynnifrea's power was coveted by every witch alive. When she died, I knew they would eventually come for her. I also knew that in defending her remains, I would eventually be exposed and *you* would find me. I had to get far away. So, I managed to gain passage on a voyage."

"You came to the New World," Lazlo closed his eyes and shook his head. "Of course."

"I knew you would eventually make your way over, but I thought if I knew the land better than you, it would make it more difficult to track me."

Xabier's fear of discovery by Lazlo was matched only by his fear of failing his friend, who had entrusted her final wishes to him. Those wishes included the safeguarding of items that unlocked the door to great power. It was a power Wynnifrea was uncomfortable passing on to the witches of her time.

"Before she died, Wynnifrea spelled several items. Knowing her death would break any spell she cast, she had to bind her spells to a celestial event. She said the power of a celestial event would maintain the spell even upon her death. On May 24th, just a week before she died, there was a lunar eclipse that lasted an hour and forty-six minutes. Wynnifrea spelled several items in that time, and gave me specific instructions on how to activate the spells."

Lazlo nodded in understanding. "Cloaking spells."

"Exactly. She was afraid of witches fighting over her spell books and relics, so she wanted me to hide them and activate a spell that would keep witches from locating them."

Xabier explained the trip he took across the Atlantic in 1584 was commissioned by Sir Walter Raleigh. The captains, Philip Amadas and Arthur Barlowe, were easy enough to compel, along with their crew. Under cover of darkness, Xabier got Wynnifrea's coffin aboard the vessel. After crossing the ocean, he compelled everyone involved in the voyage to forget about him and his "baggage."

The ship had landed just off the coast of Virginia. Xabier made his way west, finding the Mississippi River. He'd imagined de Soto's discovery of the river, just forty or so years before, and wondered if the Spaniard was as awestruck by the great river as Xabier had been. Instead of going south, where he knew the warmer weather was, Xabier traveled north, to what was hopefully more rugged territory. Ultimately, he came to what would later be dubbed "The Driftless Area."

"It's a mountainous wasteland covering tens of thousands of square miles. When I stopped to rest for the night, I explored a little and found vast mountains, and, more importantly, hidden caverns leading to underground caves. I knew I'd found the place for Wynnifrea to rest in peace." Xabier shrugged. "So, I brought her to a cavern I knew would be almost impossible for someone to find intentionally, and took her as far underground as I could go."

Lazlo pursed his lips and nodded. "Hidden for all eternity." He held up a finger. "Though a witch's essence cannot be eliminated. Her people must have sought her out."

"They did," Xabier said. "They got as far as Louisiana."

"New Orleans," Lazlo said, nodding and closing his eyes. The pieces were falling into place. "Of course. That is why you reacted upon hearing that my brother was seeking out the witch community in New Orleans. You suspect they might have some idea where to look?"

Xabier shrugged. "I have no idea. To be honest, I watched them for years when they first made it across the Atlantic, but in their insanity, the witches brought hell down upon themselves from the humans and the Kharashuoa witches were hunted and killed. Even the other witches hated them. After that, I figured Wynnifrea would be forgotten and her remains safe forever."

"Until now."

Xabier nodded "Until now. If Benyamin has a Kharashuoa witch, we cannot let them get their hands on the contents of that crypt. It contains everything they need to reopen the portal to Purgatory, and that isn't even the scary bit."

Chapter 15

"Bad day?" Frank, the bartender, poured him another glass.

"Yeah, you could say that."

Nico downed the double shot and gestured for more. Frank chuckled, pouring another generous portion. He placed the bottle in front of Nico and winked. Nico smirked, closed his eyes, and pressed his hands together, resting his forehead against his fingertips. The pressure was building. He felt like his veins were swollen. His heart thudded like a jackhammer and a bruising sensation began to spread outward from the center of his chest.

A "bad day" didn't begin to cover the kind of day he'd had. He'd accomplished nothing. The Russian sex-trafficking operation continued unabated. Nico had been threatened by an archangel, effectively abandoned by his best friend, who was still incommunicado, and his angel-friend was nowhere to be found. No doubt, Zha'riel was trying to talk his way back into Heaven, something Nico couldn't begin to comprehend. The angels turned their backs on Zha'riel for the egregious sin of fighting against evil. Nico knew they were dangling the carrot of Zha'riel's reinstatement. If he could steer Nico in the "right" direction, they would pull some strings.

He'd had a long talk with evil personified, whom, he could hardly forget, had spared his life some months back. The worst part of it all was Lucifer was the only one who seemed to be looking out for him. Zha'riel and the angels of Heaven only cared about whether Nico was behaving, meaning he wasn't allowed to kill sex-traffickers. The irony of Heaven protecting the lives of those animals was not lost on Nico. Rafael certainly failed to see any irony. Then again, Rafael was a stiff, like a by-the-book FBI agent who wore dark sunglasses and always had a grim smile plastered on his face.

Then, there was Tatiana, his beautiful Tatiana, who only wanted to know what was wrong. Their relationship was so new, and she was so oblivious to the world she was rubbing up against. How could she fathom the realities he faced, and was *he* right to get so close to her? After losing one girl to a supernatural fate, how could he justify putting another in danger, especially when the threat had never been eliminated? In fact, with the knowledge he had gleaned earlier from Lucifer, it was a good bet the danger was light-years greater than he could ever have imagined.

Their fight had lasted only moments and it left Tatiana petrified and in tears, but it was necessary. He had to get Tatiana out of this situation, and he had to do it without explaining it. She provided the perfect opportunity when she pressed him to "let her in" and to "let her help him." He'd tried to tell her to leave and he didn't want to discuss it. He assumed, so early in the relationship, she would take that as a sign that he was emotionally unavailable, or whatever girls thought when the guy wouldn't talk about his problems.

But she was persistent. When he withdrew, it frustrated her even more. Nico tried to ignore her but Tatiana wasn't the type to be ignored. She finally pushed just a little too hard and Nico snapped. He managed to regain control of himself before he struck her, but the damage was done. Her eyes had been wide as saucers when he'd finally regained focus, and she backed away from him in horror. When he tried to reach out to her, she threw herself backwards and slid along the floor in fear, her hands shaking and legs coming up until she was in the corner of the room in a fetal position. Nico hadn't wanted that, but it was all for the best. He'd left her alone.

"Damn, Nico," Frank said, picking up the half-empty bottle. "Slow down. You've only been here for twenty minutes."

Nico nodded, though the effects of the alcohol were only beginning to touch him. It would take a great deal more to impair him. Such was the cost of his transformation to the supernatural. Drunkenness took far longer and cost far more money these days.

"Don't worry, Frank. I've got him."

Nico closed his eyes at the sound of her voice. "Tatiana. What are you doing here?"

She slipped into the seat next to him and asked Frank for water. Turning to Nico, she touched his face and gave him a rueful smile.

"I know I probably *shouldn't* be here," she said. "Everything in me tells me I should run screaming before I get in too deep."

"You should listen to your gut," Nico said.

One corner of Tatiana's mouth turned down as her smoky, green eyes searched his profile for any indication he was joking. Nico stared anywhere but at her face.

"Maybe I should," she said with a shrug as she put her purse on the bar and crossed her legs. Even in a simple pair of black jeans, the movement of her perfect legs stirred Nico. She smiled as his eyes flicked down at her legs just for a second. "But I can't. I can't stand the thought of waking up tomorrow anywhere but in your bed."

Nico shook his head. The mere thought of being with her made his skin tingle. The connection he felt with Tatiana was stronger than anything he had ever felt, even with Stephanie. That thought alone terrified him. He wasn't sure he would survive losing Tatiana the way he'd lost Stephanie. She deserved to know what she was getting into.

"Tatiana, being with me is dangerous. You saw what could happen." He glanced over his shoulder and around the bar. No one was close by. "I don't want you to get hurt."

She smiled and put her hand on his. "Then let me help you. Talk to me. Tell me what is going on with you. That's what real couples do."

Nico shook his head. "I wish I could. I really do. But I can promise, you wouldn't believe me if I told you."

Tatiana grabbed his chin and pulled his face to look at hers. "Nico, you would be surprised at what I would believe."

Nico smiled. Without Zha'riel to talk to, and no Xabier to bounce ideas off, he felt only the building pressure deep in his core. Should he tell her about the wayward angel he was friends with? Or perhaps she would be interested in his vampire best friend. He had no idea when and where the angels were watching. Maybe he could tell her about Rafael's threats. Or even better, maybe she'd be interested in the chat he had with Lucifer just a few short hours ago.

He shook his head. How could he even consider that discussion? He'd made that mistake before and the girl stuck by him, costing her an agonizing death.

"Tatiana," he said. "I just can't. Please, just…please understand. It's just too—"

"Complicated?" she smiled wryly.

He nodded. "I'm sorry."

"Don't be." She ran her palm over his cheek. "But I'm not going anywhere. When you get home later, I'll be there, waiting."

She got up, kissed his lips softly, and pressed her forehead to his. "Just so you know…I could love you, Nico…if…if you gave me the chance."

As Tatiana made her way toward the exit, she had to wipe tears from her eyes. She couldn't believe the words that had come out of her mouth. Of all the things she could have said, those words implied a commitment she had no business making. She had a job to do, and while earning his trust was certainly a plus, she didn't have to go about it that way. The problem was, those words, which should have been empty promises, designed to allay suspicious, were nothing of the sort. She gasped as she realized a terrifying thing: those words were absolutely true. She was falling in love with Nico Scarlatti.

Nico downed another scotch and sighed. Tatiana was going to stay. He should have done more to scare her off. This was guaranteed to end badly for her and send him even further into the darkness he was now convinced was beginning to envelope him.

He became even more despondent as he pondered the implications of what Lucifer had divulged. He was in far greater danger than he ever thought possible. On one side, Heaven hated him, while powerful fallen angels hated him on the other. Lucifer's intentions were unclear, though it was easy to see he wanted Nico on his side. He offered friendship and protection, but who can stand against Heaven?

"Such a pretty young thing."

The hairs on the back of Nico's neck stood at attention. A chill raced down his spine and his blood cooled. If there was one thing that haunted his dreams, it was that voice. He turned his head slowly, feeling the rush of power surging through his body. With the pressure already peaking, Nico felt as though his veins were about to explode. He had to get control.

When their eyes met, Nico thought he was looking through a golden lens; everything was in razor sharp focus, but bathed in gold. Then, the golden hue faded. The figure standing before him looked different than when they last met. No longer dressed in his warrior's robes, he looked strange in a pair of loose-fitting black jeans and an untucked, white, silk button-down. His jet-black hair, previously tied back, hung in loose waves, framing his face. The white glow of his eyes faded to a piercing deep blue. His casual smile was new, yet there was a soullessness behind his icy countenance.

"Azazel," Nico hissed. "Come to finish what you started?"

The cold stare-down continued for a beat. Nico couldn't help but shrink a little. Azazel was far more experienced at inducing fear than Nico, and he had little to fear from a human, even one infused with the blood of Lucifer. Even without the white glow, Azazel's gaze was terrifying. The tension in the room was palpable.

Azazel's eyes began to sparkle and he cracked a grin. "What *I* started?" He leaned his hip on the bar. It was such a casual stance, he looked like a guy, chatting with a buddy, at the bar. "Please tell me you're not still angry with *me* over the consequences of *your* actions."

"*My* actions?" Nico's eyes bored into Azazel's. "You murdered my girlfriend right in front of me after torturing her for an entire day, you psycho!"

"Ahh, yes," Azazel said lazily, as though the memory had somehow slipped his mind. He nodded and bit the tip of his finger. "I can see how that might create friction between us."

"*Friction?*"

Nico fought the urge to lash out. He could smell the scent of ozone in the air. He felt the crackle of electricity at the tips of his fingers. Nico had grown far more powerful than he had been the last time he faced off against the ageless archangel, but he wasn't delusional. A fight with Azazel equaled suicide. The archangel would squash him like a cockroach and they both knew it.

"You forget, my insolent human friend," Azazel said in his haunting monotone. "That you incurred my wrath only after you murdered my son." He leaned a bit closer, his eyes flashing silver. "You would do well to remember, it is *his* essence within you, not yours. What you have...is stolen."

Nico couldn't be certain, but he thought he detected a bit of sorrow in Azazel's voice. It sounded strange, and Nico wrote it off as his own imagination. In all the stories he'd heard relating to Azazel, there was never a single instance of him demonstrating any emotion other than rage and hate. The loss of his son should only increase the intensity of those emotions. Now, Nico wondered if there was a heart deep down inside that was just a little bit broken. It didn't make him feel sorry for Azazel. If anything, it comforted him that he could bring pain to one who had hurt so many.

Azazel straightened and smiled grimly. "Anyway, I am not here to rehash old disputes. I am here with an offer."

"An offer," Nico said with a sniff. He was not only skeptical of whatever the offer was, but he couldn't help glancing all around the bar, half-expecting to see Seir lurking in the shadows, waiting for a signal from his master. The whole scene felt like a sick game. "You can't be serious."

"Really?" Azazel tilted his head. "Let me ask you this: How many allies do you have?"

"Allies?" Nico frowned. "What kind of..."

"How many?" Azazel repeated. "By now you must realize that, like it or not, you are part of a war. What you may not be aware of is there are many sides to this war, many factions vying for supremacy. I can tell you, each of these factions knows about you. At some point, they will come for you, either to recruit you or to kill you, whichever one benefits them more at the time." He rubbed his chin with his hand. "So, I ask you again, who is on *your* side?"

ᚦ ᚪ ᛝ ᛦ ᚷ

"I don't understand, Sire."

"What confuses you, Abdiel?"

Lucifer's eyes glimmered with amusement at his new apprentice's bewilderment. Over the past few weeks, they had spread word throughout the underworld that anyone who was found assisting Azazel in his efforts would be dealt with. Lucifer had already dispensed fast and harsh judgment upon three entire cohorts of demons, and their generals, who he suspected of working with Azazel. The message should have been clearly received, yet Azazel continued in his efforts.

"New Orleans, Sire?" Abdiel frowned. "They found Kharashuoa witches in New Orleans and are now seeking the tools they need to continue their search for the portal."

"Yes," Lucifer nodded. "Everything is right on schedule."

"You don't want the portal open!" Abdiel exploded. At Lucifer's raised eyebrows, he lowered his head in contrition. "I apologize, My Lord. I just…"

"You cannot see the full picture."

Abdiel's frustration was boiling over. He was expected to carry out plans straight from the mouth of the Master, yet he was not given the full picture. He had no idea how to operate under such conditions. On the battlefield, things were far simpler. They had a task, a mission, and they would fulfill that mission by any means necessary. Now, *he* handed out the battlefield orders to others while the more esoteric functions were left in his hands.

Azazel used to be the one to handle this kind of work for Lucifer. He had a knack for the artistic and was able to execute Lucifer's desires without worrying about whether he was accomplishing specific desired goals. Or, perhaps Lucifer trusted him with the information he constantly withheld from Abdiel.

They sat alone in the great throne room. Lucifer's eyes never left Abdiel, who could not sit still under his gaze. He paced the floor from one end of the ornate ancient Persian carpet to the other. His eyes roamed the intricate battle scenes depicted in the design. It matched the décor in all Lucifer's rooms, probably as a subtle reminder that no matter what was going on, no matter how quiet things may be, they were always on a war footing. Abdiel was fine with that. He just wanted to be included. Lucifer's inner circle was always small. Without Azazel, there wasn't much of an inner circle left, but Abdiel thought he would at least be in on the overall plan so he could support it.

"I would like to see the full picture, My Lord."

Lucifer folded his hands on the heavy wood table and leaned forward slightly. "The full picture for you is to keep the pressure up on my old friend without engaging him directly and without being too obvious about it."

Abdiel nodded. "Yes, but to what end? If we want to crush him, why hold back? If we want to stop him from fulfilling his plans, why…?"

His eyes widened. His mind raced through every conversation Lucifer and he had regarding Azazel and his supernatural coalition. The realization dawned on him. It was so simple, yet so equally brilliant.

"You don't want to stop him."

It was one of those things that, in the fast pace of life, one could easily miss. Abdiel had certainly missed it. Suddenly, everything began to come clear. Lucifer's half-smile told Abdiel he was right. He had the what figured out, but that was only one piece of the puzzle.

"Then...why fight him?"

Lucifer shrugged. "Consider who we're talking about, Abdiel. What motivates our old friend more than anything else?"

Abdiel sat down across from his master, his elbows resting on the table and both hands folded under his chin. He considered every piece of information he knew of about Azazel. The only thing that stood out was his thirst for blood, his love of vengeance. Azazel was unstoppable when it came to dealing out punishment.

Abdiel ran a finger over his upper lip. "He's just defying you?"

Perhaps," Lucifer shrugged. "Perhaps he really wants to succeed. I'm sure he has plans. He certainly has been seeking allies since our confrontation. I suspect Loki is at least passively assisting him, but what Azazel needs is an army."

"An army of supernatural creatures is not going to help him fight our demon army."

"No," Lucifer agreed. "But he is addressing that as well, isn't he? "How many cohorts did we annihilate this week?"

"Three," mumbled Abdiel. The sting of betrayal still bothered him. Treason among his ranks was a personal insult and he'd made it clear he would be merciless should another example be required.

"Azazel is working behind the scenes," Lucifer said. "Make no mistake. He is not hiding from me. He wants me to know what he is doing." He leaned forward. "Which means even more activity is lurking beneath the surface."

"He's playing the same game we are."

Abdiel leaned back in his chair and smiled in admiration. Azazel had nerve, Abdiel would give him that much. Anyone else would find a quiet place to hide out and do everything they could not to draw attention to themselves. Defying Lucifer to his face and surviving a one-on-one confrontation should have been enough, but Azazel apparently wanted to play in the main arena against the champion of evil.

"So, we just let him off the hook?"

Lucifer shook his head. "He is serving a purpose, for now. We'll let him open the portal and get his alphas out."

Abdiel nodded. "Okay. What about Mr. Scarlatti?"

"Nico is well on his way."

"Yet he hesitates," Abdiel said. "I must admit, I thought he would come around much faster once your blood was in him."

Lucifer shrugged. "Remember, he has the essence of a powerful mage in him as well. Perhaps he is fighting the good fight. Not to worry, my friend. He will succumb, and we will be there to free him from the burden of terror Heaven has placed upon him. We will allow him to freely express his true nature and unleash his full potential."

Abdiel grinned. "You really think of him as a game-changer?"

Lucifer's eyes flashed that brilliant gold hue. "What I saw when speaking to him face to face was a man with power so great, his vessel was scarcely able to contain it. If he doesn't act on his impulses, he will crack under the strain."

"That would be a bad thing, right?"

Abdiel wasn't certain how that worked. Power usually resided in those who were created for it. Sometimes power could be learned. Humans were created with the ability to exercise power, yet they seldom did. Those who tried often became outcasts in human society and ridiculed. In any case, the power humans wielded through study, took years to build and the human body adapted slowly over time, strengthening like a muscle to contain the power as the abilities grew.

Nico had the essences of two powerful beings in him, and his body was struggling to adapt. When a human goes to the gym to lift weights, he doesn't just put hundreds of pounds on a weight bar and start lifting. They start small, adding weight as the muscles grow and strengthen. What Nico's body was feeling was the supernatural equivalent of a man trying to bench press a thousand pounds on his first day in the gym. It wasn't going to work out well for him.

Lucifer contemplated the question. "It would not be the ideal outcome, but if it happens, I can put him back together. Ideally, he will come to me long before he gets to that point."

"We need to apply pressure," Abdiel insisted. "We need to threaten him daily, and force his hand, either by angering Heaven or by showing him that Heaven can't or won't help him."

Lucifer shook his head. "The young man is already isolated. He is already threatened by Heaven. All we need is to keep him isolated. We need him to feel alone, and threatened on all sides."

Abdiel frowned. "More than one enemy? How do we accomplish that?"

Lucifer smiled, his eyes flashing gold, the brilliant hue practically blinding Abdiel. "Oh, I've already set that in motion, my friend. Apparently, my old friend failed to inform his son's mother of the demise of her only child. I have recently remedied that oversight.

Chapter 16

"A thought keeps recurring in my mind."

That can't be good.

Xabier focused on the road. They were on Route 151, just outside of Cedar Rapids, Iowa, less than ninety minutes from their destination, Mineral Point, Wisconsin. Following their previous confrontation, they'd ridden in glorious silence for almost eight hours. He'd hoped to make it two more hours and then it would be all about Wynnifrea's tomb and getting her remains and personal effects secured somewhere safe. Leave it to Lazlo to blow that plan up.

Lazlo looked over when Xabier didn't answer. "I keep recalling Gepidae. Remember?"

Xabier remembered. The incident took place in late sixth century; it was one of their last adventures together. The Gepids were a harsh people living in a remote part of Europe, in what is now known as Western Romania. The Gepids had raided a western outpost of Italia, taking many prisoners, mostly women and children. The children would be sold into slavery and the women…no one liked to think about what the Gepids would do with the women. Lazlo and Xabier were nearby when word of the raid came. The villagers, a peaceful people, who had no hope of winning a fight with the Gepids, were terrified. Without hesitation, Xabier and Lazlo stole into Gepidae and found the village where the raid had originated. Within twenty minutes, they had laid waste to the entire village, killing everyone they saw, freeing the prisoners and returning them to Italia.

When Xabier's eyes blinked with the recollection, Lazlo grinned. "Heheh, you remember."

"I remember, it was one of the few times the people we killed actually deserved it."

Lazlo rolled his eyes. "Ahh, the song of the righteously indignant. Have you convinced yourself you didn't enjoy those days? That you didn't relish the havoc we wrought?"

"Oh, I enjoyed it all right." Xabier nodded. "You turned me into a bloodthirsty ripper."

"*I* did that?" Lazlo laughed. "How easily you shift blame to assuage your own guilty conscience. Vampirism, as you are well-aware, amplifies the characteristics you *already* possess. The ripper always inside you."

"Yeah, well, it turns out I kill a whole lot less when you're not around."

Lazlo shook his head and returned his gaze to the road. Xabier thought he saw a hint of nostalgia in Lazlo's eyes. It was hard for Xabier to think of his former friend as anything but a heartless killer. Lazlo had never exhibited the slightest remorse for the lives he had taken and he never seemed to regret his decisions no matter how destructive to his relationships. He was as stubborn as he was ruthless, as unfeeling as he was vicious.

Lazlo turned back to him. "Remember the con artist in Vasconia?"

Xabier snorted. "The short, fat one who waddled into town and scammed the peasants out of their goats?"

"That's the one." Lazlo slapped his knee. "Remember when we cornered him behind the wall?"

"I thought he was going to try to take us both on."

"Until *you* showed him your fangs. Then he wasn't so brave."

"And you just sat there laughing the whole time."

Lazlo was laughing as hard as he had been on that day, over fifteen hundred years ago. Rather than killing the rolly-polly sleaze-bag, Lazlo and Xabier compelled him to return everything he'd stolen and admit his wrongdoing to the townspeople. Needless to say, the people of that small village in Vasconia were not particularly forgiving, even though the man appeared to be turning over a new leaf. He barely made it out of town alive. Lazlo and Xabier chuckled all the way through the poor thief's humiliation.

Over the next hour and a half, Xabier felt much like had fifteen centuries before. They reminisced about the adventures they'd had over the years, the places they'd visited, and the people they'd encountered. From kings and queens, at the height of the Roman Empire, to Pope Gregory and the creation of the Latin church, from Emperor Heraclius in the Persian Empire, to the doomed Arab attack on Constantinople, Lazlo and Xabier witnessed it all. Often, they were right at the center of the action. There was even the ironic encounter with a cannibal tribe in the African jungles.

"Now *that* was funny," Xabier said. "Letting them capture us and tie us to those posts in the middle of their village was brilliant."

Lazlo shook his head. "It brought the whole tribe together, didn't it?"

The BMW sped through the last several miles of Iowa, crossing over the Mississippi River and into Southern Wisconsin. A tingle crept up Xabier's spine as he reentered a part of the United States he hadn't visited for over three hundred years. Keeping his promise to ensure her final resting place remained secure and secret, Xabier remembered his friend from afar. He'd always made certain his travels never brought him close to her. There was nothing in his life that could possibly divulge her location, only his memories.

He could see Lazlo watching him intently as the emotions caused a change in Xabier's demeanor. He felt a melancholy come over him as he realized they were in a race to disturb the resting place of his friend. It wasn't right, and it wasn't something he was going to allow. If someone was going to disturb Wynnifrea, it would be someone who loved her, who cared enough to protect her legacy.

Driftless Rivers National Park was a massive wasteland with a landscape as diverse as any in the world. There were rolling plains, broken up by tributaries forking off the Mississippi River. There were mountain regions with high peaks and deep underground caverns alongside deep-carved river valleys, but there was also plenty of forest and grasslands. It was an ecological goldmine, which boasted a range of wildlife and vegetation in unusual proximity.

Xabier steered the car as far as he could into the park, but ultimately, they had to park and trek the rest of the way on foot. He was glad it was just him and Lazlo, both vampires, making the hike. They could move faster without humans, and they could deal with the harsh landscape far easier. Vampires were less sensitive to extreme weather conditions than humans. They can handle the cold, the wind, and the rain, as easily as the native creatures lurking in the wild. Xabier often wondered if that meant vampires were closer to the rest of the animal world than they were to their human roots.

"You remember how to get there?" Lazlo asked. "It's been centuries."

Xabier held up his right hand, showing him a ring with a stunning center. It was a simple, smooth, jet-black stone. Lazlo's keen eyes took in the vivid colors buried deep in the center of the stone.

"What is that?"

Xabier looked at it. "Black opal. Wynnifrea made it for me to replace my old daylight ring. She thought you might be able to get a witch to track me through the old one."

Lazlo's eyes widened and he pursed his lips. "I should have thought of that," he mumbled.

Daylight rings allowed vampires to walk in the sun without damage. Vampires are a cursed species. Because of their need to feed on human blood, they became a danger to humanity and nature, along with those charged with protecting the Earth and its children, found a balance. The result was a curse upon the entire vampire race. The sun became their enemy. They were relegated to a life of nocturnal hunting, separating them from humanity.

The original vampire family, however, was somehow exempt from the curse. While they operated as any other human, the rest of their kind were forced into the shadows, doomed to hunt those who used to be their own. They never stopped trying to find ways around the curse. There were ways to persuade witches. Some could be bought, others threatened or coerced, still others befriended. If a vampire was fortunate enough to know someone who knew a witch willing to help, they could obtain a ring personalized to them that would enable them to survive in the sun while they wore it.

"This one is also spelled to tell me when I am near a certain relic," Xabier explained. "An amulet."

Xabier's eyes widened. He grabbed Xabier's arm and stopped walking. "Are we talking about what I think we're talking about?"

Xabier raised his eyebrows. He didn't need to affirm the answer. There was no other amulet that would matter. Wynnifrea's amulet was passed down through the millennia. Made of a complex combination of gold, silver, and bronze threads, woven together and intricately braided around a quarter-inch thick sliver of rainbow moonstone, Wynnifrea's amulet was a testament to prehistoric metallurgy and, if examined and tested, would stand modern archeology and scientific dating methods on their heads.

The rare combination of so many elements, combined with the etched spell on the moonstone made the amulet one of the most powerful items of witchcraft ever created. In the hands of a true Kharashuoa master, it could provide almost limitless power. To most witches, the amulet was little more than legend. To the Kharashuoa, it was all too real, and an item they were all too eager to recover.

"Wynnifrea trusted no one in her final days," Xabier said as they hurried, deeper and deeper, into a river bed, following an ancient dried tributary.

They were just a couple miles in but the landscape had completely changed. What started out as forest was rapidly giving way to rocky terrain. The trees still dominated but mountains rose on either side of the two vampires as they made their way deeper and deeper into the Driftless Area.

"She had no apprentice, no one to pass her craft on to." Xabier's pace was quick, his eyes alert, but his heart was heavy. "There was never a shortage of power-seeking witches who wanted to learn at her feet." He shook his head in disgust. "They all just wanted to worm their way into her good graces, hoping one day, Wynnifrea would hand over all her power to them."

Lazlo nodded. "I can certainly see how one such as Wynnifrea might have to be selective about those she chose to teach."

"In the end, there was no one she deemed worthy." Xabier sighed and spread his hands. "She left it to me to protect her legacy."

"What legacy?" Lazlo asked in amazement. "She died and took it all with her."

"She died and kept it out of the hands of those who were unworthy," Xabier insisted, "someone who would undo all the good Wynnifrea had done in her life."

Lazlo stopped, holding his hand up for Xabier to remain silent. Together, they crouched in the falling darkness. Lazlo, his senses picking through the sounds of the landscape, kept his eyes closed. Even in unfamiliar territory, he was skilled enough to pick out any out of place sound. After several moments, he shook his head.

"What?" Xabier asked.

"Nothing," Lazlo shrugged. "I just thought…"

Xabier frowned. "Thought what?"

Lazlo wasn't the type to spook. Xabier trusted his senses. Lazlo could pick out an individual pulse from a half-mile away. If a twig snapped, out of place, Lazlo would know it. If he heard something, chances are it was real and not his imagination.

"Do we have company, Laz?"

"I thought so," Lazlo said, scanning the surrounding area through squinted eyes, "but if someone's out there, they're being *extremely* quiet."

Ђ ᴀ ᴣ ѱ ᴄ

"I think it's a mistake."

"What you think is not important. You have your mission. Your job is to execute your orders."

I'll tell you what I would like to execute.

Tatiana fought to control her response. Why was it the powers that be always refused to listen to those on the ground? Sometimes, the ones in the trenches had a perspective which could not be seen from those so far removed. Sometimes, the plan needed to be changed in order to accommodate a fluid situation. In her opinion, a good leader was secure enough, and had enough sense, to listen to those around him, particularly when they had first-hand insights.

"I understand my job," was her terse reply. "I'm not a child. I'm simply telling you, I see things you are unable to see, and I'm telling you—"

"And *we* see things that *you* cannot see from *your* vantage point, Tatiana, and irrespective of your situation, the overall picture is changing rapidly. We must act now to stay ahead of it."

Tatiana closed her eyes. She had no idea how to do what she was being asked to do. She'd pressed Nico once, a few days before, and it had blown up in her face. She'd almost blown her mission. Fortunately, he was so demoralized by his own struggle, and his friends' absence, he didn't suspect her decision to remain at his side. If she pressed him again, she couldn't be sure it would stay that way.

"I don't care what you have to do. You've gotten him this far and he is none the wiser. Nico is already leaning. He is being worked from all angles, and Heaven has done itself no favors. He stands on the precipice; you need to bring it home."

Tatiana thought of all the times Nico's dark side showed itself. Sometimes it manifested in a seething rage. Other times it was cold night sweats as he fought his inner turmoil in his sleep. Mostly, it was in his demeanor. She could see the darkness cloud his face and shine though his eyes, searching for a way out. In those moments, she let Nico know how much she cared about him. His confusion was no doubt tied to the fact that he associated her affection with the darkness inside him he was so bent on fighting.

When she didn't respond right away, she heard a huff on the other end of the call. "Tell me you are not..." He almost growled at her. "Tatiana, are you falling for him?"

"What?" she cried, a little too forcefully, before reigning her emotions in. "What are you talking about?"

"I am talking about what sounds like a lack of commitment on your part. Perhaps you are too emotionally involved."

She took a breath and looked at her hands. They were shaking. She was glad the call was not a video chat. She wasn't used to the feelings running through her body. While she was an expert in the art of deception, her skills required a certain detachment, a detachment she was suddenly missing.

"That is ridiculous," she said.

"Good. Because you know he will not respond favorably should the truth suddenly come out."

She didn't disagree with that. Nico was loyal, and he expected loyalty from his friends. Nico had no idea who she really was, no idea she was a part of his secret world. The deception had gone on for so long, she had no idea how to end it without bringing the entire relationship to a screeching halt.

The sound of a car pulling up brought the conversation to an abrupt end. Tatiana signed off with a promise to report back within twenty-four hours. She ended the call as Nico opened the door. He greeted her with a quiet nod and brief smile before muttering that he was going to take a shower.

Things were hanging by a thread. Since their last conversation in the bar Tatiana had given him space, not wanting to further upset him, but now she was under pressure. She needed results and she couldn't wait for Nico to come around. With his friends out of touch, he was losing perspective. Somehow, she needed to connect with him. Nico was unaware he was with another supernatural being; that was her biggest obstacle. He thought he was in a relationship with a regular human woman, which was also the reason he was so fearful for her safety.

She trotted up the stairs and stepped into the master bedroom. Nico hadn't bothered to turn the lights on. She heard running water and leaned her forehead against the wooden door until the water was turned off. She heard Nico open the shower door and the rustling of a towel as he dried himself off. That sound alone dropped her façade.

Tatiana felt her resolve crumble. It had been a few days since she'd felt his touch, since she'd felt his skin under her fingers. There was tension between them. At times, she thought he resented her presence, as though she was making life even more difficult for him, but mostly, she got the impression he was grateful to have someone who cared enough to stand by his side.

She was startled when he opened the door. He put his hands out to steady her as she stumbled forward. The warmth of his touch caused an instant reaction in her heart. She felt it flutter and pulse rapidly. She wasn't sure if it was anxiety over her conflicted interest in him, or because of the desire her body refused to ignore. When her eyes met his, she lost all ability to speak.

"Hey," he said, a weak but amused smile tugging at the corners of his mouth.

The deep violet of his eyes sparkled even in the dim lighting. He didn't wait for her response, instead he wrapped his arms around her, pulling her close against his bare chest. Tatiana's body reacted in an instant and she pressed herself even closer. She tilted her head up, her lips parted slightly, a soft moan escaping from deep within her. His lips met hers and she was transported to a place where all her cares meant nothing and the only thing that mattered was the connection she had with the man who owned her heart.

She awoke hours later, her head on his shoulder, her right arm draped across his stomach. Their legs were hopelessly intertwined with the bed sheets. She had no idea how they managed to fall asleep tied together like that. She closed her eyes and tried to drift off. She would rather lie in bed with Nico and sleep forever than to rise and deal with the issues between them.

She felt movement. His right arm was wrapped around her and his hand was stroking her back from the base of her neck to the small of her back, and beyond. His left hand ran from her right wrist all the way up her arm to her shoulder, where his thumb reached out to stroke her cheek, causing her to smile. She squeezed him.

"How long have you been awake?" she asked, her voice husky from sleep.

He sniffed. "Never fell asleep. I've just been holding you, thinking about you, touching you."

"Mmmm." She kept her eyes closed. "Well, don't stop. The touching is my favorite part."

He chuckled, and she imagined the cocky smirk on his face. He ran his hand up her back and squeezed her neck right at the base of her skull, causing her to groan in pleasure. He grasped her hair lightly and tilted her head so he could kiss her lips.

"I'm glad," he said. "Because touching you is my favorite thing to do in the world."

Something in his eyes caused her to pull herself up on her elbow and face him. "Talk to me, Nico."

He held her hand, bringing it to his lips. "Sweetheart, I wish I could, but there are things I couldn't even begin to explain to you. I wouldn't even know where to begin."

She cupped his cheek in her hand and stroked it gently, her eyes never straying from his. Her heart skipped beats as her mind through all the possible scenarios connected with what she wanted to say. As frightening as it was, she had to make things right with him. She didn't want to hurt Nico, but the longer the deception continued, the worse the end result would be, and she wanted to believe their relationship could be salvaged. She didn't want this night to be their last together.

"Nico," she said whispered, her breath becoming ragged as her throat tightened in protest. "I know you. You think I don't understand, but believe me I do."

He narrowed his eyes. "I wish that were true, but—"

"Nico" Tatiana said, her eyes meeting his. She tried to convey in her gaze everything that she was feeling in her heart. "Before we go any further…before you say another word…I need to tell you about *me*."

Chapter 17

"You have you orders. I expect results."

"Yes, Prince."

Abdiel nodded toward the door. "Now go."

Ten generals nodded in unison and left the throne room. Abdiel leaned back in his chair and sighed. He was at the right hand of power. It was a position of extraordinary prestige and one that was both coveted and feared. When he thought about the one he had replaced, Abdiel wondered how he could be expected to succeed. Azazel had been Lucifer's closest friend through the ages. How was Abdiel supposed to compete with that? He closed his eyes and tried not to think about it.

"It is lonely, no?"

The last time Abdiel heard that voice, he was in the same room, only his skin was melting off his bones. He spun around, leaping to his feet at the same time. He wasn't sure what he intended to do. He wouldn't stand a chance against Azazel, but he knew he would rather have the archangel in front of him than behind, for all the good it would do.

Azazel stood, eyes glimmering in amusement, hands clasped together, as he regarded Abdiel's anxiety. The former general, now elevated to second-in-command of the Dark Army, continued to wither in the face of the archangel. He managed to get his feet under him and stand at attention.

Azazel laughed. "You are far too tense, General." He strolled around the great table and breathed in the air. "Ahh. It feels good to be back. I've missed this place." He held up a finger as he turned back to Abdiel. "You know, General, it is amazing what one misses. The smells, the particular atmosphere of a place. This room." He spread his arms. "This room is special."

Abdiel stood his ground. He knew the archangel was toying with him, flaunting the fact that he could simply enter Lucifer's throne room with impunity. Abdiel could see Azazel mocking him with his eyes, those glowing white eyes that flashed silver and could reduce even a man of Abdiel's stature to little more than a petrified child. Abdiel wanted nothing more than to eye him defiantly, but couldn't bring himself to do so.

Instead, he asked the obvious question. "What do you want?"

Azazel smiled. "Right to the point, General."

"I am no longer a general," Abdiel pointed out.

"Oh, really?" Azazel smirked. "And what exactly are you? I mean, other than a cowardly fool. What title has our dear lord bequeathed upon you?"

Abdiel bristled, but there was little he could do. He gritted his teeth and muttered, "Prince."

Azazel leaned forward. "What was that?"

Abdiel stood a little straighter, lifting his chin and meeting the archangel's gaze. "Prince."

"Ahhh!" Azazel's eyes widened.

Abdiel knew it wasn't news to Azazel. There was no way he was in the dark about who had taken his former post at Lucifer's right hand.

"So, I guess my old friend has really gotten desperate, hasn't he? Tell me, are you responsible for the same duties I was?"

Abdiel granted him a curt nod and Azazel laughed.

"Ha! I bet the enemies of Satan quiver at the sound of your throaty roar!"

Abdiel again gritted his teeth. Azazel was baiting him, coaxing him to make a move, to do anything that would justify Azazel's wrath. Abdiel wondered why the game. It wasn't like he, or anyone close by could stop Azazel from dishing out whatever punishment he chose. Lucifer was not around. Azazel had free reign until his return and he knew it. He must also know, Lucifer wouldn't return for some time.

"What are you here for, Azazel?"

The archangel regarded him with one hand across his stomach and the other on his chin as though he was trying to determine whether to talk to Abdiel or tear him apart limb from limb. Abdiel cringed inwardly as Azazel stretched the moment out several seconds longer than necessary. It was a technique the archangel used often. Azazel was a master at creating atmosphere.

He finally pressed his lips together, smiled, and said, "Very well. It is actually quite simple, General…ahem, I mean, *Prince*. I have a question for you."

"A question?" Abdiel frowned. "For me?"

Azazel shrugged. "A man in your position has certain…information."

"All you want," Abdiel asked with a skeptical squint, "is information?"

"I can think of nothing more valuable in this, or any other world," Azazel noted, "than information." He raised his eyebrows. "Can you?"

Abdiel blinked and gritted his teeth. He hated the condescending archangel, and not just because Azazel had tried to fry his insides. Azazel was used to being the one in charge. He was used to striking fear in everyone he came across, particularly those in his command. He ruled through fear. Abdiel wished he had the courage not to be afraid.

"I think you know…"

"I know you can't tell me anything," Azazel finished. "I am not asking you to betray your allegiance to my old friend." For the first time, Azazel's voice was reassuring. "All I want is to understand what his interest is in my…project."

Abdiel shook his head. "I don't know what you're talking about."

"Please," Azazel said softly. "All I want is a reason. Don't make me extract an answer."

Abdiel felt a chill run down his spine. He had a good idea what the "extraction" would feel like. He also got the impression that while Azazel was acting calmly so far, it wouldn't last if he didn't receive the information he sought. He assumed Abdiel would have the information because if Azazel was at Lucifer's right hand, *he* would know.

"I have no idea why he doesn't want you to succeed," Abdiel replied. "He hasn't told me."

Azazel shook his head sadly and pointed a finger at Abdiel. "It is a simple question, really. There is no reason not to tell his...*prince.*"

"But he *hasn't!*" Abdiel insisted. "All he said was that you will not be allowed to…"

"I will not be *allowed?*" Azazel exploded.

Abdiel knew this moment would come. Azazel was losing his patience and Abdiel had nothing to give him. The reality was that Abdiel *should* have the information Azazel wanted. The right hand of the master should be clued in, not just to the when, where, and how, but also the why. However, when it came to Azazel, Lucifer was playing a different kind of game and holding his cards close to the vest.

"It doesn't make any sense to me. I think he just wants to spite you."

Azazel, poised as though he was about to unleash a punishing barrage of ferocity, paused and stared at Abdiel. "Spite?" He tilted his head and thought about the possibility. "Could it be that simple?" He turned from Abdiel and paced the floor. "Of all the rationales I have considered, spite was not one of them. Yet, it is the one that makes the most sense."

Abdiel was spared whatever was to come next when the buzzing of a cell phone interrupted the moment. Azazel stared at the screen, his eyes a mixture of annoyance and interest. Without wasting another moment, he glanced at Abdiel.

"It would appear I have business elsewhere." He smiled. "We'll meet again."

ᛒ ᴀ � ᶃ

"Woman, you don't summon me, do you understand that?"

"And yet you come."

They met at Shalimar Bagh, the stunning Mughal garden near Srinagar City in India. Standing under a brown stone pavilion, Azazel tried to maintain his contemptuous attitude but failed as the corners of his mouth turned upward. As quickly as the lighthearted moment came, it passed. Azazel's expression darkened and his eyes flashed silver. He stared out over the two pools, watching the fountains erupt, sending their geysers thirty feet into the air and then abruptly shutting down and the thousands of droplets of water cascaded back to the pool.

"I intended to come see you."

"Oh, you *intended*, did you? You *intended* to come tell a mother that her son was dead? Tell me, Azazel, just when did you *intend* to tell me about Sansata?"

Azazel put his hands on her shoulders and stared into her eyes. The low angle of the sun created shadows that slanted across her face, making her grief appear that much more vivid. She struggled against his grasp, tears flooding her eyes. Within seconds, she worked herself into a violent frenzy, flailing against his chest, landing repeated blows. Azazel, rather than fight back or even defend himself, allowed her to work through her grief, pounding on the only one who could possibly understand her loss.

She was every bit as beautiful as the moment they'd first met. Her riveting, almond-shaped, brown-almost-black eyes always melted his harsh persona. Thick locks of silky, black hair were clasped loosely together and fell to the small of her back. She wore the traditional robes of ancient Hindu culture, the clash of colors somehow working together in what should have been an unlikely juxtaposition. Her brown skin and full, pinkish lips glowed with an inner beauty Azazel knew far exceeded the stunning exterior. Her pain, so evident in her eyes, cut Azazel deep in his heart.

"I am sorry, my love."

"You left me!" she cried. "You left me and took my son and now he's gone!"

"Parvati," Azazel pulled her close. "Please. You know I had to leave. I had no choice."

"You could have taken me with you."

"And risk the treaty?"

Parvati's eyes lowered and she pressed her forehead to his chest. Her fingers clutched at his cloak. Of all the angels who fell from Heaven on that dreadful day, there was none she loved more than Azazel. She'd told him that over and over during their time together and he always took it for granted.

The war had gone on for ages, spilling over into the created world. Lucifer's enemies, calling themselves Titans, were relentless in their efforts to destroy the one who had brought judgment upon them. They blamed him for their decision to defy their Almighty Father. Without the Father's will guiding them, anger and wrath filled their minds and they descended into madness. They couldn't stay together. The larger factions split into smaller factions that battled one another as much as they fought Lucifer.

Their inability to maintain a cohesive alliance almost handed Lucifer victory. The only thing that saved them was Lucifer had similar problems within his own ranks, though he managed to keep his army together. The opposing factions did reunite as allies with a common enemy and fought Lucifer to a stalemate.

At some point during the ages-long war, an unlikely love story took shape. Azazel and Parvati found one another in the fog and uncertainty of war. Though they were on opposing sides, they refused to fight one another and their affair lasted through the ages. While the fighting raged around them, they discretely stole away, finding moments of tenderness amidst the turmoil and chaos of war.

And then, Sansata was conceived. Azazel and Parvati had a son amidst the swirling hate and rage that propelled the fallen angels to kill one another. Sansata was both unexpected and dangerous, as Shiva, Parvati's husband suspected her infidelity. The only thing that saved her infant son was that Shiva was a warrior, fighting at the front. He like Azazel, had an insatiable thirst for blood and vengeance, and fought with an unmatched intensity, rising above his peers. He was not around to punish his wife. Had he been present, Shiva likely would have ended Parvati and her unborn son before he had the chance to breathe earthly air. Fortunately for Parvati and her infant, more important events consumed Shiva's time. He was the leader of an army, and the war was about to end.

It was agreed that a truce was needed to end the war. They needed a neutral location for the negotiations. The ancient city of Susa, modern day Shush, Iran, was chosen as the meeting site. Over a period of two weeks, the various factions met and debated over who would be recognized as legitimate. Once those negotiations ended, the world was divided up amongst the factions.

Shiva was a member of a trio called the Daevas, who secured for themselves a small bit of land, modern day India. They were almost cast aside in the negotiations, as the land they controlled was so nominal and unimportant. The other factions held highly populated regions, such as modern day Greece and Rome. The Greeks and Romans banded together and took the entire Mediterranean region, which was the most populated area. Other factions took far larger areas, as was the case with the Amatsu-Kami, led by Izanagi, the fourth angel, also known as the baby brother of Michael, Lucifer, and Gabriel. The Amatsu-Kami took all land east of modern day India, and reaching north deep into modern day Siberia. The Yazatas took land northwest of India, reaching as far west as modern day Iran and including all the modern day "stan" countries.

Shiva and the other Daevas never attempted to expand their land holdings. They fought their war simply to keep from being taken over. They had to fight on all fronts and never lost a single inch of land. They understood something that seemed irrelevant to many at the negotiation table. It was easier to hold and control a small area than a larger one, something all the other factions would learn later. They were nearly discarded and their land sold off to the highest bidder when Shiva spoke up.

Noting that throughout the entire war, no one had been able to encroach on their land, he made it clear that anyone attempting to enter their land would face their army. The Daevas refused all offers to join other factions and, in the end, were left to their own devices. Bordered by enemies on all sides, it was assumed the Daevas would one day become weak and weary of defending themselves. To end the conflict, and rest from war, they were left alone to govern their tiny parcel of land. They then withdrew and began the task of building a society.

Azazel, under orders from Lucifer, was forced to leave Parvati. Shiva would not let her go and to sneak her out would have created a firestorm no one was willing to risk. Lucifer knew the treaty hung on a tenuous trust between all the factions. Shiva and the Daevas were a violent lot and held their honor in high regard. Shiva was already threatening to destroy the bastard child. Azazel convinced Parvati to let him take Sansata away and out of danger from Shiva. Parvati agreed, and saw her son only rarely as she continued at the side of a husband who didn't particularly care for her.

Now her son was dead. "He is gone," she kept repeating, her voice muffled because her face was buried in Azazel's robe.

He held her close and let her cry, remembering the last time he held her so tightly. It was the day he left and the scene was not so different. She cried and he stoically hid the bitterness in his heart, knowing he would probably never see her again.

"I want his head," she mumbled. When Azazel didn't respond, she pulled back and looked into his eyes, her own eyes flashing a deep crimson. "His head," she repeated, her demeanor turning on a dime from a weeping and helpless to vengeful and impatient. "You will bring me the head of the one who dared raise his hand against my beloved. Just like my old friend, Salome requested, I now ask of you. You will bring it to me, won't you, Azazel?"

He let her go and let out a long, deep sigh. Azazel had known all along Parvati would desire swift vengeance. He had wanted the same thing in the immediate aftermath of Sansata's demise. The first impulse of a parent has got to be to lash out in vengeance. He wondered if Parvati was aware of his failed attempt on Nico's life. Had she known that he and Lucifer had already faced off once over Nico Scarlatti, and he nearly lost his own life, would she still demand he pursue their son's killer? Azazel hardly knew where to begin.

"Parvati," he began. "There is much you do not know."

"What could possibly overshadow a father's duty to avenge the murder of his son?"

Azazel shook his head. He told her about his skirmish with Lucifer, how close Nico had come to dying that day. He ended with the most important bit of information about the day he almost killed Nico Scarlatti.

"And Lucifer fed the human his blood rather than let him die."

"*What?*" Parvati's eyes widened and her mouth dropped open. She shook her head. "But...*why?* What is so special about this human?"

Azazel shrugged. "Two opposing essences is intriguing, no? It has never been done before. I witnessed, first-hand, he has extraordinary power within him. If he learns to contain it before it destroys him..." He shrugged again.

"So, the Morning Star desires a protégé," Parvati nodded, her eyes flashing in amazement. "I know of only one time he has ever shared his blood."

Azazel nodded. "Yes. She was...*special*...to him."

"She was also very powerful."

Azazel didn't respond. He let Parvati work through it.

She sighed. "This boy has that potential?"

Azazel nodded. "He had it before Lucifer infused him. Now, his potential has increased a million-fold. If Lucifer converts him, it will shift the balance."

Parvati shook her head. "If we destroy him, Lucifer cannot have him."

"You know Lucifer would simply resurrect him." Azazel sighed as Parvati's eyes told him she was not ready to discuss the matter. He smiled in understanding. She just needed time to grieve. "In any case, Scarlatti is now under Lucifer's general protection, as well as the uncertain protection of Heaven, so he is not easily accessed. And now I have a new focus. I am building for the future." He nodded to her. "And I think you might have a role."

Parvati turned to look at the flowers to her left. The pinks and whites stood out in stark relief, surrounded by the lush greenery. She leaned on one of the columns, feeling its cool textured surface with her fingertips. The sounds of the geysers erupting once again filled Azazel's ears as Parvati dried her tears. He knew, she was used to pushing her emotions down and focusing on things she could control. She straightened and turned back to Azazel, her eyes meeting his with an inquisitive stare.

"Tell me."

He told Parvati of his efforts to reopen the portal. Her eyes widened as she realized his plan was to defy Heaven, albeit indirectly. There was a reason the portal had been created in the first place.

"You wish to release the alphas," she said. It wasn't a question. "To what end?"

"It is not just the alphas," Azazel insisted. "All these disparate groups are now working together."

"For now," Parvati observed. "Once they get what they want, they will return to their common squabbles."

"Perhaps, not. I have also struck an alliance with the Kharashuoa witches. After I free the alphas, I will join all the world's supernatural creatures into one army."

"It still won't be enough," Parvati said. "Angels and demons versus human mutants is no contest."

"The army is not for a stand against the gods," Azazel replied. "It is an army *for* the gods." He smiled. "Or rather…*one* god."

Parvati's eyes widen. "So that is why you wish to turn this Scarlatti boy. You wish to rule."

Azazel shrugged. "Though I could be persuaded to share power."

"*Share* power?"

A flash of realization crossed Parvati's face. Azazel grinned as her voice stuck in her throat. He knew the Daevas were under intense pressure. The world was collapsing around them and their society was threatened like never before. Perhaps it was time to expand their holdings. It would involve breaking an ancient treaty, but no treaty was forever. Perhaps it was time for hostilities to resume. Parvati met Azazel's eyes.

"I will set up the meeting."

Chapter 18

"I don't trust him."

"He has no reason to lie."

Nayra stood at the entrance of a cave at the base of a mid-sized mountain. She closed her eyes and focused her thoughts deep inside the cave. Benyamin watched for the tenth time as she attempted to "see" deep within the underground cavern. He knew to shut up when she was trying to focus. After several silent moments, she opened her eyes and shook her head.

"Not here." She turned to look out at the rugged terrain. She'd explained earlier to Benyamin, she was trying to hear Wynnifrea's voice calling from the ether. "My dear," she mumbled. "Where you are? I am here. I am the one you have been waiting for."

She turned to Benyamin. "Your angel seeks only his own interests."

He narrowed his eyes and thought about it. Azazel had struck a deal with the witches. He stepped in like a savior, as though he'd known what was going to happen, and used the event to further solidify his position with Nayra and Benyamin, while gaining allies within the witch community, a task not easily accomplished by one with such dark energy. The Kharashuoa had been so slighted by the rest of the supernatural, and human communities, they were quite willing to accept Azazel's olive branch.

Nayra was changing right in front of him. After agreeing to Azazel's offer, the witches in New Orleans took her to a secret place outside the city to "prepare her" for her journey to seek out Wynnifrea. Many had taken the journey before her; none had returned. They had all been too weak, too selfish, or too evil. The witches couldn't be sure, but they were clear that approaching the Driftless Area was dangerous for any witch. Not one had gotten more than ten miles into southwest Wisconsin before bad things began to happen, and everyone who had tried to continue beyond that point had disappeared, never to be seen or heard from again.

Three days after disappearing with the witches, Nayra emerged. At first, she seemed her usual self, but she spoke a little differently and her eyes always seemed to be looking at a point far off on the horizon. It was as though she had aged fifty years while looking a decade younger. It was in her steel-grey eyes, years and years of knowledge that hadn't been there before.

"He will cast us aside," Nayra continued, "the moment we are no longer useful to his ends."

Benyamin chuckled. "I knew that the moment I accepted his help in the first place."

"Mmm." Nayra nodded absently. Her eyes searched something in the distance. She pointed. "That way."

They trekked in silence. Benyamin made the hike easily and wondered the whole time how the older witch managed it. The air was beginning to cool, and the terrain was rugged. He worried about how quickly she would be able to move across the rocky landscape once darkness fell. It didn't seem to concern Nayra as she led the way through the rocky riverbed.

"He speaks of a union between his demon army and us." Benyamin hated the idea of being beholden to any power higher than himself, but Azazel had offered something big, something that could solidify the supernatural for centuries to come.

Nayra shrugged. "He must know, eventually the witches must stand between the humans and the supernatural. What then?"

"You don't believe the supernatural can coexist peacefully with humans?"

Nayra's eyes never wavered, but nonetheless, Benyamin caught her skeptical demeanor. Of course, a witch would think that way. Most supernatural species posed imminent danger to humans. Vampires, for one, required blood to survive. They could subsist on animal blood, but nothing compared to human blood. Werewolves craved human organs, such as livers, kidneys, and hearts. Those that didn't feed on humans were dangerous in other ways. It was a delicate, tenuous balance, and witches, no matter how corrupt, had an instinctive kinship with nature. They would ultimately tend toward balance, and *that* meant, at some point, they would become enemies to the supernatural.

"Remember," she said. "This world was created for the humans. It was placed in our care. It is the duty of the witches to ensure the balance does not tip away from humanity."

Before he could respond, Benyamin felt a tingle in his spine. He grabbed Nayra's arm and stopped her. Holding a finger to his lips, Benyamin signaled for silence. They stood absolutely still as he strained his hearing to its limits. Nayra stared up at him, an expectant look crossed her face, though she refrained from speaking.

Benyamin leaned in very close to her ear. "My brother."

She felt her heart pick up pace but Benyamin squeezed her arm. "Control that," he hissed. "Lazlo will key in on a human heartbeat."

As much as he wanted to believe Lazlo hadn't been alerted to their presence, he knew it was hopeless. The one thing Lazlo had over all his siblings was the predator's senses. His were so finely honed over the centuries, it was impossible to beat him in the open wilderness. Lazlo was a born killer and an even better predator.

"We are not here to kill Lazlo," he said softly to Nayra.

"He stands against us."

"He is my brother."

Nayra sighed. "Fine. I will not harm him…permanently."

Ђ A ⅔ Ψ Ϛ

"This is it."

"You're certain?"

Xabier stared at Lazlo with tired eyes and held up his ring. The colors deep within the black opal were lit up like neon swirls of orange, yellow, blue, green and. red. Without bothering to wait for Lazlo's acknowledgment, he turned away. They had just sprinted, at full vampire speed, to the mouth of a cavern which was indiscernible to the human eye unless one was standing right in front of it. He didn't have time to deal with skepticism. If Benyamin was nearby, chances were, he was not alone. That could mean a psychotic archangel and demon sidekick could very well be lying in wait. They had to move. Wynnifrea's final resting place had to be cleared out and her effects hidden away. Her spell was designed to keep her possessions and remains invisible to supernatural prying eyes but there was nothing to guard against someone from *physically* getting to her, provided they knew where to go.

He took off into the cavern with Lazlo on his heels. Vampires at full speed were almost too fast for humans to see. If Benyamin was with humans, he would be moving at a much slower pace. Xabier and Lazlo had a head start but not much time to work. Deeper and deeper, Xabier led the way underground through a maze of natural tunnels and caves. Finally, they came to a halt at a large boulder.

Xabier paused. His heart was breaking over what he was about to do. He closed his eyes and shook his head. Leaning on the large rock, he pressed his forehead to it and whispered, "I'm so sorry."

With that, he shoved the boulder to the side and peered into the inky blackness. The musty odor of underground filled their nostrils. The cave hadn't been filled with fresh air in centuries. Xabier's ring cast a glow, enabling them both to see as Xabier grabbed a lantern off a ledge on the wall to his right and lit the candles inside. He handed it to Lazlo, who held it up and looked around the room.

"My god!" he said under his breath.

They were staring at what amounted to a shrine of witchcraft. Crates of handwritten scrolls, journals, and books lined one wall. The other wall boasted a series of heavy, makeshift, wooden shelves. The shelves were packed with everything, from ceramic and clay jars containing animal and human blood to bones of all shapes and sizes, from mixed potions and powders to the ashes of various animals, herbs, and woods. More ceramic and clay jars were filled to their brims with jewelry, clothing, masks, chalices, even daggers and knives.

"You carried this all by yourself?" Lazlo asked.

Xabier shrugged. "It wasn't so bad, once I found a horse to pull the wagon."

He stepped to the back of the cave where a simple wooden coffin lay covered by a heavy purple drape. Several pieces of ornate jewelry lay atop the drape. Xabier placed a hand gently on top of the coffin. He shook his head, hesitating to disturb his friend any more than they already had.

Turning to Lazlo, he asked, "Do you think…?"

"I think we have no time," Lazlo said, placing a hand on Xabier's forearm. "This isn't your fault. We have to get her out of here."

For the first time since he began investigating the supernatural coalition, Xabier wished he'd had Nico with him. Getting Wynnifrea to safety would be a question of minutes. His friend would be able to orb every piece out of the cave without any danger of being intercepted. Lazlo mentioned that hours before, but Xabier rejected the thought. Nico was a powder keg of pent up aggression. His essence, dark and uncontrollable, was pushing him dangerously close to the abyss. Azazel's involvement put them all at risk, but Nico was almost suicidal in his desire to avenge Stephanie's death. He wasn't ready to face the archangel again, but he didn't seem to care. Xabier knew, putting his friend in Azazel's path would end in disaster, but by *not* calling him in, he was putting another friend at risk.

"Okay. Let's move."

Lazlo froze, his head tilting to one side. Xabier could see his jaw muscles clench in the dim lighting. He knew what it meant, and his mind raced to figure out their options. He came up empty. The only choice they had was to stand and fight.

Xabier heard a scuffle outside the entrance to their little side cave. He took a defensive stance, wondering if today would be his last. He could think of no better way to die than defending a friend, yet he hated the idea of going into battle knowing he had no chance of success.

"Brother!"

The voice came from outside the cave. It was Benyamin. Even after centuries, the eldest of the Maccabee siblings carried a refined and dignified authority. Even Lazlo reacted to the sound of his brother's voice.

Benyamin stepped into view at the entrance. He scanned the room. Seeing his brother tensed and ready to attack, he held up a hand.

"Please, brother. I do not wish to fight."

"No," Lazlo spat. "You wish to set me against our father once again."

Benyamin sighed. "You are far too short-sighted, Laz. Please join me. This does not have to end badly for anyone."

Xabier, seeing the two brothers engaged with one another, took the opportunity to slide to his right, flanking the elder Maccabee. Lazlo's face was a picture of rage, which became more and more menacing the more Benyamin tried to convince him. Xabier knew it was just a matter of time before Lazlo attacked. Benyamin had to know it as well.

Benyamin continued. "Do not make this harder than it has to be. We need not contend against one another."

"*You* contend against *me, Brother!*" Lazlo spat out the last word and strode toward Benyamin until just three feet separated them. "Shall we get on with it then?"

ﬡ ﾑ ﾝ ﾈ ﾁ

"Come on, dammit. Answer the phone."

Nico let the phone drop onto the bar and picked up his third scotch. He sipped it and shook his head, trying to piece together the brief conversations he'd had with Xabier over the past few weeks, the vague texts, and the long periods of silence. Nico was pissed. They were supposed to be friends. He was going through a lot of things, things a best friend should be around to help with. What was Xabier going through that he couldn't share with Nico? He didn't know what was worse, not being there for a friend, or not letting a friend be there.

He downed his drink and signaled Frank for another. Frank, as he was becoming accustomed to doing, poured the drink and left the bottle out for Nico.

"Looks like that kinda night," he said with a sympathetic smile. "He placed a menu in front of Nico and said, "You need to eat something."

Frank had terrific instincts. Nico hadn't eaten since the night before, when he had completely melted down over Tatiana's revelation. The lies, the deceit, the manipulation…She'd been quick to tell him her original intent had been to get close to him so she could push him toward darkness, but then she'd developed real feelings for him, which overpowered her loyalty to the mission. She had fallen in love with him.

It didn't matter. At that point, his heart was so filled with anger and resentment, nothing she said could overshadow his bitterness. He was too beaten down and miserable to think clearly. Rather than explode outward, which was what every instinct in his body screamed for, Nico simply told her to leave. To her credit, Tatiana was understanding and gave him his space.

Now he was alone. The one person who had been there throughout the past few weeks, who had filled the void left by Nico's absentee friends, turned out to be nothing more than a plant, a phony, who wanted only to manipulate his emotions. And what *about* that? What does one do when everyone is deceitful and no one is worthy?

"You are predictable, Nico. You might seek to remedy that."

Nico's heart skipped a beat and fear coursed through his veins as the eerie monotone droned from behind him. Just as quickly, his fear turned to wrath, and he had to struggle to regain his calm. He wasn't sure what the psychotic archangel had up his sleeve. Azazel's previous suggestion, that somehow, they could make peace and work together, seemed suspect, to say the least. It was far more likely the whole thing was some elaborate trick to toy with him before exacting vengeance. In any case, Nico was not about to give him the satisfaction of watching him squirm.

"Twice in one week?" he said, wrinkling his forehead. "To what do I owe the honor?"

Azazel's eyes flashed silver but not in their usual menacing way. Nico had always assumed that brilliant metallic flash was a signal of the archangel's anger. Perhaps it signaled other emotional reactions, including amusement.

"If I am not mistaken, "Azazel said, "I left you with a proposition."

Nico chuckled. "Yeah, you suggested two mortal enemies could somehow become best friends, or something like that."

Azazel smiled, pushing his long dark hair out of his face. He took the bar stool next to Nico and sat down. Frank set a coaster in front of him and held a rocks glass up. Azazel nodded and Frank poured from Nico's bottle. He took a small sip, narrowed his eyes as he considered the taste.

"Not the worst."

Nico sniffed. "Glad you approve."

Azazel chuckled, showing Nico yet another aspect of his personality he hadn't seen before. "You know, Nico, I was serious when I suggested we do not have to be enemies."

Nico blew out a long, slow breath. "What is it you want from me?"

"You think rulers rule alone? You think armies are led by lone commanders?" Azazel sipped again from his glass. "Nico, I am going to tell you something I doubt anyone else has told you. You *have* to choose a side."

Nico laughed. "Of course, I do. Why wouldn't I join forces with the one being in the universe who has made it abundantly clear he wants to peel my skin off and roast my organs while I'm still alive?"

Azazel let out a chuckle. "What if I told you, everyone you have lost could be restored to you?"

Nico stared at him in disbelief. From the moment Dominick was found dead, his primary concern had been to find a way to bring him back. Xabier knew of no way to resurrect a corpse. Zha'riel explained to him that only archangels possessed the power of resurrection, and no angel in Heaven would consider bringing Dominick back to life. When Stephanie was taken, Nico, stricken with grief, called out to the darkness for Lucifer to help, but he was never answered.

"He never even gave you the choice, did he?" Azazel asked. "And isn't that all you really wanted?"

It wasn't untrue. Lucifer had never asked Nico what he wanted. He'd just laid out the consequences in a way that made it impossible to choose without being selfish and soulless. It was a manipulation, no different than all the rest of the manipulations Nico's so-called friends had put him through.

The thought that Lucifer could actually be his friend, sickened Nico a little. He couldn't imagine being friends with the source of all evil in the universe. He downed the rest of his scotch and poured himself another. He wondered how it was that the supernatural world could be so convoluted, the bad guys seemed like good guys, while the good guys acted like tin-pot dictators, threatening those weaker than them. Nico wondered how he was sitting in a bar having drinks with the monster who had killed his girlfriend.

"I'm right, aren't I?"

Nico could see Azazel wasn't bragging. He wasn't dredging up the past to cause him pain. He was simply stating facts. Lucifer never offered, and Heaven didn't care.

"If you ask, *I* will do it." Azazel put a hand on Nico' shoulder. "Lucifer didn't lie about the consequences, but you never had the opportunity to choose, so I will offer you that choice now, as a show of good faith."

Words failed Nico. Thoughts of seeing Dominick and Stephanie alive and well flooded his mind. It was a warm feeling, but one he knew he could never act upon. As much as he wanted to see his loved ones again, he didn't want to visit the same pain upon others that he felt every day. That he now had the choice at least gave him a sense of power. It was something he *could* decide to do for himself. Only he couldn't.

"Heaven would descend on me if they found out I did something like that."

"Understand, Nico," Azazel insisted. "It doesn't matter in which direction you turn. *Both* Heaven and Hell want you for their own ends. Just look at how they manipulated you with Tatiana."

It stung, but it didn't sway Nico. "And *you* don't?"

"Of course, I do," Azazel said, "but I am the only one offering you the thing you want most of all."

"You think the thing I want most of all is to resurrect dead loved ones?"

"Of course not." Azazel waved a lazy finger. "I know you see the error in that path. You are not me. You could never live with the guilt of destroying innocent life." He nodded in understanding. "What I am offering is far more important."

"I can't wait to hear this." Nico downed another drink. "What exactly are you offering?"

"Complete and total freedom to live as you choose."

Silence hung in the air between them. Azazel sat with the look of a man who'd just laid down a royal flush. Nico flicked his eyes from the ice in his glass to Azazel's eyes. He couldn't hold the archangel's gaze for long. It felt too much like Azazel could read into his soul.

"You cannot continue to live as you have been." Azazel pursed his lips and leaned with his elbows on the bar. "Heaven will destroy you if you continue to kill. Lucifer will eventually make demands. Nico, you need friends if you intend to stand against them all. You will need more than a single angel and a loyal vampire."

"You say complete and total freedom," Nico replied. "But you will also make demands."

"I would only require that you stand with me against my enemies." Azazel smiled. "It shouldn't be too hard, seeing as my enemies happen to be yours as well."

It was a dubious proposition, but Nico had problems greater than he could handle. His were supernatural problems, and they extended beyond those manifesting themselves physically in his body. He had the most powerful beings in existence preparing to squash him the moment they realized he wasn't on their side.

"Okay," Azazel continued. "I am prepared to accept that you didn't know what you were doing when Mattaeus coaxed you into his little experiment."

"Experiment?" Nico frowned.

Azazel tilted his head, his forehead puckered. "Did no one tell you?"

Nico felt a burning sensation radiate from the center of his chest. Azazel could very well be playing a game, but something in the archangel's surprised expression told him that was unlikely. With multiple groups vying for his loyalty, he couldn't understand why one of them hadn't stepped forward with explanations and answers. Instead, information pertinent to his life, his survival, was being withheld. It was par for the course at that point, but Nico was getting closer and closer to throwing in the towel and telling all of them to get lost.

"You are the first of your kind," Azazel said, swirling the scotch in his glass and watching as it ran down the sides. "It had become a joke, Mattaeus' idea to combine the essences of good and evil. He believed two opposing essences could exist inside one person. It was insane...until you."

Azazel poured another round for them both, and they each took a sip, sitting in silence as the seconds ticked away. Nico wondered how a homicidal psychopath such as Azazel could seem so normal. The animosity between them should have kept them at each other's throats, but somehow, they were two regular guys talking at the bar.

Azazel continued. "Nico, you possess the essence of my son. What you don't understand is that one's essence is *visible* in the supernatural world." He sat up straighter and gestured to his own body. "What you see here is a physical vessel. Humans are focused on that because they have forgotten how to see past the physical. When other angels, or even demons, look at me, they see my true form."

"Which is what?"

Azazel sniffed. "Something far greater than this, I will tell you that much."

Nico frowned. "Are you saying when you look at me, you see Sansata?"

"Not purely," Azazel said in a near-whisper. "Remember, you now have *three* essences within you, but I do see my son in you."

"And because of that, you don't want to kill me anymore?"

Azazel shook his head. "What I want…is to help you."

Nico laughed. "Oh, my God." He looked at Azazel's eyes, seeing them flash brilliant silver. "You're serious."

"Nico, the truth is, you are an addict. You don't know it yet, but you are. That power inside you? It was never designed for the human psyche. The human body *can* change and the brain *can* adapt to contain it, but the pressure builds and must be released. The compulsion to kill is weak right now, but it will only grow stronger, and the paradox you find yourself in is this: The more you kill, the stronger the next urge is, just like a drug."

Nico scratched his chin. "I can just stop now, while the urge is weak then."

Azazel chuckles. "You can try. Perhaps you will even succeed, but too many have a vested interest in you. They will push you and you will crack, but even if you do not, one day, when you least expect it, you will snap. On that day, the pressure will be so immense, you will inflict damage unlike anything you have ever imagined possible, to anyone unfortunate enough to be in the vicinity, innocents and deserving alike." The archangel gripped Nico's shoulder and tilted his head. His eyes held the faintest hint of white glow. "Now, wouldn't you rather channel that destructive impulse toward those more deserving?"

Chapter 19

Benyamin's eyes flicked to the cave entrance and he leaned his head forward. "*Please*, brother," he begged. "Do not stand against us."

"Us?" Lazlo laughed. "Who is this us?

"Enough is enough."

Benyamin's head snapped up as a figure entered the cave, followed by another. Xabier instantly recognized most of them. He knew Jargis, the vetala, who led the way. He was followed by Yarrid, a shapeshifter, currently in the form of a tall, muscular man with brooding eyes. Shapeshifters only had to touch another person to assume their shape. The humans were usually killed to preserve their identity. The transition from one form to another always left a disgusting pile of discarded skin, sort of like a snake molting, only much messier.

Lazlo laughed as the group filed in one by one. "Some crew you've assembled, brother. It looks like you've scraped the bottom of the barrel this time. Perhaps after I dispatch with these fools, you and I will have a go."

Xabier stood at the ready. He heard a sound behind him and whirled around to face a shadowy figure.

"Ktulis?" he asked. "How did you get mixed up in this?"

Ktulis was a wraith, a shadow person. Wraiths lived in the shadows, at the periphery of human life. They drew all their power from the darkness, but they were not helpless in daylight. By instinct, they moved just outside the peripheral vision of humans, making them seem invisible. When caught on camera, they appeared to walk just like any other person. Their brains enabled them to choose the perfect path to leave them virtually unnoticed. Ktulis was once a friend of Xabier's. The look in his eyes told Xabier their friendship was probably over.

"I could ask you the same thing." Ktulis cast an ominous stare at him. "Have you come to face all the species you betrayed?"

Xabier's secret was out. He was likely the most hated supernatural creature on the planet. He always knew this day would come. He wished now, more than ever, that he'd called Nico to help them. His hands went to his waistband, where he'd secured his silver daggers. At least he came prepared.

"Oh, you brought the whores along," Lazlo prattled as two females entered the cave. "Hello, ladies. Perhaps we can have a bit of fun after I take care of your pathetic little gang."

Xabier recognized Angela Bracci and Genevieve. Angela was a succubus. The succubae were known in the supernatural world for their stunning beauty. They survived by tricking men into sexual encounters, after which they plunged a tubular pronged tongue down the throat of their victims, sucking all their inner organs out and leaving the bodies empty shells. Sirens don't feed on humans, an unusual thing in the supernatural world. Their bodies feed normally, but they have a psychological impulse to lure men into sexual encounters and then, once they hook their prey using their sexual prowess, they use the power of suggestion to entice them. Men, once under the siren's influence, will do anything to please the siren. They are given increasingly dangerous suggestions, until the victim is killed, often by their own hand.

When the next figure stepped into the cave, Xabier recognized the lanky form with the long, gaunt face. He had no idea how Benyamin managed to track down the wendigos. The cannibalistic clan kept far from view, straying out only during late evening hours, when they hunted. They hated all other life forms, and lived under the code that anyone who got too close had to be killed and eaten.

Lazlo chortled at the sight of the gangly cannibal. "Daggnat? Is that you? You stoop to join with these half-wits?"

"My people are nearly extinct," Daggnat replied in his gravelly voice. "I do what I have to."

"You're enthusiasm is contagious," Lazlo replied with a wide grin. "Allow me to suggest you turn around and save yourself. Your position is about to become untenable."

Benyamin faced Lazlo. "Brother, I beg you, don't make this a fight. You are overmatched."

Lazlo smiled. "Is that right?"

He looked over Benyamin's shoulder and his eyes widened. His brother caught the subtle look and turned to see what was there. Lazlo moved like lightning, snapping Benyamin's neck and flinging him to the side.

Xabier's mouth dropped open as Lazlo stood defiantly in the middle of the underground room. He had seen Lazlo's ruthless nature on countless occasions, but never had he seen Lazlo attack his own family with such gusto and fervor, first Riva, back in Arizona, and then his oldest brother, Benyamin, both mere hours apart.

Lazlo, his head bowed, eyes flicking from one supernatural creature to the next, stood in a ready posture. The grin on his face said everything Xabier needed to know. He gripped the silver daggers in his hands and readied himself, waiting for Lazlo's cue.

Lazlo smiled. His maniacal gaze held back anyone who thought about making the first move against him. "Well," he said. "Now that my loquacious sibling is resting peacefully, shall we continue this conversation affray?"

Without waiting for an answer, Lazlo dashed through the crowd of supernatural creatures to Daggnat, the wendigo, who never saw the attack coming. Xabier watched as Lazlo's hand tore into the tall creature's chest. Dagnat's eyes bulged as he realized Lazlo's fingers had a grip on his heart. Lazlo smiled as he twisted his hand. Daggnat screamed. It was the last sound he would ever make. Lalzo met his eyes as he ripped the heart from Daggnat's chest.

He didn't stop to gloat. Lunging toward Yarrid, his hand shot out once again, aiming for his chest. Yarrid was quicker than Daggnat, pivoting on his heel and driving his fist into Lazlo's stomach. Lazlo doubled over but quickly recovered, grabbing Yarrid's arm and flinging the shape-shifter into the jagged cavern wall. Yarrid fell to the ground, dazed. Jargis darted behind Lazlo, grasping his head. He lost his grip in an instant when Lazlo spun away, the dagger in his hand slashing across the vetala's chest, slicing him almost down to the bone.

It was nowhere near as serious a wound as it would have been for a human; vetala healed quickly, but it hurt like hell. Jargis screamed, baring his fangs and lunging for Lazlo. One bite and Lazlo would be incapacitated within seconds. Vetala produced paralyzing venom that rendered the victim unconscious and kept them weak even after they awoke. Lazlo jabbed with the dagger but Jargis blocked with his arm and moved to bite Lazlo's neck. Just before the teeth sank in, Lazlo spun, bringing his left hand up to Jargis' neck. He chopped hard against the carotid artery and Jargis went down, stunned.

When Lazlo made his move on Daggnat, the whole room froze. It was a common event in close combat, when a group wasn't used to fighting alongside one another. Unfamiliar teammates often equals slower reaction times. Xabier didn't have that issue. While everyone was riveted on Lazlo's actions, Xabier was moving. The silver dagger in his left hand found a home deep in Ktulis' chest, missing his heart by inches. Ktulis was that close to death. A last second flinch made all the difference, but he wasn't out of trouble. Silver wreaked havoc on a wraith, even when it wasn't fatal. Xabier punched several additional holes in Ktulis' torso in rapid-fire succession. None of his strikes pierced the heart, but Ktulis went down hard.

Genevieve had her own silver blade, and lunged toward Lazlo. Xabier saw, and moved with lightning speed across the room, just in time to jam one of his daggers into her neck. When he yanked it out, blood spurted all over his arm as she fell to her knees. He was about to finish the job and remove her head when her friend, Angela, jabbed her own silver knife into his side.

Xabier grunted and gritted his teeth as the silver flooded his bloodstream. He felt the familiar burning sensation, instantly recalling his near-death experience Seir's hands all those months ago. Had he been facing the other way, Angela's blade would have pierced his heart, ending his life in a matter of minutes. Instead, he suffered a very painful wound. He slashed with his right hand, the long, thin dagger cutting halfway through Angela's neck. She too, crumpled to the ground.

Before Lazlo could acknowledge Xabier, the room swarmed with supernatural creatures. Xabier and Lazlo didn't stop to think about it. They knew how to fight against larger numbers. They waded into the fray, using their vampire quickness to slash from one end of the room to another. Xabier plunged his silver daggers into the hearts of everyone he got close to, darting out of reach before anyone could get their hands on him. Lazlo chose to fight hand-to-hand, ripping out heart after heart as he moved through the crowd of ill-prepared creatures.

Bodies began to pile up, and the crowd thinned to the point some decided enough was enough, and escaped through the cave entrance. Covered in blood and carried by their adrenaline, Xabier and Lazlo fought them all the way out the mouth of the underground cavern, and into the main tunnel. They caught up to a couple stragglers and ended their lives for the sheer pleasure of it.

Xabier, gasping from the exertion, grinned at Lazlo who held up the heart of the last vetala he killed and grinned back at him. The whole scene had lasted a matter of minutes, but the flurry of mortal combat had taken its toll. Both vampires suffered from silver-bladed stab wounds. They both had silver searing through their veins and, as the adrenaline backed off, the effects of the silver began to grip them. They rested, waiting for the silver to pass through their system. Their wounds would heal, but not until the silver was gone.

Lazlo closed his eyes. "Just like old times, Xabier."

Xabier was so exhausted he couldn't speak. He just nodded and grinned weakly. But then he frowned and peered into the inky blackness as a figure took shape in front of them.

"Maybe not *just* like old times," came the familiar voice.

Xabier gasped. "Nayra?"

Before the witch could respond, he lunged, his vamp-speed closing the distance in a split-second. Lazlo, reacting to Xabier's lead, didn't hesitate. He was on his feet in an instant, joining the attack. Just as Xabier's fangs exposed and he was about to sink his teeth into Nayra's slim neck, a piercing sound filled his ears and dropped him to his knees. His hands went to his ears, trying to block the sound, but he knew it was futile.

Xabier heard Lazlo's cries of anguish and knew they were doomed. Nayra stood over the two writhing vampires and shook her head.

"Abominations," she said. "I should rid the world of you both right now."

"You will do nothing of the sort, witch."

It was another familiar voice. Xabier would have looked up to see who it was, but the sound kept him curled in a ball, his arms and hands doing their best to cover his ears and head. It didn't matter. The voice spoke again and this time it was right in his ear.

"We meet again, *Fang*."

Seir.

Azazel's demon finally found him. The last time they met, Seir had him seconds from death. Now, with his head about to explode from the pressure of the maddening sound, Xabier almost wished Seir would just end it all for him.

"Don't worry, Fang," Seir hissed into his ear. "I'm here to save your pathetic hide. You will live to see tomorrow."

Xabier felt a searing burn around his right wrist and his arm was jerked down and behind him. His left arm received the same treatment. He felt a rope wrap around both wrists and jerk tight. His skin burned as though acid was eating through it.

Vervain.

Seir chuckled. "Vervain rope with a little silver thread running through it."

He trussed Xabier's ankles so that they were connected to the ropes binding his wrists. Any move Xabier made only served to tighten the knots. Seir left him and tied Lazlo. After, he signaled to Nayra, and the piercing sound ceased. Xabier felt instant relief, but soon endured the full effects of the vervain and silver. Vervain was like a tranquilizer to a vampire, and on top of the burning pain, the strength sapped from his body.

Seir came back to Xabier and kicked him hard in the stomach. He picked Xabier up and slammed him against the wall of the cave repeatedly, flinging him from one of the tunnel to the other. He pulled several slim wooden stakes from a duffel bag. Without hesitation, he drove one deep into Xabier's shoulder, just inches above his heart. A stake to the heart would kill Xabier within seconds, but this wound was just extremely painful.

"You're a bloody coward!" Lazlo spat. "Having a witch do your wet work."

Seir's eyes glowed red as he turned to face Lazlo. "Well, well, well. Lazlo Macabbee. An *original* vampire." He held a stake in front of Lazlo's eyes. "I've heard of you. I admire your work. I would think you'd appreciate the pain I'm causing your...*friend*, is it?"

Lazlo bared his fangs. "Untie me and we'll see how appreciative I am, *demon.*"

Seir drove the stake into Lazlo's heart and watched as Lazlo's eyes bulged. Xabier knew the wooden stake wouldn't kill Lazlo. The original vampire family couldn't be killed as easily as their descendants, but Lazlo wasn't immune to the effects of wood puncturing his heart. He gasped and coughed, blood sputtering from his mouth. He strained against the vervain ropes as his body reacted to the wood particles now running through his blood. His face grew ash-gray and veins appeared from his neck and ran all the way to the top of his head. After several seconds, Lazlo went limp.

The red-eyed demon turned back to Xabier. "Now," he said, pulling another stake. "Where were we?"

Nayra passed by them. "We have more important things to do, demon."

Seir's red eyes flashed and for a second, Xabier though he might take the witch's head off. Instead, he calmed himself and shook his head with a grin. "She's right." With that he jammed several more stakes into Xabier's torso, front and back, before punching him several times in the face and stomach. He left Xabier, barely conscious, on the floor of the tunnel next to Lazlo.

Through his pain, Xabier listened to them taking Wynnifrea's possessions out of her tomb. It made him sick that he was powerless to stop them. He strained against his bindings, but he was far too weak to make any real effort. Moments later, Seir came out and stood over him.

"Well, Fang, it looks like our fun is over for today." He knelt close. "See you soon."

ᛒ ᛅ ᛋ ᛩ ᚷ

"I've waited for this day for a very long time."

Shiva, the Hindu "Destroyer God," stood with muscles tensed. Azazel let his arms drop loosely at his sides as he struggled to maintain his patience among the ruins of the great temple at Nalanda Mahavihara. The massive, twenty-seven-year-old stone structure had stood the test of time well and the Hindu deities could do a lot worse for their earthly gathering site. Azazel ran a hand along the surface of a twenty-foot statue of one of the lesser-known Hindu warrior gods. The face of the carving looked vaguely familiar to Azazel. He let his eyes roam over the musty room before leaning on a stone altar adorned with a multitude of intricate carvings along the sides and base.

"Well, Shiva," Azazel replied with a grim smile. "Here we are, but I am not here to fight you. I am here for a peaceful visit."

Azazel knew he wanted nothing more than to unleash everything he had on the one who had soiled his wife, and Azazel half-wished he would just get on with it. He couldn't remember a time when he didn't want to kill Shiva. The arrogant pseudo-god refused to let Parvati go even though he didn't really love her and could no longer stand the sight of her. Of course, Azazel, as the primary reason for those feelings, tried to restrain his own contempt. Instead, he focused on the reason he'd asked for the meeting with the three Hindu gods.

"An interesting turn of events," Shiva said. "The homicidal maniac suddenly turns peaceful."

"He has become a leader," Parvati said proudly, drawing Shiva's ire-filled stare.

Azazel smiled at her and turned to Brahma. "Despite your impetuous partner's disdain for me, I think we can be of mutual benefit to one another. Is it not time to expand your holdings?"

Brahma was the leader of the Hindu gods. He was the "Creator God," and he looked the part. He flipped his long, braid over his shoulder, and it fell to the small of his back. His deep-set, dark brown eyes flicked from Shiva to Parvati, and back to Azazel as he stood tall, midway up a flight of forty steps, cut into the stone. His black eyebrows stood out against his dark brown skin, making the skeptical furrow of his brow even more pronounced. He wore a crown of pure gold which framed heavy, purple fabric. The crown was intricately carved and adorned with massive rubies and emeralds. Royal robes, purple and white completed Shiva's ensemble. He knew how to play the part.

"We have lived in relative peace for centuries," he said to Azazel. "I don't see why we would choose to upset that peace now."

Vishnu, from his perch higher up the stone staircase, agreed. "Too, even with you and your considerable power, we simply do not have the numbers."

Azazel sighed. *Coward.* Of course, the "Preserver God" would opt for the status quo. Vishnu was dressed similarly to Brahma, in robes and a crown, but his face always had a bluish tint to it, which Azazel found disconcerting, and he always wore heavy gold necklaces…*many* heavy gold necklaces. It was ridiculous. No wonder this clown car only managed to scrape together the tiniest morsel of the Earth. As much as he hated to admit it, Shiva was the only one of them with any real balls. If the Parvati situation wasn't such a blasted mess, Azazel was fairly certain the two of them would see eye to eye on almost everything.

Of course, nothing was ever that simple.

Shiva glared daggers at Azazel, his dark eyes filled with hate. "You think you can entice us into handing over our thrones? To *you*?"

Azazel resisted his initial impulse to reach through Shiva's chest and pull out his spine. If Azazel wanted their ridiculous throne, he would just take it from them. Who were they kidding? It wasn't like they'd ever been truly threatened. They were lucky the rest of the factions chose peace, otherwise these goofs would have ultimately been crushed. That they survived, and held their morsel of land, blinded them, in Azazel's opinion, to reality.

They were bold and fearless, which was what Azazel needed. They also had a massive inferiority complex. Why else would they grow a human population of over a billion people? One sixth of the world's population in such a small area was insane, but that was how the three Hindus played their game. While they did not want to fight a war they could not win, they understood they could spread their influence without ever exerting military force. They grew a population of devout followers, who spread out past the boundaries of the nations to which they belonged.

"I don't want you to hand over anything," Azazel said. "What I want is to join you. Your plan is working, but it has not gone unnoticed. How long will it be before the Amatsu push your people back? How long before they see through your façade of peaceful coexistence?"

Azazel knew the Hindus were already in trouble. Allah and Muhammad, the most unhinged of all who secured land in the treaty, had grown a massive population of true believers, willing to die, and take as many of their enemies with them as possible. They employed a similar model in that they sent out their followers to spread the religion, but where Hindus sought to spread by expanding from their center, India, the Muslims planted their people all over the world and grew individual culture centers. Their religion spread, and sympathizers, especially in the west, advocated for them when things got rough. Pretty soon, there was enough of a population to affect change, and the cycle continued. What started as a small thing, buried within the Jewish and Persian cultures, grew into a monumental powerbase, giving Allah great power and influence. The Hindus coveted that power and influence.

"What is it that you three want more than anything else?" Azazel asked.

Brahma didn't hesitate. "We want the Middle East and the East."

Azazel chuckled. "You think too small, my old friend."

Shiva's eyes narrow. "*You* wish to settle old scores."

It wasn't a question. Azazel had a long history of settling old scores. It should have been obvious he would want to do so. However, Azazel had even bigger plans.

"More like a new one," Azazel shrugged. "Look, your model works, just not fast enough. Islam is knocking on your door."

"They would argue they never signed that treaty."

Azazel glared at Vishnu. "So, will you allow them to take from you what you fought so hard to protect?"

Shiva, for all his bluster, saw where Azazel was headed. "And what do you propose? Shall we descend upon the humans to push them back?"

Vishnu shook his head. "That would bring Heaven down on all of us."

Azazel held up a finger. "Precisely. What we need is an army, on the ground, which would secure our victory."

"You have such an army?" Brahma asked, and Azazel knew he had him hooked.

He smiled. "What I have is the largest coalition of supernatural species ever assembled. And pretty soon, I will have the most powerful witch on the planet at my beck and call." He folded his arms across his chest and looked at the nails of his right hand. "So, you see…I am prepared to strike a deal."

Shiva shook his head. "There is no deal to be struck. We will handle *our* problems *our* way. We don't need Lucifer's outcast to steer us through trouble. Look at the mess you're already in. I'm surprised you even survived." He glanced at Parvati, who sat in silence, off to one side. "I wish you hadn't."

Azazel had enough. He said what he had come to say. His cards were on the table. Theirs were on the table as well, whether they realized it or not. The one thing they absolutely could not afford was for Azazel to strike his deal with the Muslims. If he really had the army he claimed, no one would be able to stand against him. The Hindus knew Azazel was a game changer. Even without the supernatural army, he was formidable. With a coalition of supernatural creatures affecting change on Earth without bringing Heaven down on them, they would rule the Eastern Hemisphere. Why should he continue to listen to Shiva's petulant comments?

"Shiva," he said. "Perhaps you and I need to settle our differences once and for all."

"Perhaps we should."

Shiva stretched out his hand without warning and a clap of thunder sounded. Azazel felt the force of the blow in the center of his chest and he was knocked clean off his feet, flying twenty feet across the room and slamming into the wall behind him. The impact shook the ancient building. Azazel had known the blow would come and he'd chosen to let it happen, though he didn't realize how hard the Hindu Warrior God could hit. The blow felt like a jackhammer and the pain radiated out from the middle of his chest.

"This is ridiculous," Vishnu said, stepping between the two, but Shiva pushed him aside.

"This does not concern you."

Azazel picked himself up and wiped the dust from his robes. He strode back to where Shiva was waiting. Shiva didn't hesitate, stretching out his hand once again. This time, Azazel didn't stand there and take it. When Shiva's hand extended, Azazel grabbed it and pulled Shiva toward him, driving his own hand into Shiva's chest. Shiva screamed in pain as Azazel unleashed violet-hued bursts of electrical energy. Holding Shiva off the ground, Azazel watched his eyes as his entire body was enveloped in torment.

Shiva's screams were bloodcurdling. Azazel chuckled and tossed his limp body aside. It took Shiva several moments to recover enough to stand, but when he did, he raised both hands above his head. Without waiting to see what it was Shiva had in store, Azazel flicked his right hand and Shiva's neck snapped, and he collapsed to the ground.

He stood over Shiva's lifeless body. "Typical." He looked over at Brahma. "When he awakes, tell him to never let his guard down. There is no excuse for an angel to have his neck snapped." He looked at Vishnu and Brahma. "Where does this leave us?"

"Obviously," Brahma said, "we must consult with our brother." He glanced at Vishnu who shrugged his consent. "But I think we can work with you."

"Excellent," Azazel said. He straightened his robes and prepared to leave. "I will be in touch." He was about to orb out when he saw the proud look on Parvati's face. "There is one other thing," he said. "Think of it as a non-negotiable gesture of good will."

Brahma frowned skeptically and hesitated for a beat. "Yes?"

"I want Parvati.

Chapter 20

"How could you allow that to happen?"
"I'm sorry. It just…happened."

Abdiel slammed his hand on the giant table and swept the stack of documents off in one swift motion. His dark eyes flashed ominous red in the dim lighting. He closed his eyes and struggled to regain control of his breathing. He hated that he just lost control in front of a subordinate. It made him want to smash something.

As a general in Lucifer's army, many of his demon charges failed him from time to time. Abdiel was known throughout the ranks as a strict disciplinarian. No one wanted to report failure to him and he always got results. His teams always outperformed their peers. Now, Abdiel was responsible for all operations personal to Lucifer, and there was nothing closer to Lucifer than influencing Nico Scarlatti.

He glared at Tatiana. He wanted nothing more than to string her up and make an example out of her, but he couldn't do that. *She* knew it too. The fear she was demonstrating had nothing to do with anticipation of Abdiel's punishment. Unlike the rest of the Dark Army, Tatiana was untouchable. Her punishment would come from Lucifer himself. That was Abdiel's only leverage.

"It did not just *happen*," he snapped. "Tell me Tatiana, how did he… "figure it out," as you say?"

"I don't know, I…I just don't know." She shook her head. Tears filled her eyes, threatening to spill out onto her cheeks which were already rosy from previous bouts of crying. "He's going to crack and we'll lose him forever."

Abdiel closed his eyes and shook his head. "This is pathetic, Tatiana. You are like a teen-age human. Where is your fortitude? Or did you lose it the same night you jumped into bed with your target?"

She lowered her eyes. "That is not fair, Abdiel, I…"

"*PRINCE!*" Abdiel slammed his hand down on the table. "You will address me appropriately!"

The command in his tone triggered the military training in her. Tatiana straightened her slumped posture and brought her eyes forward. "I apologize, Prince. I meant no disrespect."

Abdiel knew she wasn't lying. Tatiana was loyal and had great respect for her superiors. Her performance in the past was always exemplary. She was the very best there was at moving about in the human world, influencing events, and bending people, men and women both, to hers, and ultimately Lucifer's, will. Through the centuries, Tatiana had more direct influence on major events than anyone else in Lucifer's stable of specialists.

Now, Abdiel was supposed to believe suddenly she had grown incompetent? That she had *accidentally* broken cover? That, after centuries of veritable perfection in her craft, Tatiana had made a mistake? He was an understanding leader and willing to hear reasonable explanations. The goal was always to avoid future mistakes and to correct, if possible, current ones, but a professional like Tatiana would have never let her guard down. She would never have broken cover. She would never have done anything to compromise her mission. She would never fall in love with her mark.

Yet, Abdiel suspected she had, this time, and it was completely unacceptable. Lucifer was keeping a close watch on the Scarlatti situation. They were at a point where every second counted, and Lucifer wanted Nico influenced via multiple sources. He was even personally involved in that process, encouraging Nico to take his time and be sure he was doing the right thing. Nico's body and his psyche were working against that very process, acting against his desire to be good, affecting his judgment of right and wrong. Tatiana was supposed to be there to encourage him in what Heaven considered to be his failures. She was supposed to support him as he rebelled, intentionally or otherwise, against Heaven's decrees.

"You must fix this, Tatiana," Abdiel said. "You must be on the inside of this for us to be successful."

Tatiana sighed. "I know, but he hates me."

"Fix it."

Abdiel wasn't in the mood to hear all the reasons why the plan wouldn't work. All he wanted to hear was that things were back on track. He wanted to hear Tatiana say she would go back to Nico and make him change his mind.

"How can I fix this?" Tatiana asked, her voice shaking.

Abdiel pursed his lips. "I honestly don't care how you do it. If you were not...who you are, I would have already made an example of you. Now, since you broke your cover, and fell in love with the boy, I suggest you go back to him and make him love you back."

He could see the uncertainty in her jade-green eyes. Was she unconvinced Nico would ever listen to her again, or was she really prepared to go back and play the double agent? Abdiel was taking a risk sending her back in. She hadn't blown her cover entirely. Her revelation to Nico was that she was half angel, not where she came from or where her loyalties lie. She could go back and use her femininity to win his heart over. Nico was a man, after all, and in the thousands of years Tatiana had spent with the Dark Army, Abdiel knew of no man who had ever successfully to resisted.

"And if I cannot?"

Abdiel licked his bottom lip slowly. "Then you had better think of a better story than the nonsense you just spouted to me."

Ђ A Ʒ Ψ Ϛ

"Nothing?"

"Nothing at all."

Nayra and Benyamin were locked away in their secret headquarters in Ladakh, India. Thiksey Monastery was a massive structure, located approximately 18 kilometers from town of Leh. A masterpiece of monasteries at Ladakh region, Thiksey was initially built at Stakmo by Sherab Stangpo of Stod. However, Spon Paldan Sherab, the nephew of Sherab Zangpo, reconstructed the monastery in the year 1430 AD. The new monastery was situated on a hilltop to the north of Indus River. Thiksey is one of the finest examples of Ladakhi architecture.

The pair went through all Wynnifrea's possessions secured from the tomb, and found a treasure trove of Kharashuoa spells and techniques, but after three days of searching, they hadn't come across a single item related to the portal. They hadn't even found a reference to it. It was as though Wynnifrea had taken everything related to the portal and destroyed it, or hidden it elsewhere.

"I don't understand it," Benyamin said. "Witches *never* destroy their own work. There is *always* a loophole, *always* a way to reverse a spell or..."

"Or open a sealed box?" Nayra asked with a grim smile.

Her grey eyes were red from lack of sleep, but she was wide awake. The truth was, even without the portal information, the tomb of Wynnifrea provided a treasure trove of Kharashuoa teachings Nayra would spend the rest of her life unpacking and mastering. She would bring her new family back from the brink of extinction and their craft would once again maintain the balance between the natural and the supernatural. Of course, to do that, she would have to extricate herself from the tentacles of one of the most feared beings in existence. Until she figured out that all-important piece of the puzzle, it would serve her best to be a willing participant in the opening of the portal...*if* they could figure out how to do it.

Benyamin sighed. "How can there be nothing at all related to what had to be her greatest work?"

"Perhaps she didn't want it repeated. It took a great effort to get capture them. Witches have no reason to want creatures like that running free."

Nayra struggled with her commitment to opening the portal. It ran counter to everything she had ever been taught. She was not supposed to help these creatures. Her duty was to ensure they did not ravage humanity as they once did. Humans, with the help of Heaven, managed to incarcerate the most powerful of the supernatural, but then humanity turned its ire on *anyone* who exhibited supernatural abilities. Witches were out in the open in those days, and when the tide of public sentiment turned against them, many were taken completely by surprise. In the New World, they were burned at the stake or jailed. In Europe, they were hunted down and destroyed in gruesome ways.

For this reason, witches existed in solitude, or in close-knit covens, where they practiced their craft and spurned outsiders. Many continued to protect and defend humanity, but others refused, turning their backs on the race that sought to destroy them. The Kharashuoa suffered greatly under the Trials. They were the most powerful, but also the closest friends to humanity. They assumed the people would stand up for them. The people did not. Arrests were made based on mere *accusations* of witchcraft. People were tortured and killed who had nothing to do with the craft. No one wanted to be associated with an accused witch, and this often led them to make accusations against their neighbors in the hopes their accusations would insulate *them* from suspicion.

Now, Nayra had the opportunity to return witchcraft to the mainstream. It would be a long, arduous task, and she would require a measure of protection, especially while she mastered her craft. Azazel offered her that protection and what *he* thought was a wonderful opportunity to be a part of his kingdom. Nayra didn't care about his kingdom at all. What Nayra wanted was to become a Kharashuoa master and lead her adopted people out of the shadows. A partnership with the dark angel was a necessary means to an end, but if she couldn't open the box, and then the portal, her usefulness would come to an abrupt end.

Benyamin paced the floor. "We're missing something. I know it's here; I can feel it. We're just…missing it."

"I don't know where it could be." Nayra flipped through the pages of the grimoire she was holding and tossed onto the stack in front of her. "We've searched through every document, every trinket, every clay jar and urn. It's like she took the secret to her grave."

Benyamin frowned. His cold brown eyes widened in disbelief. His mouth dropped open and he shook his head. "Could it be that simple?"

"What?"

Benyamin strode toward the door. "Come with me."

Nayra followed him into the hall. They passed several Buddhist monks as they made their way down the outdoor stairway and towards the dwelling units at the base of the hill. They had been given a small, two-story building with two units upstairs and two more downstairs. Benyamin and Nayra each took one of the downstairs units. The two upstairs units were left unoccupied save for one item. When they opened the door to the upper unit, Benyamin led Nayra in and they stood in the center of the main room, looking at the final item retrieved from Wynnifrea's tomb.

Nayra's eyes widened as the realization struck her. She pointed a finger at it. "You mean…"

Benyamin shrugged. "We have no other alternative."

"We've already removed her from her resting place," Nayra said. "Now, you wish to disturb her remains?"

"Perhaps if we simply opened the coffin and looked," he suggested. "If it is with her, we should be able to see it."

Nayra closed her eyes and shook her head. "This is evil."

"We have to exhaust every possibility."

Nayra nodded, her reluctance etched in deep lines across her face. She felt sick, her stomach souring as she realized what they were about to do. It wasn't the disturbing of the dead that bothered her. She'd done that before, but they were about to disturb the remains of one of the most revered witches who ever lived. Some things were simply out of bounds…or they ought to be.

Benyamin took a breath and pulled one end of the coffin lid. The old nails broke easily under an ancient vampire's strength, and he lifted the top off. Nayra peered into the coffin, her eyes refusing to open at first. The mere act of looking upon the remains of such a great woman shamed her, but she finally managed to lift her eyelids.

"Oh," she said immediately. She pointed a tentative finger.

The ornate amulet, still adorning the neck of the great witch, was held by what appeared to be a tanned leather strap, or more accurately, several leather straps in a complex braid. The amulet was obscured by the bones of Wynnifrea's hands, which were folded together with the amulet tucked under them. It was as though she was clutching it, protecting it, even in death.

Benyamin held out a hand to Nayra. "I will handle this."

Nayra was relieved. She wasn't sure she could bring herself to reach down into the coffin and touch Wynnifrea. Benyamin had no such reservations. He reached in and gently removed the amulet, sliding it from under her fingers. He then slid the leather cord from under her skull. When he was done, he handed the amulet to Nayra and placed the lid back where it belonged. He would have to get some nails to reseal it. Then, they would have to find a permanent resting place for her.

Nayra studied the amulet in the light of the sun, glaring through the windows. The three rings contained carvings on both sides. Her lips moved as she read every word on every ring. Her eyes were then drawn to the centerpiece of the medallion, a perfectly smooth, quarter-inch, perfect-circle moonstone. She could see a thin outline of a pentagram with pink stones set at each of the five points. All of this was somehow *inside* the moonstone. She could think of no way even a master Kharashuoa witch could get one stone inside another, but she was looking at stunning work. Also inside the moonstone, was an etching which she was able to translate. She had been looking at the words for months at that point.

After several moments, she smiled and held it up for Benyamin to inspect. He turned the amulet over in his hands and shook his head. He looked at Nayra with questioning eyes. She smiled and nodded.

"Then what are we waiting for?"

They hurried back to their secure room at the top of the monastery. Benyamin unlocked the large safe in which they stored their more valuable items. He pulled out the sealed box and handed it to Nayra. She placed it in the center of the table and pulled out her translations from around the box. Her eyes bounced back and forth from the amulet to the paper as she scribbled on a notepad. She checked her notepad and then checked it again. Then, she checked her pronunciations. Finally, she looked up at Benyamin and smiled.

"I am ready."

She placed her hands over the box, keeping them a few inches above and closed her eyes as she mumbled a few chants, pulling chakra from the earth, feeling herself connecting to the common thread of life. When she opened her eyes, she was in a hypnotic state. Her voice was deep and throaty as she began the incantation.

"Ghalat imprison sunfo seecht krey seelet open mushrat karcha darghan yot pweret yuocha seegit ka kymr morenat zhost talome gome ur inchide cuma tobaha mhur wrendt sunfo rom deschnide ikandt!"

She opened her eyes and placed her fingers atop the box. She pushed to the right and the top slid easily. Benaymin stepped closer and they looked into the box together. It was the culmination of a long journey, undertaken together, yet they were aware the journey was just beginning.

Benyamin smiled at Nayra. "Well done. I'll alert the others."

$$Ƀ \; A \; \v{Z} \; \Psi \; Ç$$

"What a bloody shambles that was." Lazlo groaned as he tried to sit up.

"At least we took out some of theirs."

Still bound in the tunnel outside Wynnifrea's tomb, Lazlo and Xabier struggled to free themselves. The braided vervain ropes not only kept them bound, but sapped their strength as well, making them weaker than even a normal human. The wooden spikes Seir stuck into them caused searing pain. They struggled to sit up in the inky blackness, leaning against the cave walls for support. Xabier grimaced at the stinging sensation that was constantly with him as the vervain seared the skin around his wrists and the agony of the wood clouded his mind.

Xabier was mortified at the realization Wynnifrea's remains had been disturbed. He began to struggle violently against the rope, lurching from side to side, trying to draw enough strength to break them the way he would if he were at full strength. It didn't work and he found himself even more uncomfortable than before as the cords dug even deeper into his wrists and the wood shifted in his chest and back.

"Now what?" he asked Lazlo. "Can we rub them against a sharp stone?"

Lazlo shook his head. "I tried that, but the bastard wove metallic threads into the rope. I'm working on mine but it will take days."

Xabier closed his eyes. "I can call someone."

"You can reach your phone?"

"No. It's not that kind of call."

Xabier did not want to make the call but he could see no other way. He and Nico hadn't been on the best of terms with Zha'riel over the past few months. The angel's preoccupation with getting his exile lifted had turned him back into the stiff he had been when they'd first met. The current situation was so dire, Xabier had to bite the bullet and swallow a little pride.

"Zha'riel!" he shouted into the air.

There was no answer. He called out again. Nothing.

"Perhaps he's angry with you," Lazlo joked.

"Well, he needs to get over it. This is too important. Zha'riel! Come on, you damn stiff! Get off your cloud and get down here!"

"If you want my help, you might think about showing a little respect."

Zha'riel strolled down the tunnel and paused when he saw Lazlo sitting opposite Xabier. His face contorted into a disgusted frown. Xabier could see the recognition on his face. It wasn't much of a surprise as Lazlo was certain to have gotten the attention of Heaven just by virtue of his existence.

"So, you teamed up with one of the greatest abominations in history this time?"

"Just shut up and get us to Nico," Xabier snapped. "We don't have time for your righteousness today."

Nico was not thrilled with his best friend.

"Where the hell have you been?"

Xabier nodded and held up a hand. "I'm sorry I haven't been…"

"You know I've been trying to call you. I've texted, sent emails. I was just getting ready to resort to smoke signals."

"I know. I'm sorry."

"The whole point of a cell phone," Nico said in a dry tone, "is to be able to get in touch with someone."

He felt his hands shaking and the blood in his veins felt hot. He thought of the various phrases referring to "boiling blood" and felt like he understood why they were so popular. The pressure in his brain increased with every passing moment, and he knew he was nearing the end of whatever rope he was clinging to. The relief he felt at finally seeing his friend alive and well was overshadowed by the bitterness filling his heart. He felt dark, and, in spite of his boiling blood, he felt the familiar chill spread throughout his core.

Xabier sighed. "If you relax for a minute, I'll tell you the whole story."

Nico felt control slipping away. He didn't want to do it but he knew he had to get some help and he had to do it immediately, otherwise, he would lose focus, and he knew Xabier had something important to tell him. There was a situation, that much was obvious. Xabier had needed Zha'riel to get him home. There was no way Xabier would have ever asked Zha'riel for anything unless it was absolutely necessary.

"Fine," he said. "Just…give me a second. I need to make a call."

He left the room, ignoring the disbelief on everyone's' faces as he pulled out his phone. He didn't care. He felt like he was going to die sooner rather than later. If he didn't gain some control, he would be unable to function.

"Hello?"

Nico sucked in a breath, trying to steady himself. "You told me to call if I ever needed help."

"Of course. Does this mean we are leaning towards a decision?"

Nico knew he was being asked, extorted really, into making a life decision that he really didn't want to make. "Let's see how helpful you actually are and then we can talk about the future."

He explained how he felt.

"The problem is your vessel, your body, is not made to contain such a powerful essence. The pressure you are feeling is the essence expanding to its natural state. Remember, an essence is organic. It isn't simply something you have or don't have. Left to its own devices, it will always seek its natural state."

"Like possession."

"Not exactly, but if you don't get control, it *will* corrupt your mind, and then you will never regain control. You will become fully dark."

"How do I stop it?"

"Simple. You stop fighting it."

"That makes no sense"

"Nico, your mind can only take so much. Right now, you are like a man fighting a split personality. At some point, one side or the other will win out. Believe me, the supernatural essence *never* loses. If you want to survive, you must stop trying to keep your supernatural essence from becoming."

"So, what do I do?"

"Start by embracing what you are."

When Nico returned to the room, he felt the pressure subside a bit. He wasn't sure he had fully accepted his dark side, or that he really wanted to. He did accept the darkness within him. It wasn't something he was pleased to have to admit to himself. He wanted to believe his urges came from an innate goodness, but now he understood, it was a mixture of innate goodness infused with darkness. He had to come to grips with the powerful nature of the darkness within him, perhaps even more powerful than the good.

The others were deep in conversation. Nico, distracted by his own thoughts, kept hearing the term "alphas." Xabier and Lazlo were arguing with Zha'riel about how to stop some portal from opening. They talked about witchcraft, some sort of supernatural coalition, past treachery on the part of Xabier, and the release of the alphas.

He sat down on a couch and leaned forward, rubbing his temples. "Okay, catch me up. It sounds like we're in for a long night." He looked at Zha'riel. "What the hell are alphas?"

Chapter 21

"So, they've opened the box?"

"They have. They believe they have everything they need."

Azazel nodded and smiled as they walked through the small trellis and into the pavilion courtyard. The multicolored bushes, purple, yellow, white, and red, lined both sides of the courtyard. A variety of trees filled the space on one end of the yard, and more sculpted bushes and trees formed a perimeter around the entire park. It was a beautiful, serene setting, nowhere near what he used to roam in Paradise, but Azazel found gardens peaceful. He could think better when he was surrounded by the natural world. It was odd, that he took pleasure in the very creation he had spent eons trying to destroy, but nevertheless true.

Everything was coming together. The box was finally open. Nayra had what she needed to decipher the next move. The portal was about to be opened. He could feel it. Seir was building an army, and Azazel had a deal in place with the Hindu gods. All operations were now in secure territory, and all of it had been executed in near complete secrecy.

"You did not kill the vampire."

Seir chuckled. "No, Sire. I took the liberty of inflicting a bit of pain, but left them tied up in a cave. They probably called the angel for help by now."

Azazel laughed. He was in good spirits. His eyes glowed fierce white, only they held a rare glimmer of glee. He sent Seir away with instructions to carry on as planned.

"Be sure you are cautious in your recruiting," he said, "but inform them they will be a part of a great future." He grasped Seir by the shoulders. "It is almost time, my friend. Prepare for war."

Azazel wandered. He wandered throughout the Chambal Gardens. Located on the banks of the Chanbal River, it contained some of the rarest flowers in the Himalayas. The freedom he felt gave him a sense of peace he had never experienced in his time with Lucifer He wondered if this was how his old friend had always felt. He couldn't be sure. Lucifer was consumed with rage. His calm demeanor hid it most of the time, but Azazel knew how bitter his former friend really was. Losing Heaven turned him into a shell of his former self. Now, all the once great archangel had left was his anger and his mission to destroy the creation of his enemy.

Azazel understood anger, bitterness, and everything that came with them. He knew what it was like to focus his hatred on one being. He also knew how to compartmentalize. He knew how to save his real emotion for the day he would face his most hated rival.

He felt free…free from Lucifer and his rule over Azazel's life. He felt free to roam the Indian countryside without fear of Lucifer attacking. For the first time in his life, Azazel was making his own decisions and planning for a future with his own interests at the forefront. His mind wandered to thoughts of the future.

"Tell me what you are thinking."

She was smiling as Azazel snapped back to reality. His eyes roved over her, trying to determine if she was real. She was dressed in flowing white sheer over white robes with a silver floral pattern and silver trim. Her jewelry was simple, all silver, including the thin chains she wore over her hair, which she had up, revealing her slender neck. Several stray tendrils fell on either side of her face.

Azazel's breath caught in his throat. He remembered the first day he ever saw Parvati. She was the most beautiful thing his eyes had ever seen. As she stood before him in the garden along the Chambal River, he wondered if there was anything more beautiful in the entire universe. He held out his hand and she came to him without hesitation, collapsing into his arms.

"Thank you." Her words were muffled as she buried her face in his robes, but he understood. "Thank you, my love. I knew one day you would return for me."

It was the icing on a very sweet cake. Azazel had to make hard decisions in the past regarding Parvati. He'd chosen to submit to the wishes of his master. Too often, peace was broken because of the infidelity of a wife or husband. Lucifer had asked him to bide his time. He'd promised Azazel, one day he would be able to return for Parvati. That day had never come.

When Azazel formulated a plan to partner with a faction not sympathetic to Lucifer, he knew he would start with the Hindus. He also knew Parvati would be a part of the equation. He knew Shiva would challenge him. He knew he would easily defeat Shiva. The only surprise was that Shiva gave in so quickly. Azazel suspected he had to be convinced by his peers that there was no upside to refusing Azazel. In the end, Azazel accomplished for himself what Lucifer had never delivered.

He cupped Parvati's cheek in his hand and kissed her forehead gently. "This is just the beginning. Are you ready for what is to come?"

She rested her head on his chest. "I am ready for anything that comes as long as we are together."

Ђ ᴧ ᷎ Ψ Ģ

"Human love is tricky."

"She should have controlled herself," Abdiel huffed. "Imagine...falling in love with a human."

In the wake of Tatiana's failure with Nico, Abdiel made the decision to inform Lucifer. His master was bound to find out about the mess his prized asset made, and then Abdiel would have to explain why he wasn't more forthcoming. It was the kind of thing that could get one's organs fried.

"Nico is an enigmatic person," Lucifer said. "And he is hardly *just* a human."

He raised his eyebrows at Abdiel and gave him a knowing smile. Abdiel had the distinct impression Lucifer knew more than he was letting on. Lucifer had an infuriating habit of knowing everything before he was told by his team.

Abdiel stared out at the Atlantic Ocean as the sun began to peek out from beneath the horizon. The glare was only just beginning to sparkle across the waves. The sky was bright blue, not yet fully lit up but promising a crisp, clear, fall day. He breathed in the salty ocean air and shook his head.

"She must be punished."

Lucifer frowned. "Yet you did not punish her."

Abdiel didn't usually give Lucifer funny looks. His position was not equal to that of Azazel. He did not have millennia after millennia of friendship behind his relationship with his master. This time however, Lucifer's suggestion bordered on provocative, so he risked it. Lucifer suppressed a slight chuckle and patted Abdiel on the shoulder.

"Of course, you didn't." Lucifer pursed his lips. Abdiel could feel his thought process. Lucifer was enigmatic, even when he was merely thinking. Abdiel wondered how he did it.

"Everything is fine," Lucifer told Abdiel. "This is not unexpected."

It was a strange thing to say. Abdiel narrowed his eyes. "Wait a minute. You *knew* all this would happen!"

Lucifer shook his head with a wry grin. "Your problem, Abdiel, is you wish to *control* everything. You do not allow for the natural progression of things."

Abdiel frowned. "Natural progr…"

"If I have tried to teach you anything, it is that *true* power comes, not from one's ability to bend others to their will. Rather, it is one's ability to place what is necessary in the paths of others and allow events to transpire."

Abdiel thought back to all their plans over the past few months. It was true. Lucifer almost never made demands of others. Sure, he gave orders, but those orders were all about position, all about strategy. For all his power, all his ability to wreak havoc on the natural and supernatural worlds alike, Lucifer seldom exercised it directly.

Abdiel leaned on the cool iron rail, his eyes drifting from the water to the sand directly below where they stood. His own mind raced to keep up with the events Lucifer so easily kept straight. His patience with the Scarlatti kid should have been enough of a tip-off. Lucifer had never forced the issue. When he'd first found out about Nico, the orders were simply to watch and report. They never made a demand. They never attacked. Abdiel was dispatched to befriend and to lend support. He was there to teach Nico just enough to make him crave more, but more importantly, he was there to present an alternative to the intimidation tactics and threats of Heaven's angels.

When Lucifer and Azazel parted ways, everyone knew Azazel would go after Nico. When he did, Lucifer was there. Using his own blood, he placed within Nico something that would cause discomfort the longer Nico fought against his essence. It was like steroids to an essence that was already raging within him. With that in motion, he then sent Tatiana, the beautiful distraction, who would report from within Nico's inner circle, and also influence with subtle hints and suggestions. Abdiel couldn't believe he never glimpsed the larger picture.

"So, all of this was part of the plan," he said, shaking his head.

Lucifer clasped his hands in front of his stomach. "*Everything is part of the plan.*"

$$ Ƀ A Ʒ Ψ Ç $$

"The alphas are a special group of supernatural creatures."

Nico frowned and leaned forward in his chair. "Like another species?"

Xabier shook his head. "No, not another species."

"In some respects, they are." Zha'riel held up a finger and looked at Xabier. "They are not a specific species per se, but they all have the same thing in common. They are all the first of their kind." He held up both hands as Nico opened his mouth to respond. "Let me start from the beginning."

Zha'riel began by explaining the alphas were individuals which came about at various times throughout history. Like every other species in the biological world, there was a first. The alphas were the originals of their various species, but not *all* alphas were success stories. He looked in disgust at Lazlo and nodded in his direction.

"His father is the last of that line that survived."

Nico frowned. "That *survived?* What does that mean?"

"Not all newly created species were viable," Zha'riel said. "Think of them as experiments of a kind. Some lasted. Others failed and went extinct as quickly as they were born."

These created species all had three things in common. First, they were all once human. Second, they were virtually immortal. Third, they required proximity human beings for their survival. Some needed humans for things like rituals and used people for their sources of energy. The rituals never ended well for the human. Most needed humans for far more grotesque purposes.

"Some feed on human blood," Zha'riel said. "Vampires, vetala…others feed on human organs. Others may not feed on humans but use humans for their own ends, and often, death follows every instance, or at the very least, enslavement."

He explained that while each species was unique, both in their needs as well as in their abilities, they all were dangerous to humans. They were usually much faster and stronger physically. They were also immune to most human weapons. Each species had at least one fatal weakness, but it wasn't always easy to exploit those weaknesses.

"And the alphas do not always share those weaknesses with their descendants." Zha'riel locked eyes with Lazlo. "The original of the species is always the most powerful and produces the most powerful offspring. The farther the line gets from the original source, the weaker the next generation becomes."

Lazlo shook his head. "None of this is important. Why are we wasting time with a history lesson?"

"Because not all of us knows what the hell we're talking about," Nico shot back. "Maybe if you two idiots would have thought to pick up the goddamn phone, I would have gotten filled in a little sooner."

Xabier sighed and got up. He went to the bar in the corner of the room and poured drinks. He held one out to Lazlo with a look of warning. They didn't need to alienate Nico any more than he already was. Xabier never gave Nico much detail about his past. Nico was so new to the supernatural world, and had so many questions about his place in it, Xabier had never found the time to explain himself.

He handed a glass to Nico who gulped it down in one swift swallow. He knew Nico was still annoyed. His last comment, while directed to Lazlo was really meant for Xabier. Nico wasn't really mad though. Xabier knew that. He was hurt, which was worse. He was disappointed, which was *far* worse.

"The key point," he said to Nico, "is to know that the alphas are very powerful and very ruthless."

"That is correct," Zha'riel agreed. "They were put away for a reason."

Nico thought for a moment. "Okay, these alphas...where do they fall on the scale of powerful beings? I've met archangels, regular angels, and demons."

"The alphas are nowhere near as powerful as any of those," Zha'riel replied.

Nico looked at him skeptically. "Okay, maybe I'm missing something here. If they're not all that strong, how bad could things get if they get loose?"

Xabier shrugged. "Ever hear of the Dark Ages?"

In the years following the rise of the Roman Empire, the supernatural world grew exponentially. As Rome spread throughout the immediate region, the population of the world began to rise as well, providing ample food for the supernatural. They grew far more aggressive than ever before, and far more willing to decimate large populations. The losses became noticeable and humans began to investigate.

"Suddenly," Zha'riel said, "species like vampires and vetala were caught in the act. This led humans to wonder what else might be out there."

"Their worst fears were realized," Xabier added. "The further they dug into the supernatural world, the more truth they uncovered. All our lore, myth, religion…it's real stuff, for the most part. The things that scare humans the most usually exist in some form or another."

"So why not just kill them all?" Nico asked Zha'riel.

"It does not work that way. Angels are not permitted to interfere with the affairs of humans unless specifically directed to do so."

But at one point, that was exactly what had happened. The supernatural reproduced at a rate exceeding the humans. By 500 AD, the alphas were on the brink of tipping the balance of nature. A decree was handed down in Heaven. The supernatural were a threat to creation. Heaven mobilized, but the angels were not allowed to intervene directly. The humans needed to be taught how to deal with their supernatural cousins. They enlisted the help of the most powerful witch in the world to help them create an earthly portal to Purgatory.

"Purgatory?" Nico frowned. "Isn't that where you go when you die?"

Zha'riel shook his head. "That was the story handed to the masses to protect the reality. You see, it was determined the supernatural problem was too much for simple people to have to deal with. The reality is, Purgatory is a prison."

One by one, the humans subdued the alphas from each supernatural line and cast them into the portal. Without the alphas, the supernatural would weaken, little by little, with each generation, eventually dying off and becoming extinct. Those still alive could be hunted and driven back.

The humans took care of the rest, training and sending out "hunters" to track down and kill supernatural beings. The supernatural bloodlines weakened without the alphas. Nature's balance was restored, and the threat to the Earth was put down. The humans continued to populate the planet while the supernatural maintained their place among them. As long as they didn't get too out of control, the humans were generally content to live in peace, allowing the reality of the supernatural to fade into myth and lore.

"That's insane," Nico said.

"But true, nevertheless."

Nico's cell phone began to vibrate. He glanced down at the incoming text.

Tatiana: McGillian's? Please, Nico.

He closed his eyes and shook his head. That made twelve texts since the morning. He was aware all eyes were on him but he didn't care. Tatiana really wanted to meet him. He still wasn't sure he wanted to talk to her, but she had a piece of him that wouldn't let go so easily. Every time she texted, a little more of his resolve melted away. He knew as soon as he looked into her eyes, he would be a goner. He didn't want to put himself in that position, but hadn't figured out how to completely cut her loose.

Nico: Be there in a few.

He put his phone in his pocket and looked at Xabier, then at Zha'riel. "I have to run out. I'll be back later."

Xabier shook his head. "This is a pressing matter."

"To *you*." Nico stood up. "Look…if they get out and become a problem, I'll think about stepping in. Otherwise…I have my own problems."

"Nico…" Zha'riel began.

"See ya."

Nico orbed out, leaving Zha'riel and the two vampires staring at one another in shock.

"Was he serious?" Lazlo asked.

Chapter 22

"This is a fascinating country."

"It is that."

Nayra stood on the roof of one of the buildings near the top of Thiksey monastery, looking out over the rugged landscape surrounding the hilltop structure. Benyamin stood behind her, his hands folded in front of him, trying to maintain his patience. Nayra's eyes were closed. She gave the impression of a woman in meditation, though her face was anything but serene. If anything, Benyamin thought she looked agitated.

He and Nayra had worked so well together ever since New Orleans, he'd started to believe they were on the same page, working toward the same goals. She'd attacked the puzzle of opening the box with gusto, distracted only by the treasure trove of Kharashuoa witchcraft paraphernalia. Now that the box was opened, Nayra, to Benyamin's dismay, seemed to withdraw. She seemed interested only in studying Kharashuoa witchcraft. She poured over Wynnifrea's grimoires for hours on end. He gave her space, assuming she would circle back to the task at hand, but she remained withdrawn, her focus on magic instead of their shared mission.

It was Benyamin's intention to keep the peace between them. Azazel had made it clear she was far too important to his cause to alienate her, so Benyamiin was forced into a façade of diplomacy. He was well-suited to it. Throughout his life, he'd learned the art of refinement, of influencing others to follow willingly rather than feel forced, but time was important, even Azazel had to admit that. They could not wait for Nayra to circle back. They needed that portal opened.

"This country is steeped in mysticism," she went on. "Can you feel it, Benyamin?"

He sighed and licked his lips. He didn't have time for superfluous conversation. "I only feel time," he replied. "As it slips through our fingers."

Nayra opened her eyes and took in a deep breath. She shook her head as she turned to face him. Benyamin had one consistent thought about her, and witches in general. They all tended toward the eccentric. Power did that to a person; he understood that. When a person could draw upon the power of the Earth, and that power ran through their body, it made sense it would affect them, but all too often, witches grew arrogant, and it seemed to Benyamin, the arrogance was in direct proportion to the amount of power they wielded.

Nayra had exhibited immense power. Benyamin knew she could do him great harm anytime she wanted, but she couldn't kill him, at least, he didn't think so. What *she* didn't seem to realize was that all it would take was a simple snap of her slim neck and that would be her last breath. She would do well to remember that, but such thoughts were not productive.

"You have something to say?" she asked.

"I would like to focus more intently on the portal spell," he replied. He wasn't about to make a fight out of it, but it was reasonable to request a little more focus on the task at hand.

Nayra's eyes bored into him. Benyamin returned her stare with one of his own. It wasn't an aggressive stare, but it wasn't meek either. He just wanted to get to work, and he needed Nayra to pull her weight.

"You are so focused on pleasing the one who cares nothing for you," she said. "Why is that?"

Benyamin sighed. It was a question he'd asked himself more times than he cared to discuss. "Remember, I began this quest long before I ever met Azazel."

"Yet you continue even after he is of no further use."

"I made a deal. It is a matter of honor."

"Honor?" She raised her eyebrows. "What good is honor when you are a slave to the one you obey?"

"I am a slave to no one," Benyamin hissed, his eyes darkening. The veins in his face became visible under his skin as his frustration began to boil over. "We have a deal. Azazel has fulfilled his every promise, including saving our lives back in New Orleans. We must hold up our end." His eyes bored into her. "And my *reason*…is because I want to free my father."

When she didn't respond, he asked, "And what of *your* involvement? I have family involved, but you…you're supposed to be a servant of nature. Where is your loyalty to humanity?"

Nayra's eyes blazed. Her jaw clenched and she gritted her teeth. "My *loyalty* diminished when humanity tried to stamp out my people. Now, I am loyal only to the earth and to my family…my Kharashuoa family."

They stared at one another for several seconds. Nayra was the first to blink, and she simply shrugged and brushed past him, leading the way to their study room. Everything was laid out and organized on tables. The contents from the spelled box were given their own table. There were five pink stones tinged with yellow. Benyamin identified them as poudretteite, one of the rarest gemstones in the world. They were about five to six inches in length, two inches in diameter, and looked as though they'd just been plucked from the earth. Benyamin estimated them to be between fifteen hundred and two-thousand carats apiece. He placed the value of the collection at twenty-five to thirty million American dollars.

There was another stone. It was eight inches in length and more than two inches in diameter. It was darker than the other five, a deep red-orange hue. It took Benyamin three days to identify it. It turned out to be an even rarer gemstone than the other five. It was called painite. It was so rare, there wasn't even a real value guide for it. He found a few smaller pieces but nothing substantial. The most consistent value he could find was in the neighborhood of fifty-thousand dollars per carat. He estimated the value of the stone at well over one hundred twenty-five million dollars.

The rest of the contents of the box consisted of a sheaf of animal skin documents with writing in Wynnifrea's hand, and another skin which Nayra believed was human. That skin was a three-foot square. It was folded neatly and put into the box. When Nayra removed, and unfolded it, they found there wasn't a single crease. After seven hundred years, the skins came out of the box like they were brand new. It had to be a spell.

They spent the next few hours reading and rereading every word on every page from Wynnifrea's box. Benyamin squinted at the paper and shook his head. He referenced something on another sheet before setting them both down and leaning back in his chair, rubbing his eyes.

"We're looking for *six* cities," he said, squeezing the bridge of his nose. "Not just one.

"What?" Nayra frowned.

Benyamin held up one of the animal skin pages. "The portal location is in a place called Farduzes." He pointed to the map. "Right here. I did a little research and it turns out the medieval city of Farduzes is actually the modern-day city of Vaduz, the capital of Lichtenstein."

Nayra pursed her lips and moved to peer at the map. "Okay, but Farduzes is the only city mentioned in the papers. Where do you see five others?"

Benyamin read from one of the sheets. "She talks here about something called 'the point.' And then she mentions on this page, another reference to 'a point.' And then again here and here." He showed her the pages with the references. "But if you look *here*," he pointed to a place on a third sheet, "we get a more specific number. She writes 'points of five.' See? Five points."

"And we have five small stones," Nayra added. She sighed. "But *five* points? How are we supposed to know…?"

"It's in there," Benyamin said. "Wynnifrea buried it. We just need to figure out her thought process, her code."

Nayra tilted her head and closed her eyes as she digested the new information. "Five more cities," she mumbled. "Five cities…five…why five?"

Her eyes flicked over the pages in her hand and then to the other items on the table. Her gaze rested on the amulet. Benyamin watched as she stared at the amulet in silence for several moments. She seemed drawn to it and he began to wonder if she was slipping into one of her trance-like states. If so, he could be in for a long wait.

She reached for the amulet. "The pentagram has five points," she said softly. "Five points, five points, five points…"

Her voice trailed off and Benyamin saw her eyes widen. She studied the amulet.

"Five points!" she shouted. "I need the map." She glanced up as Benyamin stared back at her. "*Quickly*! Where is the map?"

"Here," Benyamin said as he snapped back to attention and pulled the map around to face her.

Nayra peered at the moonstone in the center of the amulet. It was stunning, translucent, milky-white, with an etched pentagram inside the stone. There was no earthly way the etching of the pentagram or the incantation could have gotten *into* the stone, so it must have been another spell. There was a small dot etched at the precise center of the pentagram and Nayra placed the dot over the city of Farduzes. Benyamin watched as she slowly rotated the amulet, keeping the dot right over Farduzes. Without warning, the pink stones, much smaller versions of the poudretteite, began to glow bright pink. When Nayra rotated too far, the glow faded. When she rotated the amulet back, the glow returned. With the stones glowing their brightest, she left the amulet in place and smiled at Benyamin.

"Your five cities."

He looked at each point in turn. "Ulm, Brixen, Milan, Geneva, Strasburg."

"We have our locations," Nayra said.

"Now we just need to figure out what we're supposed to do with them."

Nayra nodded. "The spell calls for each point to be lit. That probably means that each of those stones goes somewhere in each of those cities. The clues to the locations are probably in there." She gestured at the stack of skins Benyamin had been perusing." You have six pages. I think each page deals with a specific location."

Benyamin held up one of the sheets. "It doesn't seem like it."

"She was crafty," Nayra said. "She buried the information in riddles. We must match up the pages with the cities."

They spent the next few hours researching the cities Wynnifrea had designated as the portal points. Thousand-year-old cities have a lot of history, and not all of it is accessible online. Azazel left them a number to call should they need anything. After several calls, Benyamin had stacks of old European texts in front of him. He and Nayra researched every word on every page and endeavored to match them up to a specific city.

That was only the beginning. Wynnifrea also disguised the specific location of each point in her prose. They had to go deeper into each city, searching for clues, landmarks, buildings, anything that might match up to something Wynnifrea wrote. Over the course of the several days, the unlikely pair left the research room only to sleep and eat.

On a cool, gray day, Benyamin strode into the research room to find Nayra already deep in her research. He looked over her notes and nodded in approval. They were almost finished. It would take a quick visit to each site to confirm their conclusions, but he felt good.

He sat in the seat across the table from Nayra and held up a sheaf of pages. They were scans of the original animal skin pages. "I was reading Wynnifrea's spell again, trying to dissect it, bit by bit, to see if we missed anything."

Nayra's forehead wrinkled as she tilted her head to one side. "And?"

Benyamin frowned and shook his head. "I keep coming back to her references to power. The first was when she wrote, "…power that is the envy of the gods." A rather vague and strange phrase. Later, she writes, "…the power of a thousand worlds." Finally, she gets a little more specific: "…the power placed in the heavens…the power of the tides." What do you suppose that all means?"

Nayra smiled. It wasn't her smile that tipped Benyamin off. It was the knowing glint in her grey eyes. His mouth dropped open.

"You already know the answer."

"Mmm," she said. "But before I tell you the answer, let us consider the entire picture."

Nayra had been at work, laying out the full sequence of events, like an itinerary of steps they would need to take to prepare for the final ritual. It was all information pulled from Wynnifrea's animal skin pages.

"These two pages," Nayra said, holding them up. "Contain the sequence and the spell."

She walked him through the lighting of the points. The order was specific. The second point would not light if the first was not already lit. The timing had to be handled just right. There was a limited amount of time to get everything lit and prepared for the opening of the portal itself.

"How much time?" Benyamin asked.

"Three days."

"And how do we know this? I saw nothing in the pages about a time constraint."

Nayra held up a finger. "That is where Wynnifrea's references to power come into play."

Nayra explained, the amount of power required to create a connection between two worlds was vast, far more than anything humans could generate. The world was orders of magnitude short of the necessary power.

"A trillion nuclear warheads wouldn't get us ten percent of the power we need."

"The envy of the gods," Benyamin murmured.

Nayra concurred. "Indeed. She refers to power only a god can create."

"But," Benyamin frowned, "Azazel made it clear the so-called gods were merely fallen angels. None of them would have this kind of power."

"No," Nayra agreed. "But God *Himself*...would."

Benyamin let out a breath. He closed his eyes in thought. It made sense. Only the Creator could create. If He created Purgatory it stood to reason only His power could be used to open the door between that place and earth. What would God have created, powerful enough to accomplish the task, yet that was still accessible to humans?

"Power of a thousand worlds," he mumbled, his lips barely moving as the words slid out. "Power envied by the gods...power placed in the heavens...the heavens. It could be..." His eyes widened and his head snapped up to look at Nayra, who was smiling. "Is it that simple?"

"I believe it is."

He raced to the computer to, but she stopped him.

"Tomorrow," she said. "It begins tomorrow. Tell the dark angel we open the portal in two days' time."

ℏ ᴀ ᔓ ψ ɢ

"You did well, my friend."

"Thank you, Sire. I think most of our new recruits are excited. Once we got the first few, it was easy to bring more on board."

Azazel gazed out over his army, and recalled the masses he used to command when he was with Lucifer. What he had now was a fraction of his former command, but this army was all his. *He* made all the plans. *He* gave all the orders. They all ultimately answered to *him*.

Seir had brought him sixty red-eyed demons. They were the highest rank of demon and the most powerful of all the demons. They were followed by yellow-eyed variety and then the black-eyed demons were the lowest level, the foot-soldiers. The red and yellow-eyed varieties were used for special operations; their skills were often highly specialized, especially among the red-eyed, but as good as they were at their craft, they were never given commands of their own. Demons, even the higher-ranking ones, weren't leaders.

Azazel disagreed. Seir had proven himself time and time again. For centuries, the red-eyed demon struck fear into the hearts of all Azazel's enemies. Azazel even heard there were certain angels among the heavenly ranks who feared Seir. It was understandable. It came on the heels of Seir's and his team's successful assassination of two angel soldiers on the same day. It was Seir's planning, and his leadership that made the effort successful.

The trouble with demons, in Azazel's opinion, wasn't that they were unable to lead. It was that they weren't known for their loyalty. It was not uncommon for demons to abandon their army and strike out on their own. They were usually pretty easy to find, and the penalties for desertion were always severe.

Seir's mission was to find demons willing to leave their armies and join Azazel's. It might appear counterintuitive to seek out willing deserters, but Seir was the kind of demon other demons respected and feared. Everyone understood desertion in this army would be met with punishment more creative and severe than anything they could possibly imagine. Desertion was not expected to be a major problem.

"Tell me about your structure."

Seir handed him a printout. "We currently have sixty red-eyes. Each one will command a team of ten yellows. Each yellow will command a company of one hundred black-eyes. Obviously, those numbers will increase as we recruit more."

"There are no battalion commanders? Regiments? Brigades?"

"As we discussed, Sire, those positions will be filled by angels." Seir gestured to Azazel. "When we decide to finally start recruiting them."

"Good." Azazel smiled as Seir lowered his eyes. "Seir, you have built us an army."

The demon shrugged. "It is modest at best, Sire."

Azazel tilted his head. "Only if one intends to take on the armies of Heaven or Lucifer directly." He smiled, his eyes flashing silver and then receding to their normal pearl white glow. "Which we do not."

"We don't?"

"Of course not." Azazel laughed. "That was never the plan."

Seir nodded. May I ask what the plan is, Sire?"

Azazel smiled, his eyes flashing once again. "We will fight from the shadows. We will not engage unless we can win decisive victories. The lives of our soldiers will be guarded. We will not waste resources on suicide missions. We will do exactly you and I have always done, only on a much larger scale." He turned to Seir. "You will teach them. And you will lead them...*General.*"

Seir's eyes widened in shock. His mouth hung agape. "I-I-I...Sire, I don't understand."

Azazel nodded. "You have been at my side for centuries, Seir. You have my complete trust and confidence. I have only placed complete trust in two beings in my entire existence. You are the other one."

Seir's breath caught at the import of Azazel's words. Azazel pulled a gleaming short blade from his robes and held it up for Seir to see. "Do you know what this is, Seir?"

"Of course, my Lord. It is an angel blade."

Azazel turned it from side to side so that the light played off it. "These blades are the only items in existence that can kill me. I am susceptible to the powers of other angels, and particularly archangels, but only one of these swords, crafted by a Heavenly metal, can cause fatal damage." He held it out in both palms. "This one belongs to you."

Chapter 23

"Please, Nico, just listen to me."

"Tatiana, how many times do we have to do this?"

She stood on his doorstep for the first time since Nico threw her out of his life. That he opened the door at all was a positive thing, in her mind. They'd met a couple times at McGillians, but only one meeting had been planned. After he'd told her he never wanted to see her again, she'd resorted to...well, stalking. She'd approached him at McGillians the previous night and he didn't run away. The conversation ended just like it had the previous times they talked, but she'd felt him struggling with his resolve. His pain was keeping him from taking another chance, but Tatiana was unwilling to walk away.

Heartsick and alone, she wanted nothing more than to return to Nico. She wanted him to understand, she was in love with him and would never do anything to hurt him.

"I'm never going to give up," she said. "Never. I know you don't trust me, and I don't blame you, but you need to know, I am in love with you."

"Will you stop saying that?"

His eyes flashed silver and settled into a pearlescent white glow. Tatiana's mouth dropped open. Her heart began to race and she felt sweat break out on her forehead. Without thinking she reached out her hand and touched his cheek.

"You are so beautiful."

She stroked his cheek, her hand just grazing the skin beneath it. He reached up and grabbed her wrist, pulling her hand away from his face. He shook his head. The white glow in his eyes took on a harsh quality. Instead of the loving gaze she'd hoped for, Nico stared her down with a coldness she'd never seen from him.

"You need to go."

Xabier stood in the living room and spread his arms. "Who was that?"

Nico shook his head. "Not now."

"When, Nico? When are you going to tell me what the hell is going on with you?"

Nico felt all the anger and frustration of the past few weeks bubble to the surface. He had to push it all down as hard and as far as he could, and he had to do it fast, before he unloaded on his best friend. He wasn't a hundred percent certain he could control the darkness.

He closed his eyes and took a deep breath as he fought against the tide of his anger. He exhaled slowly as he went to the bar and poured himself a drink. As he swallowed the smokey-flavored scotch, he felt the warm glow in his belly and some of his emotions began to fade. He leaned on the couch and stared at his friend.

"It's interesting, isn't it, how you manage to ask me that after leaving me out of the loop for weeks?"

Xabier rolled his eyes. "Knock it off, Nico. I couldn't take the risk. Azazel's involved. I *wanted* to call you in. I probably *should* have called you in, but I think it would have led to another showdown between you and that maniac and then you'd be dead!"

Nico stared at him. His friend had been thinking like a friend ought to think, placing himself in greater danger to protect those he cared about. Xabier, if nothing else, was honorable and self-sacrificing, but allowing the contents of Wynnifrea's tomb to fall into the wrong hands was a mistake on a cosmic scale.

"Well, it is what it is now, isn't it?"

Xabier folded his arms across his broad chest. "So, who is the pretty redhead that's in love with you?"

"She's not in love with me," Nico replied.

Lazlo chuckled. "She certainly sounded like a woman smitten."

"Yeah," Nico shrugged. "That's kinda her job." He shook his head. "She was sent get close to me, to encourage me to follow my...urges."

Xabier's eyes widened in shock. "You mean she's..."

"She's supernatural, yes."

After Nico closed the door in her face, Tatiana lowered her head and retreated to a secluded spot in the woods near his house. She leaned against a fallen tree and broke down, her tears flowing like rivers down her face. Hands on her knees, Tatiana leaned over let her hair fall around her face. She felt sick, like a part of her was twisting inside. It was agonizing and she let out an agonized moan.

"It is disconcerting to see such a beautiful creature in such distress."

She snapped her head up at the sound of a familiar voice, and instantly dropped into a defensive posture. She bent her knees slightly, and flexed her fingers. She wondered if she had any chance to get out of the encounter alive.

"What do you want?"

Azazel's eyes glowed deep white and he held up his hands. "Be still, Tatiana. I am not here to do you harm. Quite the contrary. I want to help you."

"H-help me? How?"

Azazel turned toward the house, nearly one hundred yards away. He smiled as he gestured toward the building where Nico just slammed the door on any possibility of letting her back into his life.

"I want you to get what you want."

Tatiana was desperate to win Nico back, but she wasn't a complete fool. "Why would you care? You hate him and want to kill him."

Azazel looked back at her with a kind and gentle smile. "Yes, that *was* indeed the case, but things have changed, and now my attitude toward young Nico is, shall we say...*evolving*."

"I don't know what that means."

Azazel laughed. It was an unusual act on his part. Tatiana wasn't sure she'd ever seen him laugh out loud, other than the maniacal laugh of a stone-cold sadist. Shocking though it was, she found the joyful sound of Azazel's glee, strangely soothing.

"You're different," she noted, studying his expression. "You seem...almost happy."

"Oh?" Azazel tilted his head and smiled. "Perhaps my newfound independence has given me a fresh perspective on life." He leaned closer to her. "Perhaps you need a little freedom of your own."

"What I *need*," Tatiana replied, her heart sinking to her stomach once again, "is Nico to love me."

She couldn't believe she'd said it aloud in front of Azazel. In their world, one did not reveal such weakness. All vulnerabilities were dangerous. She half-expected him to laugh and wave her off like some petulant child, but he didn't. The look in his eyes was not contempt or disgust. If anything, it felt like empathy, compassion...weird coming from Azazel, but there it was.

"Perhaps he really *does* love you. Perhaps it is the sting of betrayal, still fresh in his mind, that keeps him from letting you back in."

Azazel was right, but it didn't solve Tatiana's dilemma. After her encounter with Nico just moments before, she doubted he would accept her anytime soon. She would be lucky if he ever bothered to speak to her again based on the way head had just looked at her before rejecting her.

Azazel placed a hand on her shoulder. "As I said, I want to help you. What Nico needs from you right now is to know, beyond any doubt, that you are with him."

"How can I show him that if he won't let me near him?"

Azazel held up a small slip of paper. "Our friend is about to insert himself into a very dangerous situation. He will find himself out numbered and his essence is going to bring him to his knees. This list is a series of locations. Perhaps you can be his…backup, his…guardian angel as it were. If you are nearby, perhaps you can help him if he gets into trouble."

"Why would you do this?"

"As I said, my interest in Nico has changed. He has the essence of my son in him. I no longer want him destroyed."

ҍ ᴀ ⳠΨ ᴄ

"Ilnio estare insindio! Mori alaffectare! Sentilio mande oma astorarre!"

As Benyamin looked on, Nayra completed the incantation, and the poudretteite shard began to glow. The main cupola of the Basilica of San Lorenzo, in Milan, Italy, was bathed in a pink glow. As she uttered the final words, the intensity of the glow grew, then finally dissipated until only the center of the stone gave off light. It looked to Benyamin as though there was a tiny light, like a candle, in the center of the rough, pink stone. The first point was lit.

Following a day of searching and verifying, Nayra and Benyamin determined they had the correct locations of all five pentagram points along with the sixth location, the portal itself. Their timeline was such that they had little time to waste if they didn't want to wait another month, so they contacted Azazel, arranged for all preparations to be made. The portal would be opened tonight.

Lighting each point required an elaborate ceremony, complete with incantations and the blood of the witch performing the ceremony. Nayra knew Xabier and his friends would show up to disrupt the portal opening, so she planned for the occasion. At each point, they left a team of two Kharashuoa witches, from New Orleans. Their job was to guard the point, making sure no one pulled it from its socket.

Once the point was lit, Nayra began another incantation. Benyamin knew it was not part of the original spell. He had gone through it word for word with Nayra countless times to ensure perfect pronunciation. He knew it by heart. He frowned as she went through the extra ritual but did not stop her.

"What was that?" he asked. "Another spell?"

Nayra pressed her lips together in a thin line. "Do you really think two witches will be enough to hold off our enemies?"

ƀ ᴀ ᣟ ψ ɕ

"Just calm down."

"*CALM DOWN?* Are you joking? This is not a game, Rafael. This is *really* happening!"

Heaven was on high alert. The instant the first point lit up, warning bells sounded throughout the angelic ranks. Zha'riel was there to bring Rafael up to date. Wynnifrea's secrets were in the wind. Purgatory gate aside, there was enough in her spell books and paraphernalia to bring the world to its knees if it got into the wrong hands. They were up against a motivated group.

Rafael nodded. "Yes, Zha'riel, it is really happening. We knew it would someday."

"And...what? We're just going to let it happen? We're going to let those...*vermin* out again to destroy creation?"

"You forget our mandate, Zha'riel." Rafael put his hands on Zha'riel's shoulders. "We are not permitted to interfere in human business unless specifically directed."

Zha'riel shrugged his superior's hands off and paced the floor, his right-hand clenching and unclenching as he struggled to maintain his composure. The whole situation seemed absurd. The bad guys were about to win, and the good guys were in a position to stop it. Yet, the good guys were forced to let it all happen. There was no rhyme or reason.

"This is insane," Zha'riel said. "We threaten Nico with death for killing evil people and yet we are going to sit here and allow the most evil creatures on the planet out of their cage? A cage that *we* helped put them into? Doesn't that seem stupid to you?"

Rafael sighed. His dark eyes never wavered. While he managed to take on human personality traits at will, Zha'riel never saw him doubt his mandate. If the instructions were to let humanity suffer the consequences of the alphas' release, so be it. Rafael saw it as just another event in the timeline of creation. Something to be observed, certainly, but it would never rise to the level of concern, in his eyes, unless and until he was called upon to act.

"It doesn't matter how it seems, Zha'riel. We fight the fights we are given, not the ones we choose."

"Yes, but I think…"

"What *you think* does not matter," Rafael shot back with a cold glare. "You are to *stay out of it*. You are *not* to interfere. Do you understand?"

Zha'riel shook his head. "I need to at least warn them."

"It is a bad idea," Rafael said. "This group looks like a combination of human and supernatural. If your friend goes in there and kills a human, even in self-defense, I will have no choice but to descend upon him."

Zha'riel slammed his fist into the wall. He continued to pace as Rafael watched him with a skeptical frown. All he had to do was stay out of it, to prove that he was not emotionally invested in Nico or events related to him. If he could do that, he would gain his reinstatement and then he would get an assignment where he would not have to see Nico again. He would be free of the burden of human struggles and the relationship that had cost him so much.

He understood why Rafael didn't trust him. How many times had he run off to help Nico even when Nico was following the council of the foolish and the evil? Nico's problems were one hundred percent self-inflicted, and even deserved. The harsh reality was that all of Nico's losses were the direct result of his failure to control his evil impulses. The dark essence inside him had controlled him from the very beginning; Zha'riel could see that now. For that reason alone, he should leave Nico to his own devices.

But he couldn't.

"I'm going to warn them," he said. "I have to."

"If you interfere," Rafael warned. "You will forfeit any chance you have of returning to your station. You may impart information, but you may not assist in any way."

"I understand."

"And if Nico Scarlatti kills a human…" Rafael raised his eyebrows. "You tell him that as well."

Ѣ Ѧ ǯ ψ Ϛ

"You two need to stop this quibbling. There is no time for it."

"Stay out of it, Zha'riel."

Nico was tired of Zha'riel's angelic attitude toward everything. For a guy who wasn't around when he was needed, Zha'riel sure turned up often enough to tell everyone how to live. At least with Xabier, Nico could tell where he stood. Zha'riel was a riddle. One moment he was on board, willing to help take down those who harmed the innocent. The next he was spouting fire and brimstone about how Heaven was not going to stand for Nico's vigilantism.

"Fine," Zha'riel said. "I will stay out of it, but the two of you need to work together to stop the portal ritual."

Nico shrugged. "Talk to Xabier. I don't care if they open that stupid portal."

Xabier slammed his hand down on the kitchen table. "What is your problem, Nico? This is serious business. These alphas are not a group of supernatural bridge players. They're not gonna come outta Purgatory and play nice with others. They'll go on a rampage across this world and kill like nothing you've ever seen."

"He is right," Zha'riel said. "The Dark Ages got its name specifically because of those twelve abominations."

Nico spread his arms. "Then go stop it."

"I can't," Zha'riel said. "We are forbidden."

Nico shook his head and looked at Xabier. It was one thing they could agree on, even when they were at each other's throats. Heaven's rules governing the actions of the angels were so convoluted and twisted, it was impossible to predict where they would come down on a given issue. The only consistent thing about them was their defiance of common sense.

Xabier shrugged with a sigh. "When was the last time the halos did any heavy lifting?" He leaned forward. "What is it, Nico? Is it the redhead? Believe me you're better off without some supernatural spy in your life."

Zha'riel frowned. "What?"

Nico laughed. "Like all the other supernatural people in my life are so much better?"

"Supernatural spy?" Zha'riel asked, his eyes flicking from Nico to Xabier and back again.

Xabier rolled his eyes. "At least *we're* on your side, Nico. You can trust *us*. The last thing you need is some sexy redheaded spy twisting you up like this."

"A *redheaded* supernatural spy?" Zha'riel raised his eyebrows, his mouth agape.

"She's not twisting me up, Xabier."

Zha'riel held up a finger. "Wait a minute…"

"Only a *woman* can screw a guy up this much, Nico, and believe me, I saw her. She's not exactly hard to look at."

"*STOP!*"

Zha'riel stepped between them and held up his hands. Nico looked Zha'riel in disbelief. Across the room, he could see, Xabier had a similar look on his face. The angel was usually low-key and calm even when the sky was falling. Nico couldn't recall a single time Zha'riel had raised his voice.

"You said a redheaded, supernatural…*spy*?"

Nico furrowed his brow and nodded. "Uh huh."

Zha'riel's eyes widened. "What was her name?"

"Tatiana. Why?"

Zha'riel sucked in a breath and closed his eyes. "Nothing. I just…" He opened his eyes and grabbed Nico's arm. "Just stop them from opening the portal."

Nico stared at him. He felt, once again, as though information pertinent to him was being withheld. He shrugged in an offhand manner. "Whatever."

"No!" Zha'riel shouted. "You need to get going now! The first point is lit."

"What?" Lazlo and Xabier leapt to their feet and shouted in unison.

Zha'riel nodded. "Milan is aglow. This is happening tonight...*right now.*"

Xabier turned to Nico. "We need to get to Milan, Nico. Now."

"One minute," Zha'riel said, pulling Nico aside. "You need to be careful, Nico. There are humans involved, prepared to stand against you. You are under a microscope and all eyes in Heaven are on you. There will be no way of hiding your actions."

ҍ ᴧ ჳ ψ ɢ

"Are these numbers accurate?"

"Yes, my lord."

Abdiel stared at a sheaf of reports regarding demon slaughters among the ranks of his army. The Dark Army was not often on the receiving end of wholesale losses, especially when they were not in combat. These large losses came out of thin air and without any rhyme or reason. In the wake of a series of mass desertions, it felt like things were connected. Abdiel wondered who could be orchestrating such outlandish attacks.

He struggled to put consecutive thoughts together. He was furious; he knew that much. The whole situation made him look incompetent, and he knew those under his command were afraid. A good leader always looked out for his people. A good leader ought to instill confidence that he had everything under control. Abdiel wondered how many more desertions and deaths it would take before he would lose the confidence of his army.

"Tell me, General."

"It is...tense, Prince Abdiel. There is fear amongst our ranks. These attacks...we have never experienced anything like this."

Abdiel nodded and dismissed the general. He continued to review the reports, trying to find connections between the desertions and the attacks. It was maddening. There was no question in his mind it was all connected. He just couldn't find the thread that connected it all.

It was nothing unusual that there were deserters. Demons struck out on their own all the time even though they were eventually hunted and killed. What struck Abdiel were the numbers. They were too perfect...too symmetrical. They had lost sixty red-eyed demons, six hundred yellow-eyed demons, and more than six hundred *thousand* black-eyed demons. Those numbers added up to interesting possibilities.

Lucifer appeared in the doorway. "You are troubled, my friend."

"Arggg!" Abdiel leaned back and pressed hard against his temples. "We are hemorrhaging demons from the ranks. Desertions, and now these attacks. I know they're connected. I *know* it. I just can't figure out what to do about it."

Let me see."

Lucifer examined the documentation Abdiel handed him. Within minutes he straightened up and pressed his lips together.

"Well, well. It would appear my old friend is poaching our demons. I never thought he would want to command a fighting force of his own. He was always a loner. I suppose he decided he needed join the fray, and he's chosen to let us know it was all his doing by attacking us first."

"To what end?" Abdiel asked. "What good does a tiny army of demons do when we have angels that could smash the lot of them within minutes?"

"One thing we can be sure of, Abdiel, is that Azazel has a plan, and it is sure to be a bloody one. That we can take to the bank.

Chapter 24

"I fully understand. I will be monitoring his every move…personally."

"And if he cracks?"

Rafael pressed his lips together in a grim expression. It was the very same question he'd been pondering ever since Heaven found out Nico Scarlatti had taken in the essence of evil. He wasn't the first human to be infused with evil. There was a supernatural world, a world filled with creatures, once human, but now something different. Nico Scarlatti was different. He was filled with the essence of an angel, the son of an archangel.

The one thing that had always bothered Rafael about Nico was Nico's the ability to choose what he became. Like every other human, Nico had the ability to determine his path, and he couldn't see his chosen direction was leading him to destruction.

"If he cracks, I will descend on him, and put an end to this foolishness once and for all."

"You do not feel that is too harsh a punishment?"

Rafael's eyes lowered and his shoulders drooped. There were times when he hated the burden of leadership. It felt like a personal failure that Nico was lost to darkness. They all knew it was so. Allowing the human to play out his choices was nothing more than an exercise in futility. The moment he took in the essence of a fallen angel, he was doomed. The law was immutable.

Rafael shrugged and straightened his posture, bringing his eyes back up. "Perhaps if we did not sit back and allow him to be lost. Perhaps if we instructed him rather than let the evil one sink his claws into him. Are we not wasting an opportunity to unleash good upon evil? Hell has no rules. Why not fight them on common ground?"

"Mmmm."

Rafael knew not a moment's thought was given to his questions. The Law was not something one could question. Throughout history, similar questions were posed by inquisitive angels who wondered why humans had such different rules, and why the outcomes for humans always seemed to differ from the angels.

"Are not the rules exactly what separates good from evil? It will be those who follow the law who are rewarded."

Rafael frowned and shook his head. "That doesn't apply to humans, does it? Many will be rewarded who ignored the law."

"That is true, but humans are the exception. They do not *possess* the ability to follow the law. Therefore, we must hold those who make use of the supernatural to that same standard. If Nico Scarlatti murders one more human, he will suffer Heaven's wrath."

ᛒ ᚨ ᛉ ᚥ ᚷ

I do not want to see Nico destroyed.

Azazel's words rang in her ears long after the dark angel left her, alone, in the woods near Nico's home. Tatiana had no reason to trust Azazel, yet something in his voice, and his demeanor, gave her a sliver of possibility to cling to. Maybe there was time to prove herself to Nico. Maybe the upcoming situation would present her an opportunity. She could talk all she wanted, but Nico wasn't listening. He needed to *see*.

She glanced down at the slip of paper in her hand, and Azazel's scrawled handwriting. She frowned at the list of six

European cities. It represented what was likely to be her last opportunity with Nico. If she failed, she would have thrown away her status in the Dark Army for nothing. She was already facing a steep punishment for her failure. If Nico Scarlatti didn't land where her superiors wanted, she was going to be in real trouble. On top of all that, her heart was broken.

"Am I being a fool?" she mumbled to herself.

Azazel said his feelings toward Nico had changed now that he and Parvati were reunited. Tatiana suspected Azazel was setting Nico up for a major fall. That would make the most sense. Parvati was Sansata's mother. How could she stand to help the one who killed her son? Azazel had explained, neither of them wanted to see their son's essence lost in the ether. By the end of their discussion, Azazel had been practically pleading with her.

"I think he is in serious trouble, Tatiana. You of all people know what he is up against. If you love him, and I believe you do, you need to work with us."

Tatiana was dubious, but had no other direction. Lucifer and Abdiel were moving forward with whatever plans they had for Nico. Tatiana feared Nico was on the brink of Lucifer's wrath. She knew Lucifer well enough to know his patience had a way of wearing thin with little or no warning. If he thought, even for a moment, he could lose Nico to another suitor, Lucifer would not hesitate to destroy him.

Regardless of whether she trusted Azazel, and she most certainly did *not* trust Azazel, she couldn't ignore the possibility that Nico was about to put himself in danger. It was one thing for him to run around tormenting evil humans, even at the risk of angering Heaven. At least he had allies like Abdiel and Lucifer in that fight, but if he went into battle alone, he would find himself in over his head very quickly. She wondered if he had any idea how close to the edge he was.

She decided to stay close to Nico, even if that meant stalking him. She knew she could easily track him through the ether, if and when, he orbed. She also had his cell phone bugged. It was something she'd intended to rectify once Nico took her back. It was one additional lie she would have to find a way to explain if he ever gave her the chance, but for now it was useful to her purposes.

She looked at the screen of her phone as she pulled up the stats for Nico's cell. He was still in the house and no communication had come or gone. She closed the app and stared at the screen. The background was a shot of her and Nico sitting together, her back snuggled into his chest and his arms wrapped around her. It had been windy that day and some of her hair was out to one side, caught in the breeze. They looked happy. His smile was genuine, as was Tatiana's, though she had been hiding the secret that would ultimately bring their relationship crashing down around her.

She held the phone to her chest as she did her best to quell the tears forming in her eyes. She controlled herself. There would be no more crying. She had work to do, and her heart was a liability. She needed to be strong, prepared for whatever was to come. If Nico needed her, she would not let him down.

ᛒ A Ⰵ Ψ Ϛ

"What do ya think?"

Nico squinted over Xabier's shoulder and shook his head. "I don't see anything suspicious, but if they know we're coming…"

"They'll be lying in wait," Lazlo finished.

Nico, Xabier, and Lazlo stood atop the building, across the plaza from the Basilica of San Lorenzo. Zha'riel had told them the point was inside. He'd described what to look for, but all they could see was darkened doorways and windows. There were passers-by on the street, moving in all directions. No one appeared to be paying any attention to the Basilica.

"We need to get inside," Xabier said. "Nico, can you find a quiet corner for us to make our entrance?"

Nico nodded. He put a hand on each guy's shoulder and a second later, they were in a dark room, deep inside the Basilica of San Lorenzo. They instantly separated so as not to present an easy target. Xabier moved to the doorway and peeked around the corner. He made a hand motion and Lazlo darted forward, out the doorway, taking up a position across the corridor. He pointed back at Xabier, then at his eyes, and then down the corridor.

Xabier nodded. He whispered to Nico, "He sees the point. It's down the corridor. Come on."

He took off, stealthily, down the corridor. Nico stood shaking his head and mumbled, "You guys have hand signals? Why don't *we* have hand signals?"

He peered around the corner and watched the two vampires making their way down the stone corridor. He could see the deep pink glow coming from a room at the very end of the corridor. It was just as Zha'riel had described. He caught up to Xabier, and saw they were approaching the main cathedral from the side. He tapped Xabier on the shoulder and made a gesture which somehow Xabier understood.

Nico blinked his eyes and a second later he was standing at the entrance to the main hall. He scanned the room. There was a main center aisle with chairs on either side of the massive room. The chairs lining the gleaming, polished, marble floor were the only things in the room to indicate the modern age. The centuries-old, white, brick walls and columns towered almost fifty feet high, forming massive archways and domes. Smaller archways lined the walls on either side of the room with more archways above them, on the second floor.

The stone work alone was breathtaking. Nico, a former marble and granite fabricator, knew all about Italian stone. The stonework in front of him just wasn't seen in the modern age. The skill it took to construct such massive pieces, and then to put them all together in a work of art like the Basilica, was all but lost.

Straight ahead, he saw the stage, with the monumental, gothic-style altar, standing twenty-five feet high. Intricate carvings and statues towered over the stage. The only thing that dominated the scene more than the altar itself was the backdrop of the gigantic archway, with its dome and columns in the stunning semi-circle balcony on the second floor. It was a scene straight out of the twelfth century.

Only, it was bathed in a deep pink glow. It was a stunning sight to see such an otherworldly hue in a setting nearly one thousand years old. It also struck him that he was staring at a scene which hadn't taken place in over seven hundred years. Until that moment, Nico's comprehension of the supernatural world was limited to the present. He'd heard many stories from beings which existed before the formation of the Earth, but the reality of it all had never taken root.

Until now.

Something moved at the front of the room. Xabier and Lazlo had taken positions flanking the main stage. There was still no sign of anyone guarding the glowing point, which was somewhere behind the massive altar. Nico could see a Xabier-shaped shadow moving swiftly along the wall, slipping behind the altar.

Without warning, Nico heard Xabier wail in pain, and Lazlo, approaching from the opposite side of the altar, collapsed with his hands covering his ears. Both vampires dropped from sight, but Nico could hear their screams as some unseen force assaulted them. Nico recalled a similar moment when he and Xabier mounted their attack on Alvi Cornega's house in Colombia, almost a year ago. There had been a witch present.

He scanned the room again and saw no one. He blinked his eyes and found himself standing directly behind the altar. Xabier and Lazlo writhed on the ground in agony. Nico's eyes flicked from left to right, seeking the source of the attack. All he could see was the deep pink glow emanating from directly in front of him. He stepped toward it, but caught movement out of the corner of his eye, and a tingle at the nape of his neck.

He didn't think; his body just reacted. His right hand shot up, and a green gaseous ball shot out. Thirty feet away, the ball exploded around a figure standing in the shadows of a large archway. With a loud grunt, the figure collapsed. Without looking, Nico raised his left hand, and another green ball exploded in an archway on the opposite side of the room. He could see the other witch topple over. Xabier and Lazlo stopped squirming on the ground struggled to their feet.

"I loathe witches," Lazlo said to Xabier. "Have I ever told you that?"

Xabier stretched his neck. "You might have mentioned it."

Nico gestured to the glowing shard protruding from the mouth of a carved lion head. "Care to do the honors?"

Xabier chuckled. "Don't mind if I do."

He reached out to grab the shard. His hand got within two feet of it and shopped short, slamming into an invisible barrier, which rippled in the space around the point. He frowned and tried again with the same result.

"What the hell?"

Lazlo stepped up next to him and reached out himself. His hand also stopped short. He tried punching through the impediment but succeeded only in making it ripple in space. Both vampires repeatedly beat their fists against the invisible barrier to no avail. Nico tried various methods of his own, including pouring green electrical bolts into the barrier. He even tried fire. Nothing penetrated the invisible shield.

"This is ridiculous," Xabier said. "They spelled it."

Lazlo shook his head and grabbed one of the witches from where she lay, unconscious, in the darkened corridor. Xabier took his cue and dragged the other one over to the point. Lazlo slapped the face of one until she started to come around.

"Oi! Wake up, witch. Today is your lucky day." He shook her as her eyes began to flutter open. "Can you hear me? You're in luck, witch. You get to live. All you have to do is take down this blasted spell."

"I-I-I c-c-can't."

Lazlo slammed her against the back side of the altar. She gasped as the air left her lungs. After her head banged against the altar, she looked dazed. Lazlo held her by the chin and smiled.

"How about now, sweetheart? Are we feeling a bit more cooperative now that we've woken up?"

"T-t-the spell…I didn't cast it. It w-w-won't come down u-until t-t-t-tomorrow morning."

Lazlo's eyes flashed with anger and the witch's mouth twitched. "The spell is designed specifically to ensure no one, including us, can thwart the opening of the portal."

"You're *witches*," Lazlo hissed. "It is your duty to keep the portal from opening and unleashing that vermin upon the earth."

"Our *duty*," the witch replied, "is to our people."

Xabier shoved the other witch against the wall and bared his fangs. "Maybe we should bring this entire building down."

She didn't flinch. Her short, bleach-blonde hair was slicked back and pulled into a short pony tail. Her eyes, even with the dark makeup around them, sparkled with glee. Even with her life hanging in the balance, she seemed to take pleasure in denying the vampires.

"Go ahead," she spat. "The portal will still open tonight, and you will have destroyed this magnificent building."

Nico admired their courage, misplaced as it was. Lazlo, on the other hand, had no patience left.

"We don't have time for this," he said. "If we are to stop the portal from opening, we have to get in front of them."

With that he bared his fangs and bit deeply into the witch's neck. She gasped as her skin broke and the fangs pierced her carotid artery. Within seconds, Lazlo drained her blood and without a second thought flung her lifeless body straight up in the air. She flew limply over the altar and disappeared out of sight. Seconds later, they all heard the crash and splintering of wood as the body slammed to the ground, scattering the chairs in the middle of the room.

Before anyone could react to what they'd just seen, Xabier tore into the second witch. Instead of simply draining her blood, he ripped her neck apart with his fangs, leaving only the spinal column to connect head with body. Instead of throwing the body, he simply let her fall to the ground. He looked at Nico.

"Where to next?"

Nico looked up at the ceiling and pointed his finger. "For the record...*I* didn't kill anyone."

Instead of trying to pursue the coalition, they decided to work back in the opposite direction to set up an ambush before the point could be lit. The point site in Strasbourg was the Strasbourg Cathedral. Since it was almost midnight, it was deserted. With no innocent bystanders around, so Nico decided it was the best location to make their stand.

"It's as good a place as any," he said, looking at the massive astronomical clock located on one wall of the cathedral, standing sixty feet tall. A huge stained glass window rose above the clock making for a spectacular floor to ceiling sight. The socket was located somewhere on the astronomical clock, near the spiral staircase, according to Zha'riel.

The thing was a wonder. It was even more impressive than the altar at Milan. It didn't have the intricate carvings and artwork, but it was a *functioning* clock, originally built in the fourteenth century. It was like something out of a steam punk comic book, with a spiral staircase on one side, little angel statues all over the piece, and murals on various parts of the lower level. In the darkness, it looked like a spooky castle façade.

Xabier agreed. "At least if we fail, we can try again at Milan when they try to complete the ritual."

"Listen," Nico said. "You two head around on opposite sides of the clock. I'll blink in and snatch the stones. Cover my retreat. It should only take a second or two. Once I get the stones, we'll meet up out front and I'll orb us all out of here."

They situated themselves in secluded hiding spots with good vantage points, and awaited Nayra and her coalition. When she arrived, her minions spread out and prepared for intruders. They didn't appear to be on high alert. Nico figured they hadn't heard they'd lost two witches. He and the vampires still had the advantage of surprise.

Without any fanfare, Nayra strode through the wrought iron gate and made her way up to the clock, climbing the set of stairs on one side. She was carrying a satchel which Nico was certain contained the remaining stones, one for the Strasbourg point and another for the center portal point. He only needed to get his hands on one of them.

As far as he could see, Nayra was guarded by four witches who spread out into positions giving them clear views of the entire room. Xabier and Lazlo would have to move fast to take all four of them before the witches could pull their high frequency trick. He shrugged to himself. They all had jobs to do. His was to get the gems from Nayra. After that, if things went bad, he could orb out, stash the gems and return to rescue the vampires.

He set to blink. When Nayra unshouldered the satchel, and placed it on the floor next to her, he made his move. Had he waited another second, he would have changed the plan. Just as he closed his eyes, he heard the shrieks from Lazlo and Xabier, but by then it was too late. He was committed to his blink. Too late, he realized the witches were ready and waiting.

The moment he appeared on the clock platform, Nayra unleashed a furious assault. She was casting spells even before he fully materialized. Under the best of circumstances, any defense Nico could have mounted required at least a second or two of preparation once he blinked into position. Nayra gave him no time, and he was sent flying off the platform, sprawling onto the marble floor. He skidded to a stop thirty feet away as a furious onslaught spells followed him.

Nayra was so relentless in her attacks, Nico could not recover enough to defend himself. He was repeatedly struck and thrown, slamming into columns and walls. He finally managed to catch his breath when Nayra threw him against a column near a doorway. That was a mistake. For a brief moment, he was out of her sight and managed to throw himself behind the column. It gave his brain a chance to clear enough to preserve himself. He blinked himself to a point around the corner. Nayra wasn't able to cast those kinds of spells through walls, so he was safe for the moment.

He gathered himself and, instead of taking Nayra on directly, he launched attacks on the witches holding back Lazlo and Xabier. Two went down before the others realized what was going on. Lazlo crawled to one of them and bit into her neck, draining her blood and strengthening himself. Nico, still out of

Nayra's line of sight, took out the other two witches, even though they tried to find concealment behind columns of their own. What they didn't think about was Nico's ability to blink from position to position.

Once again, Nico had his vampire allies. Xabier, after draining one of the downed witches of her blood, used his vamp speed to dash across the room to Nico's position. They crouched in the darkness as Nayra stalked them from the center of the room. Nico was spent. He'd used what little energy he had left to free his friends and needed some recovery time.

"You two take her on," he said. "As soon as I can get it together, I'll get the stones and we'll get out of here."

Xabier and Lazlo moved out, trying to distract Nayra without challenging her directly. Nico dragged himself behind a statue and tried to will his body to recover from the beating he'd just taken at Nayra's hands. He could hear the vampires dashing from one position to the other trying to get Nayra to commit to one of them so the other could move in and take her down. Nico felt chakras begin to build up and picked himself up off the floor.

He heard a commotion from across the room and saw a swarm of creatures swarming in to fill the cathedral. They were led by a refined looking individual in what Nico imagined was a very expensive suit. He bore a striking resemblance to Lazlo. He strode confidently to the center of the room as Nayra hurried back to the platform to guard the satchel. Nico stayed out of sight, trying to figure out how to get to the satchel without inviting Nayra to launch on him again.

"Brother!" Lazlo shouted from the shadows. "Once again, you sentence your friends to death! Last time you needed your witch to save you, but today, we are not alone."

"Brother, please," Benyamin replied. "You know how this will end. Just walk away now and we will let you go."

Within moments, the room was a mass of swirling bodies as Xabier and Lazlo attacked the coalition. As the battle raged, Nayra worked the ritual to light the point. After several minutes, Nico saw the stone begin to glow. The pink light radiated throughout the cathedral. The ritual was almost complete. In a few minutes the point would be fully lit.

Nico finally his strength return and set himself to blink. A second later, he stood behind Nayra, his hands coming up as the energy crackled at his fingertips. The burst took her completely by surprise and knocked her to the ground, but at the same time, Nico felt the familiar tingle at the base of his neck just a split second before he was flung across the room. Two remaining witches in Nayra's group stood on opposite sides of the room, working together to defend Nayra.

Nico battled the two witches while Nayra steadily returned to the ritual. The stone glowed brighter and brighter. There was nothing Nico could do to stop it. The moment he tried to focus any power in Nayra's direction, the two witches combined their powers and he dropped like a stone. Nico felt the pressure suddenly return to his head and body. It came over him like an avalanche, without any warning and he felt like he was going to explode. He could hear Azazel's voice in his head, telling him to stop fighting what he is and to let his essence become.

"You must let your essence do what it was created to do."

Nico, on the edge of consciousness, closed his eyes and focused all his energy inward. Suddenly, he felt it, dark and frightening, but powerful beyond anything he'd ever experienced. He gave in. The room bathed in brilliant silver as power surged through his core, exploding outward into every blood vessel. Without a second thought, he unleashed a ferocious attack on the two witches. Unable to stop himself, he struck them with a myriad of casts until they literally came apart in front of him. He stood over the remains of one of them while the room swarmed with the raging battle. Nico dropped to his knees as he realized what he has done.

"I'm dead."

The room suddenly glowed deep pink as the spell completed and the point was secured. Nico, still kneeling in shock, took the full force of Nayra's attack. He never saw it coming. She unleashed volley after volley, screaming the whole time about revenge for Colombia. Xabier and Lazlo, though they'd killed countless coalition members, were unable to help Nico, who eventually fell as Nayra continued her relentless assault. She stood over him, her hands held out over his head, her fingers flexing as Nico writhed in pain, unable to defend himself.

Then, it stopped. Nico, his eyes blurred from pain, saw only a shadow move past him as he strained to see what had happened to Nayra. He heard Nayra's voice and the reactions from her cohorts as there was a sudden scramble. Within seconds, the room was clear.

Nico felt soft hands on his body. He felt energy transferring to him and his thoughts cleared. He saw Tatiana's frightened face staring down at him, her green eyes stricken with grief.

"It's okay, my love. I'm here. You're safe."

"Yes, he is safe, but who will protect him from *you?*"

All eyes turned to the source of the menacing voice. His eyes flashed silver and glowed bright white. Without waiting for an answer, Azazel's hand came up, and Tatiana was thrown to the ground, slamming into the base of a column.

"I think," Azazel said to Nico, "it's time to clear some things up."

Chapter 25

"It must be done."

"It was self-defense, Rafael. Surely you can see that."

Zha'riel stood in Rafael's palatial office, in Heaven's military sector. Once a paradise of rolling green hills and spectacular gardens, golden mountains and crystal streams, Heaven was now divided into sectors to keep the unfortunate necessity of its armies away from the eternal perfection and peace it was created to be. Angels underwent grueling evaluations, and operated under strict supervision. Eons after one third of Heaven's angels followed Lucifer into rebellion, Heaven was still determined never to allow such horrific events to repeat themselves.

Rafael was the commander of a special garrison, an elite squad Zha'riel was once proud to be a part of. Since his disgrace, and subsequent exile, Zha'riel had done everything in his power to gain reinstatement. Now, he was being offered that very thing.

"There can be no equivocation," Rafael said, his dark eyes boring into Zha'riel. His stare was intense but not threatening. He didn't have to make threats; he knew how to lead. "It is unfortunate, but Nico knew what he was doing. Now, you must finish him.""*Me?*" Zha'riel said. He shouldn't have been surprised. Somehow, he knew his reinstatement would come at a steep price. The real question was if he was really willing to pay this particular price. "*I* have to be the one to kill him?"

"Those are your orders," Rafael replied with a grim smile. "Welcome back, Zha'riel."

He stood up and reached for something behind his large desk. He pulled a long, slender item, covered in royal linens. He strode toward Zha'riel until they stood face-to-face. He then held out his hands, palms up with the mysterious item resting atop them. He smiled as Zha'riel's perplexed expression changed to one of understanding.

"I had this made for you," Rafael said. "It is the sword of a garrison commander. It was touched by the Father's hand."

Zha'riel unwrapped the sword and wielded it in stunned awe. He'd seen them carried by the highest-ranking officers but never held one in his own hands, and never thought he would ever earn one. He stood before Rafael, the recipient of an honor most angels never bothered to aspire to. He thought about the proposal.

"To return to Heaven I have to kill my friend." He looked at Rafael. "And if I do, I get to be a garrison commander?"

"No," Rafael said. "To get back into Heaven you have to demonstrate your fidelity to the Law. You get to be garrison commander because that is the position you had earned before you met Nico Scarlatti. I am prepared to overlook the past year, Zha'riel. We will station you in an assignment that will help you regain your perspective."

Zha'riel shook his head and turned away, still examining the gleaming illidium sword in his hand. Everything he had ever wanted was right in front of him. He had only to finish the job he'd been assigned nearly one year before. That day, he was told his assignment would end in one of two ways: either Nico Scarlatti would join Heaven's forces and fight against the forces of darkness, or he would slip into darkness, at which point, he would have to be dealt with.

Nico had never shown an interest in Heaven or its rules. In fact, he ran in the complete opposite direction. His attitude bordered on outright rebellion. Sometimes, Zha'riel thought he did it on purpose, just to get under his skin, or maybe he was just flipping off the rigid angels who kept telling him how to live.

Whatever the case, Nico was headed in the wrong direction, but there was still such a thing as friendship, and Zha'riel had never known a more loyal friend than Nico Scarlatti.

"You label him a psychotic," Zha'riel said, staring at the blade as he moved it slowly through the air. His back was still to Rafael. "But all he's ever done is defend innocent people."

"Zha'riel, we have been down this road all too often. It is this very thinking that resulted in your exile."

Zha'riel whirled around. "What thinking? Compassion? Loyalty to a friend?"

"A friend who got you *exiled*!" Rafael exclaimed. "Do you not see it, Zha'riel? You show compassion to a man who trusts the darkness inside him more than he trusts the word of an angel of the Lord."

Zha'riel pursed his lips. "Perhaps he sees morality in eliminating those who harm others."

Rafael laughed. He shook his head as he backed up and leaned against his desk. "Morality? Nico's idea of morality seems to be *killing* people. How twisted does one have to be to arrive at that conclusion?"

"How twisted is it when the solution to the whole mess is for *you* to order *me* to kill him?"

Rafael stared at him without saying a word. The tension hung in the air between them. It was so thick, Zha'riel could feel it weighing on him. His choice was simple, yet impossible. The one thing becoming clearer and clearer to him was that Heaven wanted him to do the very thing they accused Nico of doing.

"I won't execute him for defending himself," Zha'riel finally said.

Rafael's eyes darkened. Zha'riel knew him to be a patient leader, but he also knew of Rafael's temper when his patience reached its limit. It was not a pretty sight, and no one wanted to be on the receiving end of one of Rafael's rants.

"Zha'riel," he said in a steady tone, but his voice was tight with tension. "You have your orders. This is our mission. This is who we are."

Zha'riel sighed and laid the sword on Rafael's desk. "There *is* no us, Rafael."

ᛒ ᴀ ꝫ ψ Ꮹ

"We must hurry."

Nayra strode purposefully toward the glowing point in the Basilica of San Lorenzo, in Milan. All five points were lit, glowing pink. The moon was nearing its apex. Its power would be at its maximum soon. Nayra knew she would need every advantage she could get to open the portal. Witchcraft could be tricky, especially when attempting to cast spells created by others.

Her heart continued to race, even after the skirmish with Nico Scarlatti. The last time she tried to face off against him, *he* had the upper hand, and she and Alvi had barely made it out alive. Tonight, she had come close to avenging that humiliation. Whatever had swooped in to save him was far more powerful than Nayra. Fortunately, whoever it was decided it was more important to tend to Nico than stop Nayra. That hesitation allowed her to escape Strasbourg intact, and with the remaining gemstone and the portal key.

"Keep your eyes open!" she called out to the remaining witches as she stood before the glowing pink point. "We need only to complete the five points ritual and then we will be ready to open the portal. No distractions!"

Despite how she was so easily cast aside by Scarlatti's mysterious savior at Strasbourg, Nayra's confidence soared. She had grown stronger in the weeks following the confrontation at Wynnifrea's tomb, but had no idea just how strong. Now that she had real combat experience, she felt the Kharashuoa energy coursing through her veins. Her connection to nature had never been stronger.

She spread her hands and began the final incantation for the five points ritual. The remaining witches, wary of anything in the vicinity that moved, kept watch, while Benyamin and his supernatural coalition spread out around and inside the building. Everyone expected another showdown with Xabier and Lazlo, but it never came. Nayra's incantations took less than three minutes and there were no interruptions.

She finished the ritual and the point brightened. Next, there was a rumble, and the deep pink glow shot out in a single beam of light for just a second. Then everything returned to the way it was, with the point glowing just as it had before.

Nayra smiled and turned to Benyamin. "It is finished. Shall we go open the portal?"

ᛒ ᴀ ẕ ψ ᴄ

"You set me up!"

Tatiana, having recovered from Azazel's initial attack, now stood before him, shaking with rage. She had known he couldn't be trusted from the very beginning. She felt foolish enough for having trusted him at all, but now he wanted to humiliate her in front of Nico. Why? Why bother playing such trivial games?

"Nonsense," Azazel said. "*You* are the one who created the distrust between you and Nico. I am merely here to ensure he knows *all* the facts."

He turned to Nico. "I told you before, you were a pawn in a game you had no chance of comprehending, but I suspect things are clearer now, aren't they?"

To Tatiana's chagrin, he told Nico she was keeping the truth form him in an effort to win him back. As Azazel held forth with strong feelings toward lying to one's friends, and especially to one's closest love, Tatiana clenched her fists with rage. She felt the blood in her veins rise in temperature. Every muscle in her body screamed at her to act.

She slowly pulled her bright red locks of hair back and held them in place with an elastic band. She shed the dark overcoat she wore to cover her light-skinned arms. She was dressed in black leather pants with black boots hugging her claves three-quarters of the way up to her knees. A black halter top completed her simple ensemble.

Without a word, she launched herself at Azazel. Midway through her leap, a curved, jet-black sword appeared in her hand.

Azazel, his back to the furious Tatiana, managed to spin away at the last moment, and the blade slashed through his left sleeve and embedded itself six inches deep in the marble floor. Azazel let out a grunt as the blade sliced through skin all the way to bone.

He stared in disbelief at his arm and the blood pouring onto the floor. He waved his right hand over it and the bleeding stopped. He looked at Tatiana, who had pulled her sword from the floor and was now poised for battle. His look of pained shock quickly dissipated, replaced by a menacing glower.

"You dare to attack me, you young fool?"

Tatiana said nothing. Instead, she charged Azazel with lightening quickness, her sword slashing and slicing through the air in precise movements. Tatiana was a master swordsman. Azazel, without a weapon of his own, twisted and leaned to avoid her strikes. Tatiana thrust forward, her sword aimed right at the center of Azazel's chest. He slid to his left. Tatiana smirked and, without breaking her movement, shot her left hand forward. Azazel had no chance. All he could do was present his shoulder instead of his heart. Tatiana, driving the dagger upward, buried the long, slender blade all the way up to the handle in Azazel's underarm. The point broke the skin above his shoulder and blood once again dripped from Azazel's wounds.

He grimaced in pain as Tatiana continued her sword attack, refusing to give him time to recover and remove the dagger from his shoulder. Finally, Azazel grew impatient, and lashed out with his right hand. Violet electrical currents swept Tatiana off her feet, driving her backwards until she dropped onto the cold, marble floor.

Azazel removed the blade from his shoulder and his wounds healed quickly. He glanced around the room with fierce, glowing white eyes which somehow retained a hint of amusement, as though the whole scene was nothing more than a temper tantrum from an ill-behaved child rather than an attempt to take his life.

Tatiana rose to her feet, and her sword flew from the floor at Azazel's feet to her hands and she took a swordfighter's stance once again. She could see Azazel struggling to maintain his calm, cool demeanor. She enjoyed seeing the powerful archangel rattled. She knew it wasn't fear, but Azazel wasn't one to show emotion. His violent nature was always carefully controlled. He didn't lose his temper; he unleashed it.

She shook her head. "You need your magic? Come on. Draw your weapon, Azazel. If you want to destroy me then do it with…"

"Enough!" He pointed a finger at her face. "Provoke me further and you will suffer, girl!"

Tatiana remained in her fighting stance but didn't attack. Azazel wasn't going to hurt her. He still wanted to influence Nico. That was the chance she took when she decided to attack in the first place. Azazel couldn't be sure of Nico's feelings for her.

"Why are you here, Azazel?" she asked.

"I am here to stop this nonsense before Nico and his friends here get themselves killed."

Nico stood on unsteady legs. Tatiana was glad to see color returning to his face. His eyes were clear, though there was no mistaking the confusion in them.

"What the hell are you two talking about?"

"Nico," Xabier interrupted. "We don't have time for this. We have to get to Milan…*now.*"

"Hold on," Nico replied, looking at Tatiana and Azazel. "Someone wanna tell me what's going on?"

"Nico," Azazel said. "You *cannot* trust her. All I want to do is ensure you are thinking clearly."

Nico frowned. "Why do you care?"

Azazel smiled and gestured to Tatiana. "When she tells you the truth, you will understand."

"Truth?" Nico made a face. "What truth?"

Tatiana lowered her sword. "Nico, please. Can we go somewhere and talk?"

"I'm kinda in the middle of something, Tatiana."

Azazel spread his hands and his face broke into a wide grin. He told Nico how simple it all really was. How can he trust Tatiana when she hasn't even told him who she really was?

"But," he said. "Stop worrying about the portal. There is no reason whatsoever for you to get involved."

Xabier interrupted. "Nico, why are we listening to this guy? We know what he is."

"Shut up, Fang!" Azazel's glowing eyes focused on Xabier, who shrank back just a little. "Learn your place."

Azazel told Nico it wasn't important that he stop Nayra. The opening of the portal was not something he should concern himself with. He needed to focus on protecting himself. He needed friends, and not just piss-ant vampires.

"Nico, you are in trouble. You need to focus on what is happening inside you and learn how to use and control it." He put a hand on Nico's shoulder. "Listen to me. You have friends at your disposal should you choose to accept us." He nodded toward Xabier and Lazlo. "And your friends are invited, provided you stop interfering with our efforts. You can trust *me*, Nico, the father of the one whose essence lives in you. And you can trust his mother. We offer you safety, and instruction."

Lazlo and Xabier pleaded with Nico to go with them, but he hesitated. Tatiana could see he was intrigued by Azazel's accusations. He was also clearly swayed a little by Azazel's offer of protection and training. She couldn't let Nico take that road.

She lunged once again, but this time Azazel's blade came out and he easily deflected her attack. They clashed for several seconds with Azazel easily getting the better of it. Before long, Tatiana was on her knees, breathless, her sword on the ground. Azazel stood over her and held his sword to her neck.

"The foolishness of love," he said, raising his sword for the final blow.

"Noooo!" Nico lunged, throwing himself over Tatiana. His arms wrapped around her and he covered her with his body. "Please! I...I love her. I-I...I need her. I don't *care* who she is."

Azazel lowered his sword. He ran his tongue along his bottom lip and let out a long breath. "Very well, Nico. Unlike those who try to solicit your loyalty with deceit, I offer you friendship, and respect your wishes. Come talk to me after she tells you everything."

ᛒ ᚨ ᛂ ᚹ ᚷ

"Did you mean it, Nico?"

Azazel was gone, leaving only Xabier and Lazlo, both of whom stood in shock at Azazel's parting comments, and Tatiana, who still clutched the front of his shirt as though he would disappear at any moment. She was staring into his eyes, a glimmer of hope behind the fear of rejection.

"I meant it." He pulled her in close and squeezed. "We'll figure it all out. I promise."

"Nico, *come on!*" Xabier prodded, his arms spread. "Can we get on with it?"

Nico shook his head and rolled his eyes, but he got up, pulling Tatiana to her feet as he rose. Azazel's words rang in his head. Nico wasn't sure it was such a good idea to stand against him over something so insignificant.

"I don't know, Xabs. You really think it's worth taking Azazel on directly?"

Xabier shrugged. "I think it's better than lying down and letting him win. Why are you suddenly ready to jump on board that psycho's wagon?"

"I didn't say that..."

"No? Well you're sure dragging your feet here. We need to stop this portal from opening. That's from Zha'riel and me, your closest friends, and here you are, hitching your—"

"*All right!*" Nico shouted. "Let's go."

Moments later, the four walked through the Basilica at San Lorenzo. It was deserted. The bodies of the two dead witches were gone and there was no trace of any damage to the chairs in the middle of the room. Everything looked exactly like it had the first time Nico and the vampires showed up. The pink glow from behind the altar cast the same eerie shadows. Xabier and Lazlo split up and slashed through the wings of the basilica. When they returned to Nico, in the center of the main hall, they looked frustrated.

"I hope it was worth it," Lazlo said to Nico, his lower lip quivering in rage. "You and your indecisiveness."

Xabier leaned against a chair and shook his head. "I don't understand where your head is at, Nico."

"What are you talking about?"

"You made us wait while you sorted out your love life," Lazlo said in a scornful tone, his eyes drifting to Tatiana, who stared back in silence.

Xabier signaled him to back off before he turned back to Nico. "You have to admit, you're not acting normal. You're taking cues from the lunatic death angel?"

Nico stared at him. "Are you serious? You went off on your own for weeks. *You* kept *me* out of the loop. That's on *you*! How is *any* of this my fault?"

The tensions between the two friends began to bubble over the rim. Xabier's jabs at Nico for his indecisiveness and lack of enthusiasm were answered with commentary on Xabier's poor judgment and arrogance in thinking he could handle everything on his own. The two squared off as their voices rose and tempers began to flare. Tatiana and Lazlo finally had to step in to separate them.

Lazlo chuckled as he kept a hand on Xabier's chest. "I find it rather amusing that *I* am the one to call for peace."

A bright light shone and disappeared, leaving a tired-looking Zha'riel standing in its place. He looked like *he'd* been the one fighting for the past hour. Nico was about to ask a sarcastic question about his appearance but Xabier beat him to it.

"Oh, look who finally shows his face." Xabier sighed and rolled his eyes in disgust. "The halo appears when you need him least."

Zha'riel ignored him and looked straight at Nico who closed his eyes. He knew what was coming. He'd known it the second he realized what he'd done to the two witches.

"You are in serious trouble."

Tatiana placed her hand on his forearm. Nico laid his hand atop hers and squeezed.

"I know," Nico replied. "Those two witches."

"And now Heaven will come for you."

Tatiana's face fell. "Today?"

"I do not know when." Zha'riel kept his eyes on Nico's and responded through clenched teeth. "Soon."

Xabier was incredulous. "Oh, for god's sake! He was defending himself, and fighting to keep the portal locked!"

Zha'riel shook his head. "When are you going to understand, you don't get to excuse the killing of humans?"

Nico understood the spot he was in. He also realized, with finality, that he was sick of Heaven's ridiculous attitudes and rules. He was sick of angels who threatened and never followed up. He was sick of the mental anguish that went with consorting with the so-called good guys.

"Does this mean you're here to execute me?"

Zha'riel closed his eyes and shook his head. When he reopened them, Nico could see the conflict behind them. "No. Though they wanted me to do exactly that." He steadied his gaze and looked Nico in the eye. "I refused."

Nico nodded. Maybe the angel was finally coming around. "So, you're here to help us then?"

Zha'riel shook his head. "I cannot help."

"Of *course*, you can't," Xabier said, throwing up his hands. "You're never allowed to help. Do you realize that? What kind of angel isn't allowed to help anyone? I never understood the logic on that. Why don't you go back to Heaven and…?"

"Let's just go!" Nico said, putting a hand on Xabier's and Lazlo's shoulders.

Before orbing to the portal location, he glanced back at Zha'riel. Though he was grateful for whatever amount of loyalty it took for Zha'riel to refuse Heaven's orders, Nico couldn't help but feel a tinge of disgust. Like Xabier, he expected his friend to pitch in. Now, Zha'riel was going to sit on the sidelines, again, while those who stuck by him over the past year, while he was in exile, went off to fight against horrific odds.

"I hope the rules are worth it, my friend," Nico said softly, and with that, they orbed out, leaving Zha'riel standing alone before the alter in the Basilica of San Lorenzo.

Chapter 26

"Are we on schedule?"

Azazel held the phone to his ear and listened for a few seconds before responding. Seir conveyed his status quickly and efficiently, as always. Azazel nodded in approval and took a deep breath.

"Excellent, my friend…yes, it worked to perfection…the witch completed the ritual undisturbed, though I expect to encounter all-out resistance at the portal sight. We must be prepared. Have everyone in position and ready. I will tolerate no mistakes this close to success."

After a few more questions from Seir, and orders from Azazel, the call ended. Azazel pocketed the cell phone. He stared out over the rugged and gloomy landscape of Nordkapp. The black sky sparkled with countless stars and a full moon, giving the place an eerie atmosphere, which suited Azazel. He stood at the very spot where he and his former friend had fought over Nico Scarlatti. Though no one died that day, blood was spilled and Azazel felt some connection to the place.

"You seem fully in command, old friend."

Azazel whirled around to find Lucifer standing before him with his hands folded in front of his belly. Lucifer's laser-blue eyes gave no indication of the Dark Lord's intentions. Azazel felt an instinct to get away but couldn't bring himself to flee. His hands clenched and unclenched as his glowing white eyes darted from Lucifer's hands to his eyes, searching for any sign of attack, but he said nothing.

Lucifer smirked. "Considering you pilfered my army, I would think at least a thank you is in order."

Azazel closed his eyes and contained his rising anger. The elder, and more powerful, angel wrote the book on psychological warfare. Lucifer had to know by now what was about to take place. He'd waited until the night of the portal opening to confront Azazel about Seir's raids on the Dark Army. It didn't take a military strategist to figure out who was responsible for those losses. There was a showdown coming, and Azazel wondered why Lucifer bothered with discussion.

When Azazel didn't respond, Lucifer tilted his head and wrinkled his forehead. "You look troubled, old friend. Are you anxious about your big night?"

Lucifer's interest in Azazel's portal project was something that had always nagged at Azazel. He'd asked the question several times over the past months, and every time he thought he had a satisfying rationale, his mind wouldn't let it lie.

Azazel narrowed his eyes. "Why are you standing in my way on this? What do you care if the portal is opened or not?"

Lucifer shrugged. "I don't...not really. But, you defied me, humiliated me in front of my whole kingdom." He raised his eyebrows. "I was willing to allow you to live, but keeping you from getting that which you desired seemed..." he shrugged.

"Vindictive and childish?" Azazel finished.

Lucifer laughed. "Perhaps, but it amused me for a while."

Azazel bent over and picked up a stone from the rocky ground. He fingered the jagged rock as he considered his choice of words. He still wondered about Lucifer intentions. He had to be ready for anything, but he wasn't about to convey weakness. His pride wouldn't allow that kind of thing.

"Was the boy worth it?" he asked Lucifer. "Now that time has passed, and our friendship has become...this. Would you do it the same way?"

Lucifer inhaled deeply as he pondered the question. He had to be feeling the same regret Azazel felt every day. Azazel would not change past events. He could see no other way things could have gone. He had to avenge his son's murder. Lucifer saw an opportunity, and chose that over friendship and loyalty. It wasn't a complete surprise, but Azazel was left with few options as a father.

Lucifer sighed, his face filled with resignation. "You were my closest confidant. I understand what you did, but *you* need to understand what that young man could mean for our cause."

Azazel figured as much. Lucifer was still entrenched in his belief that Nico would ultimately join the ranks of his army, and potentially tip the balance. He still believed his lies and deceit would net him a victory over his enemies.

"I find it strange that you put such trust in so indecisive a man. You realize he doesn't trust you?"

Lucifer shrugged slightly. "He doesn't know *who* to trust, but he knows it was *me* who saved his life. He knows he now has *my* blood in his veins. Most importantly, he knows he can find protection from Heaven if he comes to me.

"And he is going to need it after tonight," Azazel muttered.

Lucifer smiled grimly. He pursed his lips as he stared at Azazel. "Stranger still, is *your* interest in young Nico."

And there it was…the *real* reason for this visit. Lucifer must have found out he and Nico had met. Considering Azazel's previous efforts to destroy the young man, Nico still breathing had to be confusing to the dark leader. Azazel enjoyed his own moment of psychological superiority.

"My interest is no different than your own," Azazel said. "Only I haven't lied to the boy."

"No," Lucifer replied with a smug smile. "But you *have* murdered his girlfriend, *and* you tried to murder *him*."

Azazel couldn't deny those tidbits. "Very true. However, I don't think the pretty blonde girl haunts his thoughts as much as she used to."

"No?"

Lucifer's patronizing tone irritated Azazel. He thought about letting the conversation peter out but Lucifer's smug expression was begging to be wiped off his face.

Azazel looked him in the eyes. "Was it necessary to send your *daughter* to sway him? Who does that?"

"Whatever it takes," Lucifer answered with a slight shrug, as though it was all perfectly natural. "Some things are more important than propriety. She was assigned to capture the boy's heart and guide him to me."

Azazel smiled. "Yes, well, I think your little plan has come crashing down."

"And why would you say that? Has Nico failed to succumb to her beauty?"

"No," Azazel chuckled. "Nico is quite taken with the lovely Tatiana."

Lucifer shrugged. "Than what could possibly bring my plan "crashing down," as you say?"

"I'm pretty sure *she* has fallen in love with *him* as well."

Lucifer stared at him with an expression of disbelief, but it was not the disbelief Azazel was expecting. Lucifer's expression was one of condescending sympathy. Azazel suddenly felt like the child who thought two plus two equaled seven only to have the teacher tell him he should not feel bad about being wrong. Instead, he should feel proud that he did his best.

"Perhaps we should discuss something else," Lucifer said with a barely stifled smile and a wink. Then his expression reverted to a cold, icy stare. "There is the matter of your continued insolence in raiding my armies. Do not think your silly attempts at disguising your demon's efforts have kept the truth from me. I see everything, Azazel.

Azazel stood rigid, prepared for the strike he knew had to be coming. "Shall we do battle now?"

Lucifer turned and stared at the bright full moon. After several silent moments, he raised his gaze to the night sky and watched the stars. Finally, he waved a hand and strode out over the rugged landscape, away from Azazel.

"Another time."

ხ ʌ ჳ ψ ც

"Dammit!" Xabier squinted through the night. "They've already started."

"They're not wasting any time, are they?"

They stood at a tree line, deep in the mountains of Valduz, the capital of Lichtenstein. The sky was black but clear. Stars sparkled against the perfect backdrop. Nico's mind drifted. Even under the circumstances, he couldn't help but wonder if the scene, more than seven hundred years prior, had changed much. Had anyone stood where he was standing back in 1290 AD? Was there the same sense of danger as he was feeling?

Lazlo and Xabier stood to Nico's left, hashing out a plan to get close enough to interfere with their adversaries. Nayra was working in a small cave and was surrounded by a crowd of supernatural creatures, all facing outward, poised for trouble. More creatures patrolled the surrounding area in groups of three or four. The place was locked down tighter than a maximum-security prison.

Tatiana touched his arm. "We're going to have to blink in and snatch the point or the key. There's no way those two will make it through that crowd."

Nico agreed. The supernatural coalition was there in force, and it was clear the purpose of such a large force was to buy time and keep any attackers as far from Nayra as possible, indefinitely. But something was missing. He couldn't put his finger on it, but the setup felt off.

"Something's wrong," he mumbled, feeling the tingle at the base of his neck.

Xabier looked at him. "Well, figure it out. We got one shot at this."

"If we're lucky," Lazlo chimed in.

Xabier nudged him. "At least *pretend* to be positive, Laz."

Nayra's voice sang out, beginning her ritual. She knelt with her head bowed and arms outstretched. Her voice carried but not enough for Nico to make out the words. He could hear the tell-tale rhythmic cadence of a witch's chant. Her protectors moved in closer to her, forming a protective semicircle, leaving only the space between her and the cave open.

That was the opening Nico knew they needed. He and Tatiana set to blink in. Lazlo and Xabier split up and made their way to positions flanking the mass of supernatural beings. When Nico and Tatiana blinked, the vampires would attack the nearest group loudly and violently, pulling attention to them and hopefully giving Nico and Tatiana the second or two they would need to grab the point stone or portal key and blink back out of there.

Nico glanced at Tatiana and she nodded. He held up his hand and dropped it. Lazlo and Xabier launched themselves into the open space and attacked from two different directions. Nico and Tatiana waited until just before the vampires made contact with their targets. Once the vampires engaged, they set to blink over to the cave.

Nothing happened. They tried again. They were still in the same place. They exchanged confused glances.

"What's wrong?" Nico asked.

Tatiana shook her head. "It's like there's some sort of—"

"Spell?"

The amused feminine voice came from somewhere in the darkness but the owner did not reveal herself. Nico peered into the forest behind him, but even with the moonlit sky, he could make out nothing except trees and brush. He felt the tingling at the base of his neck again and glanced at Tatiana. Instinctively, they stepped away from one another.

They were under attack, that much was clear. Tatiana held her hands out, palms up, and Nico saw the flames appear at her fingers. She raised her eyebrows at him. He looked at his own hands and held them up. Green electrical energy crackled between his fingers. He looked at Tatiana and nodded. At least they weren't powerless. Whatever the spell was, it only seemed to prevent them from traveling supernaturally, but that was enough to ruin any chance they had of getting to the portal before Nayra completed her ritual.

"That's right."

"You cannot stop us."

"The portal will be opened soon."

The voices seemed to come from all directions. Nico and Tatiana spun and scanned the surrounding area, searching for the sources. They saw nothing but forest and shadows. Nico was suddenly thrown backward against a tree. He was held in place, three feet off the ground, with his back to the tree. He couldn't move a muscle.

Tatiana crouched and peered into the darkness for the witch holding Nico, but couldn't see anything. She was struck from behind and sent sprawling. She felt a giant, claw-like grip come over her body and struggled to free herself. The grip was powerful, but no match for Tatiana once she controlled her mind. More importantly, once she felt the grip come over her, she felt the location of the source. She shattered the grip and spun, unleashing a burst of energy. The witch tumbled from her perch on a low branch, and fell to the ground, stunned. Tatiana spun to check on Nico. He was still wriggling against the grip of the witch's power.

Then he jerked from side to side, and screamed in agony. Even in the darkness, Tatiana could see his face contorted, the skin stretched tight across his skull. The witch was pummeling him from the darkness. Tatiana let loose a furious volley of energy in all directions, trying to pry loose the witch from her hiding place. It didn't help. Nico thrashed about, his head slamming repeatedly against the tree. If he didn't free himself, he would soon lose consciousness.

"Nico! Center your mind! Find your essence! Let it *loose*, for God's sake! Stop fighting it!"

Her words snapped Nico out of his daze. He let his mind go where it wanted. It headed straight for the darkness he spent so much time trying to bury. Within seconds, he felt a surge of power, as if his body was instantly renewed. He felt the crackle of energy in his fingers as the chakras surged through his veins like lightning bolts.

A feeling of despair washed over him. He was allowing himself to slide even further into darkness, just like Rafael and Zha'riel had warned. He felt as though everything that made him human was slipping into the ether, and only the darkness would remain. He wondered, briefly, if saving his own life would be worth it if all he had to look forward to was an eternity of ice-cold darkness.

Those thoughts only lasted a moment. When the dread passed, Nico saw a brilliant flash of silver and then saw the world through a pure-white glow. Without turning his head, he saw everyone. Tatiana, crouched several feet away, was scanning the trees for their attackers. Xabier and Lazlo were locked in futile combat in the field, hundreds of yards away from Nayra and her portal magic. Most importantly, he could see the four witches. The one Tatiana had stunned was back on her feet and joining the other three in their attack against him.

They meant to kill him. His mind spun, and the darkness overcame whatever tender mercies his humanity retained. He clenched his fists and flexed his muscles. The grip around his body broke and he dropped to the ground, landing steadily on his feet, in perfect balance. He kept his head lowered, letting the rage build in his core as the witches continued to direct their powers at him. He turned his head slowly, from right to left, as if stretching before an athletic endeavor.

He brought his hand up, and, in the blink of an eye, flames shot out, hissing through the trees, missing every brown leaf, every tiny branch. As though they had minds of their own, the flames sought out two of the witches, knocking them off their feet and engulfing them. He stretched his hands out once again, and the other two witches met with the same fate. All four burned for several moments, screaming in agony as the flames licked at them, eating them slowly.

"Nico!"

Tatiana grabbed his arm. When he saw the frown on her face, he realized something was wrong. She was listening closely, her eyes scanning the night sky. His eyes followed hers, but he saw only stars against a black backdrop. He thought he heard a sound like rushing air but shrugged it off. They more pressing concerns.

"What is it?" he asked. "Come on. Let's get to Nayra and end this."

He was about to blink to Nayra's position but Tatiana squeezed his arm even tighter.

"Wait!" she cried and then pointed to the sky. "Demons!"

"What?"

Nico looked up but couldn't make anything out. He peered through the darkness and then saw movement. It was like a cloud of blackness, more like a wave. It was even blacker than the night sky, causing the sky to appear midnight blue. The sound was louder, now clearly heard as the wave approached. It moved quickly, filling the night sky, blacking out the light from the stars and even the moon before breaking up into thousands of smaller balls of blackness and streaking toward the earth.

"What the hell is that?" Nico asked, his heart racing, though he felt the rush of battle more than anything resembling fear. Whatever it was, he hoped he would have the chance to kill it.

"Demons!" Tatiana shouted as the sound grew to a deafening pitch. "Azazel's army! They're here!"

ㄅ A ʒ ψ ɢ

"They are going to be killed!"

"Good," Rafael replied as they watched the scene play out from their heavenly vantage point. "Perhaps all of them will fall tonight. It will save us the time and energy of hunting them down ourselves." He spread his hands. Why are you here, Zha'riel? You rejected my outstretched hand. You chose the bastard human over the servants of the Lord."

"I did not reject you, Rafael," Zha'riel countered. "You put me in an impossible position."

The corners of Rafael's mouth turned up and he sniffed. "Perhaps."

Though Zha'riel had turned down Rafael's offer to rejoin the angelic ranks with a huge promotion, he hadn't given up on reinstatement to his old post. His limited privileges, including the ability to leave and enter Heaven and consort with the other angels hadn't been revoked following his last conversation with Rafael. He felt like there was still hope. Perhaps he could gain some support simply by talking to his former friends and comrades.

But he still felt the pull to go help a friend in trouble. Nico and Xabier were fighting tremendous odds trying to stop the reopening of the portal. The angels once stood with Xabier in his effort to imprison the alphas. Now, the alphas were about to be freed and the angels refused to stand against them.

"This makes no sense," Zha'riel said. "We should be helping them keep that portal shut and those abominations locked away. It should not matter who we side with."

"*THAT*...is the very *PROBLEM*...with your *MIND*, Zha'riel!" Rafael slammed his hand down hard on the desk, shaking the entire room. "You still fail to see that it *DOES* matter! Seven hundred years ago, we did not side with that abomination you are so friendly with. He joined up with the humans because he hated one of his own. He is not worth your loyalty, angel. He hates us. He hates everything good. He mocks you and still you fight for him! Why?"

Zha'riel shook his head and mumbled, "Because he is my friend."

Rafael gritted his teeth but remained silent. Zha'riel was always the difficult one, always ready to break from the ranks and go his own way. He was talented, perhaps more talented than any of his brethren. It happened rarely, but it did happen, that an angel rose above his peers to a level of excellence far exceeding those who were supposed to be his equals.

Rafael watched the earthly fighting, in silence, for several moments, before closing his eyes and speaking. "Zha'riel, you still have the opportunity to do what is right. You can still rejoin your brethren."

There was no answer. Rafael turned to look at Zha'riel, but he was alone in his office. His eyes narrowed and he wrinkled his brown. Closing his eyes, he pressed his fingers to his temples and shook his head in weary distress.

"Zha'riel," he droned softly. "Please don't."

ƀ ᴀ ᴣ̆ ᴪ ɢ

"Holy hell!" Nico exclaimed.

"Yeah," Tatiana said. "Something like that."

The landscape swarmed with demons, and Nico and Tatiana were surrounded and attacked without hesitation. They blasted back against the demons, discharging everything they had to hold them off. Nico spun to Tatiana.

"We don't have time to fight these idiots! Let's go get the key!"

Once again, they set to blink out, but once again, they were unable.

"Dammit!" Nico shouted, taking out another demon who thought he was sneaky, coming in from their right flank. "How many more witches are there?"

Tatiana shook her head as she continued to battle the demons to the left. "Totems," she said. "They must have set totems. It's the only way they could maintain that kind of spell after death. We need to find the totems and destroy them."

"What the hell is a totem?" Nico asked, firing a blast of energy at the demons.

He and Tatiana were under heavy attack and some of the attacks were getting through. They were well-equipped to fight demons, but sometimes numbers did matter, especially when the odds were thousands to one. They couldn't hold off the wave of demons forever, and more importantly, they needed to get to Nayra.

"It's like a little pillar," Tatiana explained. "They're set up to form a perimeter, a box or circle. The more they set, the more powerful they are. The pillars bind the spells. They should be easy to spot. They'll be burning." She nodded to him. "Go. I'll hold them back. Just find them and destroy them. Fast."

Nico battled his way through the trees. Demons saw him and pursued, but Tatiana held most of them off, leaving only a few stragglers for Nico to deal with. He didn't bother playing games. He just unleashed everything he had every time. The demons went down one by one. Nico still took a stray shot every now and then but he ignored the pain and continued searching out totems.

It didn't take him long to find one, then another. He destroyed them. Once he understood the placement, he made quick work of the rest. There were eight in all. Once he destroyed the last one, he quickly blinked to Tatiana's position. She was under siege. Nico blinked right into the center of a massive demonic assault.

"The totems," Tatiana said as she fought desperately against the swarm of vicious demons. "As soon as you took the last one down, they were able blink in."

"We need to get to the portal," Nico replied.

He took a strike in the small of his back. Then he took another. Before he could turn around to face his attacker, a third strike sent him sprawling onto the hard ground. Tatiana did her best to push the demons back, but they were relentless and their numbers were endless. For every one she took down, five more filled his place. She was taking heavy damage. Nico tried to regain his senses but every time he moved, he took several more strikes in his back and felt him mind slipping into unconsciousness.

Tatiana reached down and tried to grab his arm. "Nico! Please! I need you!"

Chapter 27

"Elementum holis tule an solarium! Cantis mayleo grudarious! Mecsara ne ingostio! Havadum nexa descartra! Inicio serventum allemas!"

The portal began to glow a deep violet hue. Nayra's hands were raised and her eyes were closed. She stood with her face lifted toward the sky. Tatiana could see the beginning of the end.

Nico had managed to protect them from the demon attack with an invisible barrier but it was sapping the little strength he had remaining. Tatiana's eyes darted from him and back to the portal. She needed Nico to be a whole lot stronger than he was.

"You need to stop this nonsense, Nico," she hissed. "Whatever it is you're holding onto is going to get you killed."

He pulled his arm away and pointed a finger in her face. "Shut up. You have no idea what you're asking me to do, what I will be throwing away."

He looked better, but she knew he was not at full strength and nowhere near the way he looked when he'd let the darkness take over. She'd watched in silence as he focused all his energy to push it back. He wouldn't be able to fight it off if he let it rage again.

"I think I can hold the shield," he said. "Let's go."

"Oh, wonderful," Tatiana said, looking back at the portal cave.

She could see Seir standing near Nayra, watching as his demon army did its work. Her mouth dropped open as Azazel appeared behind him, dressed in a crimson tunic and tall black boots. He had a sheathed sword hanging from his belt. He greeted Seir and patted him on the back, nodding his approval. He turned his back on the battle as though he had no concerns. The demons fought so hard, she knew it would take more than a miracle for them to cover even half the distance between them.

Nico's jaw clenched and Tatiana could see the conflict in his eyes. It was one thing to fight against Azazel's minions, but to see him standing there and still fight against him was causing doubt. Tatiana needed him to embrace his essence.

"Nico, please," she said. "Let it in."

"NO!"

They both turned to see Zha'riel, who had appeared next to them and flicked his hands at the demons. He sent them hurtling away from them in all directions. He held the remaining ranks back with one outstretched hand.

"Do *not* let the darkness in, Nico," he insisted. "You will not survive. I saw you struggle with it last time."

The portal glowed a deeper shade of violet, and began to shimmer. The center had the appearance of liquid. Tatiana stared helplessly as the portal opened. She could see Nayra repeating the incantation with more authority and more intensity each time through. Azazel turned to observe the disturbance on the battlefield and she wondered if he would decide to deal with Zha'riel himself, but he only smiled and waved. He knew Zha'riel was not going to attack.

"What are you waiting for?" Nico screamed at Zha'riel.

"I cannot interfere!" Zha'riel shouted back. "I am already in trouble. I'm supposed to *kill* you!"

"Oh, for God's sake…"

Nayra completed the incantation and the portal center pulsed. The liquid glow pushed outward, revealing a center of inky blackness. There was movement, a silhouette appeared in the shimmering center, and a woman emerged. The light of the full moon combined with the brilliant glow radiating from the portal provided enough light to make it feel like day time. From thirty yards away, Tatiana saw her clearly. She was about five foot, three inches tall with long, auburn hair and a frightening dark-eyed glare.

"Athalia," mumbled Zha'riel, shaking his head. "The shape-shifter."

The next through was also a female, as beautiful as Nico had ever seen. Her long, black hair fell in luscious waves to the small of her back. Her radiant blue eyes seemed to stare all the way across the field and right through Nico before she turned away. The smile on her face almost made Nico feel happy for her.

"Her name is Delilah," Zha'riel said, seeing Nico's expression. "Yes...*that* Delilah."

A third female emerged, and Nico couldn't believe it, but she was even more stunning than Delilah. Her long, brown hair was styled in thin braids and she moved like a dancer, her hips swaying as she glided effortlessly from the portal. Every curve was perfection and her face was intoxicating.

Zha'riel swore under his breath, a first, as far as Nico could recollect. "That is Salome. Trust me, Nico, you do not want to be in a room alone with her."

Nico looked at him skeptically. "Who wouldn't want to be in a room alone with *her*?"

Tatiana slapped his arm and chuckled. "Graveyards have been filled with men who had the exact same thought."

The next out was a man built like a world class athlete. His muscles bulged under what looked like heavy leather with metal plates attached. Clearly a warrior, his shoulder-length light brown hair hung in shaggy locks and obscured his face. All Nico could make out was a close-trimmed full beard and moustache.

Zha'riel shook his head. "Hydarnes." Looking at Nico, he said, "We have to stop this."

"Let's go."

Zha'riel lashed out and the demons around them collapsed. He, Tatiana, and Nico orbed to the portal opening, but Azazel was waiting. His eyes flashed silver. Zha'riel was the first to feel his wrath. The second he orbed into the clearing near the portal, Azazel stretched out his hand and Zha'riel hurtled through the air, slamming into the side of the mountain and collapsing, stunned, onto the ground.

"Nico," Azazel warned. "We are not enemies! Do not stand against me."

Nico met his eyes, trying to calculate his odds of holding Azazel off long enough for Zha'riel to get back into the fight.

Azazel shook his head. "Don't."

Tatiana attacked Azazel from behind and Nico, though he feared for her, had a job to do. He focused his attention on the portal. Nayra attacked Nico, her confidence soaring now that she had Kharashuoa experience, but Nico was ready. He blinked into position behind her and hit her with a burst of electrical energy, sending her sprawling and forcing her to lose her grip on the portal. The shimmering center went solid and began to fade.

Zha'riel recovered enough to help Tatiana, who struggled in one-on-one battle against Azazel. They fought as the demons cheered their master. Ultimately, Zha'riel and Tatiana were subdued by Azazel, who refrained from killing them outright.

"Nico!" Azazel shouted as he stood over Tatiana and Zha'riel, his hands crackling with violet energy. "Think about it!"

Nico stared at him. This was the moment he could end it all. He could kill Nayra, take the point stone, and the key, closing the portal for good, but Azazel would make him pay a heavy price. Not only were Zha'riel and Tatiana at Azazel's mercy, but Seir had delivered Xabier and Lazlo to him as well. They were all alive, but how long would that remain true if he killed Nayra?

"You can close the portal and probably escape with your life," Azazel said. His voice was calm, but Nico could hear it shake a little. "But you will have to sacrifice four more friends to do so. I did not want this, Nico! Please...walk away." He looked at Nico, almost pleading with his eyes. "I still want peace with you...you and all your friends."

Nico shook his head. "You'll kill them all the second you get what you want!"

Azazel said something to Seir. From that distance, Nico couldn't hear the discussion, but Azazel nodded firmly to Seir, who stared back at him like he couldn't believe it, but he released Xabier and Lazlo. Azazel said something to them and they walked toward Nico.

"Nico!" Xabier shouted. "What are you *doing*? You have to finish this now!"

Azazel shouted. "I give you my word, Nico, I will release my exiled cousin and your lovely Tatiana, but you must walk away *now*!"

Nico gritted his teeth but he knew he would cave to Azazel's demand. There was no decision. He held up his hands. "Okay!"

"No!" Xabier shouted at him.

"Quiet!" Nico commanded. To Azazel he shouted, "Let her go! I will release Nayra! Then you release Zha'riel and we will *all* walk away!"

Azazel conferred with Seir and nodded. "Very well."

He released Tatiana, who walked backward several yards and waved to Nico, signaling she was okay. When he saw Tatiana was safe, Nico released Nayra, who for a second looked as though she was going to attack him, but he glared back at her, daring her to give him the excuse. She turned away. Azazel then released Zha'riel. Nico blinked Xabier and Lazlo to a spot where they could regroup, but still watch the events transpire.

Within moments, Nayra had the portal reopened. One by one, the alphas emerged from the shimmering liquid-like center. Nico felt Xabier's stare. He felt the mixture of disappointment and anger radiating from his friend's core. For the moment, he chose to ignore it.

They stood in impotence as the parade of alphas continued. Nico heard Zha'riel and Xabier arguing over the merits of Nico's decision but didn't bother to engage. Tatiana stepped close to him and rested her head against his chest. He wrapped his arms around her and closed his eyes.

"Tell me I made the right decision," he whispered in her ear.

She squeezed his waist. "There is no right or wrong, my love. There are only the choices we make. At least this way, we can fight another day."

With eleven alphas through the portal, only one remained. The figure of a man appeared in the center. The man stood just shy of six feet, with long, brown hair. His dark eyes were ice cold. At a distance, Nico was still struck by his presence. Even in with Lucifer himself, Nico had never felt such bitter hatred.

The most profound reaction of all was Lazlo's, who stiffened as the silhouette filled the portal gate. When the man stepped through and into the brisk air, Lazlo's breath caught in his throat with an audible gasp. His breathing become unsteady, shaking with a mixture of fear and hatred. His eyes followed the man without blinking. When Lazlo finally spoke, fear and anger filled his soft voice.

"Father."

Within moments, the alphas were gathered up by their people. Nayra closed the portal and was instantly whisked away by a demon escort. Azazel wasted no time. Seir and his demon army converged on the supernatural creatures and as one, they all orbed out, leaving Nico and his friends alone at the portal gate.

"Well," Xabier said, staring at Nico. "I guess that's that."

ꝏ A ⸰ ψ ꟈ

"You daft bastard!"

Lazlo had snapped out of his shock and glared at Nico with fierce jade eyes. Even with his short, thick hair, his resemblance to the man who had emerged from the portal was unmistakable. Father and son had the same icy coldness in their eyes. All Lazlo's hatred of his father could not change that.

"What is the matter with you, Nico?" Xabier shook his head in disgust. "Why would you release that much evil into the world?"

Nico's mouth dropped open. "You two are incredible. You realize, you are alive right now only because of the choice *I* just made, don't you?"

"Wonderful," Lazlo spat. "Nico Scarlatti, the savior of the few."

"All right," Zha'riel stepped between the vampires and the human. "It has been a long and trying night. We should discuss this later, when we are less emotional."

He took Xabier and Lazlo by their arms and orbed out, leaving Nico alone with Tatiana. They both knew they suffered a loss that night but they were finally together and, without a word, collapsed into each other's arms. Tatiana sobbed against his chest as they sat together in the field under the light of the full moon. Any other evening, it would have been romantic.

"Are we interrupting?"

Nico's shoulders clenched. He knew the voice without looking. He turned to see the glowing white of Azazel's eyes. No longer dressed in the crimson tunic of a conquering warrior, his robes were now ankle length, flowing purple with silver trim and tassels. He no longer carried the decorative sword at his side, though Nico was certain he was not unarmed. Of course, who would attack Azazel?

What got Nico's attention was the woman standing next to Azazel. She beautiful, with dark eyes and long, thick, black hair. Her skin was a deep brown which stood out against her pale pink and lavender sheer robes. A simple pink gemstone adorned the center of her forehead, and thin silver chains with more pink gemstones ran over her hair. She had a delicate look about her that stood in stark contrast to her piercing gaze. In moonlight, her eyes appeared almost black. Her gaze sent a chill down Nico's back.

Tatiana stiffened in his arms. He could see the glimmer of recognition in her eyes as she stood. It was not a look of affection. Tatiana reacted as though she were face to face with an enemy, and that was when the realization dawned on him. The woman was Parvati, the Hindu mother of Sansata, whom Nico had killed, and whose essence Nico now possessed.

Azazel smiled grimly. "I realize the evening's events turned out…*differently*…than you would have liked, Nico, but that is war. It does not mean we cannot be civilized." He placed a hand at the small of Parvati's back and gestured with the other hand. "May I present Parvati, the mother of Sansata."

Parvati stepped forward, her piercing gaze never leaving Nico's eyes. She stared right through him and he felt as though all his secrets were laid bare before her. She was like his own mother in that way. He felt like anything he said would be scrutinized and held against him, so he remained silent.

She spoke with an Indian lilt to her voice. "*This* is the vessel?" She said it more to Azazel than anyone else.

Azazel pressed his lips together. "Parvati..."

"No," she said, holding up a finger, still gazing into Nico's eyes. "This is my moment with the one who murdered my son."

"You promised it would not be contentious."

"I *promised*," Parvati countered in a firm voice, "mish nyesto facho intare."

Nico glanced at Tatiana in confusion. He shook his head as he caught the pained expression on her face. He shrugged and shot Tatiana a questioning stare.

"Enochian," she said softly. "The language of the angels."

"What—?"

Tatiana winced. "You don't want to know."

Azazel sighed as he exchanged a few more words of indecipherable speech with Parvati. "Nico is a *friend*, Parvati. And he is *not*...a vessel."

She smiled back at him. "So, you say, my love."

Turning back to Nico, she said, "When I first heard about you and my son, I wanted nothing more than to make you suffer for a thousand years. Now that I see you in person..." Reaching out to touch his cheek, she continued, "Perhaps it would be better to make peace."

Her eyes were moist, sad in a way that revealed how ageless she really was. Parvati's beauty was that of a young woman, but her persona was motherly. Nico felt an instant connection. He had no idea why he did it, but he took her hand from his cheek and held it in both of his. He smiled his warmest smile.

"I would like that."

Parvati returned his smile with a demure nod. "I see my son in you. His essence is strong. You must learn to contain it."

"I'm trying."

Her expression never changed, but Nico knew she didn't believe him. She said nothing; her stare was enough. This was a woman who was used to deference. Nico got the sense she could stand there all night until he admitted the truth.

"I mean," he continued. "I'm trying to…I don't want to lose myself."

Parvati frowned. "*Lose* yourself?" She turned back to Azazel. "Who told him he would…" She closed her eyes and nodded with a slight contemptuous smile. "Of course. I forgot, you consort with heavenly vermin. They fill your head with silly notions."

"*IS THAT RIGHT, PARVATI?*"

The voice boomed from the heavens. All eyes turned to the sky as it lit up with fire. Thousands of angels descended like rays from the sun itself, instantly surrounding them. Rafael descended in a flaming chariot with twelve other flaming chariots behind him. They spread out and formed an inner circle with the thousands-strong army arrayed behind them.

Azazel looked around slowly, challenging anyone to look him in the eyes. He finally settled his gaze on Rafael and shook his head.

"It has been a long time, old friend."

Rafael smiled with all the confidence of a leader who had his opposition outnumbered a million to one. "We were never friends, Azazel."

"Well," Azazel said evenly. "This is quite the display. Maybe a touch overcompensating, no?"

"Perhaps," Rafael replied. "I believe in overwhelming shows of force. It makes things…easier, don't you agree?" Without waiting for an answer, he turned to Nico. "Anyway, I think it is time you and I take care of our…unfinished business, and do not bother attempting to flee into the ether like a coward. You cannot orb."

Nico slumped his shoulders and closed his eyes. He had known this moment would come the instant those two witches fell. He'd imagined it a couple times in the moments between battles. In his imagination, it was always Rafael standing there, watching, as one or two other angels executed him. He never imagined Rafael would feel the need to bring his entire army. Ultimately, he decided he was not going to go to his death feeling sorry for himself. He straightened his shoulders and took a deep breath.

Turning to Tatiana, he said, "I guess this is it."

"Nonsense," Parvati said, placing her hand on his arm.

Azazel stepped forward, putting himself between Nico and Rafael. Surrounded by countless angels, Parvati and Tatiana quickly whispered instructions to Nico. They gave him as many tips as he could handle about fighting angels while Azazel addressed Rafael.

"Are we really going to try to fight them?" Nico hissed to Parvati. "This is crazy."

Parvati shrugged. "You look at numbers, Nico. They mean nothing. We Hindus held our land when the numbers against us were five times worse than this."

Azazel stepped closer to Rafael. The closest archangels moved protectively closer to their leader. Azazel laughed as he eyed them, one at a time. He shook his head and addressed Rafael.

"How many of your numbers are you willing to sacrifice today, Rafael?"

"To take *you*, Azazel?" Rafael smiled grimly. "I am here for the human, but if I manage to take two archangels and the daughter of the Deceiver along with him?" He shrugged. "I don't take the loss of angelic life lightly, but I think we will live with it today."

The clash happened instantly. At a signal from Rafael, the angels attacked. They came straight for Nico, and he had to fight for his life. Severely outnumbered, he wondered why Azazel and Parvati bothered to stick around. Tatiana stayed close to him, and they fought well together. Eventually, the numbers began to overcome them. Though Azazel and Parvati were in no particular danger, Nico and Tatiana began to lose ground and were separated. Nico, losing strength, could no longer hold off the angels.

As he was about to give up and let himself be taken, his eyes met Parvati's piercing stare. He instantly felt the change inside him. It was as though she was pulling it out of him. His eyes flashed brilliantly, the silver shining like jewels before giving way to a pearl-white glow. He exploded in a flurry of action, striking furiously with his sword while simultaneously unleashing power unlike any he had ever attempted. He pushed back the line of angels attacking him and fought his way back to Tatiana, who grinned in relief.

Azazel and Parvati were wreaking havoc among the archangels. Then, Rafael's support showed up. The sky once again filled with heavenly fire and the fighting stopped. The angels retreated to their former positions, leaving Nico at the center with Tatiana, Azazel, and Parvati at his side. They all put away their swords.

"Well, well, well," Azazel said under his breath.

Nico could see Azazel's expression darken as the fury of Heaven descended from the clouds. The number of angels in the sky dwarfed those on the battlefield. A chariot descended from the sky and came to rest next to Rafael's. There was an audible reaction from the angels. Nico got the sense they were all surprised. He turned to see what, or who, had caused all the commotion.

He was impressive, even by angelic standards. He stood taller than everyone around him. His brown hair was perfect, falling in wavy locks to his shoulders. His piercing eyes glowed bright blue, the purest blue Nico had ever seen. He commanded attention. Even more than that, Nico could see he was revered by the rest of the angels. Even Tatiana seemed shocked.

"My God," she said, her voice betraying her awe.

Parvati shook her head in disbelief and muttered, "Michael." She put a hand on Azazel's shoulder. "He looks good, doesn't he?"

Azazel chuckled and put his arm around her shoulders. "It would appear," he said, "That I have led you to your death, my love."

"Nonsense," she replied. "You have freed me. If we are to die, I choose to die at your side, wielding my sword, and taking as many of those stuck-up, heavenly swine with us as we can."

Michael stepped off his chariot and strode to within twenty feet of Azazel. His robes were pure white with a golden belt. He wore no decoration, nothing to indicate his station. He was the most powerful being in existence, short of the God he served, yet he accepted no accolades, not even the recognition of his rank and status. He regarded Azazel with a gaze as cold as it was taunting.

"Azazel," he said. "How long has it been?"

"Do what you came to do, Michael."

Nico shook with terror as he stood, watching the exchange. The last time he saw such a powerful stand-off, he'd been nearly dead. Lucifer and Azazel battled one another, and all Nico could recall about the event was how frightening it had been. Now, as he stood, shivering, in the presence of the great angel, he realized he had never seen anything like the power Michael projected.

Michael drew a gleaming sword, and stood ready to deliver the death blow. Without warning, his eyes were drawn to something far off. Nico heard the commotion behind him and turned to see what was going on. The heavenly ranks parted as a figure in a black, hooded robe made his way through. The angels couldn't scramble out of his way fast enough. Behind him, tens of thousands stood in formation, marching forward. They were all clad in black robes, their heads hooded, obscuring their faces in the night. The lone figure, led the way and Heaven's ranks were pushed back until they stood in formation behind Rafael. Then he slowly flipped his hood back.

"Lucifer," Nico breathed in surprise. He shook his head. "Can this get any crazier?"

Tatiana's face went ashen. "Listen, Nico. That thing I need to talk to you about? Lucifer...I mean, I'm his...I mean..."

"Nico." Lucifer nodded with a faint smile. He glanced at Tatiana, and Nico could see the unmistakable affection in his eyes. "Daughter."

"Father." She smiled uncertainly as he passed.

Nico wrapped an arm around her shoulders and she collapsed into him.

Lucifer's gaze fell on Parvati. His forehead wrinkled. "Interesting," he said. "Interesting indeed."

"Lucifer."

"Parvati."

The dark lord strode past them and approached Azazel and Michael. He nodded at Azazel who returned the gesture. Nico could see the uncertainly in Azazel's eyes. Lucifer's presence was a fascinating development. His reasoning could go in a lot of different directions. Nico felt like a bystander at the scene of an accident.

Lucifer turned to Michael and smiled warmly. "Brother." He took Michael's face in his hands and kissed his elder brother on both cheeks. "You look well."

"Lucifer," Michael replied. He was clearly not amused. Looking out at the sea of black-clad Dark Army soldiers, he gritted his teeth. "You brought friends, I see."

Lucifer turned and followed Michael's gaze with a nod. "Twelve legions," he said. "I thought the number was...*appropriate*. After all, it was the same number your master had at his beck and call the day we nailed his vessel to a stick outside of Jerusalem."

Michael closed his eyes. "You should learn respect."

Lucifer stuck a finger in his face and hissed, "I respect those who *deserve* it." He let out a calming breath. "I promised myself I wouldn't get upset." He turned his head slightly and threw a wink toward Azazel, who stifled a grin and held a finger over his mouth. Lucifer turned back to Michael with a friendly smile. "Anyway...how is Father?"

Michael ignored the question and continued to scan Lucifer's army. Was he calculating his odds of victory? Parvati had told him the numbers didn't matter, but he could see Michael come to the same inevitable conclusion Nico came to. Lucifer followed Michael's eyes and raised his eyebrows. Michael gestured to Azazel.

"You stand for he who betrayed you?"

Lucifer stared his brother in the eyes, matching Michael's ice-cold gaze. "Our business is *our* business, brother. You intrude where you do not belong."

He let his answer hang in the air for several tense moments before spreading his hands.

"Shall we do battle, brother?"

Michael, though clearly a revered and valiant warrior, was not suicidal. In the end, he signaled his army for a retreat. As the angels began to depart the field, he took one final look at Lucifer.

"Another day, brother. Another day."

Epilogue

"Are you sure about this? I have a bad feeling."

"Would you rather run around with a big red bull's eye on your back for the rest of your life?" Tatiana smiled as she looped her arm through his and rested her head on his shoulder.

Nico couldn't argue with her logic. Lucifer's massive show of force succeeded in pushing Michael's legion of angels to retreat, but Nico had no illusions that Lucifer, or Azazel could or would be able to guarantee his safety. He needed to get off angelic radar. He used various warding tactics to remain invisible to Heaven's spies, but they were all temporary, and easily overcome once discovered.

He needed to make other, more permanent, arrangements for his safety. Parvati provided the best possible solution. Unfortunately, she couldn't guarantee Nico would survive the procedure. He was a unique being. All she could do was facilitate the meeting. After that, it was up to Nico to determine whether he wanted to move forward and take his chances. He figured it was worth the risk. He was dead anyway.

The Farum Brigantum, also known as the Tower of Hercules, was located on a peninsula, in A Coruña Harbor, in northwest Spain. Built in the year 1 BC, it was believed to be modeled after the lighthouse of Alexandria, one of the wonders of the ancient world. It was the oldest Roman lighthouse, still in use, and stood as a monument to ancient longevity and craftsmanship. Two thousand years of weather, war, and daily wear would have reduced any modern structure to rubble, but the ancient Romans were master builders. Their structures stood the test of time.

"Now what?" he asked. "Does he just show up?"

Tatiana scanned the surrounding area. "I don't know. Roman gods aren't exactly my specialty. I spent most of my life in the West."

"Have you ever met him?"

"Mercury?" she shook her head. "No, but I've heard all about him. He's real old school. To be honest, I can see this going a lot of different ways. Not all of them are good, Nico."

Nico chuckled. "That's reassuring. Thanks a lot."

They checked the lighthouse and found it empty, except for a few tourists walking out. There was a keeper, but he wouldn't be back until sundown. The interior was a strange juxtaposition of metal and stone, glass and clay, modern and ancient. The Spaniards had erected a walkway through the lower level of the tower, so tourists could view the excavated parts without endangering them. It was a double-edged sword, the preservation of ancient sites and the desire to allow people to see and enjoy their history.

From the top of the tower, they saw the entire entrance to A Coruña Harbor, a strategic point on the sea route linking the Mediterranean with northwest Europe. It was also a deceptive and dangerous waterway for ships, making the lighthouse a key tool for sailors, even in modern times. After waiting for several minutes with no indication they were in the right place, they descended the two-hundred-thirty-four-step spiral stairway to ground level and exited the ancient tower.

They wandered around the grounds, drawing nearer and nearer to the coast. The smell of the salt air and the mist from the waves lapping at the shoreline reminded Nico of the beaches back in New Jersey. They walked through Sculpture Park, an outdoor museum of Stone Age art. After seeing all the pieces, they walked over to the giant Compass Rose, over eighty feet in diameter. They stood on all seven of the Celtic symbols before shrugging and heading over to the Shell Horn, a giant mollusk shell made of Cor-Ten steel. It had the appearance of rusted metal, but that was by design. It spun in the wind and captured the vibrations of the sea. Nico couldn't figure out the point of it, but it was one of those impressively large sculptures that didn't require any purpose.

"Maybe we're wasting our time," Nico said with a shrug.

He stared out at the harbor as the mid-afternoon sun sank toward the western horizon. The November air was cool and breezy, and felt ten degrees colder than what showed on the digital display back in town. Nico had trouble adjusting his mind to the west-coast sunset. He was used to the sun rising over water and dropping behind the landscape.

Before Tatiana could respond, they felt a sudden presence behind them, like a slight gust of wind. They turned to see a petite female, dressed in a flimsy, sky-blue garment which covered her narrow shoulders and fell to just above her knees. She was fair-skinned, with rosy cheeks. Her eyes glowed a gentle blue-green hue, matching the color of her hair. Nico couldn't tell if the hair was naturally that color or if she dyed it to go with her eyes.

"Egeria?"

Tatiana's face lit up. For a moment, the girl tilted her head to one side at the mention of her name. Her lips parted in surprise and she broke into a broad smile.

"Tatiana?" she said with a giggle. "Is that you?"

"It's me!"

Egeria spread her arms as Tatiana approached. Nico's apprehension diminished. The two embraced with laughter and exclamations of surprise. They held one another's hands as they caught up on the high points of hundreds of years of life.

"So," Tatiana said. "You're working with Mercury?"

"Well," Egeria said slowly. She winked at Tatiana with a conspiratorial look in her eyes. "I do not know if I would call it *work.*"

They devolved into more laughter. Nico felt like a third wheel for several minutes until Tatiana turned to him with an apologetic expression.

"Nico, I'm so sorry," she said, coming to him and taking his arm. "Egeria, meet Nico Scarlatti. He's—"

"—the human who defeated Sansata," Egeria finished for her, turning her eyes on Nico with an alluring smile. "Everyone knows about *him*."

She practically sighed when she said it. Her long eyelashes fluttered in star struck awe. Nico suddenly felt like the only guy in the world. Egeria had a radiant smile, made even more captivating by her sweet disposition. He felt light-headed and sweat built up on his palms. He caught Tatiana's amused grin and shot her a helpless look. She laughed and came to his rescue.

"Egeria, you're making him nervous. And besides, he's mine."

"Really?" Egeria pouted. "How come *you* get all the good ones?"

She put a hand on Nico's arm. "Tatiana is an old friend, so I won't steal you away from her."

"*Egeria*," Tatiana replied pointedly, "is a little flirt. Don't mind her. Besides, it sounds like she's already *with* someone."

"Alas," Egeria said in resignation. "It is true."

"So," Tatiana said. "Will you take us to him?"

Egeria's expression turned serious. Nico saw a better indication of her age when she was not playing the flirt. She eyed him with suspicion and doubt. He got the impression Egeria, despite her sweetheart act, was far more than a lover and errand girl for a Roman god. She was a gatekeeper. In the supernatural world, Nico could only imagine the dangers a job like that entailed.

She folded her arms across her chest. "What is it you want, exactly?"

"Nico needs to be invisible."

Egeria frowned. "Invisible."

Tatiana nodded. "Invisible to the prying eyes of Heaven's angels."

"Ahhhh," Egeria nodded her understanding. "That makes sense. After all," she said, her brilliant smile returning to her face, "you *are* consorting with Satan's spawn." She laughed as Tatiana shook her head. "We can help you. Come, friends. Follow me."

She led them back across the grass to the lighthouse. There were people milling in and out of the ancient tower, so Egeria simply walked into the lighthouse with Nico and Tatiana in tow. She waited until no one was around, and placed her hands on Nico and Tatiana. A second later, they were in a different room, one that was inaccessible from above.

"A few years back, they excavated some of the rooms above and we thought they might dig deeper and find this room."

Egeria held her hands over a large, green gemstone in one corner of the ancient room and it began to glow brighter and brighter.

"Thankfully, they didn't. We would have had to move the portal." The now-familiar liquid-looking center formed and then appeared to stretch taut. Egeria gestured to the portal. "After you."

They stood in a palace. It was the most magnificent structure Nico had ever seen. He spun in a circle with his head tilted up, looking at the monstrous archways and domed ceiling. He was certain there were no earthly structures like it. Human engineers wouldn't know where to begin with such a design. Tatiana explained, they were no longer in the earthly realm.

"You've heard us speak of the ether?" she said.

Nico nodded in awed silence.

"Well," she pointed her finger and gestured all around them. "Everything you see is in the ether. You are in the angelic realm. Welcome to Mercury's palace."

Nico thought about the crash course in Roman god history Tatiana had given him. Mercury was the messenger god. Throughout the ageless wars between the fallen angels, Mercury, along with his brother, Hermes, developed systems of coded messaging. They were also called upon to break the codes of their enemies. When the Roman deities split from the Greeks, many friends and family members were forced into unpleasant decisions. Mercury pleaded with his younger brother to come with him, but Hermes, seeking status of his own, saw the opportunity to emerge from the shadow of his brilliant elder brother and remained with Zeus. Though they operated in close proximity, the two seldom spoke after that.

Nico saw a man coming their way and knew instantly it was the messenger god. He stood about five foot eight inches tall with a thin frame. He moved with the grace of a dancer, appearing to glide as he walked toward them. His smile appeared pasted on and his glowing amber eyes were locked on Tatiana. Nico was glad he'd agreed to bring her along. She was adored and respected everywhere she went. It didn't appear to matter that her father was reviled outside his army. If Mercury wasn't pleased to see her, at least Tatiana would have some idea how to handle it. It was unlikely anyone would do anything to provoke Lucifer, so Nico felt safe in her company.

"You are the daughter of the Morning Star?" The man didn't bother to acknowledge Nico.

"I am," Tatiana said, bowing her head in deference. "Thank you for seeing us."

He didn't respond. Mercury stood before them, regarding them with darkened eyes. Nico's hands began to shake. So much for a warm welcome. The man's smile was gone and he appeared to be looking for a reason to dismiss them. He nodded at Tatiana and the corners of his mouth twitched.

"Your reputation precedes you." He tilted his head. "And your father? He is well?"

Tatiana nodded. "He is." She didn't mention that her relationship with her father was up in the air. They hadn't spoken since the confrontation with Michael two weeks prior.

Mercury pursed his lips, his head continuing to bob up and down in slow, steady rhythm. "So...why are you here? What can I do for the daughter of an old friend?"

There was an edge to his voice. Nico was aware of the general history at play among the fallen angels. Lucifer was persona non-grata outside of those still loyal to him. He was respected because of his tremendous power. He was even loved still, by some, though those who felt any affection for him were not outspoken about it. Choices were made and sides were taken based on short-term thinking and situational strategy. Most of the fallen angels looked out for themselves, and did what was necessary to survive in the days following their fall from grace. Mercury seemed to be playing it safe, treating Tatiana as visiting royalty, though not necessarily a friend.

She knew it, and used it to her advantage, taking a direct approach. "My friend requires your special abilities."

Mercury looked Nico over, acknowledging him for the first time. "You are the human who brought down Sansata." It wasn't a question. He looked Nico up and down with a curious expression. "I understand you wish to become invisible to the angels of Heaven. Are you under sanction?"

Nico didn't know what that meant. His confused expression caused no change in Mercury's posture. He just stared at Nico and waited for him to catch up. Tatiana affirmed with a nod of her head.

"It means Heaven has sanctioned your execution."

"Oh," Nico nodded. "Then yes, I guess I'm absolutely under sanction."

"The excitement two weeks ago," Mercury asked. "Was that all for you?"

Nico shrugged. "Among other things."

Mercury pursed his lips again. He rubbed his palms together slowly and made a clucking sound as he thought. Nico understood the position such a request put the angel in. Mercury was a careful operator. He had to be, since it was his job to evade the opposition and get vital messages safely to their intended targets. He didn't need to provide his enemies any additional motivation to seek him out.

Nico was asking him to defy Heaven. Even those who hated Heaven and wanted nothing more than to destroy the angel army, knew better than to arouse the ire of its commanders. Nico wouldn't be there if he wasn't under pressure. A great deal of attention was directed toward Nico. Mercury had no reason to risk his own security helping an outsider, even one accompanied by the daughter of Lucifer himself.

Mercury's eyes glowed amber and he granted a crooked smile. "I can help you."

Nico breathed a sigh of relief. There was no way to predict how much hatred the fallen angels directed toward Heaven. Based on Mercury's expression, he reveled in the idea of sticking it to his former mates.

"Thank you," he said, closing his eyes and sighing. He might actually have a shot at survival.

"But you must understand," Mercury continued. "Such a task comes with great risk to me." He made a sweeping gesture. "As you can see, I do not want for riches. In return for my help, I would ask for your loyalty."

Nico frowned. That could be a dangerous debt. His mind went to all the ways a promise like that could backfire. He shook his head.

"I am loyal to my friends," he said. "But I will not be played against another friend."

Mercury nodded. "Agreed."

He took Nico into a back room while Tatiana looked on from a corner. Nico could tell from the look in her eyes it wasn't going to be a pleasant experience. Mercury had him remove his shirt. He placed a rubber plate in Nico's mouth. That got Nico's heart racing. Mercury held a hand in front of Nico's sternum. Nico could see the tips of his fingers begin to glow.

"Are you ready?"

Nico nodded and bit down on the rubber plate.

"You might feel a little pressure."

The second Mercury's hand contacted Nico's skin, he felt searing pain rifle through his body. Nico instantly felt as though his bones were disintegrating and his insides were frying. He screamed in agony until the pain grew so intense he blacked out.

Excerpt

The sprawling ranch-style house was quiet, save for the occasional rustle of drapes from an open living room window. A face peeked out for just a moment, then disappeared, and the drapes pulled shut. Located in a rural suburb of Soroca, it was one of the nicer buildings in the area, but that wasn't saying much. Few homes in the former Soviet country of Moldova were notable. The collapse of the Soviet Union and, more recently, the nosedive of the Moldovan economy served to ravage the landlocked nation, leaving it vulnerable to organized crime of all types, including human trafficking.

A slight breeze shook the leaves around him as Nico scanned the simple home from a vantage point at the top of a hill, over three hundred yards away. He lay in a prone position, obscured by trees and shrubbery, peering through the lenses of powerful binoculars. Other than the face at the window, the only disturbance on the property was the dozen guards patrolling the perimeter in groups of three. Everything was quiet, as it had been for hours, but it was just a matter of time.

His information was good; Nico was certain of that. Over four months of hunting and interrogating Russian sex traffickers, Nico had mastered the art of extracting information from even the most hardened criminals. Some of those hardened criminals were going to meet to discuss the sudden violent ends many of their brothels had met over the past several months. It would be a short meeting.

He caught a wisp of a familiar scent. It still made his heart thud in his chest, and his eyes lost focus for just a moment. Her breath against his cheek almost sent his brain into thermal overload. A lock of flame-red hair fell across his field of vision as Tatiana's lips brushed across his temple.

"Hello, my love."

Somehow, Tatiana could turn the most lethal situations into lust-filled moments with just a single phrase. And she meant every word. Nico knew the past four months only served to draw

Tatiana ever closer to him, while he struggled to trust their relationship. What was real? His supernatural life had moved so fast, in such a short time, he hadn't been able to step back and look at the bigger picture, and when she was so close to him, the bigger picture didn't much matter. Her scent was enough to scramble his every thought.

He masked his struggle with a slow, steady breath. "It's been quiet."

"Hmph."

She slumped enough for Nico to feel like a jerk. "Well, it's about to get more exciting." She pulled away and stretched out next to him. "Two SUVs just made the turn onto the road."

Nico felt the growing gulf between them and vowed to deal with it soon, but first, they had some mid-level scumbags to snuff out. Eight men, out of the expected ten, had already arrived for the secret meeting. Two vehicles approaching meant it was almost show time.

Nico's veins exploded throughout his body with a crackle of energy. He saw a flash of silver as the darkness within him surged forward. He flexed his fingers and let his mind flow with the river of energy inside him. With Tatiana's help, Nico had learned not to strive against his dark essence, but to embrace it. Once he did that, the pressure he'd always felt in his head faded and he could control his urges.

It didn't mean the bloodlust went away; if anything, it was stronger than ever. The cold rage in Nico's heart was all-consuming, but it was directed at the worst human beings in existence, as far as Nico was concerned, so he was okay with it, and since he was already under a death order from Heaven, Nico didn't see the point in fighting his essence. That wasn't to say he was willing to succumb to evil. He wasn't willing to give *anyone* control over him. So, he did what he wanted, and took measures to always stay one step ahead of Rafael's kill squad.

It was no easy task. Mercury's excruciating technique of carving Enochian warding sigils on all of Nico's bones served to cloak Nico from the prying eyes of the angels of Heaven. With that security, Nico ravaged the Eastern European human trafficking market, destroying countless brothels and killing hundreds of the most despicable human beings Nico had ever met. Pure evil, those men…not even human, as far as Nico was concerned. He looked at them as insects, a scourge on humanity, and he was the exterminator. As Nico's body counts climbed across the European countryside, Rafael and his kill squad increased their efforts to apprehend him, but so far, Nico's luck was holding.

The two trucks arrived and pulled into the driveway. Four armed men got out of each vehicle and joined their colleagues, taking up positions in and around the building. Out of each SUV stepped a man dressed in an expensive suit. The men embraced, cast nervous glances over their shoulders, and proceeded to enter the house.

Nico watched the men outside as they reconfigured their perimeter. They were vigilant; he had to give them that. They were far more professional than their counterparts at the lower levels of the organization; not that it mattered. They were on the lookout for human intruders. They were helpless against Nico's overwhelming powers. He pitied them not in the slightest. They targeted the most helpless victims they could find: young, naïve girls. They hurt them, drugged them, used them, and sold their virtue without a second thought to the horror they inflicted.

The thoughts caused a violent surge of energy in Nico's heart. He smelled the ozone as the energy made it all the way to the tips of his fingers. He had to get out of sight before he lost control. The element of surprise was what made it so fun. His eyes flashed silver as he pushed himself deeper into the woods. When he stood, Tatiana was there to grab his shoulders and steady him.

"Easy, my love." Her riveting green eyes calmed his rage enough to fade the silver glow of his eyes. She smiled and touched her fingers to his lips. "You mustn't draw too heavily."

She was right. His chakra pull was a homing beacon for Rafael and his team. He needed to maintain control or the archangel would show up before Nico could dispatch his targets. Thanks to Mercury, Nico was almost untraceable by the angels of Heaven…almost. He still had a unique pull on the binding force of nature. Chakra would be his undoing if he wasn't careful.

He grabbed Tatiana's hands and squeezed. His eyes, back to their normal deep violet hue, met hers and he leaned in. When their lips met, his heart once again raced like a thoroughbred. How could he deny his feelings? How could he doubt her? If she didn't really love him, Tatiana was the greatest actress ever. He hated to pull away from those soft lips, but they weren't in Moldova to make out in the woods.

She sighed when he ended the kiss, and Nico chuckled.

"Later," he promised as he stroked her cheek with the backs of his fingers. "We have work to do."

Less than thirty seconds later, the men outside the house were all down, their windpipes crushed to silence their screams. They all died slow and excruciating deaths from precision-inflicted internal wounds. Nico joined Tatiana and nodded as they joined hands.

Tatiana blinked and they orbed into the center of the meeting. The ten gangsters were stunned, but reacted faster than their guards. They all carried semi-automatic pistols and, although Nico and Tatiana ravaged the group, one managed to get off several shots, burying three slugs in Nico's chest. Nico sprawled onto the carpet as blood gushed from an arterial wound.

It was the first time he'd been shot since his early training, with Abdiel, in a warehouse back home. He'd forgotten how painful bullet wounds were. As the blood flowed, Nico felt his consciousness slipping and wondered if he really was immortal or if it was all a psychological ploy to make him reckless. As confusion raged around him, all Nico could do was lie there, watching the pool of blood around him spread into the carpet.

Ᏸ ᴧ Ȝ ψ ᶃ

Xabier crouched with his back against the garage wall. He squinted, closed his eyes, and listened. Other than the chirping of crickets in the distance, and the scurry of tiny animals in the bushes, he could hear nothing out of the ordinary. He peered around the corner. Nothing moved. He focused his gaze on the white rancher attached to the garage. There was no movement or sound from within.

His prey was nocturnal. There ought to have been lights blazing and sounds of life in that house. Instead, it looked deserted. It could be a ploy, some trick to lure him into complacency. After all, he'd been tracking them for three months. It was possible he'd been spotted. He hadn't spotted any of *them*, *that* was for certain. Maybe they were on to him, and waiting until he was tired and frustrated, or maybe they were just toying with him.

Something moved on the other side of the house. Xabier caught sight of a pale hand raised in a fist. Lazlo. He squinted in the darkness and raised his own hand. With a quick gesture, he pointed at the house, then pointed two fingers at his eyes. Lazlo twirled his index finger and crept along the wall toward the front door. Xabier made his way around the house to the back door. He waited until he heard Lazlo crash through the front door before throwing his weight into the door in front of him. The scent of death struck him the moment he entered. They had the right place. Within seconds, the two vampires swept through the single-story home and met in the living room.

"Nothing," Lazlo said with a shrug. "Other than the smell. We are fast approaching ridiculous."

Xabier pressed his fingers to his temples and collapsed onto the plush leather couch. "The two dead guys in the bedroom agree."

Lazlo raised his eyebrows. "Both drained?"

"As usual." Xabier groaned. "We're always a step or two behind." He looked up at Lazlo. "We used to be pretty good at this, Laz. Why can't we catch up?"

Lazlo clucked his tongue and blew out a breath. "We are hunting alphas." He looked around the room and clucked his tongue. "There is nothing more to do here."

They left the house and drove back down the mountain to the city of Missoula, and found the Doubletree Hotel, right on the Clark Fork River. Lazlo opened the door to their room, and went straight for the minibar. Xabier opened a set of heavy curtains and stared out the massive windows overlooking the river. The sun peeked over the tree line as Lazlo poured two Scotches, handing one to Xabier before perching himself on the arm of the sofa.

Xabier sipped the brown liquid and let it run over his tongue and down his throat in a long, smooth swallow. He watched as a golden eagle swooped in low, following the winding river, and skimming the water. When it rose from the surface, it clutched a fish in its sharp talons. It soared down the river and over the trees. Xabier watched in glazed detachment as the mighty warrior bird disappeared in the distance with its dinner.

So simple is the life of the predator.

So far, Xabier and Lazlo had spent three months tracking and chasing the most violent predators the world has ever known, and hadn't so much as glimpsed a single one. It was maddening. Xabier sighed, and closed his eyes again. Three months of searching...three months of wild-goose chases all around the world...three months of mind-numbing frustration, and they had zero to show for it.

"We're going about this all wrong."

Lazlo chuckled behind him. "You're just *now* coming to that inevitable conclusion?" When Xabier didn't answer, he chuckled again. "My old friend, you are losing your sense of humor."

Xabier almost grinned, still staring out the picture windows at the river sunrise. The two-thousand-year-old vampire might have a point. So much had happened over the past year, and very little of it smile-worthy. Xabier couldn't recall the last time he'd let out a genuine laugh.

"Maybe you're right," Xabier replied. "But we still need to find them."

Lazlo snorted, shook his head, finished his drink, and left the couch for another crack at the minibar. He emptied a couple small bottles of whiskey into his glass and dropped in two square cubes from the ice bucket.

"Why do we need to chase them? They've gone underground. They're not causing any real chaos." Lazlo spread his arms and shrugged. "Why poke the hornets' nest? Perhaps a little live and let live…"

At that, Xabier did let out his own derisive chuckle. "Live and let live." He cocked his head to one side and scrunched his brow. "Are you drunk already?"

Lazlo shot him a rueful grin. He held up a hand in surrender and they both fell silent. While Lazlo opened Xabier's laptop, and began searching national news for indications of supernatural activity, Xabier checked his phone. No new messages or missed calls. He pursed his lips. It had been three months since he'd spoken to Nico. The night the alphas made their escape from Purgatory ended in a shouting match between the two friends, and Xabier had left in anger. There had been no contact since.

"Call the man," Lazlo implored as he tapped away and scrunched his brow as he scanned the screen. "Apologize if necessary, and implore him to assist us. At least then we'd be able to travel faster."

Faster travel *would* be better; had they possessed the ability to orb, he and Lazlo might have been able to catch up to the elusive alphas. Xabier finished his drink and set the glass on the table. He pushed himself away from the window and walked the perimeter of the room in silence. He stretched his neck from one side to the other. His muscles ached and he felt the incessant urge to crack his neck. Never, in the centuries since Lazlo had turned him had he felt such human discomfort.

He breathed out a long sigh and leaned against the wall with his head tilted up to the ceiling. "I wouldn't know what to say to him."

"Well, well, well," Lazlo said as he tapped the screen, almost toppling the laptop. "It appears we have options."

Xabier rolled his eyes. "Don't we always?"

Lazlo put a fist under his chin and stared at the screen in silence. He went back to tapping away and Xabier went back to brooding against the wall. Within seconds, curiosity got the better of him and he stepped around Lazlo to peer over his shoulder at the plethora of news articles displayed on the screen. It was the same story, or stories, all over again. There were inexplicable animal attacks here, strange psychic phenomenon there, a series of skinned bodies on one side of the country, and...

Xabier whistled through his teeth. "Whoa."

Lazlo tilted his head and pursed his lips. "Yep."

"Unreal," Xabier said as he shook his head. "Why didn't we think of this earlier?"

"Too easy?"

Lazlo had a series of news articles laid out along the bottom of the screen in chronological order. All four articles told the same story. Two men were found dead in hotel rooms with no apparent cause of death. The men had no apparent connection to one another and there was no sign of foul play. Xabier knew better.

"It looks like our succubae are at it again."

Lazlo nodded. "And the best part about *that* is they're close." When Xabier nodded, he got to his feet and rubbed his hands together. "I'll bring the car around."

Xabier shook his head. "I have a better idea." He gestured at his duffel bag. "Grab the map."

He sat down behind the laptop and closed out all the tabs except for the ones relating to the succubae. He then searched for additional, similar stories, and noted the locations. Lazlo opened the map and began penciling in dots in each general location. By the time they had ten locations dotted, the pattern was visible.

Xabier leaned back and looked at Lazlo. "I think you can bring the car around now."

The trail lead Xabier and Lazlo south, out of Montana and into Idaho. They stayed on the major highway until they found the offshoot route, leading through the mountains, to the city of Sun Valley. Lazlo pulled his silver Jaguar F-Type convertible up to the valet, at Sun Valley Lodge, and the vampires got out. After checking in, they found their suite and settled in.

Xabier checked the time and rubbed his hands together. "Might as well get out there. No telling when they'll show."

Lazlo had already collapsed onto a bed, one of his legs dangling over the side. He sighed and groaned his displeasure, but pulled himself to a seated position.

"Where do we start?"

Xabier pulled up the local night life hot spots on his computer. Sun Valley boasted a thriving arts culture. Though its native population was nominal, there was always a steady stream of tourists. The winter brought skiers and snowboarders, while the warmer weather meant hikers and mountain campers. In all weather, there was never a shortage of visitors, and that meant the hunting ground for predators was always ripe. It was far better to hunt tourists than locals as it took longer for them to be missed.

The vampires made the rounds of the local night clubs until they came across the Duchin Lounge, located in Sun Valley Resort, not to be confused with Sun Valley Lodge, where the vampires were staying. The instant Xabier walked through the doors, he knew they had the right place. A simple glance at Lazlo confirmed his old friend/nemesis felt the same way.

The bar was lit with dim perimeter lighting. Several table lamps were set on end tables, scattered around a couple of comfortable couches, in the center of the lounge area. The floor was a dark-stained hardwood, while the walls were mahogany-paneled and featured outdoor-themed pictures. A small jazz quartet played in one corner as a hipster crowd milled about. It was exactly the type of establishment their targets would frequent in search of prey. Xabier and Lazlo took up positions on opposite ends of the bar and ordered drinks.

It took the better part of the night, but sure enough, well after midnight, the energy in the room, which had been lively and carefree all evening, suddenly grew more focused. Xabier didn't have to look at the door to know what was happening. It was as though all the oxygen was sucked from the room. He glanced at

Lazlo, who gave him a quick nod and cast his gaze over Xabier's shoulder. It was all Xabier could do not to turn in his seat to see what was happening.

His patience was rewarded as everyone's eyes tracked the movements of the newcomers. They took seats at a small table just in Xabier's periphery. The sight almost took his breath away. Her body was a portrait of feminine perfection. Her every curve was accentuated by the silky material of her simple black dress. Her long, luscious, black hair fell over one shoulder and gleamed, even in the dim lighting, but her most prominent feature was her eyes, clear-blue and inviting, welcoming. Xabier let out a long, slow breath and struggled against his natural impulses.

"Delilah," he murmured. He'd forgotten what her presence alone was capable of.

The sexual energy in the room was palpable. Even the women seemed affected. All eyes focused on Delilah. No one in the place had any idea who...*what*...she was. Xabier did; he was well-aware of the danger. Delilah was one of the oldest creatures in existence. The biblical seductress hadn't aged a day in the three millennia she'd lived. Xabier mused at how she'd spent hundreds of years in Purgatory and still looked like she was twenty-five years old and vivacious. Little did the local testosterone-crazed men know...

He sat and watched, doing his best to avoid eye-contact with the seductive woman...women. Her companion, Angela de la Barthe was almost as beautiful, and almost as lethal. Xabier kept his head down and let Lazlo take a position behind them. It wouldn't do to have Delilah see him and recognize the one who'd helped put her away for seven centuries.

Within an hour, the succubae hooked their prey for the evening, and left with the unsuspecting fools in tow. The handsome, well-built young men were outdoor types, probably up in the mountains for camping and fishing. They had no idea how quickly their trip was about to come to a screeching, and final, halt.

Other Books by Christopher Merlino

A Quiver of Cobras Series
Follow a group of Kendall High School students as they navigate their high school social scene, experience new relationships, and test the bonds of friendship and love.

> **Beginnings**
> **HEAT**
> **Broken**
> **Desire**
> **Limbo – Coming Soon**

The Zak Fischer Chronicles
Zak Fischer is a teen age musical prodigy who is on the verge of fame and fortune. He is also a strong Christian kid with beliefs that are contrary to the pop culture world he wants so badly to be a part of. As he and his band rise to national prominence, Zak must deal with all the temptations that come with it.

> **Viral – Coming Soon**

Nico Scarlatti Novels
Follow Nico Scarlatti as he struggles to navigate a world few ever get to see. With enemies on all sides, and a darkness inside him he can barely control, Nico.

> **Essence**
> **The Alphas**
> **Mother of All – Coming Soon**

The Collide Series
The story of Harper and Riley. She is the number one female artist in the world and he is a nobody who writes a little and plays music with his buddies. She hangs out with the most talented and recognizable people in the world. He has a close

circle of friends, none of which have ever graced the cover of Vanity Fair. A chance meeting brought them together. They both knew it could never work. But the attraction was too much for either of them to resist. The only question left is, what will happen when two vastly different worlds collide?

Worlds Collide – Coming Soon
We Collide – Coming Soon

About the Author

Christopher Merlino is married to Charmine Merlino, and the father of three beautiful girls, Alexis, Cecilia, and Isabella. He makes his living selling cars and insurance. He has a Master's degree in English and Creative Writing. In addition to writing, Chris spends his time in his woodshop, making things like pens, bowls, and other knick-knacks out of domestic and exotic woods.

Chris is a fan of most genres of books from non-fiction historical and theological to fiction drama, action, fantasy, and comedy. He enjoys music and golf…well…who really *enjoys* golf? He *plays* golf from time to time and generally refers to the game as "The Refiner's Oven." He was born and raised near Atlantic City, New Jersey, and currently makes his home in Egg Harbor Township, New Jersey.